BOOKS BY
C. W. SMITH

FICTION

Thin Men of Haddam
Country Music
The Vestal Virgin Room
Buffalo Nickel

NONFICTION

Uncle Dad

BUFFALO

NICKEL

C. W. Smith

POSEIDON
PRESS

NEW YORK LONDON TORONTO SYDNEY TOKYO

Poseidon Press

Simon & Schuster Building
Rockefeller Center
1230 Avenue of the Americas
New York, New York 10020

POSEIDON PRESS is a registered trademark
of Simon & Schuster Inc.

POSEIDON PRESS colophon is a trademark
of Simon & Schuster Inc.

Designed by Barbara M. Bachman

Manufactured in the United States of America

1 3 5 7 9 10 8 6 4 2

Library of Congress Cataloging-in-Publication Data
Smith, C. W. (Charles William), date
Buffalo nickel/C. W. Smith.
p. cm.
1. Kiowa Apache Indians—Fiction. I. Title.
PS3569.M516B84   1989
813'.54—dc19   89-3683
CIP
ISBN 0-671-62447-4

A portion of this manuscript appeared
in *Southwest Review* (Autumn 1988).

Acknowledgments

Although this is a novel, I am indebted to various sources for the Kiowa lore, legend, and history adapted for fictional use in it. Two volumes in particular proved invaluable: *Kiowa Voices: Ceremonial Dance, Ritual and Song* and *Kiowa Voices: Myths, Legends and Folktales*, both edited by Maurice Boyd and published by Texas Christian University Press. However, the work of many other scholars and writers on Native American myths and history also influenced the shape and content of my story: Dee Brown, *Bury My Heart at Wounded Knee*; Isabel Crawford, *Kiowa: History of a Blanket Indian Mission* and *The Joyful Journey*; David Dary, *The Buffalo Book*; Angie Debo, *And Still the Waters Run* and *The Road to Disappearance*; T. R. Fehrenbach, *Lone Star* and *The Comanches*; Carolyn Thomas Foreman, *Indians Abroad, 1493–1938*; Grant Foreman, *A History of Oklahoma* and *The Five Civilized Tribes*; Ralph and Natasha Friar, *The Only Good Indian—The Hollywood Gospel*; Martin Garretson, *The American Bison*; G. B. Glasscock, *Then Came Oil*; Mody C. Boatright and Bill Owens, *Tales from the Derrick Floor*; Elinor Gregg, *The Indians and the Nurse*; Lawrence Kelly, *The Assault on Assimilation*; Alice Marriott, *The Ten Grandmothers* and *Saynday's People*; Alice Marriott and Carol K. Rachlin, *Native American Mythology*; John Joseph Matthews, *The Osages*; Mildred Mayhall, *The Kiowas*; N. Scott Momaday, *House Made of Dawn*, *The Names: A Memoir*, and *The Way to Rainy Mountain*; James Mooney, *Calendar History of the Kiowa Indians* and *The Ghost Dance Religion and the Sioux Outbreak of 1890*; Rev. J. J. Methvin, *In the Limelight* and *Andele, the Mexican Kiowa Captive*; Wilbur S. Nye, *Carbine and Lance* and *Bad Medicine and Good*; Elsie Parsons, *Kiowa Tales*; Florence Patterson, *Survey of the Conditions of the Indians in the United States* (Senate Hearings, 1929); Polingaysi Qoyawayma, *No Turning Back*; Jane Richardson, *Law and Status Among the Kiowa Indians*; Carl Coke Rister, *Oil: Titan of the Southwest*; Mari Sandoz, *The Buffalo Hunters*; and Zitkala-Sa (Gertrude Simmons), *American Indian Stories*.

To this list I would add the work done over so many decades by the writers and editors for *Chronicles of Oklahoma;* I'd also point out that any student exploring the field will, if lucky, soon stumble upon Francis Paul Prucha's *A Bibliographical Guide to the History of Indian-White Relations in the United States.*

To Elaine

——for her abiding faith——

PART

ONE

1904 – 1907

1

That year we rode so far south in Mexico we came upon little men who
jumped around in trees. We tried to get the little men to speak Kiowa
or Comanche but they did not know it. Hears Wind and I spoke a little
Spanish, so we talked it at them, but they did not answer back. They
did not know sign language, either. We killed one and scalped him.
There were also birds in those jungles with huge beaks, and we shot
two for their colorful feathers. I was only fifteen summers, and my
amigos, Lone Wolf's nephews, they were young, too. When we got back
to camp and showed that scalp to our to-yop-ke, he said we should have
stolen those little men's horses, too, and all the warriors laughed big at
us.

That was our first adventure out of the raiding camp alone and we
young men wanted to prove ourselves and get the notice of some warrior
who would ask us into his society. I wanted to be in the Black Legs.
Back then, a young man had to earn his honor by fighting or getting
horses from an enemy. He also had to go on a quest to a sacred place
where he would fast for four days until a spirit vision gave him strong
medicine for his life as a warrior.

But I am telling about your mother. We rode west for a few days and
into the desert. We came to a big hacienda where the Mexicans had a
horse herd in a corral, and our chief decided that we would raid and
take the horses and whatever we could find of value in the house because
it did not seem to be guarded very heavily. We waited in the darkness
and just before dawn some of our band slipped into the corral and
unlatched the gate and ran the horses off. Of course, the Mexicans heard
this and sounded the alarm. We got on our horses and rode as fast as we
could into the courtyard of the hacienda. Hears Wind wanted to be the
first inside to look for gold, but when he ran into the hacienda a Mexican
shot him in the throat with a pistol. The Mexicans and their servants
were scurrying about with their clothing dragging or flapping in the air.

I ran inside and found a Mexican stuffing two pouches into saddlebags, but when he saw me he dropped them and ran. I took them—they were full of silver—and went back and mounted my horse because I wanted to be in on the chase and get a scalp.

I saw a girl running across the courtyard in her nightshirt. Her hair was in two long braids and she was barefoot. She was running away from me. I rode right past her and I would have kept on going but she cursed me in Spanish. I didn't know a lot of that tongue then but I knew from the sound what she meant in her heart about me. I turned around and looked. Aii!

Well, you have seen her picture. What a prize, I thought. Much better than the silver. So I turned around and went riding up behind her. I leaned over and caught her around the waist and threw her up over the neck of my horse, it was easy, she was not much heavier than a dog. But she swung at me with her fists and even kicked at me and tried to knock me off the horse. She cursed and screamed. I put my hand over her mouth and she bit my flesh clean through. I threw her onto the ground and sat on her and tied her up with rawhide and had to stuff a bandana in her mouth to keep her quiet.

I kept her tied up for three days while we rode. I took out the bandana to feed her and give her water and as soon as she had her fill she would curse and scream and I would have to put it in again. Everyone teased me. They said, Throw that one away! She makes too much noise! She will be a terrible wife! Stumbling Bear said, You will have to sleep with your ears covered! But with your eyes open! But with your eyes open!

But I did not want to throw her away. She was much too beautiful. If I had met a girl like that from our band or another at a Sun Dance I would not have been able to have her because I could not have given her parents enough horses or gifts to satisfy their honor. Once in anger I said to a warrior who was kicking about her noise, You want me to throw her away. You have two wives waiting for you in your lodge, but I have none.

I also said that everyone envied me, that they wanted me to throw her away so they could pick her up. They laughed big at me again. Someone said, Everybody knows you don't bring a captive woman to your lodge who is better-looking than your wives.

Soon we were so far away she would not know the way back to her hacienda. I untied her. She did not fight now, but she sulked. Quit eating. She could tell who the leaders were, too, she was very smart, so to stab my heart she made up to the older warriors. They took her to the bushes. If she had to be a captive, she wanted to belong to someone with many horses, I could see that was her way. She wanted to be a chief's main sit-by wife and I was only a pup.

Everyone scorned her for her tricks. At night she kept running off even though her feet were cut and bruised, and I kept going out after her in the mornings and tying her up again. Then we were in Ute country and my chief, he said, If she runs again let her go. Throw her away. He was not joking. We had a fight with some Utes, and when it was over I knew she had escaped during the confusion. We rode east for a day, and my heart was sore. On the second day, I asked my chief— this was No Moccasins, he was a Tai-me keeper then and a very smart man—if I could go back for her. He thought I was foolish. But he said, Take food and give it to her when you find her. Tell her she can come back in peace with you or she can walk to Mexico. Give her moccasins. I said, Thank you. I will pray for good medicine so she will choose to come back. He smiled and said, Do not pray to be given what you want. Pray to be granted what you need.

She was not hard to track. When I found her, she looked pretty hungry, so I gave her the food and told her no more fighting. I made signs to show I would not come looking again. I had the moccasins in my pouch on my horse, and after a big fight inside myself I got them out and gave them to her.

Then I rode off a way and sat down to eat. When I was through and was ready to go, she walked over to me. She hung her head and showed me she wanted me to take her. I said, That's good. But if you make up to the other warriors, I will cut off your nose and no man will want to look at you again.

I named her Runs Off Slow. She was faithful to me, except for once, and then I did not have the heart to cut her face and throw her away, I only whipped her and the man she was with. Later, she became a good wife, a manly-hearted woman, very brave and full of strong talk, and soon she forgot about having been a Mexican. She was a hard worker. We had your older sister, then those children you never got to know because they died, the ones your mother grieved for by cutting off her finger in the Kiowa way. When you came she named you Sand because there are so many grains, maybe death would overlook you. Well, it saw her instead.

I did not get a scalp that trip—that monkey did not count. Some of *my companions did, though. But I had fought with honor against the Mexicans and the Utes, and I had captured the silver and the girl. We had lost no warriors, even Hears Wind's wound had been healed by Iron Lance, the Buffalo Medicine man riding with us. So when we returned, there was a scalp dance for us, and No Moccasins changed my name to Went on a Journey. That was many summers ago, but soon there was no more raiding and fighting because the white men came with their medicine and drove away the buffalo. Then they put up the wire-that-has-teeth all across the prairies. After the Wrinkled-Hand Chase, they sent me to prison in Florida, and that's why my lungs hurt and I am too weak to stand.*

I am telling you this now so you will know about this name, Went on a Journey. I want you to take it before I die so that it may be spoken. If we were rich or there were more of us, we would have a dance and give-away for this, but I am too poor now. I will take my old name, Red Earth.

There is a song, I know you have heard the men sing it even though they cannot go out for buffalo or scalps any more or ride as far as they want.

This is it—

> *Going far on a journey . . .*
> *Going far on a journey . . .*
> *That's the only way for a young man*
> *to get fame and many horses . . . .*

After they had buried the boy's father, his older sister, Standing Inside Lodge, sent word to the missionary school just south of Anadarko that a child was ready. Most people knew that Went on a Journey had kept his son at home because three other children had contracted measles in a white man's school, and when they were sent home sick they had died and passed the contagion on to Runs Off Slow, who was weak from having borne the child named Sand.

Standing Inside Lodge dressed the boy in her husband's best beaded moccasins and buckskin leggings and shirt. She braided his hair and greased the strands with tallow and decorated them with otter fur and colored ribbon. As she watched him pack his few belongings—extra clothing, a knife his father had given him, an old photograph of his mother and father together, a few plugs of cavendish tobacco—in an orange crate, she realized he was troubled. *What is it?*

He said, *How long will I be well before I am sick?*

Not everyone dies from going to a white man's school, she said. *Am I dead?*

She watched from the yard as the boy walked to the corral and stood looking into the empty ring of muddy earth as if searching for the two horses which had recently occupied it. They had been buried with his father. Then he went into the brush arbor beside the house. She could see his moccasins and his shins; he stood without moving. When she heard him trying to stifle his sobs she went into the house to give him privacy.

Hits Again, an old warrior now serving as a truant officer, came in a wagon to take the boy to Anadarko. On the way, the old man said, "Good chuck," in English, jerking his chin vaguely toward the north to indicate the school. The boy gave him a puzzled look. The old man said, "Many children." He was trying to reassure the boy, who was obviously terrified. *Do you know any of the white man's language?* the old man asked. The boy shook his head. *You will learn. I never said a word of it until I was sixty winters old. It will come fast for you at the school.*

The year was 1904, and the school term had just begun. Hits Again parked the wagon outside the school's biggest building and went inside. The boy waited stiffly on the wagon seat, as stolid and unblinking as the horse that was hitched to the wagon. The school grounds consisted of tall red brick buildings that to his eye seemed as numerous as those of cities he had heard described. Without turning his head, he could see a field beyond the buildings where huge sunflowers stood like thin men with dark faces fringed with yellow feathers. Beyond, low on the horizon to the south, lay the familiar blue outline of the Wichitas.

Across the road from the school was a patch of corn where boys were moving up and down rows with hoes in their hands. They looked like Kiowas, but their hair was short and they wore overalls and brogans like the white farmers.

He heard tittering, and he cocked his head slightly. On a second-story balcony several girls were shaking out white cloths the size of soldier's tents. The girls also looked like Kiowas, but they were wearing blue chambray smocks. They were not looking at him; they were looking all around him, and if their gazes had been filaments of spider web he would have been laced in place. As if on a dare, one girl called down something in English, but he pretended not to hear.

Hits Again and a smiling fat white woman came out of the building and escorted him inside. Just before they went through the door, Hits

Again leaned over and said, *We're going to see the chief. Leave your funny outside.* Down a hall more white people were walking, and the rumble their hard-soled shoes made was loud as thunder. A pretty girl who was carrying some books boldly inspected him as she passed. The children here seemed rude; they acted like white people, as if they didn't respect another person's privacy.

They led him into a room where a white man with a beard and spectacles rose from behind a desk and shook his hand. Hits Again said, *This is the chief here. He is a Jesus man. We call him Big Whiskers, but his white name is Reverend McKnight. Do what he says.*

The white Jesus man said, *Get down*, in Kiowa. The boy guessed he meant to invite him to be seated, so he said *Thank you* and eased down onto the edge of a wooden chair. The whites and Hits Again spoke English for a while. When the white woman went out of the room, Hits Again said, *They ask me your name. I tell them Went on a Journey. They ask do you have a Christian name, and I say no. They ask your father's name, and I say Red Earth.* The boy inwardly flinched to hear his dead father's name spoken aloud. *They ask about your mother and your father, and I say they are dead. The white woman is a Jesus lady like the man only she never shouts at the children. She says to call you by the white name David.*

The man behind the desk said "David" and smiled, but he also stopped combing his beard with his fingers.

So the boy said, "David."

The man nodded with satisfaction.

The white Jesus lady returned carrying a narrow strip of stiff white paper with a single string tied to each end. When she approached him gently, reaching over to drape the string around his neck, he was startled by her closeness—her large pigeon bosom loomed in his vision like a pillow. She held the paper in her hand and turned it to show him the face. There were black marks.

"David," she said, pointing to the marks. "David Copper-field."

Later, she and Hits Again walked him to the carpentry shop, the blacksmith shop, and the barn, introducing him to other boys and grown-ups. The boys were polite, but he didn't trust their public display of courtesy.

Hits Again told him that everybody went to class in the morning. In the afternoon, the boys worked and learned white man's tools, while the girls washed clothes, linens, and dishes and sewed and learned to make quilts. The boy was shown where he would sleep in a long room with a wooden floor and beds covered with ticks of straw. It was very neat and clean. Hits Again told him he could take his belongings from the orange crate and put them in a trunk that was his to use.

Next to the long room was a smaller one where Hits Again showed him the washbasins and how to turn the water on and off and how you sat on the little chairs to do your business then pulled the chain. They washed their hands at a basin. Hits Again said, *The Jesus people here have rules for all the children. The children all say,* "We must have clean hands, clean faces, not have sores on our bodies, not have bugs on us, wear clean clothes, polish our shoes, have our hair cut, not be ashamed to speak English and not be afraid of white people."

The boy said, *I am not afraid of white people.*

Hits Again chuckled, thinking this a boast. The boy meant he was afraid of the children, of measles and smallpox and of being alone.

Hits Again said, *They say here that the Devil made the whiskey road, the dance road, the card road, and the mescal road. They do not let children smoke. Also they do not like the Feather Dance people here.*

The smiling Jesus woman led them down the hallway to the big room where the children ate. It was time for supper. Several other white people came to meet the boy and to inspect the hands and faces of their children who entered the room. The boy noticed one white woman had an eye that did not move and another walked with a cane, and one white man had a withered hand; they all smiled at him and said the name on the card around his neck. The children stood behind chairs at the long tables. The boy stayed beside the fat Jesus woman. He was the only child in the room dressed like a Kiowa.

After Big Whiskers prayed, the children pulled out their chairs and sat. The boy's stomach growled, but the food seemed strange, like weeds. There was a meat he had never seen before, and he longed for fried bread and boiled beef and coffee with sugar in it. He thought about how no one had offered a prayer by tearing off a piece of meat and holding it up and thanking Daw-k'hee, then burying it. With that, he saw his father's face, and he couldn't eat.

Later, the white Jesus woman took him outside where some childen were playing tag near the steps of the chapel.

Someone asked in Kiowa, *You don't speak any English?*

The boy shook his head.

Is it true you are twelve summers old?

He nodded. They seemed skeptical; the other boys his size were at least three years older than he. Somebody, it was a girl, he thought, said something in English, and everyone giggled. The white Jesus woman looked angry. Another voice said *sa-bodle-te* in Kiowa—oaf— and he felt his face heat. These were rude and noisy children whose manners had not been improved by their having gone to school here. They looked you in the eyes and said impolite things to your face.

A bell clanged, and the children suddenly took flight like a covey of quail toward the chapel steps. The white Jesus woman and he walked behind, and the fat woman's hand burned like hot metal atop his shoulder. A girl broke away from the group and darted back to where he and the missionary were walking. It was that pretty girl with the books in the hallway.

She looked at his face but not his eyes and said, *I am Set'Alma, Bear-Chased Girl. My school name is Iola.* The girl walked beside him for a moment, then she reached into a pocket of her blue chambray dress and drew out something round and orange and held it out. *My grandfather gave this to me today, but I am not hungry for it. Will you please take it?*

Dumbfounded, the boy held out his hand, and the girl put the orange in it. Nothing within his field of vision—not the buildings or the fields or the trees or the sky or anything the children were wearing—was even remotely as bright and so very *orange* as this fruit.

Aho! he said, thanking her.

Then she was gone, skipping ahead to join the other children.

"Iola." He spoke only to try forming the word in his mouth, but the missionary instantly responded.

"Yes!" she sang. "Iola!" She sounded immensely pleased.

For an instant the boy presumed the missionary was praising his performance, then he realized he had been momentarily forgotten: the girl was *ade*, favored child.

They cut his hair; they gave him hard-soled shoes and woolen stockings, drop-seat underwear, overalls for work, and a gray wool suit for dress-up, with a red stripe down the side of the trousers, brass buttons on the coat, and a matching cap. They gave him the number 79 and put that number on everything issued to him.

He was assigned to the blacksmith shop, but soon he was also working in the fields, where his size made it easy for him to do his share and sometimes that of others. He was as large as most of the men at school, but he was placed in a class with younger children because he knew little English. This, together with his shyness, gave the other children the notion that he was backward, slow. That first label of sa-bodle-te stuck to him.

In some ways, his size was an asset. He was always chosen quickly for football; he rode the smaller children on his back; people turned to him when it was time to heave this limb or that washpot or anvil; like a burro, he came in handy when the cook needed a sack of flour toted from the wagon to the kitchen. To David, his size was a tool for others to use, for which they paid in the coin of acceptance.

When the first year was out, he was pushed ahead to the upper class. Among his classmates were the girl named Iola, a year younger than he, and her cousin, Morris Twohatchet, a year older and a leader among the boys. David had suffered the smaller children's fear of his size and the rumor that he was backward; now, placed with older boys, he risked being exploited because of his innocence.

Morris quickly took charge of David, encouraging him to help gouge out a chink of mortar in a wall of the lady teacher's lodgings so the boys could peek at Miss Roberts while she lowered her nude elephantine form into a galvanized-tin washtub. No one was surprised when David Copperfield was the one caught and the one to take the punishment for Morris and his friends. Again and again, the older boys made him do things they knew would get him into trouble and laughed at him for his gullibility. Then they accepted him for having obeyed. Never once was David fooled; being caught and punished was living up to his part of a bargain. Better to be a fool than to be alone.

When the Reverend McKnight was informed that David Copperfield had made the peephole, he called him into his office, sat him down and showed him a picture from a large Bible. It was the Devil. The boy sat frightened with his hands gripping the lip of the chair seat and looked at the red creature with sharp cow horns, glinting teeth, ears like a wolf's. Its eyes were glowing yellow.

The Devil has fur-covered paws and talons like an eagle's, and when boys are bad he will come in the night while they sleep and snatch them up with his claws and take them away to his fiery hole below the earth where they will burn, Big Whiskers said. When you feel temptations of the flesh, you must say, "Get thee behind me, Satan!" and pray to stay pure.

His official punishment was to apologize to Miss Roberts, stand in the corner of the classroom with his face to the wall, and to write "Lust is a sin. The wages of sin is death" on his slate one hundred times. Except for the damage to his pride, David felt this was a small price to pay for the chance to show his loyalty to Morris and the older boys. But in bed at night the darkness would fill with images of the creature with the burning yellow eyes who might come for him when he fell asleep. The Devil was watching him because he had seen Miss Roberts take off her clothes. She had a bushy patch of hair between her legs and large drooping breasts. He could remember seeing them, and when he did, he would tremble. What was "lust"? Was it the surprise he had felt on discovering that beneath her clothing the white missionary was made exactly like a fat Kiowa woman?

He had not eaten the orange. He had kept it in his trunk until it stank and a strange green dust covered it.

For a few days after she had given it to him she tried to lead him around and show him to other children as if he were some exotic breed of dog. He resisted, and she let him melt back into whatever anonymity he could summon. After that he was no longer the new child to her but only another fool and tormentor like Morris, and soon he believed that she had dispensed the kindness of the orange with merely an even-handed impersonality.

The first year at school, David would sometimes watch from a window if he saw her grandfather's red and yellow buffalo-skin lodge being put up just beyond the school grounds. Sometimes Iron Lance would stay for a week at a time, and he would give Iola presents such as the orange when Iola went to visit him. Iron Lance had been an illustrious warrior and chief, as well as a Buffalo Medicine man. Like David's father, he had been sent to prison in Florida when the wars ended. On his return he was one of ten chiefs the government had built wooden houses for on the reservation. Iron Lance never occupied the house, it was said, because it was square, and drafty and snakes lived under it. He refused to farm, but took up raising cattle and used the house as a hay barn. He had visited Washington three times as a representative of tribal affairs. He still did not walk the Jesus road, however, and was known to participate in the Feather Dance to bring the buffalo back. David had overheard the missionaries complain that it was bad for the children to have a peyote eater camping so close to the school.

Now and then if he were working close by, David would watch as Iola skipped across the boys' playground, leapt into the bar ditch alongside the road, and disappeared for a moment, then came up onto the road and over into the field where her grandfather's lodge stood. Without making the ritual encircling of the tipi, she would simply plunge through the east-facing opening. He would imagine her seated inside on the ground with the light coming in through the smoke flaps and her grandfather talking to her. Bear-Chased Girl. There was a story about some sisters; one turned into a bear and chased the others, who escaped by climbing up a cliff that suddenly started to grow until it was into the sky, and the seven girls became the stars that the white men called the Big Dipper. There was a Star Girls ceremony he had once seen, and the girls had bunches of sage tied in their hair and were dressed in white buckskin decorated with beautiful shells and their hands were painted white because the Star Girls were so bright. Girls who did this grew up well, without trouble or sickness.

David would hang about mooning dreamily until Iola emerged carrying some gift, and his attention would be attached to her figure like a cockleburr as she skipped across the road and back into the schoolyard. After a time, he noticed that her head no longer vanished completely when she descended into the ditch and when she crossed the field she seemed to stop far less often to inspect something on the ground, and her skip either quickened into a trot or slowed to a stroll.

The next year, seated behind her in class, he memorized the back of her head, the nape of her neck, her glossy black braid tied with a bright ribbon. There would be tendrils of black hair, fine and loose, and he would blow very softly and watch the hair waft in the breeze. Sometimes he would lean forward and quietly inhale her clean scent, drawing it so secretly into his nostrils it was like stealing from her. His hands would tremble on his desk. When she stood to read, he would pretend, like the rest of the class, to be bored with her ceaseless displays of superiority, but he could have spent hours looking at her deep brown eyes and her high cheekbones under them, the light color of untanned leather. He couldn't adequately define what he felt until one day he caught himself wishing she were his sister—he felt tender, protective, adoring, yet under that was something he couldn't acknowledge without feeling afraid.

Everybody said she would go from here to Haskell or to Carlisle, then become a successful Kiowa in a white man's world. A teacher, maybe even a doctor. Watching her with her family or with Miss Roberts or with the other children, it seemed to him she was complete. The circle had no opening. Looking over her shoulder, he saw the large red A's on her papers, and underneath always some comment from Miss Roberts whose meaning was indecipherable except for the exclamation point. Like everything else about her life, the red messages suggested she had a private arrangement with authority that excluded the other students.

Some nights, lying awake and thinking about Iola, he could hear his father's voice.

Once some people were camping and they grew very hungry because no one could find any meat. The chief, who had a beautiful daughter, sent the camp crier out to tell all the men that whoever could find meat for the camp could marry her. On the very edge of the camp lived a young man and his grandmother. They were very poor. The boy was barefoot all the time, his face was dirty, and his hair was all tangled. When the boy heard the crier say his message, he told his grandmother, I have the medicine to draw deer to the camp. His grandmother, she went nenenene in surprise. She said how can you do it? The young man sang her a song:

> *I lost my grandmother's spoon.*
> *Grandmother whipped me.*
> *I lay down crying,*
> *That is where I got my medicine.*

He said to her, As I was lying on the floor of this tipi crying a long time ago, a spirit came and gave me this medicine. He sang again:

> *I was wading in the water*
> *And kicked out the minnows*
> *On the banks.*
> *The minnows turned to deer.*

The grandmother was happy, and the chiefs all met to talk about it. They said maybe the boy can draw the deer because sometimes poor people have medicine. They called the boy in, and he told them to make two arrows, one with eagle feathers edged in black and the other with feathers edged in white. Then he told them to put a pot on the fire and to stir it while he sang. When they stirred, they heard the sound of a deer and when they peeped into the pot, it was full of deer blood. They all shouted. The next day he told them to make a big circle and put sagebrushes in it. When a fog came they sat around the big circle. One man held the arrows with his arms crossed, and the men next to him on either side passed them on. When the arrows had gone around in a circle and back to the first man, the fog lifted and the circle was filled with deer. The men moved in to make the circle closer while the deer ran. Then they heard a deer singing something:

> I am not crying
> Because I am going to die
> But I am crying
> For my wife and children.

They opened the circle to let him and his family in. Then they closed the circle until it got smaller and smaller and they could grab the deer about their necks and kill them. Even the women could do it now. Then they gave the young man the kidneys of four deer.

The chief said, You have saved our people from starving. Now here is my daughter! The boy was very happy, but the beautiful girl was displeased by her new husband's appearance and refused to look at him. The young man went home to his grandmother and said, Tah, Grandmother! Put a big pot on the fire! When that was done, he took off his clothes and got into the pot all the way over his head. When he came out, his grandmother said, It made you handsome! Do it again! So he did it three more times, and when he came out, his grandmother said, Oh, you are the most handsome man in the camp!

She told him to dump a bit of cloth into the pot, and when he put his hand in, he pulled out a Navajo blanket, a buckskin suit, some moccasins and leggings. He invited his grandmother to get into the pot, then, and when she did, and got back out again, he said, Oh, you look very nice now!

He went outside their lodge where he had made a beautiful spotted horse and got on it and rode into the main camp where the chief's daughter was sitting with some other girls. When the girls saw him, they said, Who is that handsome stranger! The chief's daughter saw who it was and clapped her hand over her mouth in surprise. She ran to him and held his horse while he got down. Then they went into her father's lodge and were married. Obaha—that is all.

On his slate he learned to add, subtract, multiply, and divide. If Jesus took one fish and made fifty more fishes and fed seven people one fish each, how many would be left?

On his slate he learned to present the English alphabet in cursive and to spell important words. *We say Jesus is the Son of God. How do we spell this "son"? I do not mean the "sun" as in the Kiowa Sun Dance.*

On his slate he wrote the titles to hymns, then they would sing, "Washed in the Blood of the Lamb."

They gave the children paper and had them draw whatever they wanted—a horse, a buffalo, a man doing a war dance. Or a glowing cross, the face of Jesus or Goliath or a lion.

The children said grace over their meals and prayed at their beds before the gas lamps were turned out.

Now that David had been at the school over two years, he had grown accustomed to the routine, but he had formed no opinions about religion. He dutifully followed the lead of his teachers, believing only that the white man's religion had to be learned or at least absorbed the way he had to accept the clothing and the haircut, the shelter and the food and his companions.

Morris, though, had decided to make his last year in the white men's school a test of his teachers' patience and faith. During Bible study, David would watch and listen with interest while Miss Roberts and Morris bantered day after day, Iola sitting red-faced in humiliation and anger.

Once Morris said, "My uncle, he wants to know if the Jesus book says Kiowas are supposed to have only 160 acres of land each and to walk the plow road." It was early in 1907, and the preceding year the government had sold the last of the remaining Kiowa lands to buyers under a sealed bid, which resulted in further encroachments by whites onto land the

Kiowas considered their own. While Iola glared at Morris, Miss Roberts smiled and said, "No, well not exactly, of course, but the Bible does encourage us to grow gardens and not to steal. Class, do we remember the Commandment about that?"

Another day, while Iola fumed, Morris said, "My uncle, he wants to know why the white men made Jesus ride on a nasty little mule, why not a good big war horse." The children giggled, but Miss Roberts said, "Tell your uncle that in the place where Jesus was born a mule was perfectly acceptable transportation. It would not be fitting for the Prince of Peace to be riding a mount trained for war."

On through the days of their lessons Morris practiced his peculiar brand of disruption, with Iola fretting and the fat missionary serenely responding.

"My uncle, he wants to know why white people are so kill crazy they killed their own Jesus."

Before Miss Roberts could answer, Iola, who had been squirming with impatience for weeks, burst out, "You don't care what she says! You're just being a Smart Aleck! And quit saying your uncle says these things!"

"Oh, it's all right if Morris wants to play devil's advocate, Iola," said Miss Roberts. "I don't think he'll trip me up, and faith must be tempered by doubt and reason."

Morris gave Iola a sidelong look of triumph, and, as if having been given blanket permission to frame any question no matter how seemingly impertinent, asked, "My uncle, he wants to know why it is that most of the white people who have come in the past few winters to take our land have walked the cheat road, the whiskey road, and the gamble road. If the Christians have strong medicine, he says, why are so many white people bad not just to Kiowas but also to each other?"

"Well, Morris, your uncle is a very wise man to have noticed these things and to have thought about them. I wish I could give you an answer that would satisfy you. Jesus is not just for white men, and God looks down and sees Kiowas and white men and Negroes and Chinamen and wants them all to be Christians. Some of them of all colors have found the way and follow His footsteps, but many have not yet. The Romans who killed Christ had not accepted him as the Son of God, either, and they were not Christians."

On a Wednesday in early October, he asked, "My uncle, he wants to know this, Miss Roberts—if Jesus could fill all the baskets he wanted to with bread and fishes by spirit power, why doesn't he come down from the spirit world and do this for all the people who are hungry in the winter when their gardens do not grow?"

Miss Roberts closed her eyes for a moment then opened them. It was like a slow blink. "Morris, I can't give you an answer to that in a sentence or two. Words can't answer it altogether. You're not ready for another kind of answer now, but perhaps some day you will be."

Everybody expected Morris to reveal, through a barely perceptible alteration of the line across his mouth, a sign, however small, of victory. They were disappointed.

Outside at the water tank, Iola called over from the girl's line to Morris, "You just say those things to try to make her look foolish, but you only make a fool out of yourself!"

She directed a burning, wounded look directly into David's eyes, accusing him of being an accomplice. He had done nothing, but when he bent his head to drink, he saw in the brightly quivering plane of water that his cheeks looked red.

2

The following Sunday, people sitting in church at Hog Creek heard hooves thumping on the earth outside; when they passed through the double doors after the benediction, they found three Kiowa horsemen in regalia. Iron Lance stood forward of his kin—Mark Wolf-Tail and John Hunt—on his favorite mount, a bay *t'a-kon* or black-eared horse.

The crowd bunched up nervously on the porch to watch them. Everyone—the families of White Horse, the Paudeletys, Paddletys, Buffaloes, Mopopes, Tinatones, and Twohatchets, among others—immediately remembered the winter when three boys had been whipped by a white teacher and, having run away, were found frozen to death—which prompted their fathers and uncles to ride to the school to get even; everyone recalled a big fight with the Negro soldiers on issue day when no rations were available; and there was the time a white boy shot Eleanor Big Elk near Boake's store at Rainy Mountain and it looked as though people were going to go to war until it was determined the shooting had been an accident.

So they wondered what emergency brought these three to wait at the church steps for everyone to come outside and be not so much members of a Christian congregation as people belonging to the Kiowa tribe.

But after their first alarm, people noticed that although Iron Lance wore his buffalo horn headdress and breast-plate of bone, he had no weapon, and he hadn't painted his face. Mark Wolf-Tail had no weapons either, although he wore the elk-hide sash that identified him as a select *koitsenko* warrior.

Ho, Mark! somebody called out. *Are you giving a dance?*

Mark grinned. *No, we came to get the Jesus man to dip us in the river. We're dirty*, he joked. Then he jerked his chin toward Iron Lance as if to say that their business would be announced by their official spokesman.

Iola, still inside, was waiting for her father, an elder, to collect and milk the little red money barrels for foreign missions of their copper pennies. She and her father stood behind the altar while the offering was hurriedly tallied by the Reverend Willis, who looked worried. Her father looked faintly embarrassed.

When they moved out to join the crowd, the pastor wondered aloud, "Have they come to be saved?" He didn't sound optimistic. "Invite them to join us, and we'll go back in."

Her father's face was exquisitely blank. She knew that look. *Father-in-law*, he said to Iron Lance, *won't you get down? The Jesus man invites you to his lodge for prayer.*

Her grandfather looked at the Reverend Willis, then said to her father in Kiowa, *No, thank you. The offer is good, and you may tell him it is appreciated.* The *t'a-kon* bay looked up and shook its head savagely to free its ears of flies. The old man waited, then said, *We are here to tell people that the buffalo are coming back.*

Hands clapped to mouths. Her mother, standing at the bottom of the steps, turned to give her father a childlike grin that lighted her eyes. Her father, however, like many around him, was frowning. She could guess his thoughts. Not many years before she was born, P'oinkia had preached that if Kiowas took their children out of schools and quit using matches and white men's tools, the buffalo would return and white men would be destroyed by fire and whirlwinds. He said he was the true Messiah, and people followed him to his camp on Elk Creek. Some chiefs scoffed, and troops from Fort Sill came to Anadarko in case he inspired a rebellion. Joshua Given, son of Satank and himself an educated missionary married to a white, proposed that P'oinkia let the troops shoot him—if he rose to life on the third day, everyone would worship him as the Messiah. When P'oinkia refused the test, his power vanished.

Then word had come down from the north of another new Messiah, the Paiute Wovoka. He had visions of a great earthquake that would open up a big hole for all whites to fall into, then all dead Kiowas and buffalo would come back from the spirit world. Iola remembered vaguely that there had been a big dance organized—the Ghost or Feather Dance—but the government had sent troops to stop it. Though still outlawed, it was done secretly by some, including her mother, who had a special dress for it of white buckskin decorated with suns, moons, and stars.

Iola's father looked as if he were thinking, This again?, while the old man stood silently on the *t'ak-on* bay waiting for him to respond. It would have been one thing for Iron Lance to speak of the buffalo's returning to his son-in-law during a visit inside his lodge; appearing here, though, in heathen attire, it was as if he were flouting his unbaptized state and his declaration were his final pronouncement in a long ongoing argument.

"What does he want?" asked the Reverend Willis.

Her father ignored the pastor. *Thank you, Father-in-law, for telling us this news,* he said at last. *Again, won't you get down?*

No, thank you. We must ride; there are others to tell.

Her mother stepped forward and laid her palm on the horse's neck. *When are they coming, Father?*

Pretty near the Geese-Going Moon. Few days either way.

Her father looked as if he were about to speak, but Iron Lance had lifted the reins of his horse and had nodded to his companions. His horse danced two steps sideways, and he said, looking toward Iola but politely avoiding her gaze, *You, Grandchild, will you tell the other children at the school for me?* He tossed the question over his shoulder as if it were something he had almost forgotten, and she looked down, swallowed, and forced herself to nod. When she raised her head, expecting to see him watching her, the three horsemen were bending their horses' necks and leaning to take a turn the horses themselves had not yet made: her grandfather had apparently been so certain of her answer that he had not bothered to wait for it before he and his companions rode thundering out of the churchyard.

Their haste was not necessary, even she could sense that—they were happy to be mounted and chasing something, if only ghosts of buffalo.

Her mother wanted to stay and discuss the event with her kin under the brush arbor that stood next to the church, but her father hitched the ponies to the wagon as swiftly as he could and ordered Iola and Limping Deer into it. When her mother protested, her father said that Iola had to be taken back to school immediately.

He spared Iola additional anguish by not adding *so that your daughter can do what your father wants*, although Iola suspected he was manipulating her mother with that implication.

Seated in the wagon as it rolled away from the churchyard along the dusty red road toward Anadarko, her mother fumed in silence. Often, the Sunday services were followed by an afternoon of quilting or playing the hand game or sewing with other kinswomen under the arbor; then there'd be a potluck dinner and an evening of hymns and prayer. On Sundays when Iola joined them, her mother could count on having two or three hours of visiting.

Her parents were frequently quiet with one another, but this afternoon the silence hurt Iola's stomach. Riding beside her father, she could see the knot of muscle near his gray-tinged temple throbbing, and his mouth remained twisted into a sour pucker. Her mother sat wrapped in her dark blue shawl so that only her round face and three fingers were visible. Within a few miles, though, her mother's irritation gave way to a smug serenity. Iola could tell she felt that the prophecy of Iron Lance would vindicate her in the struggles she had had with her husband over being Kiowa or Christian. She had been baptized at her husband's request, attended services faithfully, and believed there was a Heaven where their baptized firstborn, Nathan, now lived; but she stubbornly refused to give up the Feather Dance or go against her own father for being a peyote eater or having more than one wife. She was able to poise herself on the point of contradiction without feeling unbalanced, and when she listened to the Reverend Willis rant about hellfire, she would say privately to Iola, *His talk hits me like the wind. I duck my head, and it passes over and is gone, doesn't blow me over, I just wait.* If the preacher shouted at them, her mother, offended, would mutter *Zsapol!*—ogre— under her breath. Her husband, though, yearned for consistency. Like a white man, he believed the soul was the pear, sin the bruise, and the human will a sharp knife for paring away corruption.

Having left her boiled beef at the church to be shared with the families of her three sisters, Limping Deer said, *Husband, if you're hungry, we will have to go home before going to the school.*

Her father nodded. At the turnoff that went north toward the Washita, he steered the wagon onto their land. Their three allotments, one for each of them, jointly comprised 480 acres that bordered on the east with those of her mother's family, so that much of the land along the Washita east to Anadarko had been deeded to them. Her grandfather ran cattle on his, but her father grew oats and corn and wheat; he had recently experimented with cotton, and some Mexicans had come last month to pick it.

Some of the land was rolling pasture, with knolls from where you could see, to the south, the low, irregular rim of the Wichitas; facing north, you'd see a line of cottonwoods and plum trees, sycamores, oaks, elms, and salt cedars that marked the course of the ruddy Washita, where the men fished and the children swam. Iola knew it all well—in the bar ditches were snakes of gourd vines with fall-browned leaves and yellowing fruits; the poppy thistles still had white blossoms that stood out against the grainy red sand of the earth. There were terrapins, prairie dogs and skunks, mockingbirds and quail, and, in the cattails along the river, red-winged blackbirds. Now and then you could see a fox and always deer. Sometimes it was good to be here—she felt *Indian* here—but sometimes it made her squirm.

Now that he had reached his own property, her father slowed the ponies, and his earlier claim for the need to hurry seemed at risk of being made a lie. Both she and her mother knew he had only wanted to put distance between himself and the audacious claim that Iron Lance had made. Now that they were safely away from any tribal discussion of it, it wasn't so urgent to him that Iola get to school.

And that was fine with her.

Her father parked the wagon in the yard under the chinaberry tree where the ponies could drink from buckets and wait in the shade. The yard was littered with tin cans, scraps of cloth, bones the dogs had gnawed. She used to complain to her mother about her habit of chucking discarded things out the door, but her mother would just shrug and say, *In the old days, people did that and just moved their camp.*

Her mother went into the kitchen, took out chunks of jerky and put them on the table that stood in the center of the room within arm's reach of the wood cookstove. The table, Iola noted, was covered by the familiar red-and-white checkered oilcloth, and from where she stood, it appeared to have pieces of food glued to it. Each time she came home from school the place seemed dirtier.

She would not offer to help her mother prepare the meal, and her mother would not ask her to: they had quarreled too many times over it. When she came back from school a year ago and tried to make an apple pie, her mother complained she wasted food like white people by throwing away the peeling and the seeds and using three eggs to make a cake. Iola had provoked her mother by lecturing her about washing things in hot water, shooing off bugs and flies. At school the girls had to press the muslin sheets, pillowcases, handkerchiefs, and dish towels with very hot irons to kill the germs and to ward off tuberculosis. All the beds at home were covered only by dusty blankets.

Unable to bear watching her mother prepare lunch, she went onto the porch, started to seat herself on a step, noticed that the red dust was thick on it, went back inside, and got a dirty flower sack and used it to whip the boards clean. Then she tucked and bunched her dark gray skirt and petticoats under her legs and sat down carefully. The ponies, still in their traces, were nosing one another and shaking their manes. A scissortail flycatcher darted out of the burnished sumac and swooped upward in front of her and over the house, the long, delicate fingers of its v-shaped tail carving an invisible trail in the blue sky. The hand fan her grandfather had for the peyote ceremony contained twenty-four feathers from flycatchers. Twenty-four by two. Twelve birds. Knowing how peyote fans were made would not get a person very far in the world, Iola mused.

The things her mother believed in. When Iola was little and she was frightened by a storm with a big wind, her mother would light a cedar stick and blow the smoke all around her. Then she would run her hands all over Iola's body and chant, *Red Horse, we are camping, go on by!* And Iola would feel safe. Later, though, after she learned at school that a tornado was a tornado, it only embarrassed her. Last spring, when her mother had tried to do it, Iola had gritted her teeth, then bolted away out of reach. It had wounded her mother deeply, and she was sorry for that. The storm was a bad one. As she sat alone in her room listening to the trees groan and the rain drum like stones on the tin roof, she was also sorry the comfort the little ceremony had once provided was now and forever out of her reach.

After a lunch of jerky, cold beans, and fried apples, Iola and her father climbed into the wagon. She shivered as the big front wheels rolled over and the ponies stepped out toward school. People would laugh at her if she obeyed her grandfather. It seemed everybody was always waiting for her to do something foolish, *yearning* for it. Morris, the Poulant brothers, and David Copperfield would rejoice were she to repeat what her grandfather had said.

"Father, do you think it's true, what Grandfather said?"

Her question broke a silence that had lasted an hour. The bell tower atop the main school building was visible on the horizon.

"No. They are gone for good. It's just an old man's wish."

"Mother would say 'medicine people always know things before-hand.' "

Her father was silent a long time. "Something you don't know," he said. "Apiatan, he was strong for the Ghost Dance, and so he went north to hear the Paiute prophet's words firsthand. Your mother and me, we waited with all the other Ghost Dancers for him to return. We hoped in our hearts he could bring our dead ones to us. Your brother had just died and we were grieving. We were young and he was our first child. We were very sad. We didn't care much about the buffalo, we just wanted our way-behind little one back."

He looked away a moment, then shrugged and half-consciously gave the reins a little shake to hurry the horses. "When Apiatan came back, he said the Paiute Wovoka lived in a dark and stinking hovel and had dirty feet. He was not the Messiah. When I heard this, it made my heart sore and I knew our medicine had failed. Your mother, she still wants to see our boy, she don't care how. She will be a Christian in case that is what it takes, but she don't want to give up being Kiowa because that might be right."

He pulled the horses to a stop to let a carriage overtake them from behind. "Hello, John," the man called out merrily as they went by, and her father waved back. Whites called all the Kiowa men "John," and this indifference to her father's individuality pained her. As did his answering to it.

"Father, do I have to tell people at school?"

"You have to say he believes this."

"Even if people don't ask?"

He was quiet again for a while. They were nearing town. Several times her father had to rein in the horse to the side of the road to let a motorcar pass, and in the afterwash she slapped at her white muslin blouse to rid it of the orange dust.

She thought perhaps he hadn't heard her question, but then he finally said, with a chuckle, "No, not if they don't ask."

His wry smile invited her to conspire against her grandfather. Though relieved, she couldn't shake the feeling that she and her father were betraying Iron Lance, who had, after all, chosen her father to hear his news and her to spread it at school.

"Don't you think Grandfather will feel foolish in front of all the white people when it doesn't happen?"

"What they think don't matter to him."

In that case, she would feel foolish for him, enough maybe for them both.

Her father dropped her off, and, hurrying, Iola slipped quickly through the screen door into the kitchen where girls were donning aprons in steamy air that reeked of turnips. Her timing was perfect—she had missed the evening meal but would still have to help in the kitchen. Maybe while she worked she could tell someone that today she heard an old man claim the buffalo were coming back, try out the news. As she deliberated about it, the janitor and the Comanche cook sat down at the small table covered with red oilcloth, drank sweet black coffee out of tin mugs, and smoked roll-your-owns while Iola and the girls worked around them and choked.

The cook said to the janitor, "I heard today somebody said the buffalo coming back soon."

Iola closed her eyes against the smoke and steam and held a breath—the word had spread already! Her heart fell.

"Crazy talk, some Indian drunk maybe," the janitor offered.

"No, this man, he say the white soldiers are making a big corral to catch them in, a thousand acres, out in the pastures west of Fort Sill—so they must think it is true."

She left the kitchen in a state of uncertainty. The rumor had spread, but her grandfather's name was not connected to it. This "news" now seemed to be converging on the school, so maybe her grandfather had not conjured it alone out of the cedar and sage smoke inside his lodge. It *might* be true, especially if white men believed it. Her own and her grandfather's risk of embarrassment were lessened, but then, so was their glory.

Was this rumor only old men's wishful talk? Everybody knew the buffalo were—what was the word?—*extinct*. Once her father had gone east with other Indians from all over the country to a big missionary meeting in Ohio. On the way, their train stopped in Kansas, where they had many awesome experiences: going up in an elevator, talking on the telephone (*When the little black thing spoke, I jumped about a mile*, he told her.) Finally, in the rotunda at the statehouse in Topeka, they had been shown a huge glass case. Inside it was a stuffed buffalo. An old warrior accompanying them had cried out, *Open the door to this box! I want to put my arms around the neck of my old friend!* At that time, no Kiowa had seen one for a decade.

Now it would be a quarter century, at least.

Wouldn't it be wonderful to see a real one? She had grown up swimming in a sea of buffalo stories; the Kiowa language was still plump with references to them, and yet no complete and tangible object had existed in her lifetime to make them less than mythical. Only mysterious, tantalizing fragments: every Kiowa household had utensils or clothing made from buffalo horn, sinew, bone, or hide, not so much used day to day but treated as ceremonial heirlooms. It was as if before her birth, Night had contained another moon that had fallen to earth in shards that were now kept in jars and boxes and deerskin parfleches. Fragments, like the Kiowas themselves, who were now scattered over three counties and onto separate allotments after centuries of living as a tribe and moving about at will all over the plains.

Mr. Horace Williams, the old white man who ran some skinny cattle on her grandfather's land, once told her that the only way white men could understand the tragedy of the buffalo being killed would be for them to look into their wallets one morning to discover that their money had disintegrated into a fine green dust.

Her grandfather said, Now that winter has come and it is night and all the work has been done, I will tell you a story about Sayday and how he brought the buffalo to the Kiowa.

Sayday ahe, was coming along, and he came to a camp where the people were starving. Some men told him, Sayday, you must help us!

Every time we go out to find something to eat, someone warns the animals away from us. Saynday told them to move their camp, and they did but they still could not find any meat. One day while they were thinking it over with Saynday, a man in their camp walked by, and they all smelled a delicious smell. The man was carrying a koysoybi, a sacred stick, that had been rubbed with buffalo fat, and they could smell that. The man saw that they were noticing him, so he walked away fast.

Saynday said, I think we should spy on that man. So he went to Owl and Dragonfly and told them to go follow this man and come back and tell them what they saw. Owl went and watched so hard that his eyes got big and stayed that way. Dragonfly went and watched so hard that his eyes popped out and stayed that way. When they came back, they told Saynday that when the man left his lodge every morning, he turned himself into a White Crow and went out ahead of the hunters and warned the animals so they could hide. Then the White Crow would come back at night and turn himself back into a man.

Saynday told them that he would sneak into the man's lodge and find out what was going on. He turned himself into a puppy and went and lay whimpering outside the man's lodge. He didn't do a very good job of becoming a puppy, though, because he left his mustache on! You know, Saynday, he does not always get things right! The man's little girl came out and said, Oh, what a pretty puppy! She took him inside and asked her father if she could keep him, but he said, that looks like a man to me, not a dog. I want you to go kill it! But she begged and finally the man said you can keep him, but do not show him where we hide the animals.

The next day when the man went out, the little girl moved a stone that was over a hole in the floor of the lodge and told the puppy to come look in the hole. But Saynday acted as if he were afraid, so the girl took him to the edge herself, and when she did, he jumped down into the hole and saw that all the buffalo were down there. He turned himself into a man and said, Scatter! Scatter all over the world!

The buffalo started running out of the hole, but the man came back while they were still coming out, and he was so mad that he stood by the hole with his bow, ready to kill Saynday when he came out. So Saynday made himself into a cockleburr and attached himself to the hide of the last buffalo and that's how he got away.

After the buffalo had run a good ways from the man's lodge, Saynday *turned himself back and said to the buffalo, You run away now! You run north and south as far as the land is flat, and you run east and west until you reach some mountains, and no farther. This is your home, and you are to make food for people to eat and hides for them to use for their houses and clothing.*

That is all of that story. The buffalo stayed above the ground and did as Saynday said until the white men came along and started killing too many of them. Then they said, We will go hide. I had a vision, there was a mist surrounding Medicine Bluff, it was dawn, and when the mist parted, the rock had split open like a cave and all the buffalo were going down into the hole there.

That night buffalo came, huge as the engines of white men's trains, rumbling across a pasture toward a distant ridge that was half obscured in a violet predawn mist. On the ridge were gigantic boulders, and they parted as the buffalo came running, showing a hidden world behind them of high grass and sunshine and waterfalls, then the buffalo moved through the opening and the boulders closed like doors. But a few buffalo who hadn't gotten through milled about, bawling, heartbroken from being separated, and when David came awake suddenly, he felt his mouth stretching open and shut like a fish mouth gasping for air, and he wondered with a shock if he had been shouting in his sleep.

He was drenched in sweat and his heart was hammering against his chest.

Was this a vision? Would they really come? Could Iola's grandfather see into the future, as some people were saying?

He tossed the covers off and breathed deeply to calm himself. The wet collar of his long johns clutched around his neck in a cold ring. The dream shook loose memories from his father's stories that were extraordinarily vivid; he felt as if he had been present when his father fought against the Ute with only the knife that was now in locker number 79, scooped the Mexican girl who was to be his mother up from the tiles in the courtyard of the hacienda, and rode good strong horses, rode *with the sun on your face and the wind whispering in your ears and nothing but grass any way you look, and you can see a long way because on the back of that good strong horse you are the tallest creature on the land, taller even than the buffalo.*

If the buffalo came back, could he and the other young men prove themselves? Hunt, go on raids? It didn't seem likely. All the medicine was gone, his father had said before he died. A golden time had come to an abrupt end just as David and the other boys came from the womb, too late for history to call them men. In the winter of 1874 many Kiowa warriors were herded by soldiers into an unfinished, roofless icehouse at Fort Sill, where they huddled under guard and slept in pup tents. Once a day an army wagon would arrive, and the soldiers would fling chunks of raw meat over the walls. He had heard old Gotebo say *It was like we were lions*. From there the captives were sent with some Comanches and Cheyennes to the dungeons of Fort Marion. When his father returned, he regained some of his former dignity by becoming a soldier in the Indian police at Fort Sill, but all the warriors-turned-police had been discharged before David was born. Stories aside, David knew his father mostly as a man who was always tired and coughed up blood. The missionaries said drinking would kill him; he said white men's prison had made his lungs bleed and that would kill him, too. Drinking made him feel better; missionary talk did not.

David and the boys were cursed with the twofold shame of having fathers and grandfathers who had been more than the boys would ever be but who had now become less than they had ever been. Since the boys could not show their own courage, they resorted to delinquency as an unsatisfactory substitute.

Without buffalo, without raiding and fighting, you cannot get rich, David thought. He would not be able to get enough horses to get the wife he wanted. Imagine how many horses a man would need to marry, say, a girl like Iola, whose family already had remudas of them everywhere. Not that he would want to, but what could a poor young man offer a family like that to get them to seriously consider his suit?

If the buffalo could come back, though, who knew what else might happen? Who knew what young men might earn their honor and get horses enough to obtain whatever young woman they might desire?

He had almost coaxed himself back to sleep when, without his volition, he recalled how Iola had turned to walk down the aisle beside Morris at chapel earlier in the evening and the motion of her torso had brought the white muslin of her guimpe snug against her chest for an instant. Two smooth humps. Blushing with alarm, he realized that—overnight, it seemed!—she had grown breasts.

He tried to push to the picture out of mind, but it faded only when the soft white mounds ripened into yellow then turned into glowing eyes.

In the morning, he was ragged and gritty-eyed from sleeplessness. The sky was overcast, and the chilly air smelled of dust stirred up by the wind, but there was no hint of rain. It didn't seem possible on this morning that anything good could happen in his lifetime, and he was sore at Iola for having been the agent of so slim a hope.

The matron rang the gong at six. Iola removed her nightgown, folded it neatly, and placed it at the head of the stuffed cotton tick. In the washroom she stood in a row at the basins and rubbed her face with cold water, then went into a stall and sat on the ring that had been warmed by a previous occupant and peed. Everything seemed normal.

Back at her cot, she quickly brushed out her hair, braided it, coiled the braids, and pinned them up behind her head. After she had slipped into her blue cotton Mother Hubbard, she went to help the younger girls get dressed. When they were ready, the matron stood at the door and inspected them as they left for the dining room.

But everything was *not* normal. Her stomach was too nervous for her to be hungry, so she could hardly bring herself to swallow her oatmeal. She kept her eyes fixed on her food, afraid to look over to the boys' tables. She could sense their attention like a chill. After breakfast, some girls went off in pairs to remake the beds, while others dusted and collected laundry. Iola and Mary Two Crow were assigned to sweep out the dormitory and the adjacent hallways, but they each had a broom and Iola was thankful for the opportunity to work alone.

School began at eight-thirty. When she arrived at the classroom, her heart was pounding, and as soon as she entered, students looked at her with great anticipation. At the back of the classroom sat Morris, grinning, next to David and the Poulant brothers.

One of them said, "Moo!" softly.

Shortly, Miss Roberts strode into the room, her erect carriage conveying her bulk in a fashion that suggested she was on wheels. They stood, and she seated them in unison, then surveyed the class with her bright squirrel's eyes. She was actually a young woman, though to Iola her size made her seem older. Her soft parts huddled cozily as if by amiable agreement; she was afflicted with copious sweats, so her lace collars drooped limply about her neck like damp washcloths, giving Iola the idea they had drawn her perspiration upward from her body like the wick of a lamp.

"Well, Iola," she said brightly. "I've just heard that you have something important to tell us. Something your grandfather wants us to know."

Stunned, Iola stared, trying to gauge the depth of the woman's knowledge in her face. She was apparently Morris's dupe.

Iola turned and stared at Morris and David; they grinned back. How could Miss Roberts be so blind?

"Yes ma'am."

Miss Roberts waited; Morris and David and the two morons, the Poulants, waited, everyone in the class waited.

Blushing, Iola drew in a breath.

"He says the buffalo are coming back."

Miss Roberts's eyebrows shot up.

"How nice."

Iola heard snickering. She whirled and glared at Morris. Other children were holding their hands over their mouths. David scrunched down so Miss Roberts couldn't see him, put his fingers up beside his head and wiggled them, lipping a silent "Mooo!" Iola fumed, close to tears. David, always the butt of Morris's jokes, relished the opportunity to make somebody else one. He looked angry at her but also happy to feel that way—an odd intensity in his gaze puzzled and hurt her.

She turned back to Miss Roberts, whose skepticism was as apparent as her desire to hide it.

"It's true!" Iola was amazed to hear herself say. "If he says it's true, it's true!"

Before anybody could deny it, she dashed out of the room. She ran to the dormitory, where she hid in the washroom for an hour, bawling so furiously it was like manual labor. Finished, she felt exhausted, sore-boned, her brain encased in ice. She pictured David's mocking face, his lips going "Mooo!," and the injustice scalded her heart—that *he* would tease her! She had always felt sorry for him and had always been nice to him!

For the rest of her life she would have to live right here in this washroom in this stall behind the closed door. She wouldn't eat or wash herself or change clothes, and she would sleep curled about the base of the toilet. She could never come out now that she had blurted something as foolish as that. Why hadn't she just kept her mouth shut? She hadn't had to say she believed it too, especially when she could see that Miss Roberts hadn't thought it was true.

Yet so long as she said she believed it, then neither she nor her grandfather was truly a fool until it did not happen or had been proved it never would. And shouldn't people give him—them—the benefit of the doubt? Or at least until he had been *proved* a fool? Wasn't that the right thing to do?

Being right could make you feel as if you were in quarantine, she thought. That was the way those Christian martyrs must have felt, when they kept telling the Romans about Jesus and the Romans only laughed.

Something told her, though, that she had spoken not because she had had the courage to say what was truly right; she had spoken because of her terrible fear of appearing to be wrong.

Realizing she had been manipulated, Miss Roberts made Morris leave the class and moved David back to his regular seat; for the rest of the morning David stared at Iola's vacant desk before him and felt chastened.

Morris was angry at Iola for having caused him to be kicked out of class. At lunch he talked about getting even, while David cringed to imagine Iola's crying if they picked on her more.

"Let's make a cake for her out of cow doo."

"She's mad now."

"So?"

"We've already done something."

"Why do you care if we do more?" Morris looked suspiciously at David. "Are you sweet on her?"

Benny Poulant snickered, and David blushed. "Why do you want to do more?"

"Because she thinks she's going somewhere."

It explained nothing, but before he could get Morris to clarify it, the older boy was shadow-boxing with him, feinting, then striking him in his gut with his pointed finger, saying, "Come on, let's do it, it won't hurt anything, it'll be funny."

David had already guessed what his role would be. "You give it to her, then."

"Oh no!" said Morris. "It was my idea—that's my part, wouldn't be fair! And we'll all make it."

David almost said no, but he was afraid that if he did Morris would turn to Benny and Henry and say something again about his being "sweet." Had what he felt about Iola showed? Or was Morris only guessing? Or joking?

David got one of the girls working in the kitchen to slip him a dinner plate through the screen door. Later, when class was over, he and Henry and Benny met Morris in the barn where they had been given afternoon chores for the week. Morris took the plate to the stalls that held the dairy cows, gathered up a mound of fresh dung with a shovel, and used a flat stick to create a cake-shaped blob on the plate. Henry added candles he had stolen from the pantry.

"What are we going to do with it?" asked Henry.

Benny said, "I think she is with the sewing girls today."

"Let David give it to her there," said Henry.

"I don't want to be the one. I'm always the one."

"I don't mind," said Benny.

"You can't just give it to her," said Morris to Benny. "You have to have an accident with it, you see?"

David pictured the "cake" in Iola's lap.

"That's good!" said Henry.

"We'll get into trouble," said David.

Morris gave him a look of disdain. "She won't tell, she'd be afraid to."

"Maybe he's right," said Benny.

"I'll do it, then," said Morris, disgusted.

"No," said David. "I will."

Morris grinned.

They covered the "cake" with cheesecloth and walked to the main building, with Morris leading and David behind, carrying the plate. David and the Poulants waited nervously on the landing of the second floor while Morris went to reconnoiter. After a few minutes he came back, grinning.

"Hurry, the matron's out of the room."

Henry lighted the candles and David went down the hall carrying the "cake," the other three boys behind him. When he entered the sewing room, a dozen girls seated at tables or behind sewing machines in the room looked up as Morris said, "Surprise!"

Iola was seated at a table in the far corner, intent on a piece of sewing in her hands. David moved toward her, feeling his own oddly tortured smile like a strange mask upon his face. When she glanced up and saw them bearing down on her, she looked frightened, like a small child, and he was suddenly ashamed—they were bigger, older, they outnumbered her, they were boys—but Morris was right behind him and the thing had already been set in motion.

Grinning, David bent at the waist and moved aside a pile of fabric that lay on the table. Behind him, he could hear the other girls giggling and Morris's distinctive cackle.

"I made this. Now you can celebrate with your friends the buffalo." He set the "cake" down on the table before her but she had already smelled manure and jumped up. She stood with her feet apart, her fists clenched at her sides.

Her chin started quivering. Tears welled in her eyes. "I've never done anything to hurt you, David. You just did this because Morris made you! You can't stand up to him—you're a coward!"

He blushed, stung by the word. The other girls were standing off to the side in a clump watching them with greedy interest in the outcome of this drama but also without any apparent allegiance to Iola. She had been sitting alone when they had barged in to play the prank. David saw for the first time now not how different he and Iola were but rather how alike. It broke his heart how miserable her pretty face looked, and all because she had no real friends.

He looked around for Morris and the Poulants as if for a cue, but they were gone, and all he saw was the Reverend McKnight's arm; then he felt the white man's freckled hand grab his ear and twist it as if to wind a clock.

David was frightened by how Big Whiskers mumbled and muttered and lectured while tethering David with a rope to the flagpole in the dusty courtyard in front of the main building. *Animal filth! If you want to revel in animal filth, then you will be treated as an animal! You are incorrigible! Filth and corruption!* His face got red, and the sharp contrast between the white beard and the flushed skin made David think of pictures of the white man who came in winter to bring gifts to children, only in an angry mood.

"You stay here until I come back for you!" McKnight commanded.

It was midafternoon. Later, when some younger children came by taking bread from the bakery to the kitchen, he was very embarrassed to be tied to the flagpole, so he pretended to be a buffalo bull. They stood beyond the reach of the rope and taunted him, and he galloped, bellowed, and rushed at them in fun.

Playing with the children made him forget he needed to piss. When they left, the pressure came back. Needing to piss also made him thirsty. Had everybody forgotten about him? Where was Morris? He wished someone would tell the Reverend McKnight to let him go to the bathroom.

An hour dragged by. No one came. David's bladder pushed harder until it felt like a boulder in his groin, and when he couldn't hold it any longer he pissed a huge round wet spot on his khaki trousers. As people crossed the courtyard to go to dinner, he sat bunched up, feeling cold from being wet. He hoped nobody would see what he had done, but he could see them whispering.

When the Reverend McKnight finally turned him loose, he thought, he'd change clothes, gather up a few belongings, then after the lamps were blown out, he would run away. From the flagpole he could see the driveway and the steps where old Hits Again had brought him in the wagon three years ago, and it seemed that in that time he had only accomplished becoming a coward, as Iola had said. Living among strange white men could be no worse than this. They wouldn't know he was a coward. Shame was a terrible thing. His father said that once a nephew of Sun Boy took a horse without the owner's permission and was so humiliated by being reproved for it in front of people that he took a pistol and blew his brains out.

He hid his face in his hands. After a long while, he heard someone approaching. When he looked up, Iola was walking toward him, a blanket in her hands. He stiffened and drew his knees up under his chin.

"I thought you would be getting cold."

"I don't want anything from you."

"I felt bad because you were punished, so I told on Morris. He said he would have dumped it on my head. Now he got kicked out of school, and you ought to be glad. You don't have any cause to be mad at me!"

Yes I do, he thought. You called me a coward. And now you say I ought to be glad Morris won't be around so I won't have to feel bad for not standing up to him.

She dropped the blanket in the dirt and walked back to the dining hall. He let the blanket lie without touching it, and shortly thereafter Miss Roberts gave him permission to leave the flagpole, but he had to go without dinner. He took the blanket and went to the dormitory, where he changed in the empty room. He lay on his bunk waiting for dark so he could run away, but exhaustion overcame him and he slept the night through in his clothes.

He awoke before anyone else. His stomach was writhing and growling. He had been dreaming of something pleasurable, however. Though he couldn't recall anything particular, the mood of well-being persisted like the scent of talcum powder and dust that permeated the blanket Iola had given him and with which he had covered himself against the chill sometime during the night. The big room was tranquil, faintly illuminated now by the violet predawn light. He was hungry, but it was only a pleasure to anticipate eating breakfast. He curled himself into a ball, his arms between his thighs, and rocked himself, shivering with the delicious warmth under the blanket. As he gradually awakened, his groin ached. He was hard as a hammer handle. Iola had brought him the blanket. Morris was banished from the grounds. He had stood with her in the sewing room, they were alike. Yes, he had been a coward, but he also hadn't dumped the thing on her as he had known Morris would have. Maybe she had figured that out, and that's why she had brought the blanket.

An inexplicably pleasurable sensation passed through him, and tears stung his eyes.

Later that morning, a man from the Kiowa agency came to tell the class that the government had built a wildlife refuge for buffalo and would stock it with a herd that now lived in a place called New York.

After lunch Miss Roberts announced that one schoolchild would be sent with the men to bring the buffalo back; the child would be chosen through an essay contest on the subject of Christopher Columbus. Everybody groaned. The outcome was a foregone conclusion. At that moment, David renounced whatever tenuous claim his tenderness toward Iola might make—she was already hurriedly stepping into her future, away from all of them.

The herd grazed in a pasture near an earthen water tank. Several yards downwind Black Horse and Horace Williams lay prone in knee-high grass, watching them. Horace Williams had an unruly gray beard and wore stained buckskin breeches and a vest two decades out of style; he had unpacked the outfit from a cedar chest. Black Horse wore denim trousers, a white shirt, red suspenders, and a black stovepipe hat festooned with eagle feathers. At their backs loomed a ten-foot fence of hogwire they had climbed up and over moments ago; behind it Iola stood with her face framed by one large wire square as she peered at the men. She could have easily climbed the fence, but they had made her stay back.

"I'll be go to hell if they ain't real!" said Horace. "Since that feller keeps talking about bison this and bison that, I thought they was trying to pass off some kind of misbegotten mules as buffalo."

I can smell them, Black Horse said in Kiowa. *They make my mouth water.*

Two bulls stood peacefully in the herd of cows, all with coats that had begun to shag for the winter. Calves nuzzled the cows, looking fat and glossy as they grazed, faces to the wind.

"Aw God!" uttered Horace. "They make me want to bawl!"

Black Horse groaned.

Judging by the men's reaction, these buffalo, destined to be unloaded at the siding at Cache in a few days, would thrill the older Kiowas. Iola could picture the stir the buffalo would make as the animals were unloaded out of the wagons. At the mouth of the huge enclosure built south of Rainy Mountain, the people were already camping in the pastures, waiting for the buffalo, her grandfather among them.

The men's faintly religious awe disconcerted her. She was seeing buffalo for the first time, but it was hard to fit the preconceived ghostly templates scribed across her imagination against these sweating beasts now engaged in nothing more glorious than chewing their cud. To her inner eye the buffalo had always been as tall as, say, hay barns, but these standing by the water tank were only half again as big as horses.

Maybe they should have sent one of the boys instead of her. But even they might have been disappointed, for which she would feel partly to blame. Watching the buffalo graze calmly like cattle, she worried that Morris and the Poulant brothers and David would poke more fun at her. They wouldn't say they were impressed by the buffalo no matter what they really felt. Morris had easily tainted her victory: when the agent had brought the news, she had taunted Morris, saying "See, the buffalo *are* coming, he was right!" He had shrugged and said, "Only because the white men are bringing them."

Her hand rose to press against her breastbone. Under her coat she could feel a lump against her skin. Her grandfather had given her a little buckskin bundle of herbs and secret things for her to wear around the neck. It would keep her safe on her journey, he said. Many times during the trip she had felt for it but doing that only made her remember what Morris had said.

She lifted her gaze from the breathing animals and into the trees beyond, and the bright red blocks outlined above them were so compelling they might have been gigantic birds with wings of brick. She thought, if those buildings had fur and horns, and those windows were the eyes and the row below a mouth . . .

The many windows along the top floors made the buildings look like train cars linked together and stacked atop one another in the sky over the city called "The Bronx." Before coming East, she had seen pictures of New York and Chicago in books, but these actual buildings had a scale and grandeur that far exceeded anything suggested in the photographs. She loved being up in the buildings; she and the children from the other schools who had made the trip had been taken by their white chaperones to a rooftop where trees were growing in pots and you could see, stretched out below, hundreds of buildings. Black Horse would not stay in a hotel room on an upper story because it made him nervous "to sleep so close to the moon," he said. For Iola, the higher the better. The most memorable part of her trip had been trekking up the narrow stairs inside the Statue of Liberty to look out onto ocean, boats, bridges, buildings, and wharves. Some Kiowas who had been to school at Carlisle, Pennsylvania, had boasted of having seen big cities, but she had had no idea of how much land was covered with white men's houses, farms, cities, train tracks, and roads. She had seen vast stockyards in St. Louis, huge sternwheelers nudging aside the muddy Mississippi; in Indiana, Ohio, and Pennsylvania, the cities had been dark with stack smoke and the streets crowded with men who looked black but weren't Negroes. In St. Louis and in Ohio somewhere, whites hadn't let the Indians eat in their cafés, which made Iola angry. Instead, they ate in colored people's places, where the Negroes were friendly. In Liberty's crown, she imagined herself being a woman this tall; walking around the earth on legs this long, you could go anywhere you wanted to, all over the globe, you could go to Europe and say to the people, *Give me your tired, your poor, your huddled masses yearning to breathe free* . . . and hold out your long arms to gather them in.

Her grandfather had no notion of what she had been learning through this journey. Nor could he have guessed what a profound impression it would make. But, she thought, her father knew. That was why he allowed her to come. She had one eye for her father and one eye for her grandfather. The tension between the two men met in her heart: her grandfather had wanted her to learn the glory of the final chapter in Kiowa tribal life, but her father had wanted her to learn that this glorious chapter was final.

A motorcar chugged behind her and pulled to a stop with a squeal. The driver was a white man named Richards who had earlier driven them here and had then gone to take several other Kiowas to the railway siding to begin reinforcing the rail cars for the trip west. Horace Williams and Black Horse had then gone over the fence, and Iola could tell by the way the white man gripped the steering wheel and squinted through the windshield that he wasn't happy about this.

Richards jumped from the motorcar and scurried over to stand by Iola. He was wearing those strange-looking white man's shoes—they had rows of tiny perforations across the toes in swirling designs.

"They're dangerous!" he called out to the men, who were still lying in the grass. "They're unpredictable; it's not a good idea to get any closer. We can't be responsible."

Horace looked over his shoulder at Richards. With a huge, ragged grin, he pointed to his companion.

"You think you can tell *him* anything about buffalo?"

Black Horse scrambled to his feet and suddenly strolled toward the herd.

"Hey, wait!" the white man yelled. Black Horse turned in midstride, grinning.

"No English!" he hollered back.

Richards paced along the fence, while Iola watched Black Horse with increasing anxiety. The buffalo might not have been as big as barns, but their bodies had a taut, dense bulk that suggested a ton of compact meat on nimble hooves, and their black woolly faces looked angry and mean.

Walking slowly, Black Horse approached the herd. He circled until he was facing them, upwind, on the far side of the earthen tank, letting them take his scent. The buffalo lifted their muzzles from the grass and the water and eyed him, the languid rotation of their jaws now suspended. Black Horse kept coming slowly, crouching, one moccasin at a time planted in the grass before him with a gingerly probe, until, at last, he stood an arm's length from the face of a bull. The bull's withers twitched with hostility, and its tail shot upright into the shape of a quivering question mark.

"Oh Lord!" breathed Richards.

Iola's heart thumped in her breast as Black Horse bent at the waist and squinted as if to make certain his vision hadn't deluded him, almost nose to nose with the bull. All at once, he slapped the bull between the eyes, counting coup, then he whooped, "Hohe!"

Startled, the bull and the herd exploded into motion, grunting and galloping away from the tank. Horace laughed.

Black Horse trotted back to the fence with a grin, and Horace got up and clapped him on the back. Behind them, the herd circled the circumference of the pen at a run that brought them wheeling around toward the two men. Both laughing, they scrambled up and over the fence just as the buffalo thundered close by Iola, shaking the ground under her feet; suddenly, their glossy forms ballooned in her vision as they flew past in a brown blur, their hooves raising a billowing dustcloud tainted with the rich stench of dung and sweat. She jumped back from the fence with a happy yelp, clapping her hands. This was what buffalo were supposed to do!

"You shouldn't have done that!" Richards removed his hat and angrily brushed at the dust on its crown with the sleeve of his suitcoat. "You've gotten them aroused. They can't go on the train that way." As a representative of the New York Zoological Society, Richards was responsible for overseeing the shipment of fifteen buffalo from here to Oklahoma, and Horace Williams had resented his authority from the moment they had met.

"We just wanted to make sure they was real," said Horace. "We didn't know but what they had been living with you New York people so long they didn't know how to act like buffalo."

Black Horse's eyes were glazed with tears. He buried his nose in his palm and inhaled deeply.

Oh, I can almost taste that hot blood, he murmured to Horace.

"What's he saying?"

"He's just admiring them. Them are fine specimens of buffalo, they truly are."

Richards rolled his eyes. "Bison," he corrected Horace for the third time that morning.

"How many have you killed?"

"None, of course! We—"

"All right, then," Horace went on. "How many have you eaten?"

"None, thank God, our job here is to preserve—"

"Well, I've had 'em baked and boiled and fried and fricasseed and in fritters. I've gnawed their haunches and chewed their briskets and humps and sucked their marrow and my friend here is especially fond of their livers and gallbladders when he can get 'em hot and bloody right from the kill. These are the first *buffalo* we've seen in years, so if we wanna call them blue-balled baboons, it's our business, and we'll be thanking you for keeping your trap shut about it!" Horace turned back to the herd, squinting. "Pardon my French, girl," he added.

Richards transported them to where the other men and children were at a railroad siding adjacent to the zoo. After a while, the buffalo were herded into a corral at the siding, then they were driven up ramps and into large wooden cars. Horace and Black Horse licked their chops when Richards was watching them.

After the train left New York, Richards kept a fearful eye on the two men. Iola smiled as Horace Williams made a big show of strapping on his hunting knife and strolling back to the cattle cars, which forced the zoo's representative to get up and stalk behind him. When he finally returned, he would hand the knife over to Black Horse with a ceremonial flourish, and Black Horse would go off to "visit" the buffalo. They kept the New York white man constantly on his feet.

The second evening out, in the Allegheny Mountains, the two men watched with silent glee as Richards nodded off, exhausted. They let him glide into eye-twitching sleep, the kind that leaves the face numb and the mind at the bottom of a well, then Black Horse tossed back his head.

"Hi-yah, he-ya, hi-yah, he-yah! Ko-la, ko-la, ko-la!" he chanted.

Richards scrambled awake like a man dreaming of snakes in his bed. He pointed a shaking finger at Black Horse.

"What's wrong with him?"

"You'll have to excuse him. He smells buffalo blood. He hasn't seen one killed in twenty years."

"Bought Buffalo Sun Dance," put in Black Horse, whose English could show remarkable improvement at times.

Richards looked at Horace Williams as if expecting a translation.

"Back in the late eighties nobody could find a buffalo to kill for a Sun Dance, so they had to buy one off old Charlie Goodnight."

"Oh!" uttered Iola, but nobody seemed to hear her.

"You!" Richards said to Black Horse. He pointed boldly at the Kiowa. "No kill buffalo." He violently shook his head for emphasis and slashed the air before him with his stiffened arm.

"Kill *many* buffalo," Black Horse replied.

"Hundreds maybe," said Horace. "Don't call him a liar."

"No," said Richards. "Not then. *Now!* Tell him he can't kill any of these."

"These *what?*" asked Horace, laughing.

I met your father at the Sun Dance where they had to buy the buffalo from a Texan. It was the last one ever held. Some day again, maybe. Now, watch how I am staking the hide of the deer to the ground here, with the flesh side up. Here, help me.

He was of the Wild Plains band, and we were Sugar-Eaters, they called us that because we camped pretty close by the agency. You could always tell when the time came for the dance in the summer because you would see the little tufts from the cottonwood trees start to float through the air. The Tai-may keeper would send out messengers to all the bands, and if you were in your camp you'd see him come up on his horse, pretend to be blowing an eagle-bone whistle, and look up at the sun, and move his body as if he were dancing. Oh, and was everybody happy! Then he would tell people where the dance was to be held.

It was very important. You listen now. Because, you see, it was the only time all the people got together to pray and to thank the Great Spirit for the buffalo and to hear about news from your kin, see the new babies, and, heh! it was a time for young people to sneak away, too. Take this, you see those dots, that's how many years this scraper was used. The handle is bone from elk, my grandmother had it back up north where we came from. The metal's about gone, isn't it, that part used to be flint. No, child, get on your hands and knees, put your weight into it and get all the meat and tissue off. . . .

We all camped in a great circle, with each band having a certain part of the circle each year, the same place every time. It made your heart sing to look out across that circle and see so many lodges. You missed some, over here, look.

It was the second of the getting-ready days, I think, when he and some other young men were standing around joking and bragging about their fathers' ponies, and I went past them on my way to the creek for water for my mother. You know, people didn't have wells then, or water tanks with pipes, and a girl always had to go for the water. Anyway, he —heh!—was all puffed up and sticking out his chest like this! And he came and said he wanted to go with me for water. I thought he was very handsome but also very pleased with himself, he was like all young men that way. My mother had already told me that since it was my four-teenth summer that this should be the Sun Dance where I found a husband. Otherwise, it would be another year unless I wanted to con-sider some boy in our own band.

Well, I thought that if he liked me I would accept him. This going-for-water business went on for a few days, and each time I liked him more and more. My mother started teasing. She said, Daughter, if I have to drink any more water I will burst! Next thing, my father came into the lodge and said to my mother, he was smiling very sly, Looks like some foolish young man is trying to keep his horses where our lodges are! And of course we went outside and saw all the horses his family had brought over. That Spanish saddle with the silver trim? It, too. Bunch of blankets . . .

When we finish this side we'll turn it over and scrape the hair from the other side. We'll make buckskin, not rawhide, from this deer, it's a nice one. When we get the hide scraped good and clean, we'll rub it with something we'll make. They say every hide has enough brains to tan itself! We'll use the liver and brains from the deer and cook them with some fat, then we'll pound it all until it's soft and then we'll rub that into the flesh side of the hide with our hands and a stone.

Don't make such a face! What's that face for? When we finish with this hide, you'll know how to make buckskin. How will you make moccasins or shirts if you can't even make buckskin? You may be pretty but no young man is going to be interested in some girl who makes a terrible face and doesn't know how to make moccasins, let alone decorate them with beads.

You're always going to wear shoes? I see. You think things will always be just the way they are now. Yes, I know you are going to a white man's school to learn the wearing-shoes road. No buckskin or mocca-sins, only white ladies' dresses and shoes. Tell me, what will you do about the color of your skin?

•

On the third morning, the train stopped in Columbus, Ohio. Suffering from cabin fever, Iola escaped the notice of the chaperone and slipped out of the car where the children rode. She climbed the ladder of a freight car just ahead of the cattle cars and sat on the edge with her legs dangling over. Horace and Black Horse walked on top of the cattle cars, opened trapdoors, pitched down hay for the buffalo, then poured buckets of water through the slats and into a trough. The animals were mired in their own manure and hay. From her perch, Iola could see the spines of the buffalo in constant motion but without forward progress, like snakes swimming against a strong current.

Now that she was accustomed to them, they were her buffalo. She thought of how her mother described the way the Y-shaped pole in the huge Sun Dance lodge would hold the head and the hide from the back of the buffalo that had been killed in a special way, and she thought of how much work there would be in scraping, tanning, and working a hide from an animal as big as the buffalo below her feet. The women would make the lodges out of nine hides, sitting around together in a circle, sewing and cutting. That was still another chore she would not have to learn how to do. Her mother thought she was lazy, but she didn't mind work; she just didn't like to waste energy on things that would not matter.

As the train pulled away from the siding, she stayed atop the freight car watching the buildings of Columbus slide across her vision. After a while, the train was moving across the rolling countryside, and she enjoyed the sensation of height and forward motion, as if the train were a great beast and she was astride it, hurling across the earth.

The air was crisp, the sky dominated by a high-pressure dome of blue air suspended over the Ohio Valley. She wrapped her blue woolen cape more closely around her shoulders, feeling the sunlight on her face and the delicious chill nipping at the backs of her ears. To the north along the high, rolling ridge rising from the rail bed, a stand of green forest had begun to dapple, the oaks brownish-orange and the maples ruddy in the strong yellow light. A flock of crows darted out of the trees and sailed over the tracks, cawing.

Her mother said that Saynday had turned the White Crow black as punishment for hiding the buffalo from the people. He disguised himself as a dead elk lying on the plain, and when White Crow came along to start pecking at his ribs, Saynday closed his ribs around White Crow and caught him. Her mother's face always looked serious when she told this, as if these were not mere legends. Saynday gave White Crow to Spider Old Woman, who threw him into her fire—her mother's eyes would widen with the horror of this, making Iola giggle or flinch—and the crow came out black from the fire.

Alone, she wasn't embarrassed by her mother's tale-telling; rather, an image of her mother's face made her neck suddenly warm, the way it felt when, on a cold night, her mother came to spread another blanket over her as she lay half asleep.

At night when she slept now, some strange black grass sprouted glossy and downy on the meadows of her flesh without her volition. It had spread from her legs to her pubes to her armpits, growing fast and wild but fine. Strange ruddy secretions betrayed the integrity of her flesh. She had felt a certain gathering, the moonlight sinking into her joints and swelling them, her chest suddenly like a patch of earth upon which the caps of two large sprouting mushrooms had appeared. When her arms dropped to her sides now, her hands brushed her hips. These inexplicable transformations had a terrifying edge, as if the person she thought of as Iola were really only a kernel bound inside a wrapping of flesh that was constantly burgeoning in obedience to a voice that it, but not she, could hear.

No matter what, she wouldn't become a blanket Indian like her mother. But surely she would be married, have babies? Would there be some young man who had not given up and become only a drunk or a talker, some man with his own allotment who could farm and keep cows and horses and knew how to read and write? There were girls her age now who had already married, but their lives were not even as good as her mother's. They didn't have the pride and status of being married to proud men and having come from a good family. Her mother had been pressuring her to start looking about for someone to marry so she could start a family, but her father and Miss Roberts believed that such a life was too small for her. She needed more education so that maybe she could be a teacher or a doctor, even a lawyer. People always spoke of T'ow-haddle whose white name was Laura Pedrick. She had been among the first of the Kiowa girls to attend Carlisle and had married another student, who had died. Now she was married to a white man and was influential in tribal affairs—she had even been to Washington to help her brother, Apiatan, negotiate about leasing the Big Pasture. Miss Roberts talked to Iola about a Sioux, Gertrude Bonnin, who taught at Carlisle and who had written articles for important white people's magazines, and about an Omaha woman named Bright Eyes, who had gone to Philadelphia Women's Medical School then returned to her people in Nebraska as Dr. Susette La Flesche.

But it seemed to her that while people admired these women, if you told someone you planned to be like them or if they saw you doing what was necessary to become like them, they resented you for putting yourself above everybody. Her mother's sisters were all that way. They made fun of her for not knowing how to bead very well or make much with her hands. They said, What will you wrap your babies in, white man's newspapers?

Overhead, a plume of smoke from the engine drifted toward the river that paralleled the tracks. To her right, beyond the cornfield where the crows had settled like a torn blanket, lay another field where a farmer walked behind a team of mules, hands on a plow, turning under a stand of oat stubble. As the train passed, the farmer reined in the mules and watched, then returned Iola's wave. He was rooted to the field with hands curled stiff like old gloves to match the handles of the plow and the share snagged like a fishhook into the flank of the earth. He might be jealous, she thought, of her rolling westward toward an unknown future.

When she looked ahead, the sky was full of orange wings. The train had intersected a swarm of butterflies, and they made her heart leap into her throat. The turbulence stirred by the moving cars made them tumble and sail crazily in the air; some were sucked into the vortex and were plastered against the fronts of the cars. They struck her face and cheeks. A huge bolus of them was suddenly caught in the thermal uplift of the black coal smoke; it was momentarily tossed about and shredded into individual tatters, but then it reassembled before resuming its flight for the river.

They were only the vanguard; soon, she was abob in a butterfly soup. Looking north, she couldn't find a window of sky uncluttered with orange wings. Nothing stopped them, not even the train; a message in their delicate tissue drove them forward on a path already encoded in their cells.

Oh, to be a butterfly! Tell me, little brothers, how do *you* know where to go? What to be?

Sacrificing individuals, the swarm was undaunted by the passing cars. Even after the caboose had long passed under them, the butterflies still formed an arc over the empty track, an arc like a rainbow over their memory of a train.

4

When the word spread that the buffalo were returning, people put up tents and tipis in the pasture by the enclosure near Otter Creek. The men built brush arbors and sat under them to smoke and drink illicit whiskey or Perunia. Some told old winter stories, sang war or journey songs, bragged about the buffalo they had killed and the enemies they had scalped. They played three-card monte and the hand game, and gambled on horse races in the pasture. The women cooked in the old way, over fires in black pots; they scoured the thickets for late wild plums, pounded chokecherries into dried beef for jerky, and cooked fry bread; they rolled their babies about in strollers or hung them in their cradles from trees. When the children arrived, having been dismissed from their various schools for this occasion, they played Kiowas-and-Texans, did the old Rabbit Dances, and practiced their bowmanship with rolling hoops, while the older boys played football and raced their ponies.

The evening before the buffalo came, David took a blanket down by the creek to sleep, wanting to get away from his sister's family and the students from his school. He had been avoiding Morris since the cake incident; it was a form of standing up to him. He was still smoldering from his humiliation. He felt lonely, but wouldn't forsake his pride and seek out the Poulants or Morris. Instead, he lay by the creek on his blanket in the twilight and nursed his sorrow.

He was within several yards of the tipi that Iron Lance had set up to hold a peyote ceremony at the rear of the encampment. Near nightfall, Iola's grandfather and three other men—Apiatan, Dangerous Eagle, and Robert Dances Best—appeared in their full panoply of feathers, buckskin, and beads outside the lodge. They had painted their faces yellow with black chins and foreheads. Robert Dances Best held a water drum, Iron Lance a brace of beaded gourd rattles, and they all had their fans tucked under their arms.

He watched, curious, as Iron Lance led the other three men slowly around the circumference of the lodge, from the east-facing opening around to the left or south, then to the back and the north sides. They walked three times about the tipi, and then Iron Lance led them inside.

After a while, David could smell the fragrance of sage and cedar, then tobacco smoke. He guessed the men were filling the clay pipe with Bull Durham mixed with crushed sumac leaves. He knew that along with the smoking, they would be swallowing mashed peyote buttons softened with water.

During the night, the men beat an incessant rhythm on the water drum and shook rattles. They sang eerily for hours, "traveling to the moon," their voices weaving in and out of David's thoughts and dreams. He could smell the cedar smoke from the fire in the lodge. Once, he awakened and watched shadows play on the walls as one singer rose to relate his vision to the others. He was glad to be so close to these men, to this ceremony, closer to the powerful secrets of what made the world work. Some word they uttered or sung might drift like smoke into the spirit world where knowledge would be unloosened to tumble back into David's life—how to get horses, how to save face, earn respect.

Just before dawn, six Kiowa men rode to the railroad's unloading point at Cache, a few miles south of the Preserve. The train arrived just as the sun came up, and, dumbstruck, the men peered like sleepwalkers into the cattle cars at the big animals; reality and memory and legend collided at once to paralyze them, as if they had come to greet the Messiah only to see him step off the train smoking a cheroot and carrying his own bags.

After David rose, he ate breakfast with Standing Inside Lodge and her family, then returned to the creek; he wanted to be alone to feel sorry for himself for having to be alone. Midmorning, Morris and the Poulant brothers brought their horses to the creek to drink. They had been racing them. The other three boys sat a few yards from where David lay propped on his elbow, watching them. They seemed to ignore him. Surely Morris was aware that David was still angry for how they had deserted him. He wanted them to apologize; he longed for the bad feelings to vanish so that he could enjoy their company, but he would not make the first move.

"You think they'll really come?" Morris asked no one.

"Sure," said Henry Poulant.

Morris seemed skeptical. He was restless. He got up, stepped over to a willow, and cut a switch. He swatted at trees and bushes with it, then he turned abruptly to David.

"How do you feel?"

"Fine," blurted David, startled. The question resembled an apology, and he raised himself into a cross-legged sit facing the Poulants.

Morris strode over to his pony, retrieved an old parfleche that was draped over the pony's back, and returned to where they were sitting. He plopped it onto the ground and rooted about in it. Warily, David considered that the question about his health had not been an apology; it was the barb to hook him into some new game, and he steeled himself to remain suspicious.

The Poulants looked curious but also faintly apprehensive. They wore straw hats and white shirts with orange suspenders, and their school haircuts fell just above their collars. They came from a wealthy, well-known family; they sometimes gave David the impression that even Morris was beneath them and that were he not so amusing or daring they would have dismissed him.

Morris was holding a red clay pipe in one hand, and, in the other, a few small, thornless green cacti with gray caps shaped like stars.

"Where'd you get that?" asked Henry.

"Oh, don't worry!" sneered Morris. The pipe was unadorned and looked smaller than the sacrosanct pipes used by the tribe's medicine keepers.

"Moan," said Morris to David. "Make the sound of a sick buffalo!"

David had been prepared to resist, but Morris passed him an engaging smile and winked in a way the brothers could not see. Come on, he was saying. It won't hurt. These Poulants are stodgy and superstitious, but you're not.

The appeal was irresistible. David closed his eyes and bleated. The Poulants laughed. When David smelled smoke, he opened his eyes. Morris had packed the pipe with Bull Durham, lighted it, and moved over close to them.

Morris feinted toward each of the four winds, then he took four puffs and passed the pipe to Henry, who looked very dubious about the implied sacrilegious mockery but was also caught up in saving face. David enjoyed watching him squirm. Finally, Henry took a puff and passed the pipe quickly back to Morris.

"We have to make this buffalo well so he can be hunted."

David and the Poulants smoked the pipe, the Poulants taking turns sending surreptitious glances across the meadow to the camp. David felt allied with Morris. Having no illustrious family to fear, he was a fellow renegade.

Morris then plucked the star-shaped caps from the cacti and pounded them into bits on a rock. The Poulants watched with alarm.

Morris snickered. "It's mine," he said, implying he'd take responsibility for possessing and handling the peyote. It was sometimes administered to the sick by authorized priests and was taken ceremonially, but no one would applaud this frivolous use, and the missionaries had damned it as more dangerous than strong drink. Morris offered David a horn spoonful of ground-up bits moistened with water. He was humming a chant; he drew his fingers through the mud of the creek bank and moved that hand toward David's face, obviously intending to dab it with the red mud.

The spoon came farther forward, laden with the "medicine." The Poulants held their breath. David balked. Morris reached out with the splayed fingers of his left hand, and David felt the coolness of the mud touch his hot forehead, his cheeks, then the tautness when it instantly dried in the air.

Morris winked again seductively. It suggested a grand plan that might eventually unfold to the Poulants' detriment. David stared intently at the gray-green chunks of meaty substance in the spoon that were like an off-color mushroom, then he parted his lips and Morris shot the spoon forward, dumping the contents into his mouth.

He started to chew, but the taste was so bitter he gagged; on his hands and knees, he scrambled to the water and slurped up a mouthful to wash the cacti bits that had stuck in his craw. Some of it he had spat out, but at least half the dose had been swallowed.

Morris and the Poulants were laughing. He looked up from the water with a sullen glare that warned them to stop.

"Now it is time for the Sick Buffalo to rest," Morris announced, as if reciting a litany. "When he wakes, he will be well."

He pressed David's forehead with his palm, forcing David to lie back. David shut his eyes. He felt comfortable, the passive role relieving his anxiety. After a moment, the metal discs on Henry Poulant's leggings jingled. David eased his eyes into slits to see that Morris and the Poulants were walking toward their ponies.

He closed his eyes again. He hoped they were going off for a while. The sun warmed his face. Having been assigned the role of sleeping off a sickness, he lay still, locating a faint queasiness in his belly that he soothed by not moving. The tip of his tongue kept discovering bitter bits of peyote between his teeth.

For a while he listened to voices coming from the camp, children shouting in the distance, then a murmur. Crows went *kawww kawww eep*, mad at the world. A lizard skittered through dry leaves nearby, making an angry whisper. The creek sighed, burped. *Saynday was coming along, and when he reached a big creek he tried to jump over it but he broke his legs. Grandfather Buffalo came along and so he said, Grandpa, help me over! I broke my legs. But Grandfather Buffalo said, Oh no! You are too tricky! And Saynday . . .*

He might have dozed; the murmur from the camp had grown indistinct but constant, like the sound of a stream. After a while, the smell of fry bread reached his nostrils. It grew thicker like heavy leaf smoke until he thought he would choke. One moment his mouth was watering from hunger, then the next he was nauseous.

He sat up suddenly. Though he stopped his forward motion, his body kept rolling then rising into the air like a tumbleweed lifted aloft in a whirlwind. He leaned over and vomited onto the dark red sand a bolus of green and yellow bile; it was extremely colorful, almost glowing. He looked about. He didn't see Morris, so he lay back down. The sky was a hard blue that looked colder up high. Sunlight in the sycamore over his head made animated dancers of the dangling, sharp-thorned seed-balls.

He closed his eyes. His body wanted to levitate and drift away from the spot, so he plunged his fingers into the packed damp sand at his flanks to anchor himself. That felt better. Pictures of strange animals with tails thrusting out of their mouths were hurled up against the dark backdrop of his closed eyelids, then he saw the animals in the distance out on a plain and they appeared to be arguing but he couldn't distinguish their words. Then a herd of buffalo were looking at a lone bull who stood off by himself under a tree *each year at a special time the bull, he will move away from the herd and stand for days while he has a vision and that's why the Buffalo Medicine men go off alone. . . .* and the herd were all calling out to him *Wake up, old buffalo!*

"You are well, Sick Buffalo!"

The voice thundered in his head. His eyelids snapped open; above him, on horseback, were Morris and the Poulants. The legs of their horses were like tree trunks in a forest, the way they circled his head and went up into the clouds.

The boys' heads were small, far above him. They had painted their faces yellow with red stripes.

"We've cornered you, Buffalo, but we'll let you get up and run now that you're well."

Morris had an old coup stick with a rawhide thong wrapped about his wrist. He reached down and tapped David's skull with it. The pony was restless and danced on the sand near David's head. Its unshod hooves were big as bushel baskets to his eye. From somewhere in his mind came the command to avoid being stepped on.

Morris leered. The other two boys were grinning, but their lips kept curling and sliding as if trying to crawl off their faces.

"Get up, Buffalo! Run!" yelled Morris.

Trembling, dizzy and scared, he rose, fear turning into hot energy in his muscle. He bellowed, then scrambled up the embankment and galloped over the pasture. In a moment he could feel hooves at his back shaking the ground. They rode beside him, going *la la la la la* as they chased him, and he ran on, panting, his mouth open to catch the wind so that his tongue felt like a dry wooden stick. His heart raced, a strange thrill tore through his veins, and he knew he could have run for days.

When Morris whacked him on the head again with the coup stick, he spun in a rage and bellowed, then flung himself at the pony, grabbed it around its neck and wrestled it to the ground. Morris toppled off and landed on his back, and before he could get up, David was stamping his chest and ribs with his buffalo hooves; as Morris was scrambling to his feet, David knocked his head against the other boy's, giving out such huge angry buffalo brays that the Poulants stood off on their ponies staring in disbelief.

Morris yelled for help but got none. Then he dashed away after his pony. His chest heaving, David came momentarily back to himself. His fury shocked him, but between waves of hallucinatory sensation, he was sober enough to realize that the fury came from Morris's having tricked him. But being trapped inside this buffalo brought an exhilarating release: if they wanted buffalo, he would be buffalo, many buffalo.

Morris stood behind the Poulants, taking the reins of his pony in one hand and rubbing his head with the other.

Owl! he yelled angrily at David. "You're crazy!"

To test his new power, David stepped toward them and scowled. To his delight, they took off at a gallop toward the creek. A while later, skulking about the edges of the camp looking for them, he spotted them playing football in the distance. They looked very small.

He wandered aimlessly in a peculiar daze in which all objects were outlined with an astonishing clarity and their colors had a richness that made his eyes ache. He could not have said how long this went on, but he was startled when everyone around him suddenly jumped up as if by a hidden signal and ran along the edge of the enclosure; he followed without knowing why until he saw, far off on a ridge to the south, a caravan of wagons moving down the trail from Cache, their wheels raising dust. When they drew closer, David saw the high stakes jutting up from the beds and, above that, the rounded humps of brown backs. The buffalo were coming in the wagons, not by their own legs!

Were they sick or crippled?

The lead wagon was being driven by an old white man, and when he saw the people coming forth in a mob across the grass, he checked the team of oxen and waved for the following wagons to slow down. Iola was seated beside him, and David kept to the back of the crowd to hide, though once he thought she saw him but simply looked right through him as if he were no more substantial than air. Riding in the front of the caravan, she looked very full of herself.

When the first wagon had passed, David struggled up through the crowd to get closer. Listing with their weight, the wagons creaked forward through a sea of humanity. The children leapt up on the spokes of the slowly moving wheels to see the buffalo, while the animals grew frightened by the commotion. People hurried alongside the wagons and stuck their hands through the pickets to stroke the buffalo's legs and fetlocks, marveling, chanting old songs, and laughing to each other. They shouted at the buffalo as if expecting the buffalo to answer; they sang to them; the young boys hurled challenges in voices thick with bravado.

David worked his way forward until he was trotting alongside the third wagon with his hand curled about a picket. His knuckles were inches away from fur that belonged to a part of a buffalo he couldn't identify. Although he couldn't see them clearly because of the dust and the jostling of the wagons as well as his own bobbing head, their stench of sweat, wet wool, piss, and dung struck him like a blow, and he knew they were real, at last.

He leaned up close to the wagon, striding swiftly to keep up, pushing his face between the stakes. Unexpectedly, he was confronted by a large bearded face countering his own, with a nose broad as his hand and a forehead as substantial as a wood stump. The mouth opened, a large purple tongue dropped down, wagging, as if the buffalo were chuckling; when David blinked and looked again, the animal had shifted so that one wet brown eye big as a plum was looking at him, and the convex, glassy sheen of it reflected his rawhide-colored face quavering like a picture in disturbed water.

Everyone wanted to help unload the buffalo and drive them into the holding pen inside the enclosure. There was much noise and confusion until several Kiowas and soldiers from Fort Sill herded the buffalo safe behind the gate, where, once they felt the earth under their hooves, they started grazing on the grass in the pasture. In the meantime, a large, open motorcar arrived carrying a reporter from Oklahoma City, the Kiowas' agent, Hackworth, an assistant to the territorial governor, and a white lady in a blue dress who kept a pink parasol hiked over her head, even though the day was cool. They all alighted from the open motorcar and brushed at the orange dust hanging on their shoulders. The soldiers parked two empty wagons end to end for a speaker's platform, with the wire of the giant holding pen serving as a backdrop.

At the enclosure people hung on to the fence, put their faces to the wire, and gazed at the buffalo. Some children burrowed under adult legs and knelt on the ground, where the dust was thick as fog and almost hid the buffalo from their eyes. To Iola, the animals now seemed as calm and harmless as they had been in the Bronx Zoo, so she took advantage of the lull to seek out her family.

She strolled about asking people where her parents were camped. Her father wouldn't have come except for the last day or so, but her mother would have been here since Iola left. Aside from the Christmas camps many families held near churches, opportunities to gather as a tribe were rare now that the agency no longer made quarterly payments or issued goods.

People nodded and spoke Iola's name as she passed, giving it a special lilt of importance, she thought. She was no longer a child; she had been to the white man's biggest city and had helped to bring the buffalo back.

She halted beside a brush arbor where several men were whittling and talking. Nearby, her mother was sitting cross-legged on a blanket. She was pounding chokecherries into a slab of dried beef on a board held across her lap. Her black braids were tied off with pink yarn; the long, unevenly cut sleeves of her deerskin dress rose and fell with her rhythmical motion, disclosing the slash scars from when she had grieved for Nathan. The dress was old, and her father didn't like for her mother to wear it, so Iola had not seen her in it often. Looking at her seated on the ground with her face bent intently over her work, Iola felt a rush of love and contempt. Squaw. Blanket Indian. She tried to fight back a blush but couldn't.

Two of her aunts were seated nearby. Both were clad in old buckskin dresses but wore shawls about their shoulders; one was sewing shells onto the fringes of a buckskin shirt, and the other was decorating a small buckskin bag with beads—it would be used, Iola knew, to store the umbilical cord of her aunt's first grandchild, due soon to be born to Iola's oldest cousin. The sixteen-year-old had come near to creating a scandal in the family by getting pregnant before she had married in either a Kiowa or Christian way, but she and the young man, who was seventeen, had since then put things right and been married by the Reverend Willis.

The subject of her cousin's state seemed to be under discussion—her aunts were in the midst of reminding one another of how a woman who is pregnant must avoid eating certain foods so the child will not be deformed. Iola stood back slightly behind her mother, much too accustomed to being the Kiowa child at home to interrupt, even if it meant she had come back from New York after having been away for over a week and was dying to hug her mother.

When her mother looked up and saw Iola standing before her, she hastily moved the board from her lap but took care to keep the beef out of the dirt. She scrambled to her feet and embraced Iola tightly, pressing

Iola's face into the stained panel of deerskin on her shoulder. Her mother smelled musty, of dust and sweat, and Iola almost broke into tears.

Her aunts were looking suspiciously at her dark blue woolen dress and her shoes and coat. Miss Roberts had tapped a special fund at school to buy them for her especially for the trip because she was their "ambassador," she said, but under her aunts' scrutiny she felt as if she were wearing a heavy, outlandish costume.

Her mother had no curiosity about the journey. She instructed Iola to sit beside her, which Iola did reluctantly, knowing the dark wool skirt and coat would pick up the fine red dust and chaff from the grass. Her mother spoke of relatives she hadn't seen in months, of tribal gossip, babbling happily. Iola's father had decided to remain at home to study and pray. Confused, Iola absorbed the strange double hurt: her mother was too much Kiowa and her father not enough.

Soon she grew restless to get back to the enclosure, guessing that the ceremony would be starting soon, but her mother apparently preferred talking to seeing the buffalo. *Soon we will go*, she said with annoyance when Iola suggested that they walk to the pen. *When you spend too much time with white people, you always get on the hurry-up road.* Away from the buffalo, Iola had the anxiety of someone who has left a highly valued toy in the hands of other children, so after a few minutes, she asked her mother if she could return alone and received grudging permission to do so.

She wormed through the crowd until she reached the wire, which she climbed like a ladder until she was higher than the adults around her, perched on top of a big round support post. She scanned the red faces to find her grandfather but didn't see him until she looked toward the camp.

He and his companions were walking slowly toward the enclosure, making a fashionably tardy appearance to satisfy their dignity. They had spent the morning in a *seidl-ku-toh*, sweating to purify and cleanse themselves, and now the skin on her grandfather's face was tight and shiny. He had on a blue soldier's coat that a white general had given him years ago and a tall black hat, but he was wearing leggings and moccasins, and his long braids had been carefully groomed and were adorned with otter fur and ribbon.

When the men moved toward the wire, people parted to make way. Iron Lance stood beside Robert Dances Best and Dangerous Eagle, close to the fence, but he didn't put his hands on the wire. Iola dropped down from her perch then squirmed and butted through the crowd to get closer to him.

They look smaller, Dangerous Eagle was saying.

Maybe the white men made them that way, said Robert Dances Best.

Kiowas are smaller, too, her grandfather put in. The others laughed. *For the same reason.*

He rotated his head to search through the crowd, then he noticed Iola.

Come here.

She moved in front of him. A bull stood so close she could feel heat emanating from the animal. Its flank was damp with sweat and in the thick curls of wool along its shoulders insects were buzzing and burrowing. Its ears twitched away flies; it bobbed its great head and cropped the grass, the sound decisive and more voracious than that of a horse. It breathed, soughing in and out, making the sound of wind in a long tube. Although she had seen the buffalo in the Bronx Zoo and in the cattle cars and wagons, to see them this close with her grandfather was to recognize their true identity.

Unexpectedly, the bull flicked its tail and the thick, brushy knob on the end swept her knuckles as she gripped the wire. She yanked her hands away.

Her grandfather laughed.

In the old times if you stood on a hill and looked across the plains they were like a brown blanket from where the sun comes to where it goes, he said.

And when they ran they were like a flooding river. We rode our horses through them like men in boats, letting the waves crash around us, Robert Dances Best added.

You see the bone along their backs?

Iola stretched up on her tiptoes, but the buffalo was far too tall for her to see its spine.

The sinew there, said Dangerous Eagle. *We made bowstrings out of it. It was strong and springy.*

We didn't waste any part. We didn't let the carcasses rot in the sun, said her grandfather. He paused then made smacking sounds with his lips. *I'm thinking now of a slice of hot liver sprinkled with gallbladder juice.*

His companions groaned with ecstasy.

Food like that made you strong, ready for fighting and hunting.

Not like hard corn that hurts your teeth, said Dangerous Eagle. *You remember how warm the robes were?*

A lot warmer than those army blankets the white men use, said Robert Dances Best.

I wish my bones weren't so old and I could ride after them again, said Dangerous Eagle. *I wish I'd killed more of them.*

I wish I had taken more white scalps, chuckled Robert Dances Best.

Then the agent, Hackworth, came to tell them the white men were impatient to begin the ceremonies. He escorted her grandfather to the speaker's wagon, where he climbed stiffly up into the bed and sat next to the white lady, his spine curving away from the straight back of a chair, his forearms across his thighs and his palms clasped together. He looked uncomfortable up there with the dressed-up white people, and Iola was embarrassed for him.

Iola heard the muted shuffling of hats coming off behind her as the Methodist minister began an invocation. Sitting on the ground in the front row of the audience just beneath the wagons, she automatically stared into her lap, noticing the dust on her dress, then lifted her eyes to look slyly about. With her father absent, she was free to play this game without fear of punishment. Most of the Kiowas were Christians, so most had bowed their heads. The buffalo had not bowed their heads, though; they almost drowned out the prayer as they grunted, chewed, snorted, and walked about behind the speaker's wagon. A bull sent a thumb-thick stream of piss drilling loudly into the trampled dirt. Some of the children giggled. Iola cocked her head to sneak a glance up to the platform. The white lady was frowning at the toe of her shoe, turning it one way then another. Iola slid her gaze across to her grandfather. He had been watching her, and when their eyes met he winked.

Richards talked about how the white men had saved the buffalo from extinction, the territorial governor's assistant discussed the coming election for statehood, then the agent Hackworth bragged about his part in bringing the bison to this sanctuary. Iola's attention wandered back to the buffalo themselves whose shaggy forelegs could be seen under the wagon.

When Hackworth mentioned her grandfather, she looked up. It seemed the buffalo stopped chewing when it became apparent her grandfather would speak.

When he rose, a hush came to the audience, and she could feel their attention lean forward as if poised in stalking. Being the only Kiowa appointed by agreement between the tribal council and the agency to speak, he carried the burden of their hearts.

We're happy to see the buffalo, her grandfather said in Kiowa. *They remind me of the old time when the people lived on the plains before there were white people's fences. Then the wind blew free and there was nothing to break the light of the sun.*

"The Kiowa people are grateful for the buffalo," the agent translated. "They can remember when there was a lot of wind and sunshine."

Now the new times have come. The government has sold off the last of our reservation lands to white men, and they live among us as numerous as rabbit pellets.

"White people . . . now live among the Kiowas," Hacksworth began, then furrowed his brow. "As many as there are rabbits."

We're glad to see the white men repay part of their debt," Iron Lance continued. *Fifteen buffalo now stand on the land. We consider them not as a gift but as a drop of water returned from a stolen sea. If there are no more buffalo but these to come, then we will take increased payments on the reservation lands that the government sold for seven dollars an acre. Even that money is being held in Washington's fist, where it does us no good.*

The Kiowas applauded. Her grandfather turned to Hackworth. The white lady was smiling expectantly and the reporter's pencil was poised over the pad as he waited for the translation. Hackworth looked uneasy. Out in the crowd grins were splitting dusty faces; in the rear of the crowd, Iola saw Robert Dances Best and Dangerous Eagle chuckling silently.

Hackworth turned to the white guests and smiled weakly.

"The Kiowas take the buffalo to be a sign of greater prosperity for their people," he said finally.

Her grandfather then began talking about the old days. He didn't pause for the agent to translate. Not understanding what he said, the whites on the platform grew restless. He spoke of raiding and fighting and gaining honor through war, and of how the government had forced them to give up old ways to become farmers and they had almost starved. *Now things are a little better. All you young men and women, you listen. You cannot be now the way we were then. You must work hard to learn the white man's road in his schools. That will be your future whether we old men like this or not.*

Iola was surprised to hear this. When she looked about her, she saw the other children had ceased to pay attention. A low ridge cut across the northern end of the pasture close to the enclosure, and butterflies had come soaring over it in a wave a hundred yards wide and thirty feet high. They rose in the sky from the rear of the speaker's stand and crossed over the top of the holding pen, where some alighted on the heavy heads of the buffalo.

Iola's grandfather stopped speaking when he saw the children were looking at him and giggling. A Monarch had glided down to a stop on the top of his tall black hat. He stiffened and gave the children a steely look; they tried not to laugh.

Soon the assembly was swimming in butterflies. Everyone gawked skyward, their gazes tracing the flight of the butterflies as they perched like epaulets on the shoulders of the men on the speaker's wagon and snagged in the white lady's hair. As they continued to come like a steady breeze, Iola's grandfather finally realized what the children had been laughing about. So many butterflies had alighted upon his hat that he appeared to have a headdress of living decorations. His eyes turned upward into his head as if he were trying to see above the rim of his hat.

Then he gingerly grasped the brim and stepped out from under the tall black hat. He lowered it and held it before him, eyeing it as if it were an enormous cake.

He chuckled.

Welcome back, little brothers.

He stood at the wire. The sun melted his hair. His hair oozed through his sideburns, trickled down his cheeks and temples, then under his collar and over his shoulders until it formed a warm coating of fur under his overalls. *Saynday turned himself into a buffalo and lay down on the prairie so when White Crow came along . . .* Dust motes were animate; they glowed and made a noise like the hum made by a telegraph line even when there was no wind.

Near him, a bull cropped the grass with its large jaws and approached the wire step by step with its shaggy fetlocks quivering. He could have put his arm through a square and slapped its nose. It raised its head and chewed. Its near eye looked right at him, framed by the wire, egg-shaped, jellied, and glistening.

Got what yellow no! the buffalo uttered suddenly in a low voice, urgent, furtive. David flinched. He stared at the buffalo's jaws grinding the grass. The huge brown eye did not fix on him so much as its gaze threw out a net in which he was caught.

David turned to look at the adults who had crowded about him at the wire. If they had heard the buffalo speak, they weren't showing it.

Neta drum gotta shish shish! the buffalo whispered again, frustrated at not being understood.

When the buffalo took another step that put its long face almost against his own, David bolted from the wire, gouged his way through the adults until he emerged clear at the back of the crowd. He moved down the wire to the far flanks of the spectators and wiggled through to another place.

But the bull had simply followed him to his new location and was waiting for him!

What do you do out there?

You can't talk! David thought.

Uhhoooawh! the buffalo moaned. *You me hablar!*

The buffalo not only talked—it could hear David's thoughts even though they hadn't left his skull.

David looked away to the other animals in the herd; two were eavesdropping. While he kept his eyes trained on the backs of his hands as if to deny reality to the bull, it began a long speech that made him grit his teeth. The drift of it was that the bull knew about his life here at school, about Iola and Morris. Part of the speech was in Kiowa, part Spanish, part English, woven together in phrases like a piece of rope of varicolored strands.

Finally, *Chew on me, Went on a Journey!*

The buffalo knew his Kiowa name!

Frightened, he turned away. The sun beat down heavily, the yellow light growing thick as butter and swirling about his ankles. It was too bright; he hooded his eyes with his hand. Behind him, the soldiers were sweeping out the wagons, and the sound of their brooms was like steam hissing fitfully from an engine.

When he turned back to the buffalo, they had fallen silent. His head cleared. It had been a wondrous moment, but now they had lost the power of speech, or he had lost the power to hear them, and the magic had evaporated.

His life returned like a yoke laid suddenly across his neck. He was afraid to look too closely at the faces of the children seated on the ground on the other side of the platform; the awareness of his difference was like a fever rushing on him and then receding. No one else was hearing buffalo talk. Was this like the old men's visions, or was he crazy?

When the invocation began, David, upset, slipped away, striding in a quick zigzag through the now untended campfires and rolled-up blankets until he came to the creek. Downstream from the camp a boy younger than he sat under a chinaberry tree watching the horses in the remuda. Back at the enclosure, Iola's grandfather was sitting in the speaker's wagon, next to the white lady. The agent, standing, was speaking. David couldn't hear the words. The mouth opened and closed. Then Iola's grandfather rose and his mouth came open. They could have been singing a song together. Even the white people there had more in common with the Kiowas today than did David with either. He was under some spell, had blinked his eyes and had awakened to a state he had never known.

Later he could have explained what made him lie about the old man's horse, but at the time he only felt a vague desire to be helpful, to be part of the ceremony and belong. The old man wouldn't be able to ride his favorite *t'a-kon* bay after the buffalo, but surely he would want the horse to be in on the chase, wouldn't he? That there would be a chase now seemed a foregone conclusion—why else have them here, why else bring them back?

He told the boy that the old man had sent him for the horse. The boy looked mildly suspicious, but since they were within sight of the gathering, he got up, went into the herd, and came back leading the large, sand-colored horse with the black ears. David thanked him and mounted the horse. Astride it, he looked over to the distant enclosure. Could he be seen from here?

Now that he was on the horse, an impulse to have a weapon in his hand made him guide the bay over to Iola's grandfather's lodge. He slid easily off the back of the horse and walked fearlessly to the opening, ducking as he entered. Several lances with steel points stood bundled in tripod fashion near the center by the fire pit, and David quickly removed one and steadied the stack so it wouldn't fall.

Had there been someone in the lodge, he would have said the old man had sent for the lance—and meant it—because it seemed he had been sent on this mission by if not the old man's direct command, at least a voice from tribal history. But after he had remounted the bay and was urging the horse back toward the enclosure, a moment of clarity befell him: no chase was truly planned, no hunt. His heart shuddered beneath his ribs. Sweat coated his forearms, trickled through his sideburns. If they looked his way, he would be caught and he would have no explanation. If he let his momentum carry him onward, he might do something more foolish.

But he might also do something that would show his courage and earn respect. He had seen the old warriors standing at the wire, drooling. They were all much too old to ride, but he wasn't.

Did he have the courage?

The ghost of his father was looking on. Morris and Iron Lance would be there to see it, too.

And Iola would be watching.

His heart began to hammer madly in his chest, and he felt his grin spread like spilled water—This is what they felt when they went into battle! This is what they felt when there was no turning back!

Later, people said the boy unlatched the large gate, slipped inside while people were still listening to the ceremony, then he jabbed the lance into the haunch of the bull buffalo to make it run. It bellowed, jumped, and instantly the herd was alert in turn, and the boy ran screaming at them with the lance to stampede them. The soldier guarding the pen later claimed that he shot off his pistol to warn people, but everybody believed he was frightened because the buffalo were running toward him.

The pistol shot created pandemonium. A second after she heard it, Iola leapt to her feet and tried to peer through the wagon wheels, where she saw a blur of shaggy brown legs in motion and several soldiers running. A man screamed something in Kiowa at the buffalo.

Squealing and roaring, the buffalo milled furiously, their hooves pounding the earth and strewing clods and bits of manure into the crowd outside the wire, their turmoil tossing up clouds of butterflies. Then they untangled and made for the opening. They bunched up a moment in a bottleneck, then they knocked a gate post loose, the fence surrendered, and they surged through the gap and thundered out into the world.

Iola heard a great whooping and hollering. Many Kiowa men were running for their horses in the corral, and moments later they were flying past the speaker's wagon on the horses with their braids snapping and their horses parting waves of butterflies; their whoops rose over the drumming of hooves, and their laughter crackled in the air as they slapped at their horses' rumps with their quirts and charged after the stampeding herd.

Iola scrambled to the top of the fence. Across the pasture dust clouds rose red in the morning light as the Kiowas on horseback rushed out to chase the buffalo. Through a haze of butterflies, Iola could see that the buffalo had galloped all the way to the northern ridge and were now veering off to the left along a creek bed, running hard, throwing their back feet in front of their fore feet, heads low to the ground. They didn't stampede like cattle, with a point flowing back into a wedge, but rather with a wide fan of four buffalo across the front.

"My God!" screamed Richards. "They're coming back this way!"

Iola caught her breath as the fan of heads in the pasture grew more distinct; their horns swayed back and forth as they galloped, their shaggy leggings flashing black, their beards swept under their chins by the wind, and their maddened groans and bleats sent chills through her veins.

They struck the camp like a tornado. A cow crashed through a tent, its rear hooves hooking a guy rope and dragging the canvas across the ground into a fire, where the canvas caught and became a burning sled. The herd struck her grandfather's lodge, the top of it swung over into the thick dust and the poles jutted crazily into the air before disappearing; a brush arbor folded over into a cooking fire and the dry boughs burst into flame; a copper pot flew upward spewing out a brown streak, the pot handle hooked on a horn and its copper flashed in the light as the buffalo charged on; bedrolls were pitched up and rolled in the dust like tumbleweeds before vanishing under the hooves, then, just before they cleared the camp, the herd crashed into the motorcar and overturned it.

Meanwhile, the butterflies had kept coming. Over this bedlam they hovered like a moving orange net, blanketing the sky above the pasture and drifting south like slow horizontal confetti. Iola saw, ripping through the scrim of butterflies behind the herd, a man on a bay that looked very much like her grandfather's horse. The man was wearing overalls and was waving a lance in the air with one hand while clutching at the horse's mane with the other. He was much closer to the running buffalo than the other riders. Who? she wondered, then she knew: Big dummy! He must have done this! He had no right, they were *her* buffalo!

He had stolen her grandfather's horse, too!

She scrambled down and took off running to the south, where the creek angled away from the path of the buffalo. She guessed they would run along the creek and the creek bed would keep them contained so that they would only run west or southwest along it. And if she ran fast enough, she could intersect the herd and stupid David Copperfield, grab a rock and knock him off her grandfather's horse with it!

When the herd cleared the camp, fatigue set in and they slowed some but kept running on, driven by panic. David was not an expert rider, but when the buffalo appeared to be slowing down, he clutched the horse's mane in one hand and the lance in the other, then jabbed at the horse's flanks with his bare heel to force it up between the trailing buffalo and into the middle of the herd, where he and the horse seemed to be caught and were swept along as the herd thundered along the creek to the south.

Holding on as best he could, David drew back the lance and sighted along its shaft until the nape of the bull's neck wavered at the end of the point. The bull was flank to flank with him and his horse; David's mouth was dry and his eyes stung from wind and dust, and being trapped inside the running herd made his hand shake. He tried to imagine how his father would draw back the lance, how he would sight it, and perhaps how at *this* instant—

He flung the shaft at the bull's neck with all his strength.

It glanced off a horn and went flying harmlessly to the earth where the herd kicked it aside.

Now there was little to do but hang on. The herd pressed him in on all sides, carrying him along, and he feared falling off the horse and going under their hooves. Glancing behind him, he saw several Kiowa men on horses closing quickly on the herd, the riders grinning from car to ear.

Turning back to front, he seemed to become one of the buffalo now, hunted. The herd swept along the creek, running in a flat that flooded when the creek was swollen; looking ahead as he felt the horse beneath him tire, he saw that the herd would eventually be stopped in the distance by a line of oaks that formed a barrier in front as the creek cut between bluffs of sandstone.

Then he saw the girl. She had come running out of the woods to the left and was screaming at him and the buffalo and had something large in her hand. David thought for an instant that surely she would stop running toward them, but she didn't seem to care that the herd had now curved southward to follow the flat into the trees.

She seemed to realize that she had gone too far. He saw the object fall from her hand; she whirled and began running away from the herd, but the buffalo were heading straight toward her as she ran with her braids whipping across her back.

Forcing the horse forward with savage kicks in its ribs, David struggled to stay astride and guided the horse up through the herd until he was wedged between the four leading buffalo. Clutching the reins and the horse's mane, he kicked at the head of the buffalo near his left knee in an attempt to make it veer off course and cause the herd to split. The buffalo bleated when he kicked it again in the ear as hard as he could, then it swerved left to avoid his foot.

That gave the horse freedom to surge forward unhindered by the buffalo, and David coaxed it ahead until they were leading the herd by a length as they thundered down on Iola. He cursed the horse at the top of his lungs, kicked its flanks, pounded its neck, and the horse, terrified and unaccustomed to being ridden this way, shot forward.

They came upon Iola running, and just as the horse passed her, David leaned down and flung his arm about the girl's shoulder, gripping her under an arm, and brought her onto the horse's back and into his lap. His heart boiled upward like hot white smoke *it was easy, she was not much heavier than a dog*, the bay lurched from the weight, and they would have been trampled by the herd had it not reeled off to the west.

He held the girl tightly around her waist, her head knocking hard against his chin, but he kept driving the horse at a gallop into the trees, where he had to duck a gauntlet of drooping limbs.

He reined the bay to a halt, but it took some wrestling; the animal was crazed and overheated. Iola squirmed out from under his hold, pushed away from him, and leapt to the ground. He sat panting on the horse, his blood still charging through his limbs. He was so proud he could have burst.

She slapped her hands onto her hips.

"Those were my buffalo! You big dummy! And that's my grandfather's horse!"

David stared at her a moment. He longed to slap her.

Then he looked behind him; the men on horseback had caught up to where the herd had run into a grove. The buffalo were scattering singly into the trees, and the men were trying desperately to prevent them from escaping.

A fog in his mind was lifting. This horse belonged not to an enemy but to a Kiowa chief; this girl, his granddaughter, would be no one's captive wife. His heart sank. There'd be no dance for the fool who stampeded these buffalo and rode this horse without permission. They'd be after him as soon as they had the herd rounded up.

And then what?

He looked back at Iola.

"Next time I let them run you down."

He wheeled the horse about and pointed it north, away from where the buffalo were thrashing about in the woods, bellowing to one another. He nudged the horse with his heel, and it took a step forward.

"Wait!" screamed Iola. "Where are you going with my grandfather's horse?"

Where else could he go? He twisted about and looked at her but didn't open his mouth to utter the words running through his mind. *Going far on a journey, going far on a journey. That's the only way for a young man to gain fame and many horses!*

The men captured all but one of the buffalo in the oak grove. They happily searched for the straggler, a bull, throughout the afternoon, while another party set out to track down the boy who had stampeded them and had stolen the horse. They failed to locate either. The missing buffalo made his presence known the next morning when he stuck his head through a window at a barbershop in Apache. He glared at the customers. He shook his horns against a ragged edge of broken pane, spewing glass splinters like some Pleistocene beast waking furiously in an icy coffin, and severed his jugular in the process.

PART

TWO

1907 — 1919

5

His biceps and back were the tools of his trade and they kept him employed. He assisted a blacksmith at a crossroads livery stable just south of the Kansas line for over a year, until he toured the East in a Wild West show billed as "Heap Big Knife." Out of costume, he was the only roustabout who could wield a sixteen-pound sledge with the ease of a tack hammer. When the show came home to Ponca City, he hired on with loggers at Fort Smith, later was a gandy dancer on the Katy. Hard work was never a burden, but living under the continual scrutiny of white men who presumed he was stupid chaffed more sorely at his soul with each passing year.

In the spring of 1913, he was on his way to Texas when he walked up to a ferry crossing on the Canadian north of McAlester. At the landing stood two white men and their wives, looking helpless. The ferry operator, they said, had flung down his pole and walked away. He had left a mule standing in harness on the far bank attached to the ferry by a rope.

David picked up the ferryman's pole and waved the passengers aboard. He began poling the ferry under the cable which stretched from bank to bank and through pulleys rigged to guide it, and the mule started trudging up the incline on the road, taking the slack out of the rope so that it popped, dripping, out of the water.

David admired the mule's loyalty. When the passengers got off, he remained aboard. Operating the ferry seemed a good way to keep body and soul together, and he was looking for a temporary resting place.

During the remainder of the spring and over the summer, David and the mule slept on the landing or aboard the ferry. The elderly one-eyed mule was quite companionable, a good listener but a disappointing conversationalist. To encourage any heretofore untapped talent for speech in the mule, David amused himself on many a star-strewn night by relating stories about talkative wolves, grasshoppers, owls, and buffalo who had had instructive and troublesome affairs with Saynday the Trickster and ordinary human Kiowas.

Yo-yoing across the river imposed a pleasant rhythm on his days. On the ferry he could stand in the path of the world but not be required to set out on it. It imparted the sensation of travel without the inconvenience of it. Nothing in his heritage had prepared him for the satisfaction of providing a service for a fee, but he found a dignity here which had been lacking in his recent past. He was useful, even needed: he slid a palm under the destiny of his passengers and smoothly conveyed them on to their fates.

It pleased him to feel the thick rod in his calloused hands as he leaned his weight upon the pole and walked the length of the ferry to propel it. The pole was glossy and dark where his palms had stropped it smooth and oiled it; the sameness of the grip, the sameness of his leaning on it, and the sameness of his steps down the length of the plank-floored ferry came to be fixed in his muscle tissue like the orbits of moons. He awoke mornings with his hands already curled into a stiff pantomime of what would be required of them.

Then, too, the ferry was a slow parade. People materialized, whip-stitched themselves into the fabric of his life, then unraveled their work as they vanished into the future, going north toward Wewoka, Wetumpka, Wetoka, and numerous small Creek settlements, or south to McAlester. David enjoyed the spectacle of strangers festooned in the garb of their whimsy and babbling like tropical birds. He eavesdropped on the conversations of German and Polish farmers, Choctaw ranchers, Mexican horse traders, and British journalists to hear their exotic-scented English, the odd vowels and angular consonants carving unpredictable didoes in the silences.

But he resisted drawing them into conversation because he knew the sight of him made white men angry. He inspired a need to be on guard; they assumed that any red man of such bulk could crush them if he chose, so they bristled with alarm when he approached them for the first time. Because he understood this, David took pains to allay their fears for their safety. He called all men "sir," which delighted the Negroes and instantly lulled white men to sleep.

He could win children over by grinning and passing them a hard candy he kept for that purpose. Children who lived nearby would parade their familiarity with him before children to whom he was a stranger; sidling up to David, they enjoyed being admired from afar by their peers who lacked the courage to approach him.

The mothers would sometimes cross into the perimeter of his charm after their children had shown the way. At first, he appeared as a lout to them; it usually took some time before they noticed that his skin was smooth and clean and that he walked with a light, rolling step that looked graceful and confident. When he was in repose, his bearing would seem almost courtly to them, the line of his jaw square and surprisingly patrician, his black eyes alert like a hunter's and intelligent. Taking that second glance, the mothers would come to presume that this large, homely man with such an easy way with children must be very lonely and very gentle, a most unwarranted pair of presumptions in David's case.

During these months, he wanted nothing more than he had. He ate when hungry, slept when sleepy, and no man stood over him to tell him nay or yea; he enjoyed the supreme condition of human happiness in an age and place where the solitary life was not a pitiable aberration.

For the most part, he wasn't lonely. Since running away from Anadarko, he had learned not to try to cure his isolation by joining groups or seeking approval. He had learned to cure his isolation the way you cure meat: you hang it alone in the dark, caress it with salt until it is aged and preserved and protected against time. It was as if as a youth he had had an extra thumb that people made sport of but as an adult he had discovered how handy that extra digit could be. For a time he didn't think of his isolation at all except occasionally to feel grateful that it no longer seemed a condition that required amelioration. Loneliness had become solitude. The ferryman's job measured the precise distance David had wished to mark off between himself and others. It allowed him privacy while preventing him from becoming a hermit.

As always, nature forced a change. When the first blue norther came late in September, David knew that he and the mule couldn't go on sleeping aboard the ferry. About a half mile from the landing on the north bank lived an old Creek couple with whom he had spoken a few times when he was hunting squirrel or rabbit near their land, and he had occasionally bought flour or sugar from them or vegetables from their garden; Albert and Katie Parker never used the ferry; they got their supplies from Wetoka just north of the river, so he saw them only occasionally.

When he went to ask them if he and the mule could winter in the shed attached to their barn, he found them both bedridden with flu. David's need for shelter happened to intersect the line in their lives where their former good health had played out like a vein in a mine. He and the mule stayed in the shed, and David nursed the Parkers over that winter.

They had alternating spells of recovery as brief and fitful as spates of sickness are to the healthy. Katie was a little stronger than Albert, but for the most part they both were dependent upon David for the next year and a half. He made trips to Wetoka to buy staples for them, made broth following directions issued by Katie from her bed, chopped firewood and kept the cabin warm, and he and the mule plowed the garden plot two springs.

He came to have a deep regard for them, admiring their appreciation of each other—how each always felt more sorry for the other than for him- or herself, how each believed the other's illness was worse. When they were not sick, they were witty and good-natured. Furthermore, they treated him not only as an equal but as a godsend.

Albert died first. David built his coffin, Katie prepared his body, and they buried him behind the barn. David went into town to find a preacher to read Scripture over the grave.

"You'd just as well dig another hole," Katie said when they were walking back to the house. "Only don't bother about the preacher. That was Albert's idea, but I don't want him. Keep the ten dollars and buy yourself new overalls."

After Katie had died two weeks later, he was astonished to learn that, having no surviving family, the Parkers had willed him the cabin and the two 180-acre allotments the Dawes Commission had assigned to them in 1903.

He had a home now and a responsibility to inhabit it. For two years he had lived in the shed and had listened to the comforting cacophony of the mule snoring or grunting or grinding his teeth during a midnight repast. But now he felt obliged to sleep in the Parkers' bed and continue the life of their things—the crockery, the quilts, the pans, the books, the round hooked carpet. He was a man with possessions. He felt an ill-defined but persistent duty to the plank-top table with its three oak chairs, the dresser, the four-poster bed, the pie safe full of knives, forks, spoons, and utensils. Dominating one room was a huge black cookstove;

it was too complicated for David to use save for heating water or storing tools, but Katie had manipulated its many holes and lids and compartments where the wood and water went with the skill of a pump organist.

Now he was responsible for the glass-covered bookcase and its contents—almanacs, a hymnal, a Bible, a dictionary, several catalogues, a brace of novels, prayer books, and primers. He knew their covers better than their interiors, though Katie had used the primers to further his reading and writing. Katie read to Albert from the Bible and discussed events in the newspapers with him. At school, learning from books had never seemed important to David, but Katie had taught him how words on a page could convey the voice of the world (though it had not yet dawned on him that when you lived alone, that voice could stave off loneliness).

Living with the Parkers, he had grown used to being responsible for someone else and having them justify his existence with their regard. After Katie died early in February 1916, for the rest of that month, David ached for companionship. He found himself working harder to engage his regular passengers in longer conversations, and several times he spent the night in the shed, telling himself the mule needed his company. Fortunately, traffic on the river had increased over the past several months so that he was kept too busy to think much about his loss.

In early March, he was at the landing when a strong cold wind blew out of the northwest around noon, hinting of a blizzard, so he secured the ferry during a lull in traffic, walked back to the house, and, a little guiltily, left the mule alone in the shed.

He stirred the coals in the fireplace and soon had the cabin comfortable. Sleet began ticking on the windows and by midafternoon a darkness like twilight descended outside. David lighted the kerosene lamps, made a stew and biscuits in the Dutch oven, then, as he was setting the oven onto the coals, he was startled by a sharp rap at the door.

He opened it to find a petite woman with skin so black it would look faintly purple in strong sunlight. Shivering, she was holding a bushel basket half full of turnips on her hip.

"Ain't you the man who runs the ferry?" She seemed surprised to recognize him.

"Yes." He couldn't recall having ever seen her, and he wouldn't likely have forgotten her. She looked exotic—like a black gypsy—in a skirt of flour sacks sewn together and a white cotton blouse. Her wiry hair was flaming orange and stuck out behind her head as if she had been facing a hurricane and it had frozen that way. She wore long earrings someone had made using snips on cigarette tins. Her features were sharp and small, her nose finely chiseled.

"You need turnips?"

"Aren't you cold without a coat?"

She looked off with an impatient toss of her head and danced in place. Clearly she would rather make a sale or hear him say no than be detained in conversation. "It was warm this morning when I started."

He agreed to buy the turnips and invited her in out of the cold. For the next six months, Jenny would sometimes appear without notice to cook slabs of smoked ham, cornbread, and greens, then lie under him with her white teeth flashing. Sometimes he would go to bed alone, awaken in the night, and discover her beside him, but when he rose at dawn, she might already have gone.

Where she went he never asked. Returning home at night from the ferry, he might find that she had been at the cabin during the day and left him a skillet of cornbread.

Over the months that he was graced by these enigmatic manifestations, he presumed that she needed his cabin to escape an abusive relative or the boredom of labor. Curious as he was, he never questioned her. Learning too much might break the spell. In any case, having her present now and then allayed his loneliness.

One evening in August, he and the mule came back around twilight from the ferry to find Jenny waiting for them on the porch. She was poised to leave, as if waiting for him to relieve her from guard duty. He would have asked her to stay the night, but she had already stepped off the porch and was striding away before he could gather his wits.

"Some white man looking for you, David," she called over her shoulder. He got the impression she had been waiting on the porch just to deliver that message.

Inside the cabin there was no white man, but he found a saucepan of black-eyed peas cooked with onion and salt pork on the stove. Hungry though he was, he resented that she would spend the afternoon here in his absence then bolt as soon as he returned. He ate the peas cold, refusing to heat them, because he knew they would taste better warm.

No sooner had he finished the peas and gone out to the shed to feed the mule than he heard someone yell, "Hulloah?" from the barnyard.

The man wore high-topped engineer's boots with mud stains high on their calves, khaki trousers held up by suspenders, and a shirt that might have been white earlier in the week. His sleeves were rolled to the elbow, and his forearms were freckled and covered with curly blond hair. A straw hat such as salesmen wore was cocked back away from his face, revealing a high forehead that shone with sweat in the light coming from the cabin. He was a young man of medium height, with a wiry build that David thought made him look more Scottish than Swedish.

He introduced himself as Tom Quick and called David "Mr. Copperfield," arousing David's suspicion at his apparent research.

"I've been tramping about all over the countryside the past few days," he said, "spent some time over at Mr. Atlas Smythe's place?" Before David could nod, Quick went on, "Has a nice spread up the river from here, but I suppose you know everybody in these parts."

Quick was carrying a suit coat gripped in his fist as if it were a long, ungainly tube with limp ends, and he suddenly held it up by the shoulders, shook it out, stuck his nose into an armpit, and grimaced.

"Pee-yoo! Been on the road too long! You wouldn't happen to have a horse trough I could dip this sonofagun in, would you?"

David led him inside the barn. The man walked beside him and just to the rear, taking small light steps in a kind of dance that suggested he was longing to lead and following made him fret. Like most white men, something seemed to be leaning forward in him, and David could sense the energy churning under his surface.

Shown the trough where the mule watered, Quick tossed his coat into it, but then also stuck his head under and seemed to be screaming while submerged—at least, there were torrents of bubbles and a muffled cry.

He came up coughing and sent his hands over his head to squeeze out the water. Then he took the coat, wrung it, and draped it over the fence outside the barn, giving David the unhappy presentiment that the man intended to stay around as long as it might take for the coat to dry, which might be considerable now the sun had gone down.

David went back into the shed to bed the mule down for the night. Quick followed too closely behind him.

"What's your business, Mr. Quick?"

"Well, I'm interested in mineral rights."

"Mineral rights?"

Quick might have been a spinning top that some giant hand suddenly grasped, he became quiet and still so fast. He reached into his right pocket and drew out two cigars, one of which he stuck in his mouth and the other he held out to David. When David bit on the end of it, he could taste the sweetness of the rum it had been soaked in. He raised his guard. He had heard the Parkers discuss mineral rights and wanted to see if Quick's definition worked to the white man's advantage.

Quick sidled closer until David could see his blue eyes darting in the moonlight inside the shed. "Look, Mr. Copperfield, you got corn and oats and your vegetables on top of the land, right? But what you don't know is that under the land"—here Quick cut two planes in the air with his hands, one below the other—"you might have gold, silver, zinc or copper or coal or gas or oil. That's yours, too. That's your underground crop, you see, and if you got oil there and I can get it out of the ground for you, I can make you the richest goddamn Indian in this part of Oklahoma."

"Why would you do that?"

"Well, hell! I'd be rich, too! That stuff may be a half mile under the ground and you'd have to have somebody like me to drill for it and truck it off and sell it. We'd be partners. We'd sign a paper called a lease agreement, and then nobody else could come along and get that oil but you and me, see?"

Partners with a white man who gave out cigars!

"I have enough money."

"I'm not saying you're poor. But you'd have a fortune. You could have three cars and a house right here made of stone high as a low-hanging cloud! It'd make what white men around here live in look like a pigsty."

The picture of a large domicile suddenly standing on this spot alarmed David.

"No, I don't want that."

"What do you want?" Quick asked. "You tell me, and I can get it for you if you sign a lease with me." Quick's right hand disappeared somewhere and when it reappeared it was carrying a smoking flame through the air that stank of sulphur. He held the match to the tip of his cigar, then held out the flame, but David shook his head, content to chew his cigar. Quick's eager, sweaty face shone in the orange light for a moment, and the air was plump with clouds of pungent blue cigar smoke.

Out of curiosity, David tried to think of something to want. He needed a new rifle, but he had money enough for that. For the things he really needed, he had the means. What he lacked was the will to exchange old things for new.

"Well, what is it?" Quick prodded. "A horse? How about an automobile? I left my own down on the road, be glad to take you for a ride, tonight if you like, you could get one just like it, two if you wanted, once you try one you'll never go back to a horse." Quick's peculiar urgency and impatience made David balky. He was discovering the power he had to frustrate the white man by simply being slow.

When David didn't answer, Quick cocked his head into a wreath of cigar smoke and raised his voice. "Or how about a white woman? I can get you a passel of them to come out here and wait on you hand and foot if that's what you want. They can all be your wives, if you get my drift."

"I don't want more people," David blurted out. Though this last prospect was undeniably intriguing, Quick's suggestions conjured upheaval, crowds, unwanted visitors such as the very man who was presently drying his coat on David's fence without asking permission and who had yet to inquire if David minded having a talk about his mineral rights.

Quick sighed, backed off slightly, smoked in silence.

"What about your future?" he started up again after a moment, apparently inspired. "You ever think about your future?"

David's gaze went to the mule, who was still grinding oats between his ancient teeth.

"My future?"

Quick caught the note of uncertainty and plucked it out of the air; he jabbed his head forward and began speaking as if his words were sandbags frantically laid on a levee that might give way. "You think you can just keep running that ferry that same way? You think things aren't changing in this territory? There's oil popping up out of the ground all over, and in just a few months, before spring maybe, people'll be swarming all over this place, and they'll be getting rich from somebody else's oil! They'll be lined up at the ferry for miles back, and they'll be screaming to get across! And when you can't carry all the traffic, they'll yell for the state of Oklahoma to build a bridge—and you'll be sitting there with that pole in your hand without a passenger and not a goddamn thing to do but starve and watch somebody else get rich! Don't you see it? Don't you know that's going to happen?"

David shivered. So there was a reason for the increased traffic. He and the mule had been returning to the cabin each night exhausted, the mule growing thinner and sadder, and he had wanted to ignore this change or think of it as a temporary aberration.

That white men could change the course of history to the detriment of a red man was embedded in David's bones. But he had believed that his sanctuary by the river made him immune to history. Quick had his own reasons for conjuring up this picture, but that didn't dispel the truth of the vision. And the hint of chaos in it shook David.

To hold things steady, to be offered a snug niche from which to ambush the future, disarm it—that was something. Behind Quick's words came a relentless horde of white men sweeping across the land; yet his offer seemed a way by which the tide might be controlled, a way that might allow David to be a rock that parts the waters.

A wreath of smoke enveloped Quick's head, the smoke pale blue in the light from the cabin. It was like a dream, this moment when Quick held up the apple and David leaned over to sink a tooth into it. "You'll be a rich man," Quick said flatly. Though he sounded certain, his inflection conveyed urgency: But you'll have to do something about it right this minute, he seemed to say, things won't wait for you to take your own sweet time, because there is no more sweet time left in the world!

Quick's face was severed from his body by shadows as he bent forward in a halo of blue smoke, his brows squiggling like insect antennae while he waited for an answer. David, neither needing nor wanting to be rich, having never itched or worked for it, said to Quick, not because he was greedy or even curious but only because he was afraid of what might happen should he not:

"Yes."

The crow's nest of an oil derrick was visible above the trees across the river as Alice Roberts brought the rented team past the mule and to a halt on the south landing. A white man in shirtsleeves and a straw boater stood on the running board of his automobile and drummed his fingers on the roof while staring out to where the ferry, heavily laden, was slowly making its way toward them against the current.

"Well, I'll be. The rumor must have been true."

Iola's pulse quickened; she scanned the deck of the ferry until she spotted a large man in khaki pants and a blue denim workshirt who was pushing on a long thick pole to propel the ferry, walking toward them slowly along the rail. For a moment she couldn't quite make out his features, then he turned his face toward the landing and it was unmistakably David Copperfield's.

His features grew more distinct as the ferry gradually closed onto the landing. Iola saw the differences between the large boy of fifteen and the large man of twenty-five: he had been plump and bearish in school, but now, as he lifted the pole, laid it on the deck, and came forward to stand on the lip of the ferry in preparation for landing, she saw that his bulk had hardened to a more feline conformation, his shoulders were broader, hips narrow, arms showing tanned and gracefully rounded muscle below the roll of sleeve high on his biceps. He moved with light-footed grace for such a big man.

Alice said, "I'd have known him anywhere. He looks just the same as he did ten years ago."

Iola said nothing, surprised at this misperception. David turned to speak to a passenger, his shoulders shaking as he chuckled, head cocked back. He wore his hair short, which emphasized the solidity of his skull and made his brown eyes even larger. To her his facial features were now stronger and even more homely, but in becoming so had crossed a fine line between ugliness and beauty; it was the kind of striking and intriguing face which she thought made conventionally handsome men look spiritually bereft by comparison.

She had anticipated this meeting for many months, and so far she was not disappointed. She had only one small nagging disillusionment: she had thought the boy who was brave enough to stampede the buffalo then go out into the world would have become something more than a ferry poleman. But what? An entrepreneur? A rich rancher? In the years following his disappearance, she had had much time to consider how she had acted toward him, and she was ashamed for not having thanked him for saving her from being trampled. For the children who came to school in years afterward the story of what happened that day took on the aura of legend, and David became a mythic hero. Even the old men, after clucking their tongues, would grin. *Do you remember how they looked when they hit the white men's automobile?* they'd say. *Do you remember how that boy tried to lance that bull?* The men would laugh, slap their thighs. They had richly enjoyed rounding up the strays.

"I wonder if he has a family," Alice mused.

Iola's ear tips burned. "Please don't."

"Oh, child, would you please relax? I was just thinking out loud. Lord only knows what the boy is like."

They fell silent when he came within earshot. As the disembarking traffic went past, raising dust, he stood by the white man's automobile and pointed at the ferry, giving instructions. When the automobile chugged down the incline and onto the ferry, David turned, gave Iola and Alice a glance and a nod without recognizing them—they were both wearing hats—slipped one large hand brown as an oak leaf through a bridle, and led their horses and the wagon onto the deck.

He walked around to Alice's side and looked up into her face. A flicker of fear passed through his gaze the instant he recognized her, but then he laughed.

"Well! Teacher!"

"Hello, David," Alice said demurely. "I'm sure you recall your classmate. . . . " She nodded toward Iola, but David's quick glance had already darted across the distance between the two women, and his eyes brightened. The smile he gave her, unlike the one he had given Alice, only worked on one side of his face, and Iola wondered if he was only half as happy to see her.

"Iola." He might have been identifying some peculiar species of vegetation whose usefulness was unknown, although his eyes traveled eagerly about her face.

"David, I'm glad to see you again."

"Help me down, will you, young man? This seat is getting hard even if I do have a lot of padding."

Alice rose, held out her hand. David took it, helping her down from the wagon, then came quickly around the horses presumably to assist Iola. She was caught for a moment between waiting for him and getting down before he reached her, which she could do quite easily; she was no pale and wilting white lady! She stood in the wagon and stepped down onto the footrest, but in her haste her toe slipped; he took the distance in one neat lunge, put his hands around her waist, and swung her down before she could fall.

"Thank you," she said, feeling humiliated. Alice was smirking. The places on Iola's lower rib cage where his hands had grasped her held a disconcerting memory of the pressure. "It's never happened before," she offered to save face, but realized she had merely confessed to being flustered.

David went off to get the ferry under way. She longed to talk more with him, and after a few moments walked to where he stood slowly plunging the pole into the ruddy, opaque water.

He looked over with a crooked grin when she moved beside him at the rail.

"We didn't know if we'd find you here or not."

"You were looking for me?"

"No, no." She laughed nervously. "No, they gave up on finding you a long time ago. I meant that my father had written to me to say that someone had seen you here. Written to me in McAlester. I've been there for the past two years studying to be a nurse, and now I'm going to Wetoka to help a doctor for a while, just for more training. We just thought we might see you, that's all." The silence prompted her to answer more questions that he had not asked. "Alice got the job for me. She's going to teach at a little country school run by the county. She's left Anadarko."

He nodded, but whether he was interested she couldn't tell. When she had uttered "Alice," David had given her a little look of challenge or reproach that whisked her back to being jeered at. Teacher's pet. For a moment, she fretted with irritation, as if she and David were back at that flagpole deliberately misunderstanding one another.

"Have you been here all this time?"

"Oh no. Only the past three years or so. I was all around, I had many jobs, went back East, like you." Now he gave her a broad grin. "If you will be in Wetoka, that's only a few miles up the road, you and Miss Roberts can come back to visit and I can pay you for your grandfather's horse. You can send the money to him." He pointed to a ridge rising beyond a stand of dappled oaks on the north bank of the river. "I have a cabin up there, a nice place. You see that thing above the trees? There's a white man drilling an oil well on my land. He says he's going to make me rich."

So he had a home, land, good work. She hoped Alice wouldn't discover these things only to ask quite baldly if he had a wife and children. She looked over to the opposite rail; Alice was chatting with the driver of the automobile, though she glanced at Iola and David as if to gauge their progress.

"I appreciate the invitation," Iola finally said.

She had mentally prepared a speech were she to find him on the ferry. It had changed length over many drafts, the last one pared down a mile or so back of the ferry landing to several sentences that expressed her understanding of why he had stampeded the buffalo, of how she had "forgiven" him for it, of how the notion that they were "her" buffalo came to seem silly and childish, of how many people in the tribe had *enjoyed* what he had done, and, finally, of how brave he had been to get out in front of the herd to snatch her up.

She would not tell him how long it had taken her to appreciate that. When people called him a hero or argued that he deserved to go unpunished if caught because he had saved a little girl's life, it had made her furious. Among the things she had learned about herself since David had last seen her was that she was not, and probably never would be, a gracious loser.

Now she couldn't give the speech, she couldn't quite part her lips; her few sentences seemed too long, and he kept stepping away to pole the ferry along. Each time she considered beginning, she would look up to see the north bank growing distinct, the orange swatch of fall-dressed oaks showing yellow sycamore, green willow, and red maples among them, and the dock etched against the shore. Her speech would take too long. Having too much to say made her mute, and they spent the remainder of the trip in silence.

But just before the ferry eased into the north landing, she realized happily she would see him again, he had asked for it. And on a night when they were looking at the stars or sitting by a fire, she could give him the speech, a version as long as she liked.

Saynday was coming along one day when he saw someone's camping place beside a river. It was a single camp. Deer Woman was there tanning a skin. He stood off for a while admiring her, then he went up to her and said, Deer Woman, I have come to pay you a visit. She said, Why have you come?

Saynday said, I have been camping alone too long. Now I am looking for a good wife to cook for me, to tan my skins and make my clothing and make a tipi for me. Can you do all of those things?

Deer Woman said, I don't know. I have two children, and this morning I sent them out to look for fresh hay. What do you eat?

I eat meat, said Saynday. What do you eat?

I eat grass and leaves from trees, Deer Woman told him.

Well, I suppose if I were to be your husband, I would eat those, too, Saynday said. Will you marry me?

Deer Woman said, I don't know. I don't live in a tipi. I like to live in the tall grass and rest wherever I wish. My children have gone out to eat.

Well, said Saynday, I will go eat grass with you.

So the next morning, she said she was going out to get her breakfast. Saynday said he would go with her. She went into the field and bent her head down and began to eat the grass, but old Saynday, he didn't know how to do it, so he just stood there. When Deer Woman saw that he wasn't eating, she guessed why and said, You have to eat your breakfast! Pick up that grass and eat it!

Saynday said, I'm afraid it will give me a stomach ache!

Deer Woman, she got angry with him. You eat that grass if you want to be my husband.

Saynday wanted to marry her so he tore up some grass, made a ball with it, and put it into his mouth. He chewed on it until it was as soft as he could get it, but it stuck in his throat and he started choking.

Deer Woman! he cried. Help me, I am choking!

Deer Woman just said, He is not any good as a husband! He cannot eat grass, his legs are too long, he's ugly with that old mustache, and his voice is too high, he sounds like a mouse squeaking! While she was talking, her two sons came back, and they watched Saynday choking.

Saynday finally slapped himself on the back real big and the ball of grass popped out of his throat. He sat down and rested a moment, breathing hard. Deer Woman's sons laughed at him, so he said, Deer Woman, I don't want to marry you any more. Then he jumped up and ran away. That is all.

David recalled how her ears and ankles and the inner crooks of her elbows were delicate, her skin as smooth to the touch as rose petals, and the nape of her neck soft and rabbit-belly vulnerable. Grown, she had more roundness, with womanly hips and breasts, but, thinking back on their meeting aboard the ferry, he recalled her graceful throat, the hollows around her collarbones, her strong calves, her long eyelashes: this was a more substantial creature than the child, yet she had not lost her delicacy. Her lips were fuller, with more nuance in their expression. Her eyes were still very beautiful, dark coffee brown, not so much warm as earnest. All in all, she had grown into a very beautiful woman, but he wasn't sure he admired her beauty so much as felt it seemed merely appropriate—another prize for her.

As he poled the ferry now, her face was in his mind's eye, persistent. It was a nuisance. It aroused his desire for a companion—not for *her*, he thought, maybe simply another Jenny—and it interfered with his concentration. One evening when he had come home from the ferry, he caught himself looking around at his furnishings and wondering if Iola would find them suitable, and he asked himself, suitable for what? And when he answered, suitable to live with, he knew he wanted her. His desire felt like an illness or a lapse of a vow; it was no cause for rejoicing. It would lead nowhere, he believed; she wouldn't become the wife of a man such as he. She had not followed suit on his invitation to return, so he presumed she had either forgotten him or was having trouble with her pride—having to face an inferior who had saved her life. Even though the girl had grown into a friendly woman, he doubted she could humble herself to apologize for screaming insults at him the day he saved her. She probably believed that being friendly was as good as apologizing. She would pretend to forget their rancor so that he would have to, and she would buy the peace at no cost. But he could keep score too well for that.

His life was becoming full of nuisances. Quick's crew had built the derrick and had cut a rough truck trail down to the road to Wetoka and the ferry, and when the wind was coming out of the east at night, David was kept awake by the din of the rig's engine and the clank of pipe. The sight of the structure above the trees reminded him that white men were afoot on his property.

Quick's rig had attracted curiosity-seekers, speculators, and geologists; no sooner had David come home after working long hours than some white man would be camped on his doorstep or snooping around his barnyard.

Two weeks after Iola and Alice had come, David was midriver when he felt a strange vibration in the air. From the ridge over the river's north bank, a thick column of black slammed upward, clipped off the crow's nest of the derrick, and spewed high in the air over the rig.

"Wooooo!" a passenger shouted. "Somebody got a gusher!"

Within an hour or so, the word had spread throughout the countryside and sightseers began to arrive from Wetoka and McAlester. Those coming from the south crowded together on the landing and waited for David to bring the ferry to take them across so they could tramp about on his land looking at his gusher. David shut the ferry down at noon and hurried up to his cabin, passing a score of people strolling through his woods to get to the well. He could hear the steady roar of the gusher even after he had slammed his cabin door.

He stayed inside for the rest of the day and did not light a lantern when night came. He refused to answer frequent knocks on his door. He had deserted the mule but guessed it would not be harmed. Tomorrow he would rescue it.

The next morning, the roar was still audible when he opened the door to look out. A breeze from the east brought the stench of oil. The column, he noted, had diminished some in height and apparently in strength. From his front porch he could see down to the ferry landing on the other side of the river. The distance was too great to be able to spot the mule, but the dock appeared to be covered with a speckled blanket made of human forms. He cursed.

"David?" he heard someone call.

He turned to see Iola and Miss Roberts walking up from the road.

"We heard about your good fortune," Miss Roberts beamed. "And we just wanted to come congratulate you."

"Good fortune?"

"The oil well."

"Oh," said David. He was looking at Iola. She was wearing a light blue dress with a dark blue coat over it unbuttoned down the front. Her smile looked vaguely troubled, as if it were costing her to deliver it.

He invited them in, pulled out the chairs to the plank-top table and offered them coffee. They both took it, Miss Roberts with double the sugar Iola had, and he sat with them nursing the dregs in the bottom of his tin cup. His teacher had a lot to say and had apparently spent more time than she had a right to considering the course of his future now that he was, as she put it, a rich man. None of her words seemed remotely connected to him or to his life. He was rich? His life was precisely as it was yesterday with the exception that he was suddenly overrun with white people who trespassed upon his property and intruded upon his privacy. One other important difference was that, for the first time since he had been running the ferry, he had neglected his only companion.

While Alice talked, he slyly observed Iola, who was slyly taking a look about the cabin. He wondered what she was thinking. Following her gaze, he was aware that the four-poster's frilly valance was gray and stiff with dust. He thought of how much of the Parkers' original cutlery once stored inside the pie safe had been lost, bent, or broken when he had used the items as tools. Much of old Katie's crockery had chipped or broken. He felt ashamed of how he had let things go.

"Are those books yours?" Iola asked when the older woman paused. She jerked her chin toward the glass-covered bookcase.

"Now they are."

"How wonderful!" the teacher gushed.

Evidently, she presumed a reformation in his character from their presence, but he knew the Parkers' books were wasted on him.

He began to tell them about the Parkers, but his story was interrupted by shouting outside in the yard and insistent banging on the door.

"Copperfield! Hey, Copperfield! Open up, man! You're rich, god-damnit, you and me, we're rich!"

Both women visibly stiffened.

"That's the oilman," said David.

When he opened the door, Quick, covered in oil, tumbled inside the cabin. "Copperfield!" he crowed at the top of his lungs. Before David could react, the white man had taken David in his arms and, with a struggle, lifted him off the floor and spun him around. David smelled whiskey.

"Here! Want you to meet somebody!" He reached through the open doorway and grabbed a man by his lapels and pulled him over the threshold. He was wearing a tan suit splattered with oil which Quick's hands further soiled. "This here's a reporter for *Harper's Magazine* back in the East—" he hollered at David even though David was close enough to smell his breath, then he looked back at the reporter and hollered into his face, "And that's the World's Richest Goddamn Indian!"

"Ma'ams," the reporter mumbled as, looking about, he spied Iola and Alice and tipped his hat.

Quick saw them, now. "Whoah!" he said to himself. "Gold-darn it, ladies! Here I've gone and made a total fool of myself. Believe me if I seen you there I wouldn't a come through the door cussing like a sailor, believe me." He bowed low as if to curtsy, but when he was bent over he had to send his arm shooting out to brace himself against the door. "What if I can't get up now?" he asked himself. "Copperfield, will you help me up?"

David good-humoredly grabbed the oilman's shoulders and straightened him until he stood upright facing the women. Miss Roberts seemed to fight back a small smile of amusement. Iola's gaze was stone cold, however.

It sobered Quick. "I reckon I've busted up a private party with my bad manners," he said. "I guess I just better get to my business and be on my way. Copperfield, I got something for you here." He sent his hand into his right front pants pocket and then struggled to extract it after closing it around something. "Right here's the first of many, I hope. Just signed a deal with a fella to truck it out and refine all that gooey crude."

He held out a roll of bills tied with a string and brown with oil. David took it and looked at it curiously.

"What do you think?" the reporter asked. He had a small notebook in one palm. "How're you going to use the money? How's it feel to be the World's Richest Indian?"

"Put down Tom Quick made the discovery well," Quick said, tapping the reporter's pad with a forefinger. "Spelled just like it sounds."

David stared at the reporter.

"I say, how's it feel—"

"Aw, heckfire, he's just speechless with joy, anybody can see that, right?" Quick cut in impatiently. "But you're gonna need to know how many feet of drill stem, stuff like that, and—"

"Are you going to quit work on the ferry now?" the reporter asked.

David thought of the mule standing among strangers on the south landing, hungry and thirsty.

"You men go now," he said. "I've got work to do."

He walked with Miss Roberts and Iola down to the road where they had left their wagon and team. Before they parted, Iola said, "I've wanted to come see you, but it hasn't been possible yet. We're staying in the Baptist minister's home for the time being. His name is Tatum. You could visit with us. I'm also at the doctor's place." She gave him that troubled smile again, this time looking wistful.

"Thank you, I will come, if this Tatum doesn't mind Indians in his parlor."

"I'm there."

David chuckled. "You're no threat to his wife."

Iola laughed. "When you see her neither will you be."

David walked down to the crowded landing and ferried a load of passengers across the river to the south bank, where he took on another full load of sightseers. They all paid the usual nickel to cross. The irony struck him that now that Quick had hit oil on his land, he no longer needed the income from the ferry, yet the income from it had doubled overnight. Several people asked him if he knew whose land the gusher was on, but he just shrugged. *Lucky sumbitch!* somebody said.

David found the mule at the top of the hill. He led him back to the ferry, and, an hour later, had watered, fed, and brushed him down in the shed. He decided to stay there for the night to keep the mule company and avoid any unwanted visitors. After the mule had lain down with a groan of pleasure, David sat on the matted-hay floor chewing on a straw. He thought of Iola; her face was a small calm attraction in the center of a maelstrom, but eventually the surrounding uproar washed over it. He thought of the mob down on the landing, trooping about on his land, and he wasn't so much angry at having his peace disturbed as mystified: why did they find this gusher so *interesting* that they would come from so far to get a glimpse of it?

He slipped the roll of greasy bills out of his overalls pocket. He studied it, flipped it over in his palm. Idly, he wondered how much it amounted to but never got around to untying it. He felt the weight of the white citizenry on the landing below whispering, Lucky sumbitch! Take it, fool, sure wish I had it!

They would be shocked, he thought. He pushed aside the hay to clear a place, set the roll of bills upright on the earthen floor, took a match and struck it. The burning bills gave off a greasy black smoke like the badly trimmed wick of a kerosene lamp.

7

"Cheers!" Dr. Hartzler lifted a battered flask to liver-colored lips and swigged. The ironic toast carried its usual hint of self-pity. Why he wasn't peering into the powdered recesses of rich white people in the East, Iola didn't know.

"What's out there?"

They stood behind a muslin curtain that divided the "waiting room" of the big medical tent from the "surgical chamber," a partitioning which allowed Hartzler to practice his hacking and sawing out of sight —but not out of earshot—of waiting patients.

Iola peered into the waiting room. There were two white women with the gaunt look of oil-camp wives, one with a red-faced child bundled in a dirty quilt in her lap, and another whose right jaw was swollen and purple. An elderly Creek sat near them, his hands laid over the top of a cane. Hartzler hadn't practiced in Wetoka long, and the town's established white residents were still in the habit of going south to McAlester for a doctor. But the boom had brought in oil workers maimed by machinery or their own violent folly; their wives suffering from influenza, dysentery, or tuberculosis; or their children, who were ridden with worms, whooping cough, boils, rickets, and who, like their mothers, bore bruises made by knuckles. White misery was new to Iola, but in her six months of working here, she had been struck by how pervasive it was among the poor and by how little the unafflicted were concerned about it.

She described the patients to Hartzler.

"Let's see the kid," he said, shrugging. He was a tall, thin, ganglylimbed man who reminded Iola of a crane.

The choice was logical and predictable; to Hartzler, white men came first, their children second, wives third, Mexicans, Indians, and Negroes fourth, fifth, and sixth. That he was willing to treat the last three categories did him some credit, Iola thought.

The woman came through the curtain of sheets carrying her child.

"Three days now she's been puking and shitting," she said.

Hartzler vised the child's glands between his fingers and peered into its throat. "Putrid. Has she been immunized?"

The mother shrugged, not understanding.

"She looks dehydrated," Iola said.

"What remedy do you recommend?" Hartzler asked tartly.

"A starch enema, maybe some paregoric, aspirin, and a lot of water."

Hartzler nodded, and Iola turned to preparing the solution for the enema. She would not have intruded had she not recently become convinced that her teachers at St. Mary's would be as contemptuous of Hartzler's practice as he was of "witch doctor" medicine.

Since coming to Wetoka, she had grown further disillusioned about white men's medicine. When she had taken the nurse's-training scholarship Alice had secured for her, Iola had been certain that her people's ways of treating sickness were ineffectual. When she had measles during childhood, her mother and her grandfather had bathed her in cold water, then her grandfather donned his buffalo headdress, shook his buffalo-hoof rattle, and prayed and sang while waving cedar smoke over her body with feathers. Her father stood outside the lodge and fretted, and at the first opportunity whisked her away to the agency infirmary, where she got well.

But the white medicine she learned at McAlester seemed contradictory and constantly under revision. The student nurses were first taught to discourage mothers from buying canned tomatoes because they had no calories, then they were told the opposite when vitamins were discovered. Her supervisor, Dr. Mary Forsyth, was as harsh a critic of yesterday's methods as she was of red folk cures. To Dr. Forsyth, the past was but a series of mistakes the present was correcting, and she had as profound a faith in machinery as Iola's grandfather had in cedar smoke and gourd rattles: she had every portion of her body documented by the hospital's new X-ray machine to prove the machine was harmless and wholly useful. The nurses had allowed their hands and feet to be photographed and made jokes about needing lead bloomers around the hospital.

Hartzler, on the other hand, practiced frontier medicine, or what Dr. Forsyth contemptuously called "granny medicine"—cures such as hot chicken blood for shingles and poultices made from dirt-daubers' nests. He believed the sick should be purged, and pharmaceutical assistance with calomel or tartar emetic was applied to coax the patient to crap, sweat, vomit, or bleed out the offending material. He was also quick to sell patients a bottle of "Electro-Tonic," or "Simmons Liver Regulator," concoctions that hovered perilously close to being designated as alcoholic beverages by the Federal Drug Act.

Iola had hoped to augment her training here, but the elaborate instructions in her American Red Cross nursing text on tucking bed corners and sterilizing instruments were absurdly useless here, and after her first day she had exchanged her white uniform for a dark cotton smock that hid the dirt.

Iola gave the child an enema, administered the paregoric, then the aspirin ground into a spoon of water. She gave the mother an eyedropper and instructed her to squeeze warm water into the child's mouth.

While the woman encouraged her child to drink, Iola quietly palmed a vial of Argyrol, passed into the waiting room, and gave it to the old Creek, whose eyes were red-rimmed, watery, and clouded with pus. She instructed him to bathe his eyes with the antiseptic solution, using a clean cloth.

The other white woman with the swollen jaw had vanished; Iola was about to return to the first woman and her sick child when Tom Quick came through the door.

"Howdy, Miss Iola. I hope y'all ain't too busy." He appeared apologetic to the point of being abject. One hand was clenched into a fist, the forearm pressed to his stomach. It was wrapped in a greasy rag with ruddy brown bloodstains. She fought back a wave of hostility.

"What's the trouble, Mr. Quick?"

He raised his arm from his trunk without bending the elbow. "Oh, I did something stupid and a machine took advantage of it." His handsome face looked pinched, the features all straining toward some invisible point about two inches before the tip of his nose. She could tell he was fighting to appear unconcerned.

"It ain't much, but it's getting in my way. I don't want to take up your time if somebody else's hurt."

"Let's see that."

Iola was caught between tending his wound and making it clear that she considered him an enemy. When he held the sore arm out for her to undo the homemade bandage, she didn't make a move to do so, and he awkwardly unwound the rags himself.

There was a long, ragged cut on his forearm encrusted with pus and scabs; the surrounding skin was red and inflamed, which spelled infection. She pressed a finger on the crest of the cut, and he winced. She pressed again, more firmly.

"Tender?"

"A little," he gasped.

Involuntarily, she gave him a crooked grin. Had he been more aware of the complexity of her feelings, the grin might have told him she was confessing to having deliberately hurt him.

"It feels a lot better to see you give me a smile."

Annoyed that he had misinterpreted her expression in his favor, she turned and beckoned him to follow. When they entered the surgical chamber, Hartzler perked up: at last, a real job! Iola's irritation with Tom Quick doubled, though it was no fault of Quick's that the doctor favored white male patients. That, in essence, was the source of her difficulty with Quick: it was not so much his person she objected to, it was his type, what he stood for. To Alice, he was full of "native charm." But Iola kept her first impression of Quick as a loud-mouthed drunken white man, and her animosity had been honed to a keen edge by the leers and jibes she had endured from other white men to whom she was only a squaw to be addressed in vulgar pidgin English. That Quick was courteous did confuse her, but she took her own confusion as a form of temptation to be resisted.

It wasn't just that first impression that she held against Quick—he was, after all, the man responsible for the boom and all its squalid horrors. He was the man responsible for the changes in David's life. The changes in David himself.

"This looks pretty raw," Hartzler declared with gusto when he had inspected Quick's wound. "We better drain that. Iola, get some ether."

"I don't need no ether!" chirped Quick. "Hell, it's just a scratch!"

"When did it happen?"

"Yesterday."

"You should have come in then." Iola pointedly assigned him the blame for his condition.

"The well wouldn't cooperate."

Iola could feel herself climbing a ladder of anger. "You don't have enough oil wells already?"

Quick turned hurt blue eyes toward her, and she shifted her gaze. It has been this way the last two times they had met—Quick would hand her a doleful-puppy look in exchange for a reproach, and she detested the trap in it.

"Iola, the ether—"

"He says he doesn't want it. He's a big boy, he can take pain."

She gave Quick her crooked, sour grin again, and he laughed sadly. This time he didn't pretend it meant something other than what she intended.

"Yeah. Some pain."

Hartzler shrugged. "Okay, hang on there, lad." He dug into Quick's cut with an instrument, letting the pus and blood spring freely out of it, and Iola came close to watch. Quick clenched his eyes shut; the muscles in his jaws were throbbing, his free hand clutched tightly at the gunwales of the cot, and his sweating fingers left ghosts of themselves on the faded canvas.

After Hartzler had cleaned the wound with alcohol, bringing tears from under Quick's clenched eyelids, he sewed up the cut, then instructed Iola to bandage it. Iola took Quick's arm and held it up like a log of firewood, trying to ignore the fact that it felt like human flesh, man's flesh. The cords of muscles striating it lengthwise were firm, crossed with thick veins. His skin was deeply tanned and laced with curly blond hairs. There was a peculiar fascination in being able to inspect some portion of him so closely under an impersonal guise.

She wrapped gauze around the arm while Hartzler talked to Quick about investing in his oil company. She kept her attention on her work, but once she looked up to see his large blue eyes staring at her dreamily.

"I ain't never gonna wash this arm," he said, when she had finished.

"You better, or it'll get reinfected."

Tom Quick wore out shoes before other men did. His shirts rotted at the armpits. In his haste to get into the future, he was always leaving hats and coats behind, so it was easier to find signs of where he had been than to discover his current location. And no matter where his body stood, his mind was ranging ahead, doing reconnaissance.

But any exchange with the Kiowa nurse brought that motion to a screeching halt.

Ordinarily, he didn't mind stepping off his own train now and then, and women were a welcome diversion from work. He liked them. He wasn't a "man's man," didn't spend his leisure with his fellow oilmen, drinking, playing cards, fishing, or hunting. Mutual cooperation was necessary to do a job, but men's company bored him. However, he was also not a "ladies' man." He knew no poetry and seldom had the urge to give a lady a bouquet. He did enjoy the company of women. They were far more sensible than men, less inclined to obsession and delusion, more practical and realistic. He liked the animation in their faces, the nimbleness of their talk. He liked to draw out shy women; with forward women, he liked to keep up his end of banter and repartee.

But he had never lost his head over one. And he would swear on a stack of Bibles ten miles high that he hadn't lost his head over the Kiowa nurse: the reason he had gotten drunk this time after talking to her was because of the pain in his arm.

As he stood lounging unsteadily against a pillar on the porch of the hotel, the hootch in his system seemed to eat like acid through his defenses. Yes, she had hurt his pride. His charm simply did not work on her. But she made his knees weak and his stomach jumpy; he couldn't get her out of his mind.

But it was not love. Call it a challenge, say that he simply wanted to prove white men could be decent; he only wanted to prove that he, too, had Copperfield's welfare upmost in his mind and that he and she could be friends, that's all! He wanted to win her over only because being disliked for no reason didn't sit well. Well, he had been a jackass the first time they met, but should he pay for it forever?

He had forgotten to eat, and the rotgut was now living up to its name, burning a hole in his stomach. He couldn't face another meal alone, though. He wanted company, someone to charm. He looked down the boardwalk in the twilight. A pretty woman painted up like a whore stepped briskly out of the gloom. She had on a green velvet dress un-fashionably long, with a low neck that exposed the top of her breasts. Golden curls cascaded from under the brim of a large hat. Her mouth was a bright pomegranate red; her eyes were glittery, but when she drew close, the spidery signs of hard traveling were visible at the corners of her eyes and mouth. She carried a furled umbrella and reminded him of a madam in an Old West saloon. As she passed, he laid his fingers over the crook of her arm.

He started to speak, but she spun and slammed the umbrella across his bandaged forearm. The pain was so sharp that he yowled, stumbled, and fell onto the bench in front of the hotel windows, hugging his arm to his breast. The woman stood with the umbrella's tip resting on the boards like a cane, one hand fisted on her hip.

"I'm sorry." Her inflection suggested that she was generous enough to make an apology though none was owed. "I lost my temper. I'm sick of being pawed."

Tom tried to smile despite his pain but couldn't.

"I busted this arm today and just had it reset. I think you busted it again."

"I'm really very sorry," she said, with more feeling.

Tom rose and nested his sore arm gently against his torso, then grinned. "I ain't sure what my crime was, but my punishment was pretty severe."

"I said I'm sorry." Now the regret was mechanical. She hesitated only for an instant, then turned and stepped off the boardwalk and into the mire of the street.

Tom hopped after her. "Ma'am, I'd feel privileged if I could buy you a dinner. I know I'm not so pretty at the moment, but I could clean up."

"Just because I hit you on the arm doesn't mean I owe you the pleasure of my company."

"Didn't say you did." He tried to smile away her anger. "Let's just think of it as an odd way of getting met. My name is Tom Quick and under all this crud there's an honest-to-God rich man dying to spend some money on a pretty young lady."

She snickered. When they reached the other side of the street, she sprang up on the boardwalk and strode away, her skirt hem undulating like surf on sand. In her heels, she was up to his five-nine, but she seemed to be all leg. He was almost trotting to keep up with her.

"I can see you don't believe it. Or else it just doesn't make any difference to you. Mind telling me which it is?"

"The rich have better manners."

He chuckled. "Most of the rich people I know'd slit their granny's throat for a dime."

"Apparently we don't move in the same circles."

He had hooked her, dug under her skin.

"Name some rich men you know," he demanded.

"My friends are none of your business."

Tom laughed scornfully. "So you don't know any."

They reached the end of the block. Across the street were more one-story buildings that had been knocked up recently with a boardwalk before them. In the muddy street a string of trucks passed with equipment stacked on their beds, transmissions whining as the drivers sought to negotiate the muddy ruts without getting stuck. The woman glanced at him, furious, then bolted into the street.

He chased after her again, darting ahead to halt traffic and clear a space, and when they reached the curb where a crowd of oil workers stood cracking jokes at passersby, Tom wedged his way through them like a ship's prow and connected himself to the woman so they wouldn't harass her. If she appreciated this gallantry, she didn't show it. Following her line of sight, he saw a huge tent erected in a vacant lot. The crowd along the walk seemed to be surging toward it.

"I wasn't making fun of you," he said humbly. "But if you haven't known a rich man, you ought to treat yourself to it once in your life."

She lengthened her stride. Strong as a racehorse! Her pulse throbbed in the side of her pale neck. Vesuvius! He was perverse enough to want to cause the explosion, and widened the gap between them to stay far from her umbrella.

"You can be honest with me," he purred in a syrupy voice calculated to infuriate her. "Lots of girls fib to make themselves a little more respectable, but a fancy background doesn't mean anything to me."

"Listen, you filthy clodhopper! I don't care if you believe me or not!" She whirled and came to a stop, glaring at him. "When I was three my father gave me a birthday party. The theme was Cinderella. On the table in my grandparents' dining room was a centerpiece carved from ice—it was a coach—and there was a shoe, a giant shoe. The coach was so big that my guests could have ridden in it, you understand?"

"That's a pretty stout table," Tom put in with a grin. For a person who didn't care if she was believed or not, she was working pretty hard at making up a tale.

"Solid walnut," she went on, unfazed. She turned and resumed her walk, and he moved in beside her. "The man who carved the ice coach and shoe charged five hundred dollars for his work, but it didn't matter to my grandfather because the man did it for all his friends, and they never had a party where there wasn't one of the man's carved centerpieces."

"I reckon they've all melted by now," Tom said.

"Inside the coach sat a little prince and princess made of shaved ice that had been colored and flavored. For my birthday presents, I got a dollhouse made of teak large enough to curl up in. I got a pony, a diamond necklace, and three dresses made in Paris. All my guests got little gold bracelets and registered Highland terriers for party favors."

They had reached the entrance to the tent where a barker stood at a booth and people were in line to pass inside. Tom was amused by what he thought were the most outrageous lies he had ever heard from the mouth of a whore; the embellishments clearly marked her as a woman of imagination.

She sailed right past the barker, who tipped his hat to her.

"Evening, Miz Darby," the barker murmured smoothly, then turned to the crowd as she vanished inside the tent. "You see that lovely woman, folks? That was none other than Laura Darby, the toast of the Chicago stage! She sings like a nightingale, and she's one of many attractions onstage tonight!"

Tom was flabbergasted and not a little sheepish. Here he'd treated this "toast of the Chicago stage" as if she were one of Cheri Elena's soiled doves. He bought a ticket and moved inside with the crowd of farmers in overalls and brogans, barefoot children, large contingents of scruffy oilmen, a few townspeople in their Sunday best, Creeks from outlying settlements. He felt ashamed of himself and of the crowd, as if he were an ambassador for this rough country and his boorishness had only proved that the audience was beneath her.

The floor consisted of beat-down grass, and since recent rains hadn't seeped under the tent, dust rose as people milled about. Onstage was an upright piano and a painted backdrop of a city. When the show started, a master of ceremonies—the barker in another costume—introduced each act. A fellow and a girl assistant had five costumed Chihuahuas that jumped through hoops. "Artie's Pups" were followed by a magician —the ticket taker in another guise—who did card tricks and sawed Artie's assistant in half in a coffinlike box.

The crowd was noisy, cheering too loudly and heckling the performers. A gaggle of high-spirited, hootched-up roughnecks in the front row raised their thumbs up or down after each number.

When Laura Darby came out, she looked lovely, dressed in an old-fashioned yellow dress with a big straw hat. Artie sat at the piano; the magician and the barker came back onstage clad in tuxedos. They flanked Laura and kissed her hand while she flirted with them and sang, "Meet Me in St. Louis." As Tom watched, her magic slowly dissipated. Her smile was strained. Her eyes went out over the audience and lifted high above the tent. One of her yellow lace-up boots slipped in a dab of doo left by a Chihuahua, and the roughnecks laughed.

Why wasn't she "toasting Chicago," instead of playing to yahoos here in a boomtown a thousand miles from home in an amateur show? And if she was wealthy, why hadn't she married rich? She was a liar or had fallen a very long way. Probably the latter. And nothing could make her feel it more than having to sing for people like him in places like this.

He left after her song, cleaned up, donned a suit, tie, and hat, retrieved his Ford from the livery stable, and drove back to the tent. When the second show was over, it was late. He waited patiently until he saw her come out. She would obviously have to walk back to the hotel.

When he trotted over to her, she said, "It's you again!"

"Yes, ma'am. As you can see, I've cleaned up a bit. I enjoyed your show. It's easy to see why you're the toast of Chicago. And I'd like to apologize for being so rude." He reached inside his breast pocket and pulled out a crisp hundred-dollar bill, which he handed to her. "My calling card."

She held the bill daintily between her fingers, uncertain what to do with it. A slight smile twisted one corner of her mouth.

"You're Alexander Hamilton?"

"No, ma'am. Tom Quick." He pointed toward his car. "I've got a coach right over there. I'm afraid it's not ice, but it'll do to get you back to the hotel safe and sound and in a fashion that's more in keeping with a woman of your talent and breeding than trudging through the mud."

She looked at the car then back at the bill. Would she stuff it down her bosom or tear it up? he wondered. When she looked into his eyes and recognized his curiosity, she neatly flicked her wrist to offer the bill back.

"Nice engraving on this invitation. You must tell me who your printer is."

He took the bill with a chuckle. "Tell you what, we'll see if we can't use it all up on dinner."

Laura warmed to him over the meal. He put on his best manners, kept himself loose and casual. He flattered her by asking about her life as a famous singer and actress, pretending he had heard of her prior to this evening. The fare at the hotel consisted solely of meat and potatoes, and he had ordered the largest, most expensive steaks. He watched with fascination as Laura ate. While she had ladylike manners, she went right to the beef, taking several bites in succession—not exactly hurried, but with a controlled voraciousness, as if holding a delicate balance between feeding her hunger and maintaining a reputation as a woman of breeding. She gave him the impression that if she were eating in private, she would gnaw the bone and lick the juices off her fingers. She ate the way she walked.

He asked about her family. She passed him a glance of assessment, as if wondering how much to tell. "Not many left. Back in the eighties my grandfather invented a way of curing buffalo hides for harness leather."

Tom raised his eyebrows. "He must have made a pile, then."

"Yes." She smiled wistfully. "Then he made some unsound investments and got hit by the panic of '93. I guess if that hadn't gotten him, the automobile would have. Harnesses are a thing of the past."

Her present life was a far cry from the opulence she had known as a child. This was obviously painful, and he chose not to press her about it. Instead, he regaled her with talk about the oil fields, about characters known or invented, such as Gib Morgan, who had supposedly drilled a well to China.

"The derrick was so tall," said Tom with a wink, "that you could step off the crown block and onto the moon, and the derrick man never had to bring his lunch because he had all the green cheese he wanted. Took twenty-seven years to drill the well, and the drill stem was so long they ran out of pipe the last sixteen years and had to import snakes from the Congo and tie them together to reach the bottom of the hole. One day, though, they punched through to the other side of the earth and hit sake, about a million barrels of it, then the well commenced to cough up tons of white rice. Well, that didn't faze old Gib—he just built a pipeline all the way to New York City and another to San Francisco and put a big spigot on each end and took to selling Chinamen that sake. He sailed boatloads of white rice across the ocean and sold it right back to them."

Laura laughed.

Tom winked. "After a few years, that white rice quit coming, but just as soon as it did they hit a chop suey gusher, with noodles. That chop suey blew the top of the derrick off, and it rained chop suey all the way to Florida. Old Gib made another fortune piping chop suey into restaurants back East. And when that ran out—"

"He hit fortune cookies, right?" interjected Laura.

Tom widened his eyes in mock surprise. "Now how'd you know that?"

Laura laughed. "You're a lot of fun, Tom Quick. Most of the men I know aren't."

"I'd say that's a change of tune," Tom said dryly. "But now I'm on your good side, I wanna know how much you'd charge to give a private concert."

She winked coyly. "You mean a concert for one or a concert in a private place?"

"Both."

Her eyes rose slowly up the front of his starched white shirt, the lapels of his suit coat, the knot in his tie, until they gazed frankly and steadily into his own. Her eyes were a deep, luminescent green.

"You can have one for free."

He swallowed. She saw his Adam's apple bob, and they both laughed.

They drove through town, and while Laura chatted about the fancy opera houses she had played in, Tom observed fields cluttered with tents, lean-tos, and shacks, where the boomers had made do with whatever shelter they could muster. The town's one new boardinghouse—knocked together in a matter of days—was operating on the "hot bed" system, with one man rolling into bed as another on the next shift was rolling out of it.

The bristling energy of a boom never ceased to amaze and please him. Six months ago, Wetoka had been only a crossroad with a general store, a livery stable, a bank, and a small hotel for travelers. Now it was a hopping, roaring little burg of 30,000 souls hungry for a taste of the good life. Even now after 11:00 P.M., the streets were as alive as they had been at noon. Card games lit by lanterns hung from branches were played under trees, and men were swigging whiskey in the alleys, putting their money down on blankets, and rolling dice.

Walking around in that hot, restless energy was like downing a mug of good strong java. Any time of night you could hear singing and gunshots and hollering. Now and then you got a bad apple, that happened anywhere. Fellows got liquored up or unhappy about the way the cards turned, they lashed out. The sheriff had run out of room in his jail; with no time to build a new one, he had simply stretched a chain between two oaks and looped his prisoners' leg chains through it.

Oilmen played hard. But they worked hard, too, and Tom was proud of every one of them, proud to have lit a fire under this sleepy little hamlet by bringing in the discovery well on Copperfield's place.

When he wheeled off toward the river along the road being graded to serve as his driveway, Laura hesitated in her monologue, as if afraid, but as they turned the last corner and the mansion shone like a white Spanish castle under the moon, she sucked in her breath.

The house stood on a bluff overlooking the river like a ghostly luxury liner oddly beached. From the winding approach in front, it appeared to have even more than its three stories: his architect had a penchant for Moorish design, adorning Tom's mansion with white plaster walls, curved arches, and towers to nowhere. In the moonlight, it had a fairy-tale quality, a "Mediterranean grace," as his architect had put it. Most of the oilmen who hit it big had built large frame or brick Victorian homes in Tulsa or Oklahoma City, and their opulence was measured by the amount of gingerbread molding that festooned the windows and railings and eaves. Tom had not wanted a house that looked like a wedding cake.

A window on the top floor was lighted from inside by a lantern. Tom pulled in front of the house and tooted the horn once. Another lantern parted from the first like a cell dividing, then came weaving down through the interior of the darkened structure.

"It's a beautiful, beautiful house, Tom," sighed Laura.

"Thanks. It's not quite finished yet. I'm going to have an open-house party in two weeks. I sure hope you'll come."

He smiled, and she smiled back. Her wild green eyes had flickering orange lantern light caught up in them, giving them the strange glow that the eyes of cats and possums have when your headlights catch them on the road.

"I will," she said. She started a story about how she was soon quitting and returning to Chicago, but it sounded extemporaneous and altogether fabricated, so he hardly listened. He had offered the invitation merely so she wouldn't think that she was only an attraction of the moment, but even as he realized his motive, he also realized that she had become precisely that, only a moment's passion. It was that damned seesaw business again: as he rose in her estimation, she plummeted in his. The way she gushed praise about the house set him on edge.

He was suddenly very tired, and his sore arm ached. It had been a long, eventful day, and it had left him with a residue of bitterness and self-disgust. It had been so easy to invite Laura to his housewarming: why couldn't he have uttered those same words to Iola? That chunk of angle iron falling from the derrick had whacked his forearm only because he had been mooning. He had realized when the accident occurred that the injury was the perfect excuse to see her and issue his invitation. But he had become scared thinking about a probable rejection and let the wound fester another twenty-four hours until finally the pain had driven him in.

Then he hadn't been able to ask her! Now that he had invited Laura, could he still invite Iola? Could they both be his guests?

As his watchman emerged from the house with the lantern and walked toward where they stood waiting, Laura leaned over and took his arm in a jaunty show of approval, but it was hardly necessary— Tom could already picture himself guiding Laura through the rooms of the unfinished and unfurnished house, winding up on the balcony over-looking the river where there was a wicker couch, sitting beside her, fetching a glass of wine, kissing her, tugging down her bloomers. The certainty of it depressed him.

9

On the day of Tom Quick's party, David was bringing in a bucket of water when he heard hooves clatter on stones in front of his cabin. He carried the bucket through the back door as someone on the porch hollered, "Hullo the house!" He took his Walker-styled Colt .45 from its nail on the wall, tucked the barrel into his waistband, and unbolted the front door just as a man was shouting, "Hullo!" again.

The man wore a dusty bowler and an old camel-hair topcoat. Embar-rassed to be shouting into David's face, he broke off abruptly, and when he saw the pistol butt he lurched backward. The pistol was among the few things oil money had brought David that he did not readily curse. It did not need to be brandished; its mere presence was sufficient to encourage honesty and brevity in the speeches of strangers, particularly when his scowling face hung above it like a lighted jack-o'-lantern in a tree.

"Hullo!" the man said sheepishly. He raised his hand as if to take an oath. "White man, red man brothers!"

Behind him stood a woman who had apparently ridden up on the same horse. She wore a long rue-colored dress and a large hat which did not conceal her graying hair. She had buck teeth and small eyes set close; when David looked at her, her reddish hands met in front of her bosom as if prayer might deliver her from his wrath.

"How!" said David, biting his lip.

"Good!" The man might have been congratulating David on having the faculty of speech. "This your wife!" The man cupped the woman's elbow in his palm to coax her forward. She gave David a bashful smile.

"Me lawyer." He dipped quickly into his coat pocket and produced a folded paper which he snapped open and waved. "Me have talking paper say you and wife here marry in Kansas many moon ago." He flapped the document.

David relished how clouds passed over their faces as he dropped the heel of his hand onto the pistol butt.

"You made a mistake."

The man moved one foot backward and warily watched David's hand for further motion. "You know," he said, after a moment, "I think you're right. Fella we're needing is named something else." He pointed to the woman. "It's real likely she made the mistake."

The woman looked at the man; even with her mouth closed, her front teeth perched on the flesh of her bottom lip, giving her a pensive look but without conveying a sense of intelligence.

The man eyed David. "You wouldn't happen to *need* a wife, would you?"

"Not your grandmother there."

Ignoring the insult, the man leaned forward in a pretense of confidentiality and stage-whispered, "She's plain as a board fence, but you'd be surprised at what she knows." He squiggled his sandy eyebrows meaningfully. "You could rent her tonight just for a tryout. No strings attached. Top it off, she ain't said three words since this century turned over."

David slammed the door in his face. But he was more amused than angry. A more transparently luckless pair he had never seen, and over the past six months he had seen plenty of ludicrous guile born of desperation. He had been offered, among many other things, three barrels of high-grade Kentucky bourbon, shares in a Colorado gold mine, a house in Tulsa, a hotel in Fort Worth, two Chinese girls under sixteen skilled in the arts of cooking and matters of the boudoir, one hundred shares of Standard Oil, and a machine which restored vigor to tired members and incited passion in even the most frigid of ladies.

He went to the plank-top table and removed his shirt and the top to his long johns. Rent the bucktoothed woman for the night? The idea had a faint appeal, but it also brought a painful memory of his only visit to a Wetoka whorehouse. The would-be salesman in the bowler had indeed been knocking at the right door, but he had the wrong goods. David did need a wife now, and he was ready for one, some smart young woman who might help him keep the world at arm's length. Some woman with, say, Iola's best qualities.

He doused a rag in the water bucket and washed his face. He carried a basin to an old oak dresser, set it down, and began razoring. The silver backing on the mirror above the dresser had peeled away in patches; to shave efficiently, he had to move his face from tatter to tatter, never seeing the whole.

You could use a new mirror, a voice said.

The same voice had been talking about the pulley and rope on his water well. The voice made lists; it whispered the names of objects in his ear, and the names were all preceded by the adjective "new."

The voice disturbed him. Each time he thought about his money, he would scan the interior of the one-room cabin and remember how it looked when Joseph and Katie lived in it. He was embarrassed at how dirty it appeared now. To avoid having Miss Roberts and Iola see it, he took Iola up on her invitation and went to Wetoka to visit them in the preacher's parlor where the furnishings—draperies, carpeting, those round white lacey things on the chair arms—merely reminded him of how crude his own were.

The voice said, *You can have whatever Tatum has two times over*.

He had been uncomfortable there, with Iola sitting too quietly and the teacher talking too much and not realizing that they might want to be alone. He had been courteous but distant, tolerating the missionary's maternal regard for his welfare, though squirming when she talked of how he needed to marry. Iola had sat blushing because, he thought, she was afraid he would ask her to be his wife.

When Iola had left the room for a moment, Miss Roberts had told him how much they both admired his "strength of character"; she contrasted him to the woebegone sons of former warriors who had leased their allotments for decades in advance to white cattlemen and had soon drunk up all the lease money; David Copperfield had pride, he had not lost his sense of himself. Some of these compliments, Miss Roberts had claimed, came from Iola—Iola says this, Iola says that.

The missionary was matchmaking, surely against Iola's deepest wishes, David thought. The missionary seemed now to be trying to arrange his life the way she had arranged Iola's.

He wasn't surprised when Miss Roberts urged him to build a new school in Wetoka, and Iola suggested he build a medical facility in Anadarko. *Do good with your money, David.*

They had as much as called him guilty for having it, then offered a means of absolution. He couldn't distinguish their appeals from those of the swindlers; all assumed he was nothing more than his money, and the idea that he could possess horses, houses, automobiles, wives, schools, and hospitals merely by deciding to was still foreign.

Neither Iola nor Miss Roberts knew that he was reluctant to use the money not because he was tightfisted but because he was afraid it would involve him in the affairs of other people, would drag him into the chaos of a future whose dim outlines already made him tremble. Each time Quick appeared with more money, he would put the roll into a saucepan and hide it in the unused oven. Not spending it was akin to not admitting he had agreed to take it, even though the forest of derricks had now crept closer to the cabin and the noises they made day and night made him grind his teeth with rage; they gave incontrovertible evidence of his agreement and folly.

"Somebody's gonna hijack you sure as the dickens if they find out you're putting the stuff in there," Tom Quick had said, watching David stash a bundle of bills in the oven.

It did seem a foolish place to keep the money. Jenny might return and fire the stove, but, on the other hand, heating a skillet full of Jenny's cornbread would be the best use he could imagine for the money at the moment, if "use" meant getting pleasure from it.

The voice of the money became persistent. It spoke from inside the oven, making demands, insidious suggestions. Like it or not, he was a rich man. Yesterday, he had had his hair cut in a white man's barbershop in McAlester because he paid triple the price after regular hours; the money could alter people's attitudes about his place in the world, red man or not, like it or not.

The money had insisted it could be useful. The money had said it wanted to be a pistol, so he had bought one, and after he had chased the first intruder off with it, the money said, *See!*

The money had pointed out that his customary mode of transportation—walking—was primitive, ignoble; it was certainly not fitting for a man whose father was a warrior and hunter. So he bought a roan stallion.

While he leaned against the current with his pole and felt boneless on nights after traffic had been heavy, the money started yammering at him —*Just ride off on that stallion!* When he endured the snobbery of passengers who didn't know he was rich or the bothersome aggressiveness of those who did, the money had said, *You don't have to do this any more!*

Two weeks ago on a sleepless night he had heard the money say, *Don't lie there feeling bad—take me and your horse and go to that place Quick told you about!* So he had taken several hundred dollars and had ridden the stallion into town, where he found the house Quick had described. The woman who met him at the door told him they didn't take "his kind" there. When he unrolled his money, however, a red-haired woman standing nearby had whistled. She led him out behind the house near the privy, where she instructed him to lie on his back in the grass. She lifted her skirt, skewered herself on his erection, rode him for a few minutes, then took the bills.

Having the money instead of his old life, he had been willing to experiment to discover precisely how it might console him for all his losses. The amounts meant very little to him. But he realized he had not received full value from the red-haired whore, and for the first time he had confirmed someone's belief that he was a fool with money. The experience was bereft of intimacy, friendship, or mutual concern, and he realized his whole fortune would not have gained him anything remotely resembling what he had come to get. He knew that a very small portion of the payment was for the service itself; the remainder of it was a surcharge on the color of his skin.

When he finished shaving, he carried the basin to the door and pitched the dirty water onto the ground. He took the enamel pan to the stove, where he opened the oven and placed the basin in the front rank of pots inside. In the last row sat the saucepans in which rolls of hundred-dollar bills were stuffed. *You can see me, can't you! Don't you think anybody who looks in here could, too?*

"Today," he said.

It was close and warm in the cabin on this March morning, so David went out onto the porch, bent over and pulled off the bottoms of his long johns. He stood nude, feeling the soft balmy breeze drift between his legs, the early spring sunshine on his chest, belly, and groin. He grew hard, and for a few moments he stood wondering with amusement if the ferry passengers a half mile down the river could see him and if the sight was as effective a deterrent for unwanted visitors as the pistol. He shivered; memories of Jenny swept over him.

He reached down, took a set of new underwear out of a sack, along with khaki trousers and a blue madras dress shirt with a pleated breast. He unwrapped the new garments from their tissue paper, thinking that he'd be as presentable as anybody else at Tom Quick's party.

While slipping his arm through a sleeve, he looked down to the river again where the ferry, loaded with passengers and too many vehicles, was midstream on a trip to the south bank. *Buen suerte.* David didn't have to work, but his money hadn't caused him to abandon the ferry. A white man who had superseded him as the operator had hired two boys; David could have hired help the way his white successor did, he could have perched on the railing smoking cigars, a ferry pilot's cap at a rakish angle on his head so people would think he was indulging in a hobby or running the ferry as a public service.

On a morning only three days ago, when David was poling hard to push a load with a wagon full of machinery, he saw the mule stumble on the red road above the landing, heave over on its side, kick spastically for a moment like a dog dreaming, then lie still.

David sat down beside the animal and cried quietly with his back to the road. After a while, he dragged the mule's corpse off the road and buried him in a grove of trees. He had promised the mule a respite, and through stupidity he had lost a boon companion.

When he returned to the cabin around twilight, he noticed the side door was slightly ajar. He stormed inside, his footfalls rattling dishes. The oven door squawked on its rusty hinges, and he pawed the skillet aside and stuck his head into the cavity.

The money was still there.

It said, *I'm all you've got now. Guard me!*

Saynday was coming along one afternoon when he saw a prairie dog village near Mount Scott. He hadn't eaten since breakfast, so he was very hungry. The prairie dogs were all out of their lodges dancing and singing. Saynday stood off awhile thinking about eating hot juicy prairie-dog meat and pretty soon his mouth started to water. He didn't have a bow or lance with him, so he needed to think of a clever way to trick the prairie dogs.

He came up to where they were dancing. Hello, Nephews! he said. You look so fine and handsome while you are dancing.

The prairie dogs all said, Thank you, Uncle, because they were very proud of how well they danced.

It is a shame that you do not know the dance the prairie dogs do up north, because it is better than your dance, he told them.

Well, they all felt bad about this. Don't be upset, Nephews, Saynday told them. I will teach this dance to you.

Saynday told all the prairie dogs to join hands and dance in a long line past where he sat. He told them to close their eyes and listen to him sing and knock on the ground with a club to keep the rhythm.

So the prairie dogs closed their eyes and joined hands and started dancing right by where Saynday sat with his club. He sang—

> Prairie Dogs, Prairie Dogs, shake your tails!
> Prairie Dogs, Prairie Dogs, shake your tails!
> Now is the time to dance your best!
> Now is the time to dance your best!

Each time he said Now, he hit a prairie dog over the head with his club and killed it. He had almost got to the end of the line when one little prairie dog opened her eyes and saw what was happening. She ran off, and Saynday let her go. He said, You will be the mother of all the prairie dogs. Your children can bark at the people who are to come.

Saynday dug a hole in the ground and lined it with rocks. He took the dead prairie dogs and tossed them into the hole, covered them with green leaves and brush, then he made a fire on top of them. He sat back and thought about all the meat he would eat.

Some hungry birds smelled the meat cooking and came to where Saynday sat waiting.

Uncle Saynday, they said, What are you cooking?

I'm not cooking anything, Nephews, said Saynday.

But the birds had seen him kill the prairie dogs, so they said, Saynday, we know you are cooking some meat. Please save some for us. You have plenty enough for all of us! Don't be greedy!

But Saynday, he said, Go away, get out of here! and chased the birds away.

The birds flew off until they saw Coyote. They told him that Saynday had a lot of nice hot prairie dog meat that he would not share.

Coyote thought, Ha! I will get me some of that meat! So he got some sunflower sap and milkweed down and stuck it all over his body to look like sores. Then he sucked in his belly to make himself look skinny and got a stick to walk with like a cane.

He went limping up to where Saynday was watching his meat cook real good, and it was just about ready.

Uncle, said Coyote, What's that wonderful smell! It smells like prairie-dog meat cooking! As you can see, I am sick and very hungry. Won't you share just a bone or two? Don't be greedy.

Saynday said, No, Nephew, I am going to eat it by myself, even the bones. I am very hungry.

Well, said Coyote, Would you be willing to gamble for it?

What do you mean? asked Saynday.

I think I can run faster than you, said Coyote. So we will run a race and if I win I get some of your meat.

Saynday was proud and thought he could run faster than Coyote. He laughed and said, Nephew, you are foolish. Just to be fair, I will tie some rocks together and wrap them around me. We will run around Mount Scott and back. If I win you will go away and quit bothering me, and if you win you can have a few bones.

Coyote said that was fine. They started to race. Neither one went very fast, but they stayed right together, Coyote with his cane, and Saynday carrying rocks, until they reached the other side of Mount Scott. Suddenly Coyote put down his cane and took off running as fast as he could, but Saynday got tangled up in the rocks he had tied together. Coyote ran back to the camp and found that the prairie dogs were cooked just right. He ate all the delicious meat and left the bones covered with ashes. Then he ran away. When Saynday returned, he discovered that the prairie dogs had been eaten, and he had no meat that day.

This is what happens to greedy people. O'teha, all is told.

With the bills from the saucepans packed in his saddlebags, David rode to Wetoka. Since traffic on the dusty red road was heavy, he took the horse off to the side and along the bordering pastures. Where a farmer had had an empty oat field weeks ago lay a sea of canvas tents, brush lean-tos, autos and wagons that people were living in. Women and children were milling about; open fires sent streams of smoke into the blue sky. Beyond the pasture, above the rim of a ridge, the crow's nests of derricks were visible.

Passing through the outskirts, David noticed that several new streets had been cut to the west of the railroad station and into what had been a grove of post oak. New buildings were going up, their frames crawling with white men carrying hammers and saws. This boom, David knew, had come from the three-letter word he had uttered to Tom Quick. Quick had caught him in a weak moment, and now that he could see the results of his answer, he wasn't sure he would say yes had he the chance to answer again. What would have happened to all these people and himself had he answered no? Would the boom have happened anyway, the oil found on someone else's land? Quick had been right, at least—now people were talking about building a bridge where the ferry crossed.

At the bank, David dismounted and stood for a moment after tying his horse, half in awe of the burgeoning crowds on the streets and boardwalks. Several pretty women passed, one a yellow Negress dressed in finery, but she looked away with indifference when he smiled at her.

He had not made a deposit in the bank for over seven months. He had been in the habit of collecting the coins from his ferry passengers and hiding them in a jar under the cabin floor until they overflowed, only then making a deposit during a trip to the village for supplies.

He had never seen the teller before, but, then, the bank was full of strangers. He raised the saddlebags to the window, pulled out the rolls of bills and placed them on the ledge. He told the clerk to place them in his account.

The clerk eyed him, then uncoiled each roll by cutting the tie string with a pocket knife. Slowly and deliberately, he counted each bill and flattened it on top of the others. When he finished, he looked at David with curiosity.

"Excuse me a moment."

The clerk disappeared into an office at the rear of the bank. He returned a moment later followed by a tall thin man clad in a vested suit, string tie, and cowboy boots; his small, severe black eyes didn't match the broad grin his lips were practicing.

"Well, well, the famous Mr. Copperfield, how are you? I'm W. O. Kale!"

Kale passed his hand through David's swiftly and tentatively, the way a child might pet an unfamiliar animal.

"Let's go into my office and chat, if you have a minute. No point in your standing at the window here." Kale nodded to the teller. "Bring Mr. Copperfield his deposit record when you're finished."

The office was roomy, with leather chairs and carpets on the floor, dominated by an elephant's-foot table in the center, around which the chairs were arranged. Kale's rolltop desk was pushed into a corner, seemingly as an afterthought. On the paneled walls hung game trophies. David stared at the buffalo's head. Beside it were the heads of a moose, a deer, a zebra, a lion, and two others he didn't recognize.

"What is that?"

"A rhinoceros," answered Kale, amused. "My father shot him on his last African safari. Africa is across a big water—"

"I mean the one like an antelope." Thus he could manage to learn both by being officially ignorant of only one.

"A gazelle, a Thomson's gazelle. You like to hunt?"

"My people are Kiowas, they've always hunted."

"Ah!" exclaimed Kale. "Good people. You're not Creek, then?"

"My friends, the Parkers, were."

Kale nodded. He seemed uncertain as to why he had brought David here, and after a moment, he gestured David into a chair.

"If you're interested in big-game hunting, why then sometime perhaps we can do that. My last trip was with the Great White Father Theodore Roosevelt when he came West. My family has been here for many years, Mr. Copperfield." He passed David a curious look whose significance David couldn't determine. "We're not like these Johnny-come-latelies in the oil business. We've been friends with the red folk for many a decade now. I knew the Parkers well."

Kale opened a box of cigars and offered one. David took it. Kale's nostrils widened and closed like a rabbit's when he leaned close to light the cigar. David saw in Kale's small, involuntary reflex one creature testing another.

"They deeded their land to you, of course?"

David nodded. He toyed with the cigar, sniffing at the smoke, bit off the tip and chewed on it, rolling it over his tongue. It was sweet. He waited for Kale to ask why the Parkers would have turned over their allotment to someone who had come along out of the blue. He didn't think it was any of Kale's business. If Kale knew the Parkers well, why need to ask David?

"Considering how things turned out, that was exceedingly generous of them, wouldn't you say?"

"Where did these come from?" David held out the cigar.

"Cuba." Kale closed the box and held it out to David. "Take them, please."

David nodded to indicate Kale could place them back onto the table where he would later retrieve them.

"Thank you."

"Would you like some sherry or some cognac?"

David nodded, curious as to what this assent would bring him. Kale rose from his chair, went to a sideboard, poured two snifters of cognac, then handed one to David.

David sipped; it burned like white man's whiskey, but it was thicker. It was tasty. He downed the rest of it, and his eyes watered. Kale took his snifter and filled it again.

"I see you're a connoisseur."

When he handed David the refilled snifter, David took another swallow, then set the glass on his thigh and puffed on the cigar.

"Here, take this too, with my compliments." He passed the bottle to David, and again David nodded for him to set it on the table. There was in his refusal to actually touch the gifts a curious aloofness that appeared to disconcert Kale.

"Thank you."

"My pleasure. I like doing business with men of good taste."

David sat enjoying the cognac and the cigar, waiting for the banker to surface from beneath the courtesies.

"I'm not like a lot of white men around here. My family has been ranching in this territory since after the War for States' Rights, and we lived in harmony with red folks. Between you and me"—Kale leaned forward—"these oil people are filthy, ill-bred, and uneducated. My father sent my brother and myself east to see what civilization is like, and I can tell you that some of us feel that these oil people stick in the craw."

David was uncertain as to the drift of Kale's words; on the one hand, he seemed to be reassuring David that he wasn't an ordinary white man —and therefore wasn't to be thought of as an enemy—but the pecking order implied in the hierarchy of values sketched would most likely place a person in David's own circumstances a notch below even repugnant white men.

"You went to school?"

"Yes."

"Ah!" said Kale, too agreeably, David thought. "Education is the best thing for your people. You ever study genetics?"

A knock on the door saved David from ducking the question. The teller entered, passed Kale a paper. They exchanged a look that made David feel important. When the teller left, Kale handed the paper to David.

"Your deposit record. You'll be bringing in more later?"

Kale's cool, bland surface was ruffled as his purpose surfaced despite his desire to keep it hidden. David had understood that this white man, like the others, wanted something he had, and, for the first time, he enjoyed having something that was coveted.

He shrugged.

"Mr. Copperfield, I don't wish to presume to interfere with the affairs of a man so obviously in possession of his own sense of direction, of course, but to tell the truth, I'm a little concerned about your money."

David's eyebrows rose.

"I'm happy that we here at this bank apparently have your respect and trust, but I wouldn't ever want to stand accused of acting contrary to your best interests. Do you have an attorney who might oversee transactions such as we made this morning?"

"No."

Kale smiled broadly. "Could I suggest someone at our bank here? This might greatly simplify your affairs. You give the power of attorney to the firm, why then we could find secure investments for you, make your deposits multiply without your ever turning a hand."

This sounded faintly like the pitch Tom Quick had given him, and his face shut. Kale saw it happen.

"There's no hurry, of course," he went on in a rush. "We welcome your business any way you wish to give it. I brought it up thinking of the trouble some of your people have found themselves in because of sudden wealth. There are a lot of greedy thieves around, and the courts are beginning to fill up with meretricious lawsuits because some Creek found himself blessed with a fortune but cursed with new relatives he had never heard of. I know you're aware of guardianship and competency hearings and such."

Kale lifted the bottle and poured David another finger of cognac.

"Are you married?"

"Not yet."

"Not yet?" Kale smiled. "That's not quite the same thing as saying no, is it? You have plans, then?"

"No," David said firmly, trying to close off Kale's access to his interior.

"Well, it's something a man of your means would want to be cautious about, of course."

The cigar and cognac had settled into his blood; David felt groggy. Kale rose suddenly and extended his hand; the action seemed extraordinary and inexplicable for an instant, then David understood that Kale was finished with whatever he had set out to accomplish.

"Feel free to come in and consult me at any time, Mr. Copperfield. We consider you a valued customer."

David nodded. He picked up the box of cigars, tucked it under one arm, and grasped the cognac bottle by the neck. Looking up, he saw a flicker of satisfaction pass over Kale's face.

"Thank you for the gifts."

"My pleasure, indeed!"

David stopped in the lobby to retrieve his saddlebags and to put the cigars and cognac in them. He looked back into Kale's office and saw the banker go to a window and bat at the air with his hand.

10

Iola had been ready to go for some time when Alice, tardy as usual, shoved the Sears, Roebuck catalogue under her nose. Floridly rococo hats perched on the heads of pretty, full-cheeked women with eyes shaped like almonds.

"That's the one I got."

One hat and bearer were circled in red. *Very pretty hat for misses or young ladies.* Iola looked up at Alice, whose porcine face was creased and frowning.

"Well?"

"Where's the hat?"

"What do you think?"

Privately, Iola thought Alice would do well to reread the phrase designating the hat's intended wearer.

"Pretty."

Alice nodded, then took the hat down from a shelf of the oak armoire that held their meager wardrobes. She slowly lowered the hat onto her piled-up hair.

She cocked her head this way and that in the mirror.

"It's certainly . . . *there*, isn't it?"

The hat reminded Iola of a basket of fruit. Occasionally, Alice did foolish things beneath her dignity, though it was hard for Iola to acknowledge them.

"It's very becoming."

She was uneasy soothing Alice's vanity.

"You're ready to go, I suppose."

It sounded like an accusation. Iola glanced down at her high-button boots, the navy woolen skirt, and the lace-trimmed white blouse closed to her throat. She would wear her blue woolen cape over that, not so much for warmth but for armament. Since the outfit looked and felt too much like white people's clothes, she had combed out her long black hair, parted it in the middle, and had considered changing from boots into moccasins.

"Not anxious, I see."

Iola felt her cheeks redden.

"Why should I be?"

Alice teased her with a grin.

"Oh, no reason."

She hated it when Alice pretended to know her mind, hated it even more when her intuition was accurate. Alice knew Iola was anxious to see David at Tom Quick's party. Alice relished playing matchmaker, and Iola felt trapped: she could not bring herself to be forward with David and thought she *needed* a go-between, but Alice played the role with such gusto that Iola felt rushed and self-conscious. And enough was enough—Alice had dropped hints to David that would have penetrated the thickest skull, but still he hadn't taken the cue. When he had come to visit them, Iola's plans to be alone with David to apologize and to thank him had been thwarted, and the longer it went undone the harder it became to do.

At the front gate, Alice untied the horse from the hitch and they climbed into the buggy Alice had borrowed from the Reverend Tatum.

"I wouldn't have been late," Alice said as she passed the reins to Iola, "except that I had a mission of mercy."

The formality of missionary speech was rare in Alice and Iola turned to check her expression for irony.

"I was at a house of ill repute."

Iola guided the two-wheel buggy through muddy streets in the waning twilight. The rest of the story would come, she knew, when Alice had chewed sufficiently on Iola's silence. She sometimes felt guilty at how easily Alice could be manipulated by silences in which the missionary imagined she heard disapproval. That an educated, thirty-two-year-old white missionary harbored such insecurity about her moral state that she sought the approval of a Kiowa girl descended from "heathens" was an unexpected turn.

"Some Mexican girl had been beaten. She thought she was going to die, and she wanted to confess. I was the closest thing to a Catholic priest anybody could scare up. None of the local preachers, including our esteemed landlord, would go for fear of harming his reputation."

"Did she die?"

Alice sighed. "No, it was her first walloping. I'd guess she'll grow used to it if she doesn't break apart."

"Maybe you should have brought her in."

"And let old Heartless tell her it was due to her bad attitude? She's better off among friends. They had her cleaned up pretty well."

Iola was annoyed that Alice had not considered coming to her for help. She wondered if the missionary thought she wouldn't be competent to administer white man's medicine, though she knew the thought was irrational—Alice had seen her work.

Iola threaded the buggy through the traffic on the street, and soon they were on the road that led to Quick's house.

"Dear God, I tell you they all need something they're not getting," Alice went on. "They were spiritually starved, they embarrassed me, those girls, they were so in want for someone of the cloth to talk to. No servant of the Lord could ask for a more needy flock."

She sounded faintly defensive. Alice's superiors might be shocked to learn where Alice had been applying her zeal, but to Iola what Alice had done made perfect sense. The rules white people had for abandoning or accepting one another were still mysterious to her Kiowa mind.

"The woman in charge goes by the rather impossible name of Cheri Elena, though I'd guess she was christened—if she was christened, poor thing!—as 'Charity' or something of the sort." Alice laughed. "She told me she believed in 're-in-cog-nation.' I think she wanted to assure me she wasn't without religious feelings of some kind."

"Re-in-cog-nation?"

"Reincarnation, the belief in the Orient that one's soul moves from life to life in various forms." Alice sighed. "She told me she thought she was a dog in another life."

"Kiowas believe everything has spirit."

Alice could not consider the concepts of a heathen religion without a shadow crossing her face—it was one of her shortcomings, thought Iola.

"I told her that if there was such a thing—and I don't believe for a moment there is, of course—then I was probably an elephant." She flushed. "She got a kick out of that." She sighed heavily and gave Iola a sidelong glance. "Maybe I was an oriental courtesan so addicted to pleasures of the flesh that my present form is a kind of punishment."

The comment was an oblique confession of the sin that concerned Alice the most. Living in close quarters, Iola had discovered not only vanity but also a streak of sensuality in Alice that appeared in her gluttony and in the way she stroked her fingers lightly across velvet cushions or dabbed at her lower lip with the tip of her tongue when she was reading or thinking.

Iola hadn't known how much Alice anguished over her sensual appetite until she secretly read, with curiosity and guilt, a furiously scribbled entry in Alice's journal. Inspired by too much sherry and a mutinous meeting in McAlester with her "sisters," during which they had apparently reproached her, Alice had written: *They're so cool and angelic! So pale, so willowy, so quiet! They make me feel like one of those bovine washerwoman nuns of some German order whose sole claim to belonging to Christ lies in the ponderous dedication of their scrub boards and soapsuds. Cattle rewarded for giving milk every day. I'm too fond of the languorous wash of warm water over my skin, too fond of walking alone in the pastures on a windy day and raising my skirt to let the wind brush my thighs, too fond of stroking my hair! Too fond of feeling my skin under my fingers! Too fond of snuff! Too fond of potatoes! Too fond of sherry! (Much too!) I should not love the smell of horses and the smell of men. And the smell of tobacco and whiskey and oil and saddle leather. I shouldn't let myself love the smell of wood fires and cooking things and coffee and bacon and flowers and sachet packets and cedar! On a cold day my face takes relish in the pale heat of the sun on my cheeks! I curse my senses! I should train myself to abhor the feel of flesh. Those are my sins—loneliness and guilt are my punishment!*

So Alice agonized over her sins! That partly restored Alice to her pedestal. Alice did not cling rigidly to principle and duty; she followed her heart. Iola was willing to take Alice's sensuality as a sign of deep and joyous attachment to life.

Along the road oil workers were living in the pastures; lanterns inside tents glowed softly in the twilight. Cooking fires flickered across the fields, and on the ridges to the south, flares from the wells burned with a distant hiss. Iola watched a small boy struggle to carry two buckets of water with a board run through their handles and across his shoulders, like an ox yoke.

Driving on, they came to the oil fields. Ahead in the dimness, men worked with shovels to fill a pipeline ditch dug across the road. Iola reined in the horse to wait for the crew to finish, and Alice rose to light the lantern hanging from the hoop beside her head. The roaring cacophony of clanking metal beat against Iola's ears, and the parson's horse skittishly danced in place. Trees in the distance shimmered, oil-drenched, and the ground nearby was littered with hunks of machinery sitting in puddles of oil. The working men moved silently, humped over like beasts. It was eerie—the white men so strangely silent and shadowy, the squealing machinery; it was suddenly as if she had been plopped down on another planet where man-sized ants were toiling enigmatically to accomplish something of which she had no conception. The white man's road might as well be an avenue in the Milky Way, it was so far removed from the earth she had known.

She clucked the horse forward when a workman waved them on; they rounded a bend, and the noise fell behind them.

"Apparently David had been there," Alice said.

It took Iola a minute to understand that Alice was referring to the "house of ill repute." She felt heartsick, but she struggled to hide her feelings.

"What was he doing there?" she asked evenly, hoping that circumstances out of the ordinary explained his presence.

In the lantern light, Alice passed her a curiously maternal look.

"Spending his money, I'm afraid."

Her heart plummeted. With the local paper calling him "The World's Richest Indian," he would now be pressured by all manner of corrupting whites. In the few exchanges she and David had had since she had come to Wetoka, she had detected a subtle change in him: he had grown mulish, uninterested in her, less willing to listen. She hadn't seen any evidence of profligate spending, but he wasn't enthusiastic about using any of his wealth to help his own people, either. When she or Alice made suggestions, he grew twitchy, distracted, perhaps even bored.

Maybe her expectations had been too high. She had written her father about David, taking care not to reveal too much. She wanted her father to know she could make her own choices, and good ones. She'd be embarrassed to have her father know she had been a fool, if she had.

Was there something wrong with her? She had too much pride, her father said. His choices for her to marry had all been copies of himself, dutiful, industrious but dirt-poor Kiowa farmers with one hand on a plow and the other on the white man's Bible. She could choose between them or from among their luckless peers who hadn't been able to leap the chasm in their history and had fallen into the abyss. She could choose between two sorts of failure, two sets of dispirited men.

So even before she had met David again, his having saved her life and having stampeded the buffalo had attained in her memory the rosy glow of legend. And David was young, strong, and dignified. More than ever now she felt that she and David shared more than merely their common heritage, something more than his having saved her, more than the buffalo: it was that they had both left the tribe to seek their destinies in the world.

It wasn't only Tom Quick's bad influence she worried about. Nothing seemed to incite white fury, frustration, and avarice more than the sight of an oil-rich Indian. The Dawes Commission had broken up tribal lands supposedly so that the Indian should become restless and acquisitive and predatory in the manner of whites. Alice had pointed out to her that Senator Dawes had said that the "red man's socialism" prevented his progress. Where land was held by the whole tribe, there was "no selfishness, which is at the bottom of civilization. Till this people will consent to give up their lands, and divide them among their citizens so that each can own the land he cultivates, they will not make much more progress."

The commission left both the civilized Creeks and the warrior Kiowas with parcels of land belonging to individuals who had no understanding of the legal underpinnings, and it wasn't long before much of that land had passed into white hands. Iola believed that had been the real purpose, but Alice thought that was a cynical interpretation. Where Iola saw a grand conspiracy, Alice saw only conflicts between good and evil. Men called grafters had rounded up full-blooded Creeks, carted them into town, put them up for a day or two, took them to the Indian office where they were to receive the deeds to their allotments, gave them a small payment, and the land changed hands.

When oil hit the Creek lands to the north, white swindlers abounded. Incomprehensible fortunes were handled by white judges, attorneys, guardians appointed by the courts, or white spouses, who held the same attitude about an Indian's money as they had held about his land: namely, that any Indian who did not use it the way they saw fit deserved to have it stolen.

It seemed to Iola that stories about reckless Indian extravagance were as widespread as stories about white culpability were scarce. That a full-blooded Creek would use his fancy, newly built house to keep his cattle in made far more colorful copy than that the man's white lawyer had earned $60,000 the preceding year by keeping him embroiled in pointless lawsuits.

The Dawes Commission had done an excellent job of restoring selfishness to the territory, a fact Iola pointed out when Alice endorsed the principle without looking at the result. Only the Osages had been wise or strong enough to retain the mineral rights to their lands as a tribe and not as individuals.

She and Alice had talked about these things, but not in regard to David. Iola had been unwilling to see David as another example of exploitable innocence, and Alice was unwilling to consider Quick a villain.

Now, though, the news that David had been spending his money on prostitutes was a sign of Quick's influence. Prostitution was a singularly white institution.

"It's about a half mile ahead, turn off to the right."

Iola nodded. Her pulse quickened with a confusing mixture of anger at Quick and excitement at seeing David. Seeing him now was not just desirable—it would be a chance to check on his condition. She took several long, slow breaths to calm herself as she let the horse pick its way along the packed-earth drive. Through the foliage, lights glimmered in the darkness and some saucy, insolent piano music sailed buoyantly through the air, insulting her ears.

In the lantern light, Alice's face was beaming as she peered ahead through the trees. Iola had been about to suggest that they not stay long, but the look on Alice's face stopped her. The woman was hopelessly gregarious, and Iola didn't have the heart to dampen Alice's pleasures— talking, singing, eating, drinking, dipping her snuff. Besides, having made herself David's guardian angel, Iola could not leave until he did.

The whine of a truck transmission woke Tom. His body was shrouded in foul sweat. It had rained at dawn, and now steam was rising from the murky water of the river. Out on the lawn, workmen were preparing for the party. His blood pounding, he rose, walked gingerly into his bathroom, and eased onto the closed commode.

Where was what's-his-name?

He scanned the gilt plumbing, the sunken bath of pink Italian marble, and the wall behind it. There was supposed to be a button.

The missing button might have been an oversight of the contractor, but he doubted it. He should have bird-dogged the builders, but he hadn't. To curious cronies at the Hotel Tulsa who asked how much the place had cost, he would say, "I don't know," then chuckle. Not knowing made him just a little richer than rich men who did.

Once the horde of contractors and subcontractors saw him shrug diffidently and fail to check their arithmetic, they stole from him with great zest and awe at their luck. His accountants were too busy bending figures to their own advantage to catch the contractors' cheating. To Tom, being stolen from was a mark of greatness; parasites were part of nature.

Having money meant nothing. Spending it, the flow of monetary energy, that was the point. The things he bought never failed to disappoint him because his thrill was in the buying. There was, for instance, the Kentucky blue grass which the English landscape designer had insisted on in the formal gardens. The grass had arrived in rolls like carpet and had cost $10,000. Tom would have preferred to see those five acres in rigs or wheat or a stockyard, but the gardens were more impressive, if less enjoyable or practical. He liked paying exorbitant sums for things for which he had no use or appreciation.

He wouldn't have spent five minutes in the mansion were it not for the legion of help hired to look after needs he'd never known he had. He was accustomed to bossing his roughnecks, but the servants here had mysterious tasks, and he had no idea how to measure the quality of their labor.

Steeling himself, Tom slid down into the cold, dry marble of the tub. As it filled, the hot water set him afloat, and he dragged a monogrammed towel off the rack, doused it, then laid it over his face.

He felt better.

He felt well enough to worry.

He worried that the invitation to his party hadn't reached Iola.

Next, he worried she wouldn't come even if it had.

Then he worried that she wouldn't fit in. He had hired somebody's well-known maiden aunt to play social secretary. She had suggested he invite the region's established rich folks, then Tom had added his friends to the list. She turned peevish when he explained some people wouldn't are-ess-vee-pee because they wouldn't understand what that meant. Some would have to have the invitation read to them. He had asked three times if Iola had responded, and each time had heard "no." He couldn't ask again without showing a prissy old maid accustomed to Tulsa high society that his most prized guest was a Kiowa nurse.

Iola had such fire, such spine! Her fury dazzled him; he was frightened of her, but also drawn to her. He wanted to know why she was so set against him, feeling the perverse curiosity of one warned against touching something hot.

He sighed, burbling water lapping at his lips. He owed it to himself to propose, even if that meant humiliation. At least he would have tried.

He decided he'd do it in the library, preferably after dark, when the party was roaring elsewhere. The library might make him seem more serious and dignified.

How about his ancestry? A redskin in the woodpile? Miss Iola, I never mentioned this, but you know I am part Cherokee on my mother's side—her grandmother was the daughter of a chief in Georgia.

Horse hockey! Chief cracker, that's what! His people were Ozark ridgerunners, so inbred and ignorant and tucked away in their suspicious hollows that they actually believed the Civil War was still going on. To his knowledge he had been the only one of the clan to top a ridge and keep on going.

In a way, he and Iola were alike, both restless, uprooting themselves in search of something better.

"You're up, then?"

Tom yanked the towel from his face. The valet was still in his suspenders, coatless, his white shirt not yet buttoned at the cuffs and open at the collar. Tom could have sworn the man was fighting to hold back a snicker.

"You're not, I see."

"Well, I worried you were in need of something, sir," the valet returned smoothly. His obsequiousness reeked of mockery.

"I want a T-bone steak medium rare and a couple eggs over easy, a glass of tomato juice and a pot of coffee." He closed his eyes to conjure the food. "And toast, three or four pieces."

"Which, sir?" The valet was smiling slightly.

"Damnation, man! If there's three, I'll eat three, four, I'll have four!" The smile again.

"And what time should I tell the cook you'll come down, sir?"

"Bring it up here."

The valet nodded. "In bed, sir, or at the dressing table—or perhaps by the windows in the club chair?"

"Look!" Tom jabbed his dripping forefinger against the floor tiles near his head. "Here, I want it here."

The man's disdain flashed briefly across his features before he could mask them.

"And I want a handful of cigars and don't ask me exactly how many, and I want some matches to light them with, and I want a bottle of the best bourbon in my bar and don't ask me what brand. And I want a glass to drink it out of, and I want you to bring it all toot sweet, and when you've done with that, you can go scare up the morning paper. Then you can pack up because I'm not going to employ some silly sonofabitch who's got no more sense than to show up in his galluses and look down his nose at me."

The man was shocked, but quickly recovered, then about-faced to exit the room. Tom closed his eyes and eased the towel back over his face. Was there a school for how to be rich? It was a safe bet that J. P. Morgan or the Rockefellers or Carnegie never gave a second's thought to their valets. He wouldn't see this one again, that was sure. He needed help with his help. This mansion needed a woman to keep these people out of his hair and make things run smoothly.

Iola wasn't cut out to play a rich oilman's wife. If she *should* accept his proposal, he'd have to hire still another employee to supervise the household staff. He pictured Iola being snubbed by other oilmen's wives, the kind who knew how to supervise a household of wealth. If that were the case, then he'd become the champion of racial justice, delivering harangues about discrimination to snobs who weren't good enough Americans themselves to believe in democracy, the real democracy of a man or a woman living by their wits and getting ahead no matter what race they were! The Tom Quicks would be known for their eccentricity, for keeping true to themselves even though they were rich. . . .

Laura, on the other hand, could run the household with her little finger. The night he brought her here for dinner she had a broccoli dish returned to the kitchen then gently admonished first the serving girl then Tom for being lax in letting his cook serve him cold food.

The picture of her lying under him on the wicker couch that night on the balcony flickered behind his closed eyelids for a few moments, easing his headache. Then he was snapped to attention by a weird, garbled sound in the bedroom. A thud and then clomps. Bewildered, he watched the doorway. In a moment, his valet appeared, on all fours, the morning paper crosswise in his mouth.

He crawled to the edge of the tub and opened his mouth to let the paper drop onto the tiles.

"I need the job." The valet craned his neck and, without getting up, wiped his mouth on his shirtsleeve. He grimaced with disgust. The newsprint left a gray smear across his cheek. "Your breakfast is on the way."

"What's your name again?" Tom asked when he had recovered his presence of mind.

"Bowser. Robert Bowser. Bob Bowser. Arf! Arf!"

Tom burst into laughter. The valet continued to deadpan, however, waiting expectantly as if for a command to "heel" or "play dead."

"Do my tricks amuse the master?"

Tom blushed furiously as he laughed. The man's groveling—or the ironic mockery of groveling—shamed Tom, but he couldn't back down without appearing weak. At that moment he knew being rich was going to be harder than he had thought. He had fired roughnecks out of pique then later apologized and rehired them. But no roughneck had dared laugh at or question his methods. His authority on a rig was certain, which gave him the luxury of admitting he was wrong. Here he had to hang tough or he'd be eaten alive.

"I've already fired you," he said when he had stopped laughing.

By midafternoon Tom decided that Iola and the missionary were not going to show up, so he broke his vow to stay sober. A string quartet was playing inside, and Laura was charming his high-toned guests, so he could say that things were going well, considering. But he was tired of presenting himself to people with whom he wouldn't have spent thirty seconds otherwise, wearing the pleated shirt front of his tuxedo like a signboard advertising his attempt to upgrade his social status.

He walked down to the river, exchanging nods and murmurs, and sat on the bank sourly considering how out of place he felt at his own do. When he looked back up the slope, his "social secretary" was running like a great, crippled turkey in her high-button boots and ankle-length dress down the curving flagstones.

He had a deep desire to shed his clothes and dive into the river. He waited with increasing discomfort by a willow as she bellowed his name.

"Mr. Quick! Oh, Mr. Quick!" She halted before him and laid a palm on her large damp bosom.

"Easy now," said Tom.

"At the front door," she gasped. It's . . . three . . . Indians, Mr. Quick! Only one is on the list. And they appear to be very intoxicated!"

Tom grinned. "Are they in a yellow Pierce-Arrow?"

She managed to nod. "Their automobile is in the front *yard*, Mr. Quick! They've ruined the new sodding!"

Tom laughed. "Let them in and show them the bar. And anybody else who comes!"

"Then you hardly need me!" she sniffed.

Watching her bootheels wobble in retreat, Tom thought, Good riddance! But he felt, as well, that his sudden desire to be an expansive host had been the impetuous act of a man who seeks to ruin his possibilities before they have proved to be out of reach. Once word got out about a free shindig, the riffraff who'd show up would make him look like a saint by contrast.

Two of the three Indians at the front door turned out to be, as he suspected, Robert Big Heart and George Tall Chief, prominent and well-respected Osages. They smelled of whiskey but they weren't drunk.

The third was David Copperfield. Tom slapped them on the back and guided them to the bar. He wanted Copperfield near him to show Iola, should she come, that he was being a good host to her fellow Kiowa. After they had a few drinks, George wanted to take them riding in his new convertible. An inexperienced driver and six sheets to the wind besides, Robert drove the car through a newly planted hedge, then it rolled down the back lawn, guests scattering like quail before it, and vaulted off the bank into the river, he and his passengers howling with laughter.

Drenched, they climbed onto the bank. One look at Copperfield made Tom's heart sink. His lips were floppy, and he had mud on his bare arms. To take them offstage, as it were, and to quiet them, Tom suggested they all go into the parlor, but no sooner had they settled there than Copperfield went out to his horse and brought back a bottle of very good cognac and a box of Cuban cigars. In the meantime, more of Tom's friends had arrived, whooping down by the river. Their voices almost drowned out the piano from the "music room," where Laura had been entertaining his fancy guests.

They drank the cognac and smoked the cigars. Woozily, Tom studied the quavering lines in his parquet floor; the tiles seemed out of plumb, but he couldn't say if it was because he had been cheated by his contractor or because he had been drinking too much. His anxiety over being caught drunk by Iola made him want to drink more to calm himself. All he could hope now was to be conscious if she arrived so he could say his piece and take his lumps.

As the men sat cross-legged, talking and passing the bottle, their buttocks and heels left great damp spots on the oriental carpet. Copperfield's head was cocked in a funny way, with his ear bent toward the ceiling, while Robert and George were arguing about rich people.

"Me, I like rich people," Robert was saying.

"That's because you are one," explained George.

"What good is it?" interjected Tom.

Tom's question went unanswered.

"I want to be rich like the Creeks and like this Kiowa of yours," George said, nodding toward David, who appeared transfixed. "They're like the whites. Osages just get it dribbled out to the whole tribe, and I'd like to have mine all at once. Maybe I'd get me a fancy woman."

"You could have one if you'd quit buying automobiles," said Robert.

"I don't want a woman I can buy," said Tom.

"You'd just go out and spend it all or somebody would rob you," Robert said to George. "The tribe kept all the rights and the money gets divided for everybody's good. We won't lose our land."

"Who is singing the music?" David asked without looking at anyone.

"A fancy woman would just come along and grab your pecker with one hand and your wallet with the other," continued Robert, and they laughed.

"The problem is," said Tom, "if you're rich, how do you know if the woman is taking you or your money?"

"If she won't marry you, you know she's not liking either," said George.

Over George's shoulder, Tom was astonished to see a cow standing on the terrace. The cow was white with large black splotches on its flanks, and when it slowly craned its head to peer through the French doors, Tom saw a white froth around its lips. Hair rose on his nape. He blinked once, then the cow turned back to languidly eating a cake from a nearby table. He thought he should shoo the animal away, but it seemed too much trouble.

Robert and George started talking about the war, and Tom joined in. Copperfield kept mooning in a trance. After a burst of applause from the "music room," the door opened and several of the better guests strolled into the parlor, Laura leading them. She beamed munificently, laying fingertips across men's forearms and offering earnest expressions of appreciation for their being such a kind audience. With her billowy yellow dress and her hair done up in yellow ribbons, Laura looked girlish and springlike.

Tom rose as Laura approached with an elderly couple in tow. She introduced them as Mr. and Mrs. He Didn't Even Bother to Listen, and he made a feeble apology about being wet—"had a little accident down at the river," then watched Laura shoo them along with a gentle push.

He beckoned her back. "I want you to meet some of the finest sonsa-bitches in twenty-six counties," he said.

She gave him the condescending smile of amusement one gives benign drunks. He said, "I'm not kidding. Salts of the earth. This here's Robert Tall Chief and George Big Heart—they're Osages and friends of mine. Laura Darby." Robert and George got to their feet, slowly and not too steadily, but managed to murmur "Pleased to meet you." Tom turned to David, but Copperfield was already standing, towering over Laura.

"This here's my partner, the man whose land I hit the discovery well on, David Copperfield."

To indulge Tom, Laura did a little quick mock curtsy and said, "Any friend of Tom's . . ."

"You were singing?" Copperfield asked. He swayed a little too far forward. Laura took a half-step backward.

"You liked it?"

"Very much." He blushed. "Will you sing again?"

Laura passed Tom a glance of amusement, inviting him to share the difficulty of being far too well-bred to be rude to her inferiors.

"I appreciate the compliment, Mr. Copperfield. You're obviously a man of discriminating judgment. Perhaps I will do something more later."

She dipped her head to acknowledge Robert, George, and Copperfield, then gave Tom a wink before following the last of her audience out of the parlor.

Robert and George said they wanted to join a poker game upstairs, and Copperfield walked away while they were talking. The cognac was gone, so Tom headed for the bar outside.

His help were lighting lanterns hanging in the trees. Despair and twilight came on hand in hand, each a metaphor for the other, and he knew the ragged end of this gathering wouldn't be very impressive. Evidence that he had not hallucinated the cow was humped on the tiles near his feet. Earlier the grounds had had a festive air, gay but sedate, the acreage strewn with women cocking parasols over beribboned heads and men in vests and hats and spats. The ladies and gentlemen had been served rare beef, smoked ham and caviar, cheeses, and olives stuffed with anchovies. Black waiters in white coats had glided about in patent leather shoes bearing silver trays of wine goblets. Tom had stood here hours earlier with a cheroot between his teeth, thinking, Let her come now.

The pop of pistol shots made him flinch. A tinkle of glass, shouts and laughter—the sound of assorted yahoos having target practice at bottles tossed into the river where George's Pierce-Arrow was partly submerged. He had to hand it to his friends, they knew how to have a good time. He guessed the so-called society folk had given over the outdoors to cowhands and roughnecks now.

Behind one white-draped table two black bartenders stood immobile, faces bland with servile expectation, as if the party were still defined by their dignity. Their silence and their meticulous blindness made them a living reproach.

Tom stepped off the terrace, half tripped on a flagstone, and lurched to the bartender's table.

"I'd like a bourbon and branch, please." He spoke very distinctly, as if trying out a foreign phrase.

"Comin' up, suh." The cheerful, courteous response made Tom feel his money had been well spent. When the waiter handed him the chilled glass with a napkin, Tom beheld it in appreciation.

"Where's the host?" he asked the bartender.

Under the impression that he had just served the host, the man looked confused but swiftly slid his puzzlement under his professional face.

"Doan know, suh."

"Somebody told me he was drunk on his ass up in the house, you hear that? Maybe he's up there mooning about some woman, what do you think?" He winked, sharing his joke about the host.

The barkeep quickly glanced at his coworker, who blinked significantly. Fear of harassment was palpable on both men's features.

"Beats me, suh." The keep beamed at him professionally. "Your drink awright, capt'n?"

"Fine," Tom said, sullen. He had yet to taste it. He was frustrated; it was just such men he needed to pass judgment on the "host." He surveyed the sloping lawn. The cow's white face glowed dimly at the edge of the woods.

"Don't you think a joker who'd piss away good money for a bunch of yahoos like this is a powerfully *stupid* sonofabitch?" He waved his drink, and the liquid sloshed onto his wrist.

"Everybody got to have a good time, capt'n." The barkeep's hands were suddenly busy crows pecking ice into glasses from a bucket.

"Amen!" Tom tipped his glass to salute their diplomacy.

When he turned, he spotted Iola standing on the terrace with the

missionary. My raven-haired beauty, he thought, and instantly panicked. Her dark blue cape gave her the aura of an ominous oracle.

She and the missionary were waiting for something. The host, no
doubt. He wanted to scurry to intercept them before they saw what
damage bad companions and strong drink had done to the grounds. The
cow had tromped through the shrubbery and now stood with a hoof
poised over the edge of the terrace.

Tom's courage fell like a hangman's trapdoor.

"Mr. Quick!"

The missionary hailed him merrily, waving. An impulse came to toss
back the drink for final fortification, but he set the glass on the table,
ruefully noting that his Spartan self-denial came hours late. He quickly
wiggled his bow tie, shot the cuffs of his tuxedo coat, then made his
way up the slope with a growing despondency, feeling their scrutiny.
That goddamn cow!

"Well! Well! My guests of honor!" he crowed when he reached them.
"I'm so glad to see you, Miss Iola—" He skimmed his gaze across her
forehead, afraid to meet her eyes. "And Miss Alice. I'm sorry you
couldn't have made it earlier in the day. I'm afraid my guest list got all
swole up with a bunch of rowdies who'd be better off in a saloon, but
I'm happy to see you, anyway."

He ignored the clomp of hooves behind him. He babbled nonstop,
watching the missionary's face. Such monstrous drivel! He heard himself foolishly jabber about how rich Copperfield was, hearing his own
voice with a third ear, knowing that he was sinking hopelessly into the
mire in the mind of the woman he couldn't bring himself to look at. A
perverse impulse pushed him into acting like whatever brand of idiot
she hated most. He chattered about the trials of having servants, detest-
ing himself, and while his tongue wagged on about his British landsca-
per, he chanced a glance at Iola. What he saw surprised him; she was
looking down the slope, seemingly deaf, arms crossed over her breasts.

"I owe all my good fortune to having met your friend, Miss Iola," he
said to snag her back. "And he seems pleased to have a piece of it, too."

Iola turned; her black eyes had the cold regard of a hawk. "We've seen
him."

Alice said, without smiling, "He appears to be . . . less than sober."

Another volley of gunfire split the air, and Tom cringed. It was too
dark down on the riverbank for any more target practice, unless, of
course, they were shooting at the lighted windows of the house.

"Happens to the best of us." He laughed with embarrassment.

"And the worst too," said Iola.

The teacher had cocked her purse up to her chest as if she might carry it away somewhere. Tom wanted to be alone with Iola, despite feeling panicked about facing her hostility.

"Miss Roberts, I wonder if you wouldn't mind checking on Mr. Copperfield for me," Tom said, struggling for sobriety. "As his host, I feel a little responsible for his condition. Maybe a woman's hand . . ."

"Certainly," she responded. She moved to go, and Iola turned as if to accompany her, but Tom reached out and detained her by gently tugging at her cape. "Could I have a word with you?" he asked quietly.

She looked slightly annoyed and expectant, figuratively poised on the balls of her feet for flight after his "one" word.

"Could I get you some punch or something to eat?"

"No. Thank you."

It was neither the right place nor time, but he might as well take his whipping and finish getting "not sober." He sighed. He was about to speak when he felt the cow nose his back. He spun and shouted at it; its large brown eyes looked hurt, then it noisily thundered off the terrace and crashed though his imported shrubbery.

"One thing wrong with me is I don't have anybody around me to teach me how to act," he spoke in a rush when he turned back to Iola. "If I had a wife who could set me straight on things now and then, well, maybe I wouldn't be such a horse's hiney, if you'll pardon my lingo."

Her response was to turn as if to follow the teacher into the house, but Tom took her by the elbow to stop her.

"I don't for the life of me know why I let myself in for this, but I'm not going to let you get away before I speak my piece. You've taken a powerful dislike to me, and I swear I can't understand why or from when or for what, and I guess until you spell it out, I'll be an ignorant jackass."

Iola removed her elbow from his grasp.

"It's not personal, Mr. Quick."

"Call me Tom," he said, chuckling sorrowfully at his own bad joke.

"It's how you live and who you are and what you care for and what you don't—you understand? It's for what you're doing to David. He was content to take people across the river, he was content to be useful and worthy and what he had was noble, even though he was poor and simple, and you've poisoned his life."

"I didn't do anything but buy a lease from him and pay him every red cent he had coming to him—I've treated him fair and square!"

"I didn't say you cheated him. I believe you mean well, but our history is full of bad things that have come from well-meaning white men."

He must have looked pained; the way her brows knitted could have passed for concern.

"I appreciate how you've acted toward me. I'm not used to being respected by white men. But you can't help being what you are—you turn land and people into money."

She began walking away, and he felt helpless to stop her.

"If I give all my money away, will you marry me?" he called after her, but she had passed through the French doors and into the parlor. He didn't know if she had heard him.

Wanting to be alone, he went to the library, woozily waded through the dimness, and sank into a club chair. After a moment of sitting in the dark, he could see light from the lanterns on the lawn below spread softly across the spines of the volumes of books that had been ordered by the yard.

A ruckus rose in the hallway, but he ignored it. As far as he was concerned, they could rip the place up brick by brick. His friends. Face it. You're new-money crass.

He replayed Iola's words in his ear, her objections to him—why was she so upset about what he had "done" to Copperfield? She certainly was one to worry about him!

Then he knew—she was sweet on him! Copperfield was his competition! How could he not have seen it? The thing she most had against Tom Quick was that he wasn't David Copperfield!

His eyes felt swollen, and he began to whimper like a boy, a drunk's weeping. Almost abstractly, he listened to his sniffling, irritated and comforted by it at once. He would have exploded into sobs had someone not knocked at the door.

"Come in," he said, after blowing his nose.

Light flooding from the hallway silhouetted a large form.

"Mr. Quick?"

"Yes, over here."

He rose from the chair. It was the teacher.

"Hello," he said. "Hope you don't mind the darkness. I was just, well, thinking, I guess."

She moved closer until he could smell her lilac. Light from the torches outside made one side of her face glow. She smiled, and turned her head toward the windows.

"I would have guessed you'd be gone."

"Oh, we're leaving now, and I just wanted to thank you for inviting us."

He snuffled involuntarily, and the woman suddenly squinted into the darkness at him.

"Mr. Quick, are you all right?"

"Sure," he said automatically, then felt too weak to lie. "I mean no. Maybe. I don't know, I honestly don't know."

For a moment, he didn't know whether he should say more, but the woman's arms carved a maternal hollow in the air before her, and he fell into them without thinking what he was doing. He embraced her, bent over, and his cheek fell against her breasts. She was warm, like a radiator; he inhaled the lilac and the aroma of sweet sweat and something like fresh bread, and his sobs threatened to rise again.

She stroked his head. "There, there," she said. "You can tell me about it."

Tom burrowed his cheek farther into the woman's cleavage, hugging her, weeping quietly while still a sober part of him wondered what in the world he was doing.

Alice maneuvered herself backward into the club chair, and Tom sank to the floor on his knees. She rocked his head and crooned, "It's all right, it's all right." He lifted his palm to his eyes to wipe his tears, then it naturally came to rest on her left breast. After a few moments, he felt strangely calm and rested.

She had on a high, lace-topped blouse, but her sweat and the thin material made her flesh almost tangible to his lips as he ferreted his nose deep into her cleavage and inhaled her. His hand began circling her left breast slowly, kneading it, weighing it, his palm sliding back and forth.

It didn't occur to him what he was doing until he realized that the missionary had stopped crooning and now sat frozen in puzzlement or indecision.

"Mr. Quick, I believe you must be feeling better now." She didn't sound angry, but she had stiffened and was gently tugging his cheek away from her breasts—it seemed incredible to him, but he could very easily have immersed himself in this woman's very succulent flesh without thinking twice.

"I'm sorry," he said sincerely, but couldn't resist gilding the lily. "I'm just a sinner."

"So are we all, so are we all."

They stood, facing each other.

"Thank you for coming."

The teacher's response was to lean forward and kiss him full on the mouth. Her lips were cushiony and pliable; she kissed him with amateurish eagerness, her tongue and breath sucking at his lips as if tasting a sugared confection.

But then she broke away. "I just didn't want you to think I was being hypothetical."

He walked her to the front door, where Iola was waiting in the buggy. Iola didn't look at him as he waved good-bye, but Alice pursed her lips and her eyes twinkled merrily as she let her fingers waggle in the air. Too coy, too coy. The way she suddenly laid claim on him struck his heart with fear.

Sobered, he went back to the parlor. Laura was at the grand piano, and several people were gathered about her, singing.

Copperfield was standing with the empty cognac bottle in his left hand at the rear of the group, his face visible above the others. Tom watched Laura sing and pump the group the way you watched a spectator sport. Copperfield looked slack-jawed with adoration, and Tom wished Iola were present to witness it.

Tom moved beside Copperfield.

"Sure sings nice, don't she?"

Copperfield nodded.

"It don't exactly make a man sick to look at her, either, does it?"

And then, without really knowing why or without thinking much about it (because if he had thought much about it, he would have known why), he said, "She told me she sure admired my taste in partners. Just about made me jealous, you know, because"—he eyed Copperfield closely to see if the man was following him—"because it was a compliment to you, you see."

Copperfield looked as if he wanted to hear more, but Tom thought he had done enough damage.

He almost ordered another bourbon and water from a barkeep but changed it to plain water. He went down to the riverbank. The rowdies were gone; occasional gunshots made muffled pops in the woods, and he guessed the target shooters had gone coon hunting. He sat on the grass and watched the river lap about the flank of the Pierce-Arrow. He had just settled comfortably into a cocoon of self-pity when his reverie was interrupted.

"I set the staff to cleaning up a bit, Tom."

Behind Laura, up the slope, waiters were folding the tablecloths and taking down the tables.

"Thanks. Sit down."

She eased down beside him and tucked her knees under her chin.

"You missed my concert."

This was no reproach, but rather a cozy suggestion that they had had separate duties and that his had unfortunately kept him from the music room.

He grinned at her. "Maybe you can repeat it in private."

If she caught the allusion to their night on the upper balcony, she didn't let on. He felt vulgar. This had been a day when his lack of breeding had burst out all over him like boils. To blur the boorish joke, he said, "I really appreciate the help you've been in taking all the nice folks aside and showing them some class. I'm afraid that my own friends pretty well ruined the tone of this here august occasion," he said dryly.

Laura laughed. "Oh, I did keep most of the more tender souls locked up with me. I think most went home happy. But doing this was my pleasure."

A slight breeze out of the west brought her perfume to his nose, and he recalled with a sudden rush lying between her legs. A very pleasant oblivion from the day's disasters might be had by reassuming that position.

"I'm in your debt."

"Oh, Tom, it brought back nice memories."

"It should have been your party," he said morosely. "You enjoyed it more than I did." He winced; he had made too open an allusion to his unhappiness, and the last person he wanted to know about Iola was Laura. "I mean, you seem to be at home with this sort of thing. Me, I'm more comfortable shooting the bull with a lot of greasy roughnecks out at the rig."

"Sounds like a good team, Tom."

The significance of her display of hostess skills seeped into him. She lay back on the grass with her knees hiked into the air. Her dress hem came to her shins, but he could imagine the backs of her thighs. He lay propped on his elbow beside her, then leaned over and kissed her. She touched the tip of his tongue with hers, but sat up abruptly when his hand glided across her breast.

"Tom Quick, you're a hell of a man. I'm glad to know you, but I'm not so round-heeled that you can compromise me like this. I might have committed a single indiscretion with you, but you caught me when I was feeling low and vulnerable. I was upset about something."

She didn't seem angry, that was good—he couldn't have taken the wrath of another female tonight. But she was firm, tucking her knees under her chin and wrapping her arms around her shins, impenetrable as a rolled-up armadillo.

"Well, I don't mean any disrespect, Laura. I like you, and I'm in your debt. Being close to you, well, I get carried away. I'm sorry."

After a pause, she said, "I just got a proposal of marriage." Her snicker seemed designed to make him think it wasn't to be treated seriously. Or was it?

She kept silent; she'd make him ask.

"Who from?"

"That big fellow, the Indian."

Tom groaned. "Copperfield?"

"Yes," she said, laughing. "He was listening to me with such attention that when I was singing a German love song, I flirted with him, I thought everybody would be amused—I mean, all I did was chuck his cheek! But later in the hallway he quite literally staggered out of the shadows and stuck a bunch of flowers in my nose. Gave me quite a fright!"

"What'd you say?"

"Why, naturally, I said I was flattered, Tom. I had no reason to be rude. He's your partner."

A faint reproach was released by her inflection, but Tom couldn't quite locate the destination of the arrow.

"But you turned him down."

"Of course."

Tom joined her laughter, but it made him uneasy. He knew too well the misery of rejection and felt a twinge of guilt.

Slowly, he understood. Laura's conversation was all of a piece: I'd be good for you, good for this house. Other men desire me; you've had an introductory sample but you won't touch me again until you slide a ring on my finger.

He could count at least a dozen reasons why Laura would be a good wife. But he felt only repulsion and anger toward her, as if she were to blame for Iola's turning him down. Laura was a mirror of himself, a sign of what he was: their very compatibility damned her. She would be furious to know that as a bridal prospect she was inferior to a squaw. He thought it only fair to warn her that he would not in a million years ask her to be his wife.

"I'll tell you something, Laura," he said, leaning close and laying his hand on her shoulder the way you comfort someone stricken. Friend to friend, he meant. "It might not be a bad idea to take him up on it."

A short laugh like a bark popped from her mouth, then she read his earnest, begrieved expression. Even in the dimness, he could see her face glow with fury. She scrambled to her feet and stood over him to shake out her dress over his head; grass chaff flew in his face, and she gave him a glimpse of white thighs he might never stroke again.

Neither David nor his fellow white bachelors believed that love was necessary for marriage. Men took mail-order brides; a widower needed a woman to replace the one who left him with six children, or a young roughneck tired of living alone yearned for a woman to nest with and was happy to take anyone in a dress who could cook and bear children. Many knew they were not prize catches themselves; they were poor, ugly, and ignorant and likely to spend their youth wrestling with greasy machinery until they were too maimed to work. Among David's people, a man and his wife were sometimes in love, but it was as likely that the marriage had been an agreement between a youth with horses and the girl's father, who would heed her wishes in proportion to his lack of greed.

At Quick's party, Laura's voice and beauty were simply more unexpected pleasures for David in a day of cheerful camaraderie. Hers was no high, flitting bird's voice—it was rich, throaty, and above all, strong. Very womanly. Sitting in the parlor with Quick and the Osages, he had tried to imagine a woman from the voice; she had broad shoulders and heavy hips, good lungs, full breasts. He was all the more intrigued when Laura herself emerged, so light and willowy in her yellow dress that she could have given the appearance of flight merely by standing on tiptoe.

Her liveliness pulled him along, and he followed her about, watching her move among Quick's guests, studying the way she turned her head. Later she had gathered Quick's guests around the piano and sang a love song. He stood close to her, made brave by the cognac and by Quick's saying she admired him. And he heard his money say, *Remember how you had no need of the pistol or the horse but now you could not do without them? I can bring you what you want.* And he had thought, Iola is such a big person with the whites, she thinks, but here, look now, Iola.

At that instant Laura stretched upward from the bench while playing, released her right hand from the keyboard and sent her fingertip grazing along his cheek, her face coming closer to his, smiling merrily. The slope of her breasts showed as she bent, her full red lips parted and that strong voice came from the pink hollow of her mouth, singing words he didn't comprehend, though she had said they were words of love.

He knew then he wanted her. He went outside and sat on the terrace drinking and dreaming about her as a wife. Her strength—a man could move on her without fear of breaking something. Yet she was beautiful.

He pulled flowers from a vase and weaved up the broad staircase to the second floor, following after her then waiting for her to emerge from a bathroom. She smiled when he thrust the bouquet into her face.

He said, "I need a wife. I want you to be her."

A laugh popped from her mouth. "I'm sorry, I'm already spoken for, but the flowers are lovely, they truly are," she said. She took them from him and linked her arm in his as they went down the staircase, somehow giving him the impression she had said yes when she had actually said no.

The next morning he was tormented with the embarrassment of having proposed to this stranger, the beautiful white woman with the full strong voice and slender body. The sting of rejection was not as acute as the knowledge he had been a fool. Sober, he would not have proposed to her, and he vowed he would not touch liquor again.

He assumed his infatuation had been inspired by drinking, but after two days he could not shake off images of her that, while vague, aroused a lust and longing that were sharp and clear.

For a week, Laura's face appeared at the bottom of the tin dipper when he drank. Her hair was caught in the dried strands of feathery bluestem along the riverbank; curves of bright white cumulus took on a sensual aspect, looking like entwined limbs. His memory of her honed his solitude to a point that pierced his breast.

He decided he was touched in the head, so he made a trip into Wetoka to find Laura, hoping the disparity between his absurd longings and the reality of her would put that night, and his heart, to rest. He attended two shows in a row in the tent. Seeing her from a distance onstage was not as disturbing as having her lean forward and bathe his face with her breath and stroke his cheek with her fingertip, and he went home feeling as if the demon had been exorcised.

But that night in a dream she wore her yellow dress and they were standing face to face in murky water up to their necks; she put her hands on his cheeks and cooed, he put his hands on her breasts under the water, woke up rock hard. He went to see her again that night, only this time he realized that he was returning not so that Laura's earthly reality would chase away the teasing ghosts but in the hope that in his absence, she would magically have assumed the identity of the phantoms. He enjoyed desiring her; it made him feel alive. He wasn't looking for a cure this time.

From a café across the street, he sometimes watched her enter and leave the hotel. Frequently she was with men—twice it was the banker who had given him the cognac and cigars—sometimes she was alone. Now he wished he hadn't squandered his opportunity to propose; he would have liked to try again, perhaps after courting her. She had said, "I'm already spoken for," but he saw no evidence of it. Watching from a distance he recalled the proposal and thought with wonder that that was as close as he would ever come to possessing her. Soon, he was convinced that nothing would happen to bring them together, and he went home determined to forget his folly.

A confidant might have prescribed pitching himself headlong into a sea of women as an antidote to lovesickness. But David had no confidant, had no clear definition of what was happening to him, and so he sought to ride out his melancholy as if it were a fever too persistent to allow him to feel well but too low to send him to bed.

Ten days after Quick's party, spring had come full-blown, and David was plowing a new plot of earth, walking behind a new mule and a single-harrow plow. As the harrow heaved the chunks of topsoil aside, the aroma of the rich damp earth rose to his nostrils and made his blood surge. The sun lay on his back and the crisp air was blue despite the fumes from the derricks on the horizon. The pasture behind the cabin showed lime-green patches of grass and splotches of bluebonnet and fire wheels. He grinned, feeling ebullient, regenerated, smelling this earth, feeling the wooden handles in his grip. All I need, he thought ironically, is a Bible in hand and I would have fulfilled the missionaries' plans for me.

A buggy came up the rocky road and stopped in front of the cabin; David halted the mule, dumbfounded, with the reins in hand. He recognized her immediately, though he had never seen the driver. She waved from the seat. He waved back slowly. She was like a hallucination, his memory made manifest. He stood like a stone while she climbed down and picked her way across the furrows, teetering her arms for balance as she encountered clods in the churned-up earth.

"Mr. Copperfield!"

He opened his mouth, but his throat closed around his words. Lifting the hem of her dark red skirt, she stepped gingerly over the last furrow separating them then stood just beyond arm's reach, adjusting a dark red hat that had fresh flowers stuck in its band. Under a jacket that matched the skirt she wore a white ruffled blouse. Her cheeks were flushed.

"My oh my!" She looked about the expanse of plowed earth. "What a lot of work! What are you going to plant?"

"Vegetables." His answer seemed moronic—he couldn't very well plant deer meat, could he?

"Mercy! I'd think a man of your means could buy them or at least hire someone to do this!"

"I like the smell."

Something peculiar passed through her face before she readjusted her smile. Transfixed, he watched her hands bob, flit, alight briefly on the plow handle as if to steady herself, then fly away to her hat, where they rested momentarily on the brim, adjusting it, then buzzed across her cheeks, a finger on an earlobe, and finally roosted on opposite forearms, clinging. She looked quickly to her feet and stamped away an ant crawling across the toe of her shoe. It was the first time he had seen her close in daylight, and her skin looked dry and slightly crenelated at the corners of her eyes and mouth. She was older than he had thought. This sudden insight didn't make her less attractive, exactly, but it did reinforce his sense that he had been chasing an illusion and not a real woman.

"Mr. Copperfield . . ." She sighed, paused. He waited, wondering what had brought her here. Her eyes went everywhere except to his face, and he thought she was very courteous, modest.

"I'd like to apologize for my behavior. I'm afraid I insulted your kind proposal by appearing to treat it lightly."

His heart quickened; he grasped the reins, and the tactile presence of the leather was a vague comfort.

"Yes. Good." He meant not to approve of her apology but to say he was glad of it. "You were kind—I know what whites think of Kiowas who talk marriage to their women."

She seemed to be studying the mule's flank, where buzzing green bottle flies circled to evade the swishing tail. Watching her, David realized suddenly that she surely wouldn't have come all this way to give him a better reason for having turned him down.

"I said that I was spoken for, but the truth is that you simply caught me off guard. I've had more time to think now, and I hope you'll allow me to reconsider your offer."

He was too startled to speak. He stared at her; she was squinting against the sunlight as she looked into his face and gave him a twisted, wry little smile to acknowledge his surprise. He should have been overjoyed, he thought, but he wasn't—he was only nervous, uncertain. He had already spent too much time thinking he could never have her to allow himself to backtrack. When his mind stopped spinning, he was left with the essential mystery of her reversal—why would she do this?

As if his unspoken question formed a vessel between them that needed filling, she stepped closer, gazing earnestly into his face.

"I realize this is very sudden and that we really don't know one another. We hardly speak the same language, and I won't pretend that you and I have been swept up by mutual passion—we're no Romeo and Juliet." She watched his face. "We're not in love, that's what I mean to say. But you do appear to be a man I could come to respect, and I've decided that Copperfield is as good a name as any to tack to the end of my own." She paused a moment, then added, "I think we can be useful to one another. We can be partners."

Partners. Tom Quick had used the word that night in the shed. Ignorant of the implications, David had said yes and had come to regret it. Yet, despite their differences, a union between him and the woman had a certain logic—he needed a personal, canny ambassador to the white world, a teacher of things white. Looking at her, he imagined that his "yes" would bring specific pleasures he had already daydreamed about: listening to her sing at his whim, undressing her, stroking her flesh, watching her limbs move through the air, being absorbed by the exotic character of her otherness.

"I'd be proud," he said slowly.

"Good. Then that's settled," she said with a faint suggestion of impatience. "Shall we go?" She raised her elbow out from her body as if to allow him to take it, startling him.

"Now?"

She smiled. "And why not?"

It was his old habit of caution, resisting change. Yet wasn't this what he had had in mind when he proposed?

"Well," she sang out gaily. "Don't make me think you're a reluctant bridegroom. I do have my pride!"

Moving away, looking over her shoulder and smiling, she raised her elbow and placed it in his path, so that all he had to do was raise his hand and her elbow swung down into it, as if from a clear sky an apple had fallen there when he was merely inspecting his palm.

They walked across the furrows with Laura leading but needing assistance from David, the upchurned furrows having strangely become less negotiable for her now that he was beside her. She kept reaching over with her free hand to clutch at his biceps when a clod underfoot made her teeter, and the grip of her fingers on his muscle thrilled him.

In front of the cabin, the buggy's driver sat chewing on a toothpick and whittling on a chunk of pine with a pocketknife. He wore a derby hat and a vested suit; a burn scar like a large translucent spider lay across his cheek. David was about to send him away when Laura climbed up into the buggy's seat.

"I was going to get my horse."

"I'm afraid I'm not dressed for horseback riding, Mr. Copperfield. I would suggest that if we're going to get married, then you might clean up a bit. Mr. Shingle here will drive us into town."

The man tipped his hat ironically, using Laura's mention of him as an introduction.

"We will be needing someone to witness your X," Laura said.

"I know how to sign a white man's paper."

A trunk stood in the back of the buggy. Laura had come prepared; David was a little dazed by how moments kept opening into a maze to which she seemed to have a map.

"And not with an X," he added.

Laura's brows rose and fell. "We'll still need a witness no matter how you sign."

They were married in Wetoka before a justice of the peace. Then Shingle drove them in an automobile to Muskogee, where they were married again, Laura explaining that since he was a very wealthy man, people might seek to cheat or swindle them and disqualify their marriage.

Then Shingle drove them north, with David and Laura in the rear seat. David stared in wonder at his new bride, who watched the road through her window. He felt buoyant to have captured this wife, though she was like a gift of which he had not quite come into possession. He traced her profile, the small straight nose, the pale skin, the tendrils of blond hair falling in front of her small rosy ears. He took deep drafts of the delicate scent of her clothing, beneath which lay a musky, more fundamental scent that excited him.

Smelling her, observing her, were not enough. Once he reached over to brush his fingers along her cheek, but she winced. Tonight, he thought.

They drove all day. He was curious about their destination, but now that he possessed this woman in the eyes of the white man's law, it didn't seem to matter. They drove through oil fields and through burgeoning hamlets in Cherokee country, moving in a parallel course to the Katy railroad, through Big Cabin, Vinita, and Kelso. Shingle kept absolutely quiet, driving ahead without stopping or receiving instructions from Laura. Shingle's single-mindedness made David curious; it suggested hurry, and hurry had never been a part of his life. Out of his window, he saw the Virdigris River swollen from spring rains. They were in Osage country.

"Where are we going?"

Laura turned toward him, smiling sweetly, patting his forearm with her fingers. "Why, Mr. Copperfield!" She made his name sound like the opening to a song. "You've never heard of a honeymoon trip?" He had, certainly. But he hadn't recognized this adventure as an example of this white man's ritual.

They reached Coffeyville, Kansas, before sundown. Shingle drove them directly to the home of another justice of the peace. This time David proudly anticipated each step of the ceremony.

Coming out of the justice of the peace's house, Laura expelled a breath so large she might have been holding it all day. She grew voluble about her exhaustion and chattered merrily about how far they had driven and how many times they had been married. David was pleased that she appeared so excited.

Shingle drove them to a hotel. David would not have chosen to stay in a white man's hotel where he knew he would not be welcome, but he discovered that being married to a white woman apparently waived prejudices. The clerk appeared to have been expecting them, and, again, he was conscious that what to him had been a helter-skelter tumble of unexpected events had not come to pass from any spontaneity or impetuousness on the part of his bride. Each step had been planned by the woman who was now his wife, and he marveled at her powers of organization.

But under his willingness to let himself be led, he harbored doubts about being so passive. It went against his nature to let another human (a woman, especially) have control over his life. He would have known how to treat a Kiowa wife—what to do, how to lead—but this strange and lovely white woman had become his native guide to a foreign country. He would have to watch for an opening to become a husband in deed as well as fact.

Shingle took an adjoining room; David and Laura's room had two beds, and Laura had him put her suitcase on the bed next to the wall of Shingle's room. David sat on the other bed, grinning. He reached for her, but she skipped out of range, bustling about, digging into the trunk as if searching for something.

"Mr. Copperfield, I'm going to be needing money to pay for things such as the marriages and the hotel and the trip, you understand?"

"I have some in my cabin. The rest is in the bank."

"Yes, I know. In the future, I'd appreciate it if you would instruct Mr. Quick to make his deliveries to me so that I can take care of these matters."

In her voice he heard a minute, querulous tremor, her inadvertent admission of his latent authority. It was gratifying, particularly after a long day of being led about like a brainless child. He had known all along that his contribution to this partnership was his money; now that she had obliquely admitted it, he felt his power. He had everything to gain by withholding an answer to her request, and he felt secure in his ability to keep the upper hand by staying alert in regard to his funds.

He turned and looked out of the second-story window and down onto the cobblestone street. In the twilight autos passed, their headlamps glowing yellow eyes. Into a pool of lamplight came two dogs, wheelbarrowing. The hind dog kept hopping onto the other's haunches only to slide off.

"Look!" David laughed and pointed down into the street. "They're on a honeymoon trip." Laura snapped back from the sight with such a savage jerk that he realized he had offended her. He had only meant to make a simple joke, to be friendly and affectionate the way he and Jenny had been. He had no nervousness about taking Laura, but he was bewildered by the peculiar armor of her strange emotions; they didn't allow him a hold anywhere.

He patted his pillow.

"Come here, Mrs. Copperfield." He spoke gently and smiled. He knew already she would not take easily to being commanded. Light from the globed kerosene lamp on the room's marble-topped dresser fell across her face when she ceased stirring the contents of her suitcase and turned to peer at him, sizing his mood, the extent of the request.

"You never agreed to what I asked."

They were in a tug-of-war. "We'll talk later about that. You come here and sit beside me like a wife." He spoke more forcefully.

Her hands moved from the suitcase and crossed, palms to her breasts, one on top of the other. With a flicker of shame he realized she had no wedding ring. He felt negligent, doubly shamed when after a moment's hesitation she sat stiffly beside him, palms still pressed to her chest.

They were not touching; she presented her profile to him as a sign of her displeasure. He leaned over and put his open mouth over the ridge of her jawbone, pushing her onto her side. The proximity of her flesh, the wash of fine golden hairs on her cheek, and her musky, flowered smell stunned him. But when he moaned and shifted his body like a powerful engine suddenly cranked into life, Laura hurled herself up and strode back to her suitcase.

"One thing you'll have to learn, Mr. Copperfield, is that white ladies do not perform their marital duties during certain times of the month, unlike Negresses."

"It's the same for Kiowa women." He meant that he was accustomed to the taboo and was therefore not offended, but he was also implying that she need not think white women had any monopoly on the morality supposedly inherent in it.

"Then you understand."

After they had eaten a fried-chicken dinner which Shingle brought to them, Laura went to the community bathroom down the hall and returned ready to retire dressed in more garments than David would have thought necessary to wear in a blizzard. Not speaking, she blew out the kerosene lantern and lay without moving on her back under her covers. He had propped the windows open; the sounds from the street below seemed distant, and he felt removed from life.

Laura lay stiffly, feigning sleep. Baffled, he lay still, watching her. He had her but did not have her; she was an alien beast given over to his husbanding without instructions on feeding or caring, and he didn't know whether to milk her, shear her, let her graze, keep her barred behind a corral, or beat her. Did she bite, kick, or sting?

He grinned in the darkness, pleased with himself. He had struck a pretty shrewd bargain. Iola would not think so, of course, but then she only approved of what she thought he should do with his life. Marrying Laura Darby was like leapfrogging right over Iola and her teacher, and David took pleasure in imagining how, on hearing the news, they might be stunned. It was as if by a single stroke he had erased all their cautious advice and had proven that he could manage his life without them. As he had said to Iola the night of Tom's party, he had lived without her advice or help in the many years since he had run away as a youth, and at least he was capable of living and making decisions without constantly checking with some white for permission or approval.

He knew he had stung her by saying that, particularly because Miss Roberts was standing beside her. Both women had their backs up about the fact that he wasn't sober. They treated him like a child—and Iola was two years younger than he!

He hadn't seen Iola since that night. Now, as he lay awake in a strange hotel room next to a strange white woman, and in a strange new role, Iola's face floated into his vision. He felt a pang, a longing for something familiar, but he also felt guilty: Iola did care for him, he wasn't blind.

But they had become like warring siblings who cannot show true concern for each other for fear their weakness will be exploited. She was too proud even to admit he had saved her life.

Now, he realized for the first time that this marriage would probably mean the end of his and Iola's meetings, and he was afraid he would miss her.

As if to remind himself of what he had gained, he listened in the darkness to Laura's breathing. The balmy night air was laced with the low of a calf, bark of a dog, a coyote far off in the distance, then the yowl of cats mating in a nearby alley. Laura moaned softly. He thought of having her in his cabin, in his bed, where familiarity might give him back his sense of himself. He could easily respect her wish to abstain now, but he wanted to stroke her, lie close.

He rose, padded quietly to her bed, leaned across her body, and put his face close to hers. Washed and in repose, without the mask of consciousness and cosmetics, her face seemed to belong to a stranger who was older and softer. He could see that the mask she put on for the world was calculated to make her look younger and yet, paradoxically, less innocent and vulnerable. Having her was a great wonder; she was the most interesting thing that had ever happened to him, and he was pleased to think of her as a mystery he would be allowed to solve piece by piece over the years.

Her eyes blinked open suddenly. A flash of fear-struck disorientation whirled in them.

"What are you doing?!"

"Looking at your face."

"Oh, God!" she groaned. She rolled over on her side, facing the wall. "Go to sleep, it's a long trip back tomorrow."

He returned to the hollow his body had made in the other bed. His lifelong patience with things that didn't yield quickly came back to him, and he smiled in the darkness, imagining days and nights ahead.

The next morning Shingle drove them nonstop to Wetoka. David kept imagining his life with Laura in the cabin, a fire burning, coffee brewing. He could see that she might disrupt his solitude, but that period of his life seemed to have ended anyway when Tom Quick came. She was good at dealing with white men. That quality would be beneficial; she could be a buffer between himself and the nuisances so many whites had become of late.

In Wetoka, just before sundown, Shingle pulled up before the town's only hotel. Before David could understand what was happening, the man had unloaded Laura's suitcase and helped her out of the car.

"I don't want to stay in a white man's hotel," David told her as she stood by the idling auto. "We'll go to my house."

Laura shook her head a little sadly, bent her face into the open auto window, then put her lips up against his cheek lightly, surprising him.

"I can't live in a dirt-floor cabin, Mr. Copperfield. I'll take up residence with you after you've built a decent house."

"It doesn't have a dirt floor."

"Whatever."

He was going to explain that white men would not let him stay in that hotel, then wondered if she had managed a dispensation. But before he could speak, she had climbed the steps to the hotel's porch, suitcase in hand. Shingle put the auto in gear, and David was transported away. When they took the road south of Wetoka, it was clear that Shingle had been instructed to return him home.

Walking into his cabin, David thought white ladies had many strange requirements. But then, so did Kiowa men, and she would have to learn some of them. He scrutinized the interior of the place he had called home for three years now, wondering what it was, exactly, she could object to.

He assumed Shingle would turn the car about and leave, but only moments after David had gone inside, Shingle appeared on the threshold holding a bedroll and a small pack.

When David didn't forbid it, the man entered and walked to a corner, where he tossed the articles onto the plank floor.

"What are you doing?"

"Rich men have enemies." The scar on Shingle's cheek flexed with his half-smile. "I'm your bodyguard."

David didn't like the man's smile. It was very quiet in the cabin; dusk left only a flicker of light playing through the open door, but it was enough to allow David to see that the man kept grinning, as if at a joke. Moving quietly to the fireplace, David picked up his ax.

"Do you sleep with your eyes open?"

"Oh, I'm a mighty excellent bodyguard."

"That's good. Then you'll be able to see the edge of this ax before it splits your head open. You'll hear me when I get up in the night to do it."

He hoped the man would resist; feeling foolish at being a boy these past two days, he yearned for a chance to restore his manhood, and Shingle had provided it.

Neither moved. Then, finally, Shingle crossed the room carrying the bedroll and pack and stood silhouetted against the pale violet sky framed by the open door.

"You're the one better keep his goddamn eyes open," Shingle muttered. David waited until the auto had disappeared before loosening his grip on the ax.

Three boys in knickers and tweed golf caps came strolling out of the steam gushing from the standing locomotive. Arms linked, they were singing, "I'd Like to See the Kaiser With a Lily in His Hand" and shouting to the troops aboard the train. They walked past Iola with flushed, sweaty faces glowing with excitement.

They went to a nearby car and banged on the flank with their palms.

"Hey, Hiawatha!" one yelled to a Comanche wearing a headband, who stuck his head out of the train window and grinned.

"What do you want, boy?"

"Scalp one of them Huns for us!" the boy yelped.

The Comanche raised an ancient metal ax and waved it nonchalantly. The three boys cheered, then moved on. The Comanche turned back to his fellow soldiers, who represented several plains tribes, including the Kiowas; Iola's cousin Morris was aboard. They had sung war chants punctuated by tom-toms during the morning, alternating with snatches from the white soldiers of "Over There" and "Pack Up Your Troubles in Your Old Kit Bag" while waiting for the train to fill with recruits before it would pull out for the East. They were in high spirits, anxious to shed blood, and most had yet to open packages their mothers, wives, and sisters had packed with sluggish fingers. The train had come from Cache and other points west, where the Kiowas, Apaches, and Comanches had boarded the previous afternoon. They were on their way to join the 42nd—the "Rainbow"—Division at Camp Mills, New York.

Iola felt anxious, excited, yet not eager. Resistance to the declaration of war against Germany in April had been high in Oklahoma, where hundreds of socialists had been locked up after rioting, burning barns and bridges in protest. To Eugene Debs and his followers—and Alice Roberts was one—war with Germany was necessary only because American industrialists wanted bigger profits. Iola and Alice had watched the war progress over the summer of 1917; anti-German sentiment had risen as American boys entered the war with Pershing. From her father Iola learned that many of her former classmates were joining with patriotic fervor. The war had the feel of the hunt for them—better to fight in France than eke out a meager existence on an allotment.

The din from the train was deafening; steam enveloped the platform in white billows; women from church groups passed bundles of knitted socks and candies and mittens to the men through the windows. Pacing impatiently and peering back toward the station house, Iola smelled hot apple pie, spices and tobacco smoke, hot metallic steam, whiskey and sweat, and faint wisps of lilac perfume wafting across the platform. Her senses were sharp with expectation; she had trouble keeping her breakfast of fry bread and sausage down, and the strong odors on the platform dizzied her.

Strolling alongside the troop cars was a group of women led by Alice, who was leaning up to mouth something to each young man, then would vise his cheeks between her large hands and plant a kiss full on his lips before moving on. Not good hygiene, thought Iola, but it was certainly inspirational.

Behind Alice, wearing a lot of paint on their faces and little cloth on their bosoms, came a flock of girls from Cheri Elena's, teary-eyed and lustily kissing the troops. The men seemed more eager to receive these presents than the bundles from the church matrons, some of whom stood back in indignation as Alice's flock left lipstick roses on the soldiers' cheeks.

As Iola watched, her heart slowly swelled with grief. On the platform, couples clung desperately to one another. The sight of these tearful separations had over the past couple of hours seeped into her heart like a bittersweet poison. She watched a woman grip the lapels of her young man's suit coat in her fists and punch him sharply over and over on his breastbone as she cried.

Iola turned away in envy and embarrassment. She longed to have David embrace her, be sorry to see her leave. Whatever grief he suffered would make her own decision seem real.

She began weeping mutely, pacing beside the train, feeling the time slip away quickly and knowing the chief nurse needed her help. She had joined the Red Cross nurses' group attached to the 167th Ambulance Company, an Oklahoma outfit, because she felt that so long as men like Morris were going and would be wounded, they would need someone like Iola to look after them—the white doctors and nurses would look to their own first.

"All aboard!"

Movement on the platform quickened; the crowd began to divide. Frantically, Iola looked about for David, only to see the blue-suited conductor emerge from the mists.

"All aboard."

Alice appeared, misinterpreting her tears, drawing her into her soft bosom, hugging her, murmuring in her ear.

"Ah, child! Whatever I've done that you're angry with me for, I hope you forgive me for it."

"I'm not angry," Iola said stiffly. She resisted the larger woman's smothering embrace for a moment, then gave her a quick hug, like a jab, simply to signify her part had been done so she could win her release.

Alice blubbered, "You're my only daughter! Take care of yourself. I'll pray for you!"

Iola steeled herself against what she thought would be a last inevitable protest from Alice that she need not go to the war. But Alice surprised her, backing away, struggling to keep her composure, turning to hurry off. Iola was rattled; her right hand went into the pocket of her uniform coat where she felt the paper between her fingers wilt from the dampness of her palm. From the head of the train, a whistle blew two brief toots, then piped one long, mournful sound.

Iola felt listless and tired. She fisted her hands in her pockets, wanting to bawl. After a moment, she strolled briskly for the train.

Then, at her elbow, a man. She whirled, her heart pounding, her mouth springing into a grateful smile, only to see Tom Quick hurrying beside her. For an instant, she thought perhaps David had come with him, but no.

"I couldn't let you go without telling you again how much I admire you," he was saying, panting as if he had run to the station. "You're so noble, Miss Iola . . . I just wanted you to have this—" He held out a small wrapped package, but she couldn't quite summon the sense of purpose required to take it, and she kept moving.

"Iola!" He laid his hand heavily on her shoulder. She looked at him; he was clean-shaven, even handsome, though he looked worried. "I'll be over there with the rest of you . . . by God! It worries me something awful you going over there." He seemed panicky, his speech disjointed, but then, her own nerves were clanging like discordant bells in her ears. "I sold my place to a fella from Tulsa, and I'm just a greasy old rough-neck most of the time now," Quick went on. "When you get back—when we all get back—I just hope you'll give me another chance to prove I'm worthy of you."

He was retreating, finished with his speech, still extending the present, smiling ruefully.

"All aboard—" Metal creaked behind her, and she knew now that she would go to Europe without having spoken to David. She felt the letter between her fingers. She looked at the white man's face; she was touched despite herself by his devotion: at last someone had come to declare his sorrow at her departure.

"Thank you for coming, Tom." She tried to smile, but she was so close to sobbing that her mouth only writhed in a spasm. "Would you please give this to David?"

Her hand emerged from her coat pocket, bearing the letter; he nod-ded, took it as she handled the gift, then she ran off, clutching the package to her bosom and hoping somehow it had come from David. She was crying so hard the train looked like an apparition seen through a driving storm.

Later, after she had calmed and the train was moving slowly north with a metronomic clack, her disappointment that David had not showed to see her off turned to anger—anger partly directed toward herself for expecting him. She should have known better. She had hoped her leaving would make a greater impression on him.

At first she was angry because he had not told her about his marriage. Alice had come to Hartzler's place some ten days after it had occurred, a period during which she had worried about Quick's influence on him and about how irritated he could become when Alice and she appeared to judge him. She had been worrying that she let Alice take the lead too easily when it came to dealing with David, and she had decided that in the future whatever transpired would be strictly between her and David.

Alice said, "Dear, I have some rather surprising news. David has taken a wife, a white woman who sings with the traveling vaudeville show."

The blunt declaration, without preface, struck her like a hammer blow. She sat down on the cot in Hartzler's anteroom. For a long moment, her mind groped about this information as if seeking to identify by touch, in the darkness, some unknown object. Married? A white woman who sings? Was this Quick's doing? Why would David agree? Had he known the woman sometime in the past?

"Do you know anything about her? What's she like?" Iola finally asked.

"Very little," replied Alice. "Except that presumably she could have done better."

This comment, seemingly an effortless and natural expression of sympathy for David—suggesting suspicion of the woman's motives—kept bobbing to the surface of Iola's ruminations over the next several days, turning itself over and over until at last she defined it: to Alice, even a white whore—and Iola was convinced that Laura Darby was a sort of whore—was superior to an Indian. To Alice it was appropriate that Iola should seek to attract David as a husband because they were inferior equals, but even a prize-winning red woman such as herself was still below the rank of white prostitute in Alice's hierarchy. Why hadn't Alice said David could do better? Could have done better by marrying you?

The insight sickened her, colored her past, a past she now had to reinterpret and revise. It seemed that Alice had more in common with Laura than with Iola, and that Alice, while certainly well-intentioned and conventionally "good," could do just as much damage as a Laura Darby.

She had been cold and distant to Alice ever since. She knew that she unfairly blamed Alice for David's choice, yet she couldn't shake her anger loose. It seemed that whatever chance she and David might have had to connect had been bungled by Alice's incessant pushing and meddling, both she and David balky as mules at being pleaded for by an intermediary. It hurt their pride. Something might have grown naturally between them if Alice had left them alone and if Tom Quick had not corrupted David's life.

For weeks she tried to ignore the marriage. She tried to be reasonable: David had promised nothing, had never implied that he had any desire to marry her. He was free to make his choice, just as she was. She had no claim on him; their being together had been a figment of her fancy.

Once she had seen, from a distance, David and his wife walking together on the street. David was dressed in a suit and a hat, his wife's arm thrust through the crook in his elbow. Two greasy workmen near Iola turned to watch them pass and, grinning, nudged one another. David looked like a large pet. It scalded her heart to see it.

Then hardly a week ago she was in the bank standing in line at a teller's window when she heard a man saying, in a merry voice rich with irony, "It's a pleasure to do business with you, Mrs. Copperfield," and the announcement of the name was like a slap. Iola turned to see the woman coming out of an office and the bank officer holding open the door for her, ushering her through with a mock courtier's flourish of his arm. Mrs. Copperfield laughed much too loudly. She strode through the crowded bank with her high heels rapping sharply on the wooden floor, her nose leading the way like a gun muzzle her eyes were sighting along. She seemed terribly arrogant, but she was also beautiful. Her eyes were green. Men observed her with sidelong glances, involuntarily, like meek but covetous children. David was lost.

A letter from Iola's father arrived shortly thereafter telling of the Kiowa enlistments, and it inspired her to join. Now, though, thinking of how David had not cared enough to say good-bye, she suspected that her decision hadn't been so altruistic. She had wanted to avoid having to see him again with his wife, wanted to avoid bearing constant witness to his folly and her own rejection. She had thought by leaving she might punish him, too; perhaps he might come to realize, through her absence, what he had lost.

She had been foolish to think it would work. The best she could hope now would be to die there, then he'd suffer from the lifelong regret that he didn't see her off.

She was being childish. She couldn't seem to stop it, though. Maybe Alice hadn't told David. As the time to leave had drawn near, Iola had had to relent in her coldness toward Alice because she needed for Alice to tell David that she was leaving but couldn't make herself ask Alice to do it because her own hypocrisy galled her too much. If David didn't know she was leaving, it was not Alice's fault.

Suddenly, hardly an hour away from having parted from Alice, she felt guilty for having been so cold to her. But the last few weeks with her former teacher had been a gruesome torment; Iola had been buffeted by a squall of intense dislike for Alice's behavior—she flirted with the Reverend Tatum to his face and belittled him behind his back; she indulged herself with chocolate candy, then bemoaned her own lack of discipline; she appointed herself the spiritual champion of Wetoka's prostitutes, taking time from her own backward oil-camp pupils in her one-room school; she dipped snuff but imagined no one knew.

But nothing irritated Iola more than Alice's incessant advice about matters which Iola now suspected she knew nothing—courtship, love, marriage. "I want you to ask yourself if you are going off to Europe just because you have a broken heart," Alice had said during an argument. "Lots of girls have had broken hearts and survived quite nicely in time without having to do anything more drastic about it than to simply keep their hands and minds occupied with some worthwhile activity."

Iola had been silent, but she had thought: How do *you* know what heals a broken heart?

There were Alice's constant little lessons on manners and refinement. Or the way she presumed that Iola could not stand up to Hartzler and needed her protection. Iola had felt smothered and handled until she thought she would scream. She had become withdrawn, even rude to Alice. Now she wished she had explained or apologized for her behavior. She knew Alice would worry about it.

With a long sigh, Iola looked out the window. The train was passing through a valley between sharp-spined ridges whose woods looked baked from the heat. The soldiers had quieted. There was a conversational hum punctuated by a laugh, a stifled curse as cards were slapped down onto a table made of a suitcase flank, a single guitar and voice muffled by the crowd. And, as the miles went by, Iola's sadness and guilt seemed to dissipate. Being aboard the train brought back memories of when she had gone to New York to get the buffalo, how excited she had been to be away from Kiowa country for the first time, seeing the buildings in the cities. Now to Europe! The danger and excitement of the adventure made her tremble.

Her damp fingers had wrinkled the white tissue about the package Tom Quick had passed to her. Remembering her earlier hope that David had sent the package, she opened the small card attached to the box. "All my best wishes to Iola, TQ."

She left the package in her lap for a moment; then, because it seemed like a small piece of unfinished business that needed to be tidied before she could proceed unhindered into the future, she tugged the ribbon free and unceremoniously tore away the paper. Under the wrapping was a flat white box with the name of a Tulsa jeweler inscribed on it; inside the box was a necklace, gold links with a ruby set in an engraved gold mount. It was, officially, a "beautiful" necklace, but it didn't appeal to her, didn't fit her temperament. On what sort of occasion had he imagined she might wear this? Tom Quick had spent a lot of money, obviously, yet had not spent it well. She felt sorry for him.

Tom waited with the crowd on the platform while the train eased away and the image of the caboose gradually diminished. Children whined; a baggage wagon with squeaking axles was wheeled away from the track. Now all those left behind could do was turn away and fight off pictures in their minds of bombs and bullet wounds.

Tom felt a collective breath being taken which would not be released until they all stood on that same platform however many months or years later to greet the survivors. Some wives looked a little angry, too, maybe because their men had been too eager, though they tried to hide it. Tom felt jealous of the enlisted men. Guilt had made him utter to Iola that he would join up, but he suspected he'd be less enthusiastic when the drama died away tomorrow.

In the grieving aftermath of the train's departure, he was oddly buoyant, still caught up enough in the mood of the moment to pretend to himself he might enlist, eventually. He was glad he had come, though it had been against his better judgment. From one of Cheri Elena's whores he had learned that Alice had planned for the girls to give the boys this send-off, then he was stunned to hear the whore add, "I think that Indian girl who's her ward or something is going over there as a nurse."

His pride had told him to save face by staying back, but his gut had said, nothing ventured, nothing gained. He could replay the heartfelt sincerity of her gratitude over the coming months.

Inside the station stood a table with coffee urns and a platoon of dirty mugs surrounding plates bearing homemade cakes, all with slices gone. Three women in Red Cross smocks were shuffling listlessly about behind the table. Tom was ravenous, having risen before dawn and rushing to reach the station.

"Could I have some coffee, ma'am?"

A pretty girl with red hair to her shoulders inspected him slowly from head to toe and obviously concluded he was a slacker who didn't deserve refreshments meant for the brave boys being carted away to meet their deaths. He tried to assume a lugubrious air.

The woman reluctantly poured him a mug of coffee.

"Thanks, ma'am." He took a sip, noting how pretty she was. It occurred to him that there would be many pretty women, lonely women, around now and fewer men to give them any attention. "Don't fret about those boys, ma'am. They're in good hands. Nobody's going to best the American fighting man, I know."

The woman's quick glance revealed a slight alteration in her presumptions about him. He turned and limped across the room, dragging his right foot to a waiting bench, trading one humiliation for another, gaining face but losing self-respect.

He sat holding the mug between his palms. Thank you for coming, Tom. Using his Christian name that way. That was money in the bank.

Why had she written a letter to Copperfield?

He slipped the letter out of his coat pocket. David, she had written on the envelope, nothing more. The implied intimacy disturbed him. They were both from the same tribe, had known each other as children —they were like brother and sister in his mind. He had assumed that was why she always seemed concerned about Copperfield's welfare. Before that night at the party, he had thought perhaps they had been sweethearts, but the way Copperfield had taken up with Laura had put that out of his mind. He had thought that Iola would forget Copperfield once he married someone else.

Coffee dribbled off his chin onto the envelope in his lap. It was only partly sealed. It was rumpled, and now he had soiled it. He turned it over and held it up to the light, seeing only a faint scrawl through the paper. It wasn't any of his business. But she had made him the messenger. The envelope was already becoming next to useless—an envelope such as this could be easily lost in its poor condition. If lost, the message would never be delivered, Iola's trust would have been misplaced, he would have failed her.

It might be better to read the message in case the letter got lost: the message itself could still be delivered. Which was worse—to have violated the privacy of the message or to have failed to deliver it?

It would probably turn out that there was no reason he shouldn't know what she had written Copperfield, this man of her own kin. And it might help him understand her feelings. Possibly the letter was about Tom himself. *Thank you for coming, Tom.* Maybe she wanted Copperfield to tell him something she was unable to say—if that was the case, then he would indeed be sorry to have lost the letter.

Soon Tom grew convinced it was his moral imperative to open the letter.

He crooked a finger inside and dragged out the folded paper. The stationery was pristine, creased neatly twice to fold the paper into thirds. He peeled the wings back, saw the thin black scrawl of the few words there. The harmless, innocent salutation of "Dear David," then the black snake struck: "I know that you're another woman's husband, but she can never feel about you the way I do. Please keep me in your thoughts and in your heart. All my love, Iola."

The letter and the envelope dropped to the bench beside him. A stinging pressure rushed behind his eyes; he couldn't think and sat feeling nauseated, the coffee sloshing in his gut as he rocked slowly back and forth on the bench.

Later, when he was on the road back to Wetoka, the bitter ironies struck him. A stinking savage with no more sense than God gave a toadstool had won her heart—and to think what Tom had done for Copperfield! That's gratitude for you! If it weren't for Tom, Copperfield would still be heaving on that goddamn ferry pole and shacking up with a field nigger! Now that ignorant buck was married to a beautiful blonde who had made Tom an offer he had been too stupid to take!

Tom pulled off the road, almost diving into a muddy bar ditch, and banged his head on the steering wheel. Poetic justice! He was personally paying for the sins of the white man, and here he had had the best of intentions—he wanted to *marry* that goddamn squaw! He pounded on the rim of the wheel with his fists and roared with laughter. What a fool!

He had gone only another mile when he realized he had left the letter on the bench, and he pulled off the road again. But he didn't shut off the engine and didn't turn around, and within seconds steered the Ford back onto the road heading west. If she wanted Copperfield to get her goddamn message, she should have sent it by U.S. mail.

14

Saynday was coming along one day when he spied a beautiful woman sitting on a rock, all alone. He thought, this is the most beautiful woman I have ever seen. I will get her to marry me!

He said, You are very pretty. What are you called?

I am Whirlwind Woman, she said. I come around here in the summertime from my home in the south and west.

Well, Whirlwind Woman, I would like to marry you. You are the most beautiful woman I have seen.

Thank you, but I do not want to be married. I am too restless.

Well, said Saynday, that is good. I am restless, too. We will make a good marriage, then.

No, said Whirlwind Woman. I would not marry somebody ugly like you, with such a funny mustache and squeaky voice. Besides, the warrior who marries me has to be very strong.

I am strong, said Saynday. Test my strength.

Come hold on to my clothes, said Whirlwind Woman. If you can keep holding on to me, you can keep me and marry me.

Saynday went up to her and grabbed her around the waist, and she took off running. Pretty soon she was going real fast, then she started going around and around and went up in the air. Saynday hollered, he was scared, but he held on real tight to her dress. Then she came back down and went across the prairie, dragging poor Saynday across the dirt and rocks, but still he held on. She went flying into some trees and he knocked against them and broke many bones, but still he held on. Then she went fast through the briar bushes and the briars scratched him all over and he started bleeding. He was still holding tight, but he was getting weak now and sorry he had took hold of her waist.

Whirlwind Woman went up in the air real quick and then flung old Saynday down on the earth, where he went whump!

You are a crazy woman! he yelled at her.

That will teach you to fool with a woman you cannot keep up with! said Whirlwind Woman, and she went flying off across the prairie.

•

White ladies made peculiar brides. Laura's menstrual flow seemed interminable. For a week following their return from Coffeyville, David visited Laura at the hotel, taking meals with her in the dining room. Laura had commandeered two large rooms off the upstairs hall. He was discouraged from entering the one she used as a bed- and dressing room but was free to visit the other, where she had installed a piano. It was pleasant to sit while she sang and played and drink the thick cognac and smoke the cigars the banker had sent over for a wedding present.

With each visit, something new appeared—the piano, a walnut armoire with inlaid pearl designs, and a young Negro maid. Laura would be clothed in something different with each visit, creating a perplexing, protean illusion that made him struggle to fix her identity.

She insisted that he come daily, and he was pleased that she wanted his company. She had begun to relax a little around him. She still skittishly eluded his embraces, yet she managed to touch him every day —a finger pressed against his forearm to punctuate a moment in a song, an unpredictable peck on his cheek which left the cool damp impression of her lips and thrilled him. He thought she was familiarizing herself, whittling down her own fear of him this way.

He understood that it was important for her to control the circumstances and extent to which their bodies brushed, and he learned to stand wooden as a mule when she stood beside him and gently pressed a breast against his arm. He would be patient—they had a lifetime. He endured his frustration by reminding himself she could not put him off forever.

The passivity she had produced and exploited in him was novel and troubling. He was inexperienced; her gift of knowing what she wanted at all times encouraged him to follow her without regard for his own desire. He was very shy, and her self-possession drove him back into himself. He was aware that such behavior would make him the object of contempt in his tribe, but then, he kept telling himself, his wife was not a Kiowa, and it was not apparent yet what rules, what standards of behavior from his past, might apply here.

This new life was enormously disorienting; he had lost the paths he had established, and he had no map for a new route, let alone any knowledge of a destination beyond the vague images concerning the end of her menstrual period and their eventual life together under the same roof. He couldn't endure the idea of his cabin crawling with white men bearing hammers and saws; since their future "decent" house was a matter of concern only to her, he told her that she was free to buy or build what she liked.

After two weeks, her refusal to allow him into her bed could no longer be explained away. He had grown intolerably restless. Each afternoon when he mounted the steps to the hotel's porch, the regulars perched on the bench fell into a peculiar hush, and in their covert glances he detected a mirth that branded him a fool.

On an afternoon in mid-April, he was intercepted by Tom Quick in the lobby while on his way to Laura's upstairs parlor. Quick handed over a cashier's check with the jovial air of a man spreading Christmas cheer. As usual, Quick was clad in greasy work clothes, and he sent his merry gaze flitting over David's dark suit, the celluloid collar, the new shoes so glossy and black they might have been varnished.

He winked. "So how's married life, Copperfield?"

So, thought David, they are all laughing because they know I don't sleep at this hotel. His face must have showed his irritation, because Quick leaned closer and tapped the check in David's hand with a finger.

"A piece of free advice, Copperfield. A woman like that—you have to make them grateful for what they get. And you have to make sure they know they *have* to give you what you want."

Quick winked again, looked into the dining room, and waved. David followed his gaze; Laura and a stranger were seated at a table. Her hand went up languidly in response to the wave, and she gave Quick a flitting, ironic smile.

David slipped the check into his coat pocket, conscious of Laura's scrutiny as he strolled toward the table. She had witnessed the exchange of the paper, and he felt furtive. He had been paying her bills without question, but he hadn't told Quick to turn over the money to her.

He wasn't pleased to see her with a stranger. She had too many men in her life, he thought. People she had known from being in the tent show, he presumed, people she had known elsewhere, in those places where she had had a life altogether unknown to him. There was no way to calculate how many men she knew, how many, like him, yearned for her. Or how many she had had.

As he approached, Laura and the man broke off whispering. The man's thin cigar was posted between his fingers as if caught between the blades of large scissors. He wore a string tie, and when he leaned away from Laura, his trimmed beard caught a long wisp of her blond hair. Laura's wineglass was half full; the man was drinking something from a snifter. Plates on the table between their elbows held puddles of blood, utensils piled like bones in the juices.

When David eased into a chair at the table, Laura smiled but returned her attention to the man. They were talking of people David didn't know, and he listened in silence. As if by magic, a steak arrived beneath his face, and he cut and ate it slowly, not from hunger, but only to make the two across the table seem less rude by creating a pretext for their excluding him. The man sent him sidelong glances which flicked away the instant David caught him looking.

He might have been a large and potentially dangerous dog fed a hunk of meat to keep his attention diverted. He observed the closeness of their heads, the flirtatious way Laura twirled strands of her hair in her fingers, or emphasized a word by a pat on the man's forearm, a breast moved too near the man's bicep.

He had images of Laura and the man lying together, and his attention riveted on them. He no longer felt obliged to make himself invisible for their sakes. He sat silent but alert, clenching his jaw.

"You always did have a head for business," the stranger said with a chuckle, then he did an extraordinary thing—he reached over and touched the tip of Laura's nose playfully with his finger, as if to say "You're mine" or "I'll take that one." He winked at her, but his boldness seemed to alarm her; she leaned away from the man, and looked over at David.

"My father and his companions hunted buffalo in the old days," David said. The man's head snapped around in surprise. He might have been laboring under the impression that David was a deaf mute. David held his steak knife in the air over the table, presenting it as if it were an object for the man to contemplate.

"As soon as the buffalo was down, he and the other hunters would cut him open"—the knife made a small arc over the floral centerpiece—"and they would reach inside and cut out the gallbladder and the liver and eat them raw."

Confused, the man glanced at the knife, then at their plates, as if David's words were a non sequitur inspired by their meal. David reached across the table with his left hand and clamped the man's jaw in his grip, feeling the wiry beard in his palm. He yanked the man's head over at an angle and brought the steak knife down to the man's jugular.

Laura gasped, drew back. The blade was poised on the man's skin; his eyes widened and his hands gripped the edge of the table.

"Don't!"

Laura's shout rocketed across the room, and David suddenly felt the attention of the other diners gather at the point where his blade pressed the man's blue vein.

"Please!" the man uttered from his throat, his jaw held tightly in David's large hand.

"David! What are you doing?"

"I'm going to kill this man."

"Please!" the man croaked again.

"Please? You want to die so much?"

"David! Stop it right now!"

The man's shoulders were trembling violently; his tears were deeply satisfying to David.

"I want to see you bleed," said David. "I'm going to cut you up some. Maybe you'll die, maybe you'll live."

David cocked the knife, and before the man could struggle free, he drew the knife once quickly and lightly across the man's cheek, carving a red gash through the black beard. Blood gushed freely from the wound.

Laura was dumb with astonishment. The man got slowly to his feet, his eyes transfixed on the bloody palm he had just brought down from his cheek.

"Where's a . . . a . . . a doctor?" he whispered.

"Down at the end of the street, in a big tent," David answered calmly. "You go fast maybe you won't die."

The man broke away from their table with a strange, even walk that held his upper body like a large egg he feared might tumble and crack, pressing his palm to his cheek.

David turned to Laura. She was looking at him in confusion and fear —an improvement over ignoring him, he thought, and it was the first time she had ever appeared less than wholly composed.

But she regained her control quickly. "Am I next?"

"No, but you come to live in my house now."

"And if I don't?"

"You will."

"Why will I?"

"Because I say."

"No, not in your log cabin or anybody else's."

His anger surged upward from his gut and flooded into his chest, his heart, his shoulders, and pounded through this veins. He had been patient enough with this woman!

"Then I'll carry you there!"

Laura crossed her arms. "That's what you'll have to do, then. It'll be a pretty picture, Mr. Copperfield. A savage taking advantage of a defenseless white lady, no matter if she is his wife."

A commotion from the hotel lobby drew their attention momentarily, then she turned back to him.

"And I'd guess that you're going to be busy explaining why you assaulted a white man for no reason at all. If I'm not wrong, that'll be the sheriff in the lobby looking for you."

David bolted up from his chair and strode into the lobby, and a knot of spectators standing there scattered like chickens. The sheriff was nowhere in sight. The knifing was apparently going to go unnoticed by the law. While David stood perplexed, the hotel manager approached him, accompanied by the desk clerk.

"Mr. Copperfield, I have abided your presence in this hotel only due to the wishes of your . . . Mrs. Copperfield, but I can no longer tolerate it. Too many of our patrons have complained, and after this unfortunate incident I do not want to have to repeat my message here."

David stared down at the smaller man for a long moment.

"I'm going to buy this hotel and throw everyone out of it and live in it myself!"

The manager took the threat calmly. "Mr. Copperfield, if I had a nickel for every declaration precisely like that one from all the yokels with money they're just discovering how to abuse, I'd be rich enough myself to do it. If you care to go to all that trouble in lieu of learning manners, that choice is yours assuredly, but I think it would be better to learn how to behave."

"You mean roll over like a dog!"

David charged up the staircase and down the hallway on the second floor, banged with his fist on the door to Laura's bedroom. The Negro girl opened it and looked at him with her mouth agape.

"Go get my wife! She's downstairs!"

The girl scurried out. David strode into the room, took off his suitcoat and draped it neatly over the back of an upholstered wing chair. He took the check out of his coat pocket, unfolded it and pressed out its crease, then laid it in the center of the quilted velvet counterpane on Laura's bed. He flung himself into the wing chair and sat glowering.

After a few moments, Laura's heels rapped in the hallway, then she swung the door wide, making the knob tap against the wall. She strode into the room without looking at him and left the door ajar, going immediately to the wardrobe closet opposite the wing chair. She yanked the wardrobe door open and peered into the dark well of hanging fabric with her arms crossed and her back to him. Facing him at an angle, a beveled mirror reflected his head, large and dark against the backdrop of the wing chair. His eyes were cowish, sorrowful, and he wished his anger showed more.

In the mirror Laura was unbuttoning her high-necked white blouse. He watched as she shed it then tossed it onto the pink velvet sofa. It had been his intention to order her to undress, but she had sidestepped the necessity.

He bent in the chair, knees spread, laced hands hanging between them. His belligerence was dissipating. He didn't want to extort a payment of any kind; he wanted the gift of solace he had had from Jenny.

But how could he inspire this woman to give? Her body was disclosed in parts to him from behind the closet door, the mirror showing her bare back, the delicate wings of shoulder, white and vulnerable, then her small white waist with reddened ridges from tight clothing, her womanly hips and heart-shaped buttocks, the backs of her thighs. His heart pounded and he caught up his breath. Her hair fell across her shoulders as she reached to her head and released it.

After a moment, she appeared, wearing a long red satin robe with lapels and cuffs trimmed in black velvet.

She looked at him a moment, a flicker of hostility in her green eyes, then she eased onto the edge of the bed; the deep blue surface of the velvet counterpane was between them, the smoothness of the expanse broken only by the check lying with one wing in the air, a broken bird. She looked at it. He yearned for her to do something altogether out of character—lean over to him, cradle his head in her arms, lay his cheek against her breasts.

"For you." His head dipped toward the check. "But I won't bring you one each time I want you to share my bed."

He didn't want to sound angry; he wanted to put aside the scene in the dining room and inspire her participation.

She reached over and pinched one corner of the check between her long, lacquered nails. It might have been a large dead roach. She lifted it from the spread, folded it along the crease and eased it into the pocket of her robe.

"This isn't your money alone to give me, so you needn't treat me like a whore. In the eyes of the law, you gave me half of yours when we were married."

"What have you given me?"

She smiled from one corner of her mouth. "Look around. Better surroundings and a more genteel society. Maybe I'll teach you how to live without pulling a knife every time somebody gets your goat." She sounded calm, but he heard no melody in her voice. "Maybe you'll come to be civilized."

This wasn't what he had wanted, their tossing words like live spiders at one another. Nor had becoming "civilized" been an aspiration.

"Who was that man?"

She shrugged. "Only an old friend. From Chicago. He was just passing through. You made a fool of yourself and embarrassed us while you were at it. If he doesn't press charges for attempted murder it will only be because I talk him out of it."

"He was talking love to you and you let him. Now it's time for you to let me into your bed."

Laura looked away. After a moment she sighed, rose, pulled back the covers, and slid beneath them with her robe on, still not looking at him. She tugged the spread to her chin. Beneath the spread she dipped her shoulders this way and that and raised her hips, slipping off her robe, then she lay still again, staring at the ceiling. When she closed her eyes, he thought with surprise that she had decided to sleep him away.

"David, I want to tell you something about the world." She spoke with her eyes closed. The melody had come back into her voice, but the overtones were sad to his ear, a new sad song, not angry but resigned. Not blaming him—warning him. "Nobody ever gave anybody anything. You take what you want."

This was the most she could give, then: the opportunity for him to take. He understood that it was an oblique permission, but it also might have been her first lesson in what she claimed she was to teach him.

Trembling, he rose from the chair and shut the door to the hallway. He felt giddy with the anticipation of the moment he had been dreaming of constantly, yet her attitude troubled him. Their postponed union would be joyless.

He stripped to his underwear then eased into the bed as if she were sleeping and had warned him not to wake her. His flank tingled with the warmth her body had produced in the cavity between the sheets. He slid closer but did not touch her.

His left arm went out hesitantly and when he lowered it slowly she shivered like a horse with fly-ridden flanks. He left his hand on her belly a moment; she settled back again, but the rigidity in her body was still apparent. Her arms were pressed to her sides, hands knotted into fists that vised her thighs between them. He moved his head closer until her hair, loose against the pillow, webbed over his face, smelling of powder, perfume. He waited, listening to her shallow breathing, then he moved his hand and her skin registered his touch by rippling, pond-water response to a skating bug. He was baffled that this seemed so difficult. He was afraid of touching her. With Jenny things had been easy; they had explored the locking of their limbs with the wonder of children, but this woman was taut as a drawn bowstring.

When he raised his hand toward her breast, she giggled, then her right hand shot up from her thigh and she clamped his fingers tightly to stop them.

"None of that now!" she said.

Her eyes opened slightly, then clamped shut when she saw him studying her face, perplexed.

"Come on, get it over with, will you?!"

With Quick's help he bought the hotel and fired the manager, but he didn't evict the guests. He decided he liked to see people come and go in a place where he was the boss. He took a room that overlooked the street four steps down the hall from Laura's bedroom. Even though buying the hotel had been inspired by the incident in the dining room, Laura approved, and David allowed her to approach the banker Kale to help them with the paperwork.

Swiftly, as if doing so had been part of a plan, Laura stepped into the role of manager, and for the next year she and David settled into a routine. Laura would rise early, supervise the housekeeping staff, keep the books, and check on the state of the kitchen and dining room. Her enthusiasm in running the hotel didn't surprise David, but Tom Quick told him once, "You know, I would've thought she'd be the sleeping-in sort of woman if she didn't have to work. Just goes to show you how stupid a man can be."

David rose early also, out of habit, and ate breakfast in the dining room with the other patrons. He adopted the practice of holding a newspaper before his eyes while he drank his coffee and ate his eggs, because he didn't want to appear out of place; it was a way of looking white, of looking busy, of not appearing to need anyone's company, such as, say, his wife's. People treated him with more respect when he carried a paper. His reading ability improved with practice, soon he became addicted to following the course of the war, and he watched for mention of Iola's Rainbow Division. It had arrived in France in October, had apparently stayed behind the lines until December, made a "terrible march through a blizzard" to Rolampont, then scattered over the winter months. He felt guilty that Iola was the "warrior" and he had stayed behind. Then the thought would come—You could go anytime—but he would dismiss it: Iola might think he was chasing her. Besides, he didn't want to leave Laura for a moment, fearful some other man might possess her. It was fitting that Iola had gone off to the white man's war; it seemed her destiny to be always thrust into a future far away and very different from his own.

But he regretted not seeing her off at the station. He was convinced his invitation was simply more of the missionary's doing. Sure that Iola disapproved of his marriage, he had seen no point in walking into a bristly thicket of judgment against him. And one morning a few months ago, David met up with Tom Quick at the livery stable. Quick, drunk and morose, told him that, according to Miss Roberts, Iola had married a soldier—a white soldier—in France. David set his wagon wheel down and thought of how this was one more thing he and Iola had in common. It made her seem more kin to him even as it put her out of his reach. With all this, an intense pang of longing for her surprised him.

After David had read the morning paper, he would walk to the livery stable two doors away and see that the horses owned by the hotel's guests were fed and groomed. Guests' automobiles would be dusted and gassed up. Sometimes he would take off his coat and pitchfork a load of hay into the stable to keep from being restless or bored. In September Laura arranged to have the hotel furniture upgraded, and so he spent most of his mornings for a month supervising the moving; in October when the weather began to turn, he was in charge of stocking the hotel's coal bin.

These mornings were pleasant for him mostly because he could anticipate with relish being with Laura in the afternoon. He had negotiated with her an appointment time after she had eaten lunch. They met in her bedroom, which she had furnished lavishly with a huge oriental carpet and a canopied bed. Blue velvet curtains on sliding rings hung about the bed so that when Laura yanked the curtains closed, the interior was like a padded, scented cave or aromatic tent, and, particularly after the weather turned cold and the room contained icy drafts as active as disturbed ghosts, her bed was cozy and warm.

Waiting for her eagerly, he would draw the shades, knowing that if he didn't she would, then he would sit on the bed in his trousers and slap at drowsy flies droning around his head in the dusky light. Waiting, he could feel the excruciating crawl of time as it narrowed down to her arrival, and he would stroke some garment she had left lying about. A white bridegroom might have had to endure being teased by his peers for being overly fond of the delights of his bride's boudoir, but around the hotel, the white men's envy and indignation that a savage was bedding down a beautiful white woman kept their lips sealed. His obvious serenity infuriated them. He looked like some well-fed species of livestock ruminating on the cud of undeserved good fortune. They were not far wrong—the daily conjugal rite had over the months become an addiction whose complete grip on his attention was supremely pleasurable.

Eventually she would arrive and undress behind the curtains. He would hear rustling, creaking; when she had fallen silent, he would part the bed curtains and slide nude into the bed beside her. The linens were redolent of the sachet packets under the pillows, and their scent mingled with the warm, breadlike smell of her flesh and her winey breath.

Lying with her coiled-up hair in his face, he would unknot her sash, slowly lay back the lapels of her robe and again and again feel the awe of seeing her for the first time. He would spend breathless minutes gently passing his palms over her breasts, her belly, and her thighs while she quivered under him. At first she had tolerated his stroking her with the fitful fidgeting of a child being examined by a strange doctor, but, as the months passed, this restlessness turned into a certain attentive curiosity. He learned patience not as a means of inducing her participation but, rather, to enhance his own enjoyment of her, and in time he would eventually part her legs, lie breast to breast on her, and gently slide into her, stroking long and slowly, remaining calm on the outside because he had learned she feared him most when he was bullish and breathing hard.

Once spent, he would withdraw and return his cheek to the warm expanse of her torso made damp by his own hot flesh until she would jerk in a spasm of impatience to be free.

Their mutual silence in these couplings solidified the almost religious aspect of them. The creak of the door when she entered, the sibilant rustling of the curtains, and her labored breathing as she wrestled with her clothing—all this produced the sensation of secular mystery he had come to revere.

In the evenings, Laura retired early and gave David strict instructions not to disturb her. She altered this pattern occasionally to join him, the banker Kale, the doctor, and sometimes Tom Quick or other men for playing poker when the dining room closed. Once or twice a week she went for a buggy ride in the evenings without him, saying she needed to be by herself to think, a need for which he had a great understanding after his years on the ferry and living alone in the cabin.

Every two weeks, a bespectacled Lebanese fellow came through town to show motion pictures once the dining room had cleared out in the evening. He would hang a bedsheet against the wall and set his machinery on tables in the rear of the room. The occasion was favored by townspeople, and the Lebanese man and Laura split all ticket money.

David favored cowboy pictures, partly because he kept searching to find himself falling from horses: he had ridden in one-reelers made at the 101 Ranch after touring in the Wild West show, but these Westerns shown by the Lebanese all ran together and made little sense to him. Seeing mounted white men carrying rifles was part of his racial memory, but the Indians wore a hodgepodge of bands, ribbons, and loincloths all jumbled together without regard for tribal differentiation, and they rode poorly, like men accustomed to saddles.

Like as not, a beautiful white woman would be carried away from her log cabin over the shoulder of a brave like a sack of grain, her mouth pulsing open and closed like the bloodless lips of a fish. When a soldier raised his rifle to shoot an Indian, David would sometimes jut his hand into the beam of light to obliterate the image, causing a ruckus.

Sometimes after a poker party or a moving picture Laura would invite a select few up to her "parlor," where she would entertain until midnight at her piano. It was a delight to watch her at the piano and remember the night he saw her at Tom Quick's party, and that memory would turn to thoughts of their countless afternoons. He loved to hear Laura sing; he watched the other men watching her, felt jealousy but also pleasure and pride in knowing that the white men wanted her, but only he possessed her.

Still, he could never capture her attention the way he longed to. She was absent in spirit when he was making love to her, and there was no other time to be alone with her. He felt jealous of each person who claimed her time and grew cross and melancholy in his estrangement.

Iola was right; he had changed. He had lost the capacity to be alone. He saw people shaking hands, hugging, back-slapping—the countless, ingenious ways people had invented to touch one another in public—and he heard them telling stories and jokes to one another. Sitting on the porch, he was afloat in a sea of human interaction, immersed in it and yet separate from it. Here in the hotel, married to Laura, he felt lonelier than he had living in the cabin. There, the difference between himself and the rest of humanity was a simple matter of proximity, while here, among people, the differences were that he was Kiowa and rich, and neither of those inspired friendship.

Finally, Anna Knobel, an elderly German who was stranded by the war, came to stay in the hotel and became a confidante and friend. But until then he had to endure the discontentment of trying to fill his need for companionship through Laura.

They quarreled about money. He was generous and even unquestioning with her expenditures, but she insisted that his doling money out to her upon request amounted to belittling her, as if she were a child who needed an allowance. Didn't he trust her? Didn't he realize that with her education and knowledge of business they could take his money and make much more money with it? Didn't he realize that the oil money would run out some day? Hadn't he ever heard of an oil glut? Didn't he think about the future? What did he think he would do when the money ran out? What did he think *she* would do when it was gone?

This was the Tom Quick song all over again—the white person's mania. It was as if tomorrow the world were going to end, he thought, and Laura and Tom Quick and their ilk were always scurrying about desperately to find themselves a hole to hide in before it happened. When the money ran out he would simply go on living; he had lived well enough without the money. The prospect of losing his fortune or spending it all simply didn't alarm him.

Yet he wasn't so naive as to think that he could return to his old life. He still had his land, but now the many drilling rigs that stood upon it had stained the ground and spoiled the view and tainted the air and driven away the peaceful silences of the nights. For a while the drilling crews had used the cabin as a base camp, but then one night it had burned down. He had gone out to inspect the damage and saw that Tom Quick's prophecy about the ferry had been accurate: on both banks now were monolithic concrete supports standing like large tombstones turned orange by the sunset light. A bridge was under construction.

He had nothing in principle against making more money with his money. Laura's mistake was in not realizing that their conflict was personal; she saw him as a person who could only be manipulated through her not giving him what he wanted, and he returned the favor. He was afraid that if he gave her control of his money she would have no need for him. He did trust her; he trusted her to act in accordance to what he knew were her reasons for having married him. It had been a business proposition. And if he had any fear about being poor again, it was that Laura would not stay with him.

For the first few months after they were married, she argued with him about a life insurance policy, explaining that buying the hotel had obligated them to considerable debt and that if he were to die she would be left with it. He balked, partly because life insurance was an alien concept and because it was something Laura wanted him to do. However, Tom Quick dispelled his suspicions—life insurance was, he said, a perfectly normal thing for even a poor man to buy. So six months after they were married, he bought a policy for $100,000.

Then she had wanted him to make out a will. Again he balked. He was weary of making trips to white men's offices and signing papers he only half understood. It only made him feel vulnerable and ignorant.

But, once again, Quick told him that a will was something that any white man would have, even though, it seemed, well, superfluous: if he died, Laura would naturally get his money as his wife. When he tried to use Quick's hesitation as a reason for thwarting Laura, she railed at him, "You don't know what you're talking about! You die and four dozen of your kin will come crawling out of the woodwork and try to claim something that I've had to work for!"

He had told her he would consider it.

"You know what I hate the most about your ignorance?" she said. "It just makes you suspicious. Any white man would *want* to make out a will to protect his wife from wolves!"

That stung him. He said Standing Inside Lodge and her family were not "wolves," and if he should make out a will, he would surely include them in it. He put her off, through the summer and into the fall, but when she stubbornly withheld herself, he said he was "thinking about it more now." Still later he said he was "thinking about what he might want this paper to say."

He thought he had pacified her, but she surprised him one October afternoon. Behind the curtains of the canopy bed, she acted eager to please. As soon as he finished, she went to the window and yanked on the shade. Sunlight flooded the room, blinding him momentarily.

"Are you pleased with me now?" Her voice boomed in the silence.

"Yes."

"Good." She cleaved the bar of light from the sun-struck window in half as she passed before him. "I think it's time you trusted me a little, too. God only knows what people like that German woman have been telling you, but despite whatever you may think, I have your best interests at heart, David."

This again! "I've told you I'm thinking about this will." Disgusted, he yanked his belt tight and buckled it.

"I think you're just putting me off, stalling. It's not just the will, David. It's the way you don't trust me at all, don't let me be the guide when it comes to money. I grew up with it, I know what it can do and how to use it."

She broke off, but David knew it was only a pause—he had grown familiar with the rhythms of her harangues and knew that she usually released a short burst which he was meant to absorb before she followed it with a more intense fusillade. He took advantage of the moment to put his foot up on her dressing bench and to tie his shoe-laces. He drew inward like a creature concentrating on growing a very thick skin.

"I feel that you're cheating me, David. You take your leisure when you want it and you use your money to buy yourself this hotel and fine clothes, and you never have to spend a minute worrying about taking care of anything. You want to eat, you sit down in the dining room, you want a shave, you send for the barber, you want your . . . your conjugal rights you just send for me."

"It's my money."

"No, I beg your pardon! It's *our* money! And you act as though it's growing on trees out there. What do I get for having married you, David, answer me that! I get to manage your hotel and work my fingers to the bone supervising your household staff and overseeing your dining room—and I don't even get a salary—and then I have to *service* you whenever you get an urge, and I show you how to dress and act in polite society, and because you're my husband you've gained respect in people's eyes, but do you have any earthly idea whatsoever what most people think of a lady who marries an Indian, even a rich one?"

David was dimly aware of her question and that she seemed to be waiting for a reply, but he was still thinking about money growing on trees. It had been that way, had seemed that way, indeed. Tall trees built by Tom Quick. This, the "underground crop," he had not even had to sow.

"I said do you have any idea what people think of a lady who marries an Indian? What I have to face out in the streets when white men look at me?"

"If he's rich, they think she married for the money. They think she's smart for doing it, but maybe also not very dignified. If he's poor and she marries him, they think she is crazy. Maybe the Devil has a hold on her."

Laura looked surprised. "Yes, well, what you say about 'not very dignified' is an understatement, my friend. They think she is trash and a traitor to her race, a Judas. I'm not going to endure their looks and their whispers anymore unless I have compensation, David, you understand? I insist that you let me handle our money and give Mr. Kale the power of attorney so that we can make sound investments."

"I will consider—"

"No, no, none of that! Either you do it immediately or I'll have to reconsider my part of this bargain."

"No," he uttered without hesitation. The hard little word pecked like a sharp-beaked bird against her angry expression. He had spoken almost as a reflex to her insistence.

Unexpectedly, she gave him a sour little smile. "Well, nobody can say I didn't try," she muttered and strode out of the room.

When he finished dressing, he crossed the hallway into his own room, where he drew a cigar from a box on top of the pine dresser and lighted it. He had an hour or so to kill before Anna gave him his piano lesson, and the cigar would take a while. He was pleased with himself; although hearing Laura bring up the issue of money again had irritated him, he was proud of standing up to her.

He sat in the room's one comfortable chair, a thickly upholstered wingback—Tom Quick had given it to him when he sold the mansion —and watched the smoke make spirit shapes against the ceiling. For a time, he basked in the recollection of his firmness until it slowly dawned on him that she had threatened him with divorce. Quick had told him once that women sometimes got more of a man's money through divorce than they were ever able to obtain as wives. They had to prove, of course, that they deserved to be divorced. If she were to divorce him, there would be no more afternoons in her bed.

Alarmed, he rose and went to the door but had no firm notion of what he wanted to do. Her voice floated up from the lobby, then he heard the screen door smack its frame downstairs and her heels on the porch. He went to the window. Below, Laura crossed to the opposite corner and began walking east. Her green dress rocked like the pendulum of a mantel clock. Her back was straight, her hair pinned up, and the nape of her neck was a small, clean white line just below it.

His heart turned over. Where was she going? To some other man? Divorced, she would be free, she would have his money, and some other man would enjoy her.

But he couldn't back down without feeling like a fool. Teeth clenched, he watched her lithe figure move with her characteristically bold stride, until, blocks away, she turned a corner. Beyond where she vanished, he could see the platform of the train station, where, under the canopy, a stack of coffins was being unloaded on the cobblestones.

15

Laura Copperfield strode into the busy bank, walked to the rail that fenced off the desk of the vice-president, and asked to see Mr. Kale. While waiting, she brushed at the red dust on her dress then stood with her parasol jabbed into the raw plank flooring, leaning on the handle.

The young officer—Kale's nephew—returned after a moment.

"You may go in now, ma'am." He had a cowlick and a clean, hairless face that his high celluloid collar strained to dignify.

Kale ushered her into his office with a smile, and when she hung back and put her hand on the doorknob, he said, "Just leave it open."

He took a seat behind his desk, and she eased down into a red leather wing chair. His face was visible to anyone walking past the doorway, but the right wing on the chair partly hid hers.

She sighed. "It's still no." She spoke quietly.

Kale shrugged. "I thought so. We'll try something else."

"That sounds familiar."

"Oh now, don't be that way."

"Easy for you to say. Look what you go home to."

"Have I ever failed you?"

Laura Copperfield had her gloves coiled and gripped in one fist; with her free hand she tugged the pale leather digits one by one as if they were the petals of a flower.

"That depends on how you look at it, Bill. This wasn't supposed to go on this long. I'm supposed to be either the guardian of an incompetent or a divorcee." She looked up from her lap and fixed him steadily with her gaze. "And other things."

He glanced at the open doorway. "You have to trust me."

"No, not *have* to." She crossed her legs and looked to the wall where his glass-eyed game trophies hung as if in a state of tedious enchantment. "Maybe I'll go away, cut my losses. You seem to be happy enough, very cozy."

"Be patient."

The knobs of muscle in her temples pulsed visibly. "You were the most exciting man I'd ever met. It hurts to see you. . . . Never mind."

There was a pause, and at last he said, with a moue of disgust, "What?"

"Nothing. I can't speak my mind to a man who is afraid for people to know I'm alone with him."

"I'm not stupid, Laura. That's one thing I'm not."

"Well, I'm tired of 'safety.' I can picture you going home and sitting down by your fireplace with your pipe and slippers. It's not very dashing. I like to think of just the two of us somewhere else together, being . . ."—she smiled unhappily—"being *us*. I think I bring out the best in you."

He smiled. "Never be jealous. It gives people too much insight."

"Go to hell."

He chuckled. He reached over the desk and, without checking to see if they were being observed, patted her hand.

"Let me tell you a couple of things. I know this has been tough for you and I don't want you to think I haven't heard your complaining lately. I do have new plans.'"

"Better than the old ones, I hope."

"Well, much more . . . *definitive*, I think you could say."

She looked into her lap. They were silent a moment. Then Kale said, "You're not worrying about that, are you?"

"What?"

"A will."

"A will? No."

"Then what are you thinking?"

"I just want out of this."

"This?" Kale's gaze skimmed swiftly around the room.

"My . . . *situation*," she said. "Your big idea."

Kale grinned and stood. He held out his arms palms up, as if to encourage an audience to rise. "Who knows? Maybe sooner than you think."

She rose, but reluctantly, and stood before the desk gripping the gloves tightly in both fists.

"What will you—no, never mind." She blew out a breath. She looked at his face. "Whatever."

"Yes, *that's* it," he said. "Trust me."

"Well—" She shrugged, passed him a weak smile, then turned to go.

"The only thing is," he said, "he has to be in the parade tonight and come to the station."

"Well, yes, we were already planning on—"

"And his friend, the German woman?"

She looked at him, waiting.

"She'll stay behind, I imagine?" he asked.

"I suppose so."

"I *hope* so. We certainly wouldn't want her to go out into the street and get hurt by somebody worked up about the atrocities the Huns are committing, would we?"

She stood a moment without moving while he gazed directly at her, then, finally, she nodded. Kale looked down to his desk, and she left the office, giving the young man standing guard a radiant smile.

"Good afternoon."

"Good afternoon, ma'am," the young man returned, blushing.

At three o'clock, David walked into the parlor for his usual lessons. He sat on the bench with Anna as she played a scale on Laura's piano. Then he put his own large red hand an octave below hers in the bass to pursue her.

"David," she said after a moment. "You are gathering wool today."

Anna's profile was rounded by pouches of flesh under the jawline. A large wart stood out on her cheekbone. She raised a small hand and pointed to the music. Her nails were bitten down, and her index, middle, and little fingers displayed rings.

"I can't think today." He wanted to talk about Laura but was reluctant. He sensed that Anna and Laura didn't like each other. The night he had invited Anna to play at one of Laura's after-dinner evenings, Anna had proved the better pianist. But seeing Laura bristle, Anna had turned over the keyboard with a compliment to Laura's voice.

"You play for me."

"You mean the scale?" She was smiling.

"No."

"Ah! You mean the music that makes you think of hawks and eagles."

He nodded; perversely, she began playing scales, then abruptly stopped. "I will not play it," she chided him gently. "You must decide if you would hear the music or touch it."

He raised his huge red hands before his chest and turned the palms up. The calluses from poling the ferry had shrunk to smallish leather pads.

"I wish you could play Kiowa songs."

"Perhaps you could teach me."

"Not on a white man's piano."

"Do you want to learn to play this instrument?"

"Not today."

"Some things must be done even when the passion for them is not there, my friend."

"I'll pay."

Anna scoffed and struck a discordant cluster of notes. "Not even your money will buy you Bach, Herr Copperfield, if the artist does not want to perform. Not even torture will produce art." She smiled. "Or especially not torture." She held up a wrist spangled and festooned with bracelets that gave off a muted *chink* when she played. "The more you twist my arm, the worse the music gets, you see?"

"All right, do it to please yourself. Or me if I am lucky." Sighing, he got up and went to the window.

Behind his back, Anna played a Bach fugue, but David's pleasure in hearing the contrapuntal lines move against one another was soured by his suspicions. He stepped from the window and settled onto the chaise longue near it.

"Anna!"

She finished a line before stopping, playing to please herself. He heard a squeak as she lifted her toe from the pedal.

"What do wives want?"

Anna shrugged. "Who knows? Not yours, surely." She tapped her forehead with a finger. "She has demons, my friend. It is not what she wants. It is what they want." She smiled, proud of the insight, but he could take no comfort in it. "You are both . . . " She paused, squinting and cocking her head upward. "Without discovery? No, I mean undiscovered."

"Undiscovered?"

"History has been cruel to you. As to me." She had been stranded by the war, but he couldn't see any comparison. "It has given you this—" She waved at the room. "It has saved you from hunger and disease and war but has taken your soul, your spirit. You belong . . . where? You are . . . what is it, again?"

"I am Kiowa."

"And yet—here? A Kiowa? Where is Kiowa? You must find a new man, make him from the clay that God has abandoned, my friend. To them"—she shrugged and gestured to the streets below—"to them, your money has made you. They think if they had your money they too would be fully formed. That's what it is in America. To make this money means to complete yourself. But it is not that way, is it?" She smiled. "What do husbands want?"

"To be obeyed in all things."

Anna shrugged and turned away to resume playing, but David caught the flicker of amusement on her lips.

Was it so much to ask? The more Laura resisted him, the more truculent he became and yearned to thwart her when he could perceive what she desired. But control was not what he ultimately wanted: he wanted harmony, he wanted intimacy and affection, he wanted to halt this war without losing his self-respect. He wanted her love, and he wanted to love her.

David roused himself and vowed to keep his mind on being tutored. Inexplicably, Anna went to the door and shut it before starting the lesson, then she sat on a hassock and handed him the leather-bound volume of an English translation of Goethe's *Faust*. They had finished Book I. Faust's relationship with Gretchen had been a source of curiosity, but for the most part, David found the German poet's anguish about God and the war for the soul of Faust very . . . *white*. Anna had said, "Man must strive, man must struggle against his nature—that is the essence of Goethe." But to David, conflicts were between men; nature was a benign glue holding things together. One strived for food, clothing, for gaining glory over one's enemies. He had come to understand that at the core of every white man's mind was a dark struggle of a destructive order; inside a white man's skull was a very small stage whereupon a drama of an unharmonious universe was reenacted, and this drama supposedly documented the true state of affairs in the heavens. David had grown up believing that there could be rancor between men and tribes, but the earth and its surrounding supernatural realms were ordered and supremely serene in their workings.

David had been reading aloud from the book for only a few minutes when they heard bootsteps in the hallway.

Anna rose quickly from the hassock. "Perhaps that is enough for one day," she murmured. Frowning, she wrapped the book hastily in a shawl then stooped to slide it under the chaise longue. Perhaps the contents were unlawful for unauthorized persons to know, he thought, like the Kiowa Half-Boy medicine bundles.

"Why did you hide that book?"

She rose slowly, then sighed. "Because they are telling children that sauerkraut is 'Liberty Cabbage' now; they will not teach my language in the schools; they are telling lies about my people, that they are melting down the bodies of the dead to make glycerin for bombs, that they spear the bodies of dead babies on their bayonets." She shook her head in dismay. "With so much hatred, it is wise to be discreet. There is to be a patriotic parade tonight."

"You'll be safe here. It's my hotel."

"No one is safe anywhere," Anna said sadly. "Least of all you."

"Me?" He laughed, thinking to cajole her out of these doldrums. "I'm not an old woman quaking in her moccasins." He grinned to let her know he was teasing.

"You see the envy in their eyes, yes?"

"That is a pleasure the money buys me, Anna."

She looked at him, then with her mouth tucked tight and her large froggish eyes regarding him seriously, she drew a line across her throat with a finger. This masculine pantomime looked peculiarly incongruous acted out by a short old woman.

David left Anna and walked down to the porch where two boys were tacking a red-white-and-blue bunting onto the railing. Another was nailing a poster to the wall that showed a fetching young white girl posturing in a sailor suit. She was saying, "Gee!! I wish I were a man! I'd join the Navy!" On the bottom border, in red: "Be a man and do it!" He was pleased he could read the script so quickly. Laura always seemed curiously ambivalent about his education, even though she knew he was trying to make an acceptable husband of himself.

The boys wore filthy knickers, washed-out stockings and brogans, and the tallest had a floppy busman's hat. David's footsteps awakened a mutt sleeping on the porch. He scratched its head. *Go find my wife!* The dog rose up on its hind legs and put its paws on David's thighs.

"This your dog?" he asked the boys.

"No, sir," answered the tallest through a mouthful of tacks.

"That's too bad."

When the smallest boy turned around, the mutt trotted to him and rose to plant its paws on his chest.

"Why?" asked the tallest, suspicious.

"Because he's a talking dog."

The boys laughed nervously. The small boy backed away from the mutt so that its paws fell to the planking.

"What's he say?"

"You mean you can't hear him? He says he wants to belong to you."

The small boy scoffed. "He can't talk."

"Sure he can. He's an old-time dog. You boys were just born too late, that's all."

Their faces looked blank.

"Back in the old time everybody had ears to hear things with. All the animals had voices and everybody had ears. Trees talked too, and rocks and water."

"Crap!" the tallest boy said.

"What do you know about what it was like, then?" David eased down on the bench that stood against the wall. "My father told me about it. Back then, none of these white men's buildings were here—" His chin jerked toward the street to indicate, Kiowa style, where he meant. "No automobiles or railroads or smart little white boys walking around thinking they know everything. It was all buffalo, and they talked all the time."

A snippet of green in the corner of his eye flagged his attention. Across the street, Laura stood waiting for autos to pass so that she could walk. A parasol was cocked over her head, shading her face.

"What did they say?" asked the smallest boy while the two older boys snickered.

"They talked about everything, just as you do. And if they didn't like what they were, they could turn themselves into something else. I knew of a buffalo, for instance, that married a human woman, and he could turn himself into a man or back into a buffalo."

"That's Indian junk!" said the tallest boy.

His wife was crossing the street, her slim figure upright. The boys turned to follow his gaze. In a moment, she was stepping onto the porch, where she looked at them, folded her parasol with a deft flick of quick white hands, then used the tip as a pointer to indicate the mutt.

"That dog's been hanging about, David. Please get rid of him. He looks mangy. Some of our guests have complained that they don't enjoy sitting out here."

David smiled at her. He jerked his chin toward the small boy. "This boy will hear the dog say he wants to go home with him, any minute now."

Laura smiled dryly. "Birds of a feather, I'd say."

After she had gone through the screen door, the small boy said to him, "What about their children? Did they look like buffaloes or people?"

"Well, they had one son, a little buffalo, but he was like his father, he could take the shape of a man if he chose." The boys were still, considering this. David leaned forward, as if in confidence. There was a movement behind the screen door. "I know I look like a man to you right now, but I am the son I was speaking of. I have been the buffalo myself; I've run with them. One day a lot of us were captured and put into a place where people could look at us—"

"A zoo," said the middle-sized boy, who was blowing his nose on his shirttail.

"No, not a zoo. A field with a fence around it. I escaped by turning myself into a man. That way I can move about here without being noticed."

David looked at them intently, and with some menace; their faces showed skepticism mixed with fear. The small boy's eyes went to the screen door, where Laura stood listening. The wire mesh on the door veiled her face and dissolved the sharpness of her angular cheeks and chin.

"Have you boys finished your work?" Laura asked.

"Yes'm," said the tallest.

"Come back in an hour and I'll pay you."

The tallest one nodded, then said to his companions, "Come on, let's go see the dead soldiers," and they clambered off the porch and into the street. The small boy turned and whistled, and the mutt scrambled across the planking to follow him.

Laura came out onto the porch and stood looking after the boys.

"Well! They are a handful, aren't they!" she said with a laugh.

Her ebullience left him speechless. Smiling, Laura sat on the bench, leaving only a few inches of bare wood between David's thigh and her own. He wondered what request would follow. He had never once seen her place herself in his proximity unless it were to pursue some business. Her black shoe tapped steadily but softly against the flooring.

"Oh, David! You're going to enjoy this parade tonight!" she gushed.

She turned her head partly toward him, but her gaze remained on the street. "You're going to be one of the chief attractions, if you'll pardon an awful pun! You and I will be riding in an open motorcar *in* the parade, and all because you are the biggest buyer of Liberty Bonds in the county, David—now that's something to be proud of, and I'm certainly proud of it, too, and I'll be right there beside you!"

He peered at her face, but she was too busy looking up and down the street to return his gaze. He couldn't recall having heard so many merry-sounding words rush from her mouth in one speech, and her elation was contagious. His heart blossomed. To his surprise, he had somehow made her happy.

Just after twilight, David came down to the lobby wearing a suit and a wool topcoat. Laura was standing by the front desk listening to the Lebanese motion-picture exhibitor.

"But I've got the one with Billie Burke you've been hounding me about," the exhibitor protested. *"Eve's Daughter*. If you've asked me once, you've asked me—"

"It doesn't matter. Not tonight. I don't want this hotel in an uproar tonight. There's the parade—"

"All the better!" wailed the Lebanese. "All the people are in town—"

"No! If you want to do it, set up someplace else!"

The Lebanese removed his spectacles one earpiece at a time and blew on the lenses. Then he put them back on and shrugged. He smiled with exaggerated courtesy. "Your loss." He slammed the screen door on his way out.

Spying David, Laura said, "Don't you look dignified!" She lifted a red sash from the counter at her elbow. "Here." She unfurled the material, stood on tiptoes to toss the loop over his head, then arranged it to hang from his left shoulder. There was a yellow torch at its center over his heart. Laura clapped her palm against his sternum. "This is your badge of honor!"

Laura put on a black velvet cape and a large matching hat and they went into the street together. She slipped her arm through his elbow and his heart thumped. Already the streets were crowded with towns-people, oil-field workers, farmers, and ranchers in for the parade; vehicles choked the narrow, unpaved road between the buildings on the main street. In the growing darkness, kerosene torches made eerie orange flares, sending off curls of acrid smoke.

They passed a group of men in white robes and pointed hoods carrying torches and holding a banner that read "America First!" In the street, waiting for the parade to assemble, were knots of Salvation Army musicians; a squad of doughboys in uniform and carrying rifles with fixed bayonets; a women's church auxiliary group. They strode past a truck loaded with oil-well pipe, whose banner read "Oil For Victory!" Behind it stood a flatbed truck carrying children who waved tiny American flags.

At the rear of the parade, they reached an open motorcar. Beside it stood the stable boy clad in a long white duster and goggles. Laura got into the rear seat and saucily perched herself on the boot of the motorcar's folded top. Then she gaily patted the place beside her. "Here, David, this way we can see everybody and everybody can see us." When he was settled beside her, she produced a flask. "Here, you'll probably need something to keep off the chill while you're greeting your admirers."

David took a swig. The whiskey burned, but its pungent warmth oozed up his spine. Ahead, the band sent up a sour but happy pillow of music, then the stable boy put the car in motion.

"All you have to do," shouted Laura, "is just wave like this!" She flagged the air with her small white hands, and David imitated her. "Good! That's good!" she chirped.

They were behind the doughboys. When the soldiers appeared to the crowd on the streets, a great cheer arose, and they rode into the deafening sound. Several times the parade column bumped abruptly to a halt, and children ran from one side of the street to the other, shouting to them and the soldiers.

The parade proceeded along the road through the town's few blocks, then turned and headed south past the blacksmith shop until it stopped at the train station, and everyone coming from behind crowded into the vicinity. Minutes later, hundreds of people were milling about on the cobblestones, overflowing onto the empty track. Several boys holding torches had climbed to the roof of the station to get a better view.

Laura led David to the center of the station's platform, where wooden coffins were stacked in a large honeycomb. At the center of the noisy throng, a smaller group hovered near the coffins, hushed, some reaching forward to touch the pine boxes and weep.

Kale stood not far from Laura and David. The stationmaster and several white men in suits urged Kale up onto an empty baggage waggon, their brows earnestly knit. The crowd was surging forward, pressing closer now.

Kale climbed onto the wagon and called for quiet. He laid his hands across the rail as if upon a lectern. His gold watch chain glinted in the light as it swung. He looked over the crowd for a moment, took off his fedora, and held it over his breast. Instantly, a platoon of arms in the crowd arched up and caps vanished to disclose unkempt hair and heads slick with oil or showing bald spots.

"I guess we're all feeling pretty much the same things," Kale called out. "We're all hurt and we're all angry. I guess some of you fellows are feeling you let your country down because you weren't over there to help these boys out—I know I am."

"Tell it to Rockefeller!" cried someone, but angry shouts squelched the protest.

Kale rose on his toes. "Some of you mothers and sisters and wives and girlfriends are thinking about how you didn't want to knit that pair of socks or that sweater because you wanted to read the *Woman's Home Companion* instead. Or maybe there's been some fellow coming around in the evenings just to chat and his company is a comfort in these times. And maybe you've been putting off that letter you should have written last week, and now you're looking up here at these dead brave men and you're thinking, 'What if Joe or Bill or John dies without hearing again how much we all loved him?' "

Kale paused. Faces bowed. Men shifted their weight, hats in hands, and women drew their children nearer.

"But we can't dwell on these thoughts. These are the thoughts of the bereaved and not the thoughts of survivors who must remain strong, as strong as the men still living in the trenches and battering back the Huns! You didn't kill these men—they did! The blood of these brave boys is on their hands!"

Kale's face flushed with anger, and the crowd stirred. David felt Laura's grip tighten on his arm. The boys standing atop the station house clapped and stomped their feet.

"We have to support the boys who are still living. Let them know we're behind them! It's the boys who are still ducking the shells we have to help, we have to think of them and not about our grief and our anger! Think about it when you are warm and cozy this winter. Ask yourself, couldn't I save a little coal? After all, how warm are those trenches? How cozy is your son, your brother, or your husband? With every bite you eat, think of doing without it so that a man can fill his own belly with it!

"And Liberty Bonds! This nation needs money to finance the war, money to buy ammunition and clothing. Do it with your nickels and dimes! That Yank, Uncle Sam's pride and the flower of American youth, he's looking to us to keep him well-fed and vigorous. Wherever it's possible, friends, it must be our sacrifice and not his that brings victory! The harder we work to do our part, the fewer boys will come back in boxes like these!"

"By God!" shouted a man standing beside David, hands cupped to his mouth. "Go to Washington and tell 'em what for!"

A cheer rose, and the crowd applauded. Then Kale hushed them with a sweep of his arm.

"But that's not all, I'm afraid. Too often we've been thinking of the enemy as someone *over there*, thinking of the Huns in their helmets and their bayonets planted in the bodies of innocent children and working their will upon the bodies of our dying nurses. Well, that's the enemy our boys see. But now I'm speaking of an *invisible* enemy. . . ." His voice lowered and he leaned forward. "An enemy in disguise, a wolf in sheep's clothing, that's what I'm talking about. There are enemies right here in our midst who are killing our boys just the same as if they were in the trenches shooting at them with machine guns and killing them with poison gas!"

"Let's hang the socialists!" somebody shouted.

"I'm not talking about the slackers and socialists and the pacifists, and I'm not talking about the Bolsheviks, either, though God knows they're every bit as guilty! I'm talking about people working for a foreign nation, people whose allegiance is to the enemy!"

A silence fell for an instant, and, puzzled, several people turned to one another to murmur.

"I mean traitors!" declared Kale. He was trembling. "Right here in our town there are traitors rooting for the Huns to win the war! People who are sending messages to the Huns to let them know our weaknesses! People who are reporting our every move!"

"You know them?" shouted someone on David's right.

"We all know them," responded Kale. "All you have to do is to look around and ask who here would gain if the Yanks lose the war? Who doesn't belong? I don't have to name names or to point them out—we all know who they are!"

"String 'em up!" screamed a man clad in a white robe. The crowd roared its approval.

Laura tugged at David's elbow and pushed through the crowd until they reached the merchants surrounding Kale and congratulating him. The Baptist minister began to climb up into the wagon, but Kale reached out to stop him. "Perhaps a prayer—" the preacher said to Kale over the din of the crowd. Already people were swarming back toward the main street. "Too late!" Kale shouted into the minister's face. "Sorry."

Kale went off with other white men in suits, while David and Laura struck out for the center of town on foot. Laura's face was flushed, her lips tight. The emotional upheaval of the event was a puzzle to him—it was white men's business—and all that collective anger made him uneasy. They moved with other stragglers in the quavering orange torchlight; he heard shouts, quick footfalls of men running, vehicle horns. A single gunshot rang out above the noise, then a crash of glass. Minutes later, they saw that the window of a grocery had been smashed and the words "America First!" slashed in white paint across the front door.

At the main corner, they broke away from the crowd and walked toward the hotel. As they approached, David noticed the screen door was askew and light from the lobby fell over the porch like something spilled. Puzzled, David stepped up onto the porch, while Laura hung back, gripping his arm.

After a moment, she let him walk into the lobby alone.

The clerk was not behind the counter, and the chandelier over the lobby was swinging slightly. Puzzled, he noted a sporadic trail of white tufts like lint balls on the staircase.

"Ho!" he shouted.

Where was everyone? He took a step backward to peer into the dining room, but it was an unlighted mine of shapes and shadows, the chairs upended upon the tables by the boy who swept and mopped after closing.

"Ho!"

There was a ticking sound, like mice scurrying. He turned back to the lobby. Laura was standing beneath the chandelier, watching him, her eyes rounded, her expression curiously vacant. Her fingertips were gently caressing her lower lip, as if she had been struck there and were testing a bruise. Suddenly, he remembered Anna.

"Anna!" he shouted.

He raced up the staircase but stopped dead still when he reached the second landing. The second floor hallway was completely dark.

"Anna!" he bellowed.

"What is it? What's going on?" Laura was coming up behind him slowly, craning her head forward like a turtle.

David moved swiftly but quietly to the parlor. He stood a moment outside the closed door, listening, then swung it open and groped for the light switch.

An ax was embedded in the lid of the grand piano; the furniture was overturned, and the contents of the bureau drawers and the secretary were strewn about. A burst pillow lay on the back of the supine secretary, vomiting feathers in a long trail through the room.

"Oh!" Laura yelped at his back. "My piano!"

Anna's clothing had been taken from her room and was displayed as if laid out to dry on the furniture and fixtures. Corsets, bloomers, and petticoats were hanging or clinging to the lamps and from the valance over the window. The daybed where he had sat that afternoon reading *Faust* had been turned on end against the wall and its upholstery had been ripped. Anna's music lay everywhere, torn to pieces. Her books, piled in the center of the room, were darkly wet and smelled of ammonia.

He whirled past Laura, yelling, "Stay here!" then raced down the hallway into the room where Anna slept and snapped on the light. He was momentarily stunned by the cool order of the objects before him.

Back in the parlor, he found Laura standing in a kind of trance with a piece of paper in her hand.

"Somebody has taken her," David said.

"Yes." Laura lifted the paper for him to see. "It says that if you want to see your friend alive again, you have to bring money—there's a map." She pointed to the arrows and lines at the bottom of the page. " 'Tonight,' " she read. " 'Don't go to the sheriff or you'll be sorry. And come alone.' "

She looked up at him. She appeared to be frightened, an emotion so foreign to her features that he was struck by an unfamiliar wave of protectiveness.

She handed him the paper. The map indicated that he was to go to where his old cabin stood.

"I'm leaving now. You find the clerk, stay with him in your room." It seemed curious that the hotel was empty—where were the other guests?

She nodded absently; she seemed wholly pliable, as if drugged.

David unlocked the hotel's safe, extracted a bundle of bills—he had no idea how much was there, and the note had been strangely vague—stuffed them into saddlebags and went to the livery stable. The groom and most of the horses were missing.

Shortly later, he was riding at a trot under the light of a rising half-moon, feeling the moist breeze on the backs of his hands and insects batting at his face. The air had been still when he left, but now he could hear thunder in the distance. Strapped to his belt was a sheathed knife; he had a pistol in the saddlebags, and now he thought he should have holstered it to his hip.

After he had walked the horse through the first grove of trees off the Wetoka road near his cabin, he halted and slid to the ground. He was about to let the reins trail on the earth but remembered this was a white man's horse and instead quickly slip-knotted the leather on a low-hanging limb.

He took the pistol out of the saddlebags, slipped it into his waistband under his coat, and tossed the bags over his shoulder. He was still clad in white man's town clothing, and the tight, slick-soled shoes felt clumsy on the path. He was surprised at how quickly the path had grown strange despite his having traveled it twice daily for over three years to and from the ferry landing.

He trod carefully until he came to the clearing surrounding the charred rubble of the cabin. The stone chimney stood in the pale light; beyond it, over the trees to the east, he could discern the crow's nests of Quick's churning derricks. He hunkered in the shadows under a post oak for a few moments, watching the far edges of the clearing. He saw no unusual movement, sucked in a breath, and crept cautiously forward into the moonlight. He felt unprotected and open. Cold sweat broke over his brow and oiled his armpits. Securing the bags over his shoulder, he slid the knife from its sheath and edged the point up his cuff, the cold metal sliding against his wrist as he cupped the handle in his palm.

He walked toward the cabin, carefully scanning the clearing. When he reached the jumble of blackened timbers, he knelt with one hand on a burned portion of a porch pillar and looked about again, holding his breath to hear better.

Was this a ruse? Perhaps no one was here, had been here, or would come. Possibly, the note had been intended only to draw him away! With a shock, he conjured a picture of Laura alone at the hotel. Having tricked him away, whoever had kidnapped Anna would be free to take Laura, perhaps as punishment because she had married a Kiowa.

He was about to rise and hurry back to the horse when he noticed the strangely dappled mound in the yawning mouth of the fireplace. He stared at it for a moment, bewildered. There was a rounded hump like a large smooth boulder coated in shadows, flecked with white.

He rose and picked his way across the knee-high interstices of charred joists and broken flooring. The going was clumsy, like wading through swift water, but after a moment he realized that the rounded hump on the crumbling fireplace hearth was human. Then, seconds later, the hump became familiar. Anna was nude; the sags and folds of her flesh were basted with tar except for a patch on her buttock. Feathers stuck to the tar. Her face was skyward; she was not moving. He groaned and slammed his fist against the stone. This was his responsibility; she had asked him to keep her safe. And he had thought her fear was unfounded!

When he slipped his hand under her head to move her, she moaned softly. He bent close and put his ear to her breasts. She was breathing, but only very faintly, and her heart was barely audible.

He bent to scoop her up, but a noise altered him. He looked up, alarmed. Two men were looming over him from behind, standing on the floor joists. They wore white robes and hoods with eyeholes. One was almost within arm's reach; under the hem of his robe, David could see city-style trousers, but the man was wearing boots. The other, standing just behind the first, had a pistol with a very long barrel trained on David.

"Looks like you're a little late, but we'll be taking *that* anyway," said the one closest.

His voice was faintly familiar. He gestured toward the saddlebags tossed over David's shoulder. The other man cocked the hammer of the pistol, aimed it at David's head, and when David saw the back of the gun hand tighten, he sprang and flung the saddlebags into the man's face, flipped the knife from his cuff, and had it buried in the first man's thigh before he could back-pedal across the joists. The gunman fell backward, knocked by the saddlebags, and the hooded figure scrambled up from the ground, his hood twisted about his head so that the two eyeholes showed two shocks of black hair.

With his own pistol in hand, David vaulted over the joists to reach the man who was now tearing frantically at his hood while clutching his weapon. The man stumbled, pitched forward, and tore the hood off just as David leveled his pistol at him and yanked the trigger. The round went wide, and the man dived behind the fireplace chimney before David could identify him or shoot again. Seconds later, the man's pistol barrel winked in the bony light and two quick rounds splintered the joists near David's waist. He ducked out of sight, heard quick footfalls on the earth, then looked up to see the man running into the dark line of trees. He sprang up, aimed, and sent three wild rounds whistling into the undergrowth where the man vanished.

He crouched and waited, listening for thrashing in the woods. He heard nothing for a while, and his pulse gradually returned to a swift steady throb. He smelled tar; he reached over to put his hand on Anna's brow. Her skin was black and sticky, with small cottony tufts adhering to the pitch.

Then a stone near his feet exploded into dust and he heard the pistol shot. He jumped clear of the charred flooring, then ran from the cabin, zigging and zagging through the clearing and back to the path. As he darted away, two more shots rang out, one plucking at his jacket sleeve lightly, like a thorn snagging it.

He dived into the woods, rolled onto the ground, and lay prone with his chest heaving and his arms trembling. He peered back at the cabin, propping his pistol barrel on a rock to steady it. Unexpectedly, the man he had stabbed suddenly rose from behind the chimney, his hood gone, and, clutching his thigh, stumbled off toward the trees. David fired too quickly and the shot went harmlessly wide, but it scared the man for a moment, and he lurched about once before continuing to flee. Moonlight showed a ragged gash upon his cheek.

David waited quietly for a few moments, impatient to retrieve Anna. Finally, from far in the woods on the other side of the clearing came the muted chock of hooves on stone, and he guessed his assailants had decided against coming for the saddlebags.

He rode his horse back down the path into the clearing and up to the cabin, where he dismounted, wrapped his coat around Anna, then draped her over the horse's back. The additional weight made the old mare plod slowly back to Wetoka, though David tried to hurry her. The slow clop of hooves counterpointed his seething fury with himself for not having protected Anna better. Shingle's connection with Laura made him fear that she was in danger also—on the wedding trip the white hired driver had apparently nursed a burning hatred for the mixed-race marriage he had been paid to witness.

He reached Wetoka after midnight. The streets were quiet. In an alley, two drunken oil-field workers seated on the ground stared as he passed with the burden on the horse's back. He went to Hartzler's tent, roused the doctor, then carried Anna inside. She was still alive, said Hartzler, but she had been severely beaten.

Anxious about Laura, David hurried to the hotel. Lights were blazing in every window downstairs. The front door, usually locked for the night, opened without his key. The night clerk was still absent. He was torn between racing up the stairs to see if his wife had been harmed and making a surreptitious entry as a guarantee against another ambush. His assailants might have ridden straight back to town and could be waiting, perhaps holding Laura hostage.

In the lobby, he removed his shoes. He slipped the pistol out of his waistband and went quietly up the stairs. The wall lamp in the hall was still lighted; he moved to Laura's door, took the knob firmly in his grasp, held up the pistol, shouldered his way into the room.

Laura was standing beside the bed with a bundle of clothing bunched in her arms. When he burst in, she screamed and dropped the clothing onto the bed.

"My God!" she wailed. "You're here!"

He was so relieved she was safe that he took her into his arms. She held back a moment then pressed her body into his.

She was trembling.

"Anna's badly hurt. There were two men wearing robes and hoods waiting for me. They would have shot me, but I wounded one. It was that man you hired to drive us to get married."

Laura stiffened. After a moment, she pulled away from him and paced the room. She pointed to the valise on the bed.

"I was so scared, David, I was going to go spend the night somewhere else."

"You don't have to worry about it now. I'll watch out for you much better than I did for my friend. Something like that will never happen again." He pointed with the muzzle of the pistol toward the street. "I know now that some people might hate what we've done enough to harm you. If you ever see the man with the scar again, you let me know."

She eased down onto the bed, lips quivering, rubbing her palms together and wedging them between her thighs. After a moment, she seemed calm, even coldly angry.

"David, we have to do something. People are going to think wrong things about this! We have to get out of here!"

"Why? What wrong things?"

"Don't you see? Somebody wants *me* to be blamed for what happened! The man, Shingle!—they would know you had seen him before!"

She bent over and covered her face, breathing hoarsely and unevenly. When he moved to her and touched her shoulder, she opened her palms and peered at them with thunderstruck horror, as if her face had melted into her hands.

"David, take me away from here! Tonight! Somebody might try to do something to us, too!"

"We don't have to run away."

She bolted up from the bed and burrowed her face into his chest, clasping his torso tightly. She looked up at him; he had never seen anything in her face before that even remotely approximated this pleading expression.

"Please take me away from here and I'll be whatever kind of wife you want me to be!"

#

Vera and Rose and Iola walked arm-in-arm in the streets of Koblenz, bumping shoulders with doughboys who wolf-whistled and yakked at them. On this first night in garrison after marching to the Rhine, the Yanks were busy spending back pay on postcards, ice cream, wine, and war souvenirs hawked by jocular Germans. On doors of shops hung Christmas wreaths and in the windows candles cast a glow on furs and jewelry being sold by merchants unharmed by the war.

They were drawn into a café by their hunger and the sound of an orchestra sawing at a waltz. It was crowded; in the tiny foyer stood a hall tree festooned with a crazy mix of coats and caps of German blue and gray and American olive drab.

Cigar smoke hovered like blue gas over the crowded room. The women were given a table near the orchestra of portly, red-faced musicians decked out in tuxedos shiny with age. Koblenz girls passed among the tables selling cigarettes, candy, and matches to the Germans and Yanks alike, while officers of the warring armies sat within arm's reach and studiously ignored each other.

The three women ordered sauerbraten and noodles and a Rhine wine, then Vera and Rose began whispering about a blond German at a nearby table. The lad's gray uniform was frayed and tattered at its hems, but he still looked too beef-fed to suit Iola. He leered at Vera and cocked the lid of his stein back and forth with his thumb in an oily innuendo.

"What's he look like?" whispered Vera to Rose. Before they had gone out, Vera had removed her spectacles and let her red hair down so it fell about her shoulders; Rose, who had been drinking schnapps all afternoon, was Vera's seeing-eye companion.

"Drunk," snorted Rose. "Skull and crossbones." She and Vera snickered. To ease the pain of rejection, Vera smiled over her shoulder, her fuzzy brown eyes aimed vaguely in the youth's vicinity. Vera was giddy with expectation and the freedom from months of bandaging bloody soldiers. But to Iola, it was as if a giant fist had grasped her, shaken her hard, then dropped her, and she was still trembling from it.

Vera chattered nonstop until their food arrived. Looking down at the plate of sauerbraten, Iola felt nauseated. She picked up a chunk of dark bread and spread a pat of butter on it with the hefty, clean silver. Luxuries. They seemed oddly obscene. She nibbled from the bread, then set it down and replaced the utensils on her plate. Rose was ignoring her own food; she had refilled her wineglass and was lighting a Fatima with trembling hands cupped around a match. She flung her right arm over the back of her chair, which pulled her blouse tightly across her breasts. Her fingernails went tick-tick-tick against her wineglass.

"You know what I need?" Rose's lips set in a seesaw grin. "I need some fellow to lie between my legs and push real hard. "Then when he's got his pants buttoned back up, I'd slug him in the jaw!"

"Rose!" Vera giggled.

Rose leaned toward them. Her hand was shaking so badly she had to set her wineglass on the table instead of drinking from it. "You know what I wish? I wish the war was still on, right now, right in this room!"

Vera was startled, but Iola reached across the table and squeezed Rose's shaking fingers gently.

"Eat something," she urged. She tried to give the suggestion a professional edge; with her white companions, she steeled herself against surrendering to her compassion.

Rose withdrew her fingers and pressed them to her eyes. She took in a large breath, held it for a moment, then sighed. "But it's *Christmas!*"

A man shaped like an upright potato and clad in a dark blue suit was strolling among the customers. A medal on his lapel swung out as he leaned over to clap two German officers' backs simultaneously. He passed by a table of Yanks, hailed them merrily, then he was beside the three women.

"Ah, American ladies! On behalf of Koblenz I greet you! You are from Minnesota, perhaps? I have two cousins there."

Rose snorted. "In Minnesota? You've got to be pulling my leg!"

"Pulling the lady's leg?"

"Making a joke."

"Ah! A joke! I see."

Rose blew smoke into his face. The show of hostility gratified Iola, but the man assumed an ambassadorial loftiness. Vera squinted myopically as if he were a high-flying dirigible. Just when Iola thought the awkward silence might drive him off, he pointed to Rose's untouched sauerbraten.

"The food is not good? I will see the cook and—"

"I'm not hungry," said Rose. "It's the war."

"Ah!" His features fell into a semblance of decorum. "Vell, no more var! The Kaiser made many mistakes—the *Lusitania*, eh? So he loses the var." He smiled sheepishly and shrugged, as if the war had been a faux pas. "All good democrats now, like the Americans!"

"*Scheisskopf!*" Rose muttered.

The man only shrugged and moved to another table.

"What's the matter with you?" asked Vera. "He was just being friendly."

"I want to go home." Rose closed her eyes. " 'The stockings are hung from the chimney with care, in hopes that St. Nicholas soon will be there. The children are nestled all snug in their beds . . . ' " She looked up at Vera. "I'm tired of war and I'm afraid of peace."

"What are you talking about?" Vera said with dismay.

"Nonsense," said Rose. "Don't mind me. It's just my curse." She turned to Iola. "What are you doing after the war, dear? Are you doing anything after the war?"

"I'm going to get my old job back at Kress's," said Vera. "Until some man takes me away from all that. No more nursing."

They left the café and walked the crowded streets for a while; Iola couldn't shake the picture of the man at the table. *Like the Americans.* His voice kept sliding into her consciousness. Being in the café had once again confirmed her suspicion that the war had been a cruel game between tribes of white men, the object of which was obscure and the rules confusing. As the Third Army had convoyed across the stone bridge over the Moselle into Germany, everyone had been puzzled by the absence of hostility. Through the fall, Iola had heard the troops chant, "Then by damn! We'll all go to Germany, and God help Kaiser Bill!" They had expected hand-to-hand combat all the way to Berlin or to occupy a sulky nation of whipped civilians smoldering with anger.

As the convoys wound into hills of forest turned maroon for the coming winter, Iola had looked down into the valley matted with green winter wheat and dotted here and there with tidy houses painted blue or white. Not a single shellhole pocked the fields—the Kaiser had surrendered before the war had come to Germany. Well-shod farmers stood in their pastures and waved as the Americans passed. On the outskirts of Trier, the road crawled with German children wearing army caps and shouting fearlessly as they bartered for chocolate or sold iron crosses. Their clothing showed only the usual wear from work and play, and their faces were unmarked by the passive resignation that flattened the expressions of French children in the war zones. Citizens greeted the Yanks from doorways as they entered town. It was as if the conquering army were only passing through their terrain to a distant battle: the war was not their business, but they'd offer polite encouragement.

To Iola, this behavior made ragtag, macabre scarecrows of all the corpses; the dead were like unfortunate bystanders to a prank played by the survivors on both sides for one another's amusement. Where was the purpose of all this bloodshed? A Kiowa would not do battle unless the way he fought would bring him honor. Where was the honor in filthy trench warfare, machine guns, and mustard gas? What were the spoils? The Germans had lost but had wound up with all the butter and coffee, sugar and mutton and potatoes.

She and Vera and Rose passed by the Kino, where troops were lined up to see Charlie Chaplin in *The Tramp* and *Easy Street*, standing butt-to-belly with Koblenz burghers who placidly accepted their presence. Vera wanted to see a Chaplin show; Rose agreed to accompany her, though how Vera was going to see without spectacles nobody knew. Iola's melancholy had deepened until she was no longer fit company, she felt, so she left them at the Kino and walked alone to their hotel.

Mail had been slipped under their door. One envelope from AEF headquarters in Paris was addressed to Mrs. John Conway. She peeled it open with dread. Conway's CO, the obligatory follow-up to the death notice. He had obviously forgotten the circumstances under which Sargeant Conway had died: he addressed the surviving wife as if she were knitting stockings by a fireside in Perth Amboy and spoke vaguely of Conway's "bravery" and "courage" without providing examples. Iola knew more about her husband's death than did the officer assigned to console her.

Other letters, months old, were from Alice and her father. She didn't feel strong enough to endure the homesickness they would set off, but after a moment, she opened her father's letter. His childlike cursive evoked images of his handsome face over the white man's collar, the knot of his necktie, the suitcoat, his raven-black hair he wore cut close to his ears. Rubbing the pine pulpit with linseed oil at the church, hoeing the cemetery grounds adjacent to the mission, planting and tending the flower beds. He taught little Kiowas their psalms in Kiowa.

The garden was good this year—he was writing in September—and they had enjoyed melons and squash and corn and beans, potatoes, and unusually strong summer rains had made the pastures fit for grazing. He hoped she was well. Several persons asked about her often, among them a distant cousin, a young man who had recently finished college. (This was loaded information, she knew—apparently her father had not received the news of her marriage when he had written this letter.)

It was hard for him to say anything personal, but his character rose from the cheap paper and his unpracticed penmanship. His thick way with white words brought a rush of intimate kinship into her breast.

Her mother, he wrote, wishes she could hug and kiss her and brush out her hair for her.

Love washed over her. Her mother holding her in her lap while they sat on the back stoop, her mother's scarred forearms about her waist, her mother's hands passing over her body to protect her during a storm.

Her mother was not tormented by anything that occurred beyond the reach of her family. If Iola had remained a Kiowa woman like her mother, such happiness might have been possible for her, too.

In the beveled mirror above the dresser she saw a moon-faced Indian woman clad in a long brown wool skirt, her coat open to reveal the white blouse and dark brown army necktie. Topping her black hair was a brown garrison cap. Iola tossed the cap onto the bed, then unpinned her hair and let it tumble to her shoulders. With her hair down, she felt less like she belonged to the United States government, but still not enough like a Kiowa.

She fingered the remaining letter. Alice pretended nothing was wrong between them, and Iola had yet to say, "You bent my life the wrong way!" or "You hated the Indian in me and tried to make me someone else!" She couldn't be candid without causing pain or appearing to be ungrateful for Alice's efforts.

She blamed Alice for her being here on this alien continent of damp stone and brooding mists, cut off from her own people. She blamed the Alices for Morris's death. How could she tell Alice that Morris had died so that whites could practice their avarice and treachery on the colored peoples of the globe without interference? Like the Americans. Everybody's friends again. The Germans had made the mistake of drawing their fellow white men into war, but now that the misunderstanding had been resolved, the parties could go hand in hand about the business of carving up the world between themselves.

They were much better at killing than at healing, she thought now, holding the letter. How could she tell Alice that the medicine Alice was so eager for her to learn was just the skeleton of an umbrella raised against a torrent of death? Before coming she had had some faith in the skills of white medicine men—even Hartzler could set a bone and suture a cut—but now she believed their knowledge was scant and their techniques absurdly inadequate. Humans were thin-skinned bags of blood and crap, and it didn't take much of a rip to spill what little heat and light had been held inside from birth.

Answering Alice's letters these past months, Iola, too, had pretended not to be angry, which had produced a cool, constricted trickle of mundane information in which the struggles of her heart had been conspicuously absent. She had announced her marriage in a single sentence not in the hopes that Alice would be pleased—and if she knew the circumstances she could not have been—but so that Alice would inform David, and David would . . . would what? Tear his hair out? Shrug?

The letter said: Alice had been praying for her safe return daily; Alice had moved to Oklahoma City, where she worked for the Oklahoma Education Commission upgrading schools across the state. Tom Quick sent his regards. (Seeing the name intensified Iola's bitterness: he had stayed behind while Morris had come and died.)

As Iola moved through the letter, she identified the rest of its contents (crops, weather, Alice's work) as elements of the conspiracy of "good news only" that both those at war and at home had been encouraged to perpetrate to bolster one another's morale. Her father practiced the same deceit, though he had felt obliged to tell her months ago of her grandfather's death.

Nearing the letter's end, she was disheartened by the absence of David's name. Alice's silence made her heart tremble; if Alice was constrained by the war's unwritten rule, silence meant bad news.

Where was David? She had been in love with him, but now that love seemed pale and remote.

All she could feel were anger and self-pity. The anger was a trifle limp from overuse, but serviceable nonetheless to keep her at a distance from others. Since the end of the war in November, it had receded to a peat-bog fire in her heart, showing itself in comments her companions called cynical or melancholy. The anger never broke into flame, where it might have burned itself out, and yet it left no fuel for anything else.

She sobbed once, a small quick explosion like a sneeze, then clenched her jaw closed and ground her knuckles against her eyes. She sat frozen, waiting for the sadness to pass. Then she heard Rose and Vera clumping down the hallway. One seemed to be crying, the other complaining. She resented the intrusion, so she darted up from the window, stripped to her long woolen underwear, and slid under the comforter on the bed. She intended to feign sleep; however, they were making such a racket that she would have to feign being awakened. For an instant, she longed to tell them what troubled her. Although she had known them only a month, a month was a long time in these circumstances, and they were closer to her than anyone on the Continent, these two young women, nurses and Americans and unattached—*unmanned* was Rose's term for it—like herself. Except that they were white.

Rose was hanging onto the door as it swung open, then she staggered a few steps into the room.

Vera walked in behind her and threw her hat onto her cot.

"She's drunk!" Vera declared. "We had to leave the picture, she was carrying on so. Be glad you weren't there—the things she said to the fellows on the street!"

Rose fell onto the end of her cot and lay still on her back; she pressed her slim hands to her face and after a moment her shoulders shook.

"Really!" Vera began hanging the clothes she was removing in their shared armoire. "It was embarrassing."

Rose rolled over and managed to shrug out of her coat. She tugged the covers back from her pillow, pried off her shoes with her toes, then pulled the blankets over her head. Iola thought Rose had passed out until she heard, moments later, after Vera had turned out the lamp, choked-back sobs. Finally, Rose broke down, mewling angrily, as if she hated herself for surrendering to her sorrow.

Iola's heart turned over at the sound. She wanted to coax Rose under the comforter and hold her close. But if she moved a single muscle she might explode into sobs herself, then they'd know how she felt. Yes, Rose was also lonely and miserable and tired and afraid of the future, but the gulf between their beds was more than the distance between persons, it was between cultures, and she ached that things should be so. She finally had to do as Vera did—roll over, her back to Rose, and wrap her pillow about her head.

In April of 1919, Rose and Iola mustered out in Paris. Rose intended to take a slow way home and tour whatever part of Europe had not been damaged. But it wasn't a desire to be a tourist that kept Iola in France; it was, rather, that she had no idea of what to do should she go back to America. Her father would expect her to pursue a goal set by Alice or to marry and bear children.

She quelled her intense homesickness by pitching herself into the life of postwar Paris. She and Rose shared a flat on the quiet back side of

Montmartre, behind the Sacré Coeur, overlooking vineyards and vegetable gardens; they pooled their funds and went out to cafés together, but soon Rose went on to Italy. Iola lived on savings supplemented by her earnings as a model for a Hungarian painter. He admired her darkness, he said, she looked "tropical" (he worshiped Gauguin). Thus she briefly became part of the bohemian circle that frequented the cafés around Place du Tertre. Here no one knew her as a war widow. Viktor, a melancholy romantic whose real talent was for theatrics and not painting, threatened to leap off the Pont Neuf if she wouldn't return his love. She believed he would do it. People said he had done it before. He was an excellent swimmer. She was not particularly touched by his infatuation, but it helped her feel she belonged somewhere.

She stayed in Paris over the winter of 1919, but in early spring her father wrote that her mother had been ill. He was maddeningly laconic, with too few details for her to make a diagnosis. It could have been a sore throat or Spanish influenza. She decided to return, having grown increasingly aware that she was only marking time. And although she might have been able to blame Alice for her coming to Europe (and even that had begun to seem too simple), she had no one to blame for refusing to return home.

Viktor said, "If you leave, I will die. Before I do, grant me one night of bliss."

She found it hard to keep a straight face. She was wearing a huge gray cable-knit cardigan that came to her knees; under it, she was nude. They were resting between sessions, she drinking very hot coffee with milk and three teaspoons of sugar. The studio was cold, but the sweater and the coffee made a nice contrast. She would miss his silliness.

"Do you really love me more than all the others?"

He cocked his head, sighed, gave her a mournful look. He had black springy curls that bounced over girlish eyes.

"No," he said.

Iola laughed.

"But you are the most beautiful."

Not because she wanted to make a "gift" of herself but because she was bored with being a virgin and hated to leave Europe as one, she let Viktor make love to her. Later she would not think of it as either a pleasant or unpleasant experience; she had been neither aroused nor uncomfortable. She was happy to have made the passage from virgin to woman without much fuss, though on the ship home she had more time than she wished to consider precisely how she had dreamed she would lose her virginity and who might have had it.

On the west-bound train out of New York, Iola recalled the trip of thirteen years past, with the buffalo, when she sat on the freight car watching the cities and countryside sliding by and being pelted by butterflies. And David. She forced herself to be realistic, realizing that her plan to hurt David with the news of her marriage might have been the very reason he did not leave his wife. Even if he were unhappy in his marriage, hearing Iola was married might have simply made him give up hope of having her.

Suddenly, she was wild with eagerness to get home and find out what had happened to him, and she cursed herself for having stayed in Paris.

Her parents, overjoyed, met her at the station in Chickasha, her mother clad in her Kiowa best, her father looking like a preacher. They all cried for a bit with great gusto as if it were a form of exercise, then they got into the wagon for a few hours' ride home to Anadarko. Her father talked, catching her up on tribal news; she listened for David's name but never heard it and couldn't bring herself to ask about him.

They rolled slowly along a road that had been churned into a reddish goo by spring torrents. Streams had run red with silt and were over their banks; the willows were budding, and the sun came fitfully between ragged patches of storm cloud to warm the sprouts of lime-green grass cropping in the pastures. They had to cross several creeks in which the water came over the hubs of the wheels. The molasses-slow motion of the wagon made her restless, but by the time they reached home in early evening, she had been lulled into a rhythm of patience. Here there were no clocks, no schedules.

Her mother had prepared a cot for her in the front room of the house —they had been using her old room to store barrels of missionary clothing before they were shipped off—and she went to bed early, worn out from the train and wagon rides. She woke to the smell of coffee. On the porch she stood in her flannel shift and soaked up buttery morning light. The sky was confettied with birds, from the juncos hovering about the mesquites near the house to the buzzards spiraling in a thermal over a ridge a mile away. The air smelled of damp earth and wood. The quiet was broken only by a barely audible hum of creatures, and she was suddenly aware of how *noisy* Paris had been.

She was Kiowa again. If she pressed her ear to the ground, she was certain it would speak Saynday stories to her. If she cocked her ear to the wind, it would sing.

Hearing her mother moving about the kitchen, Iola went inside the parlor. Her underclothing lay neatly stacked on a chair. Girdle, underpants, brassiere, bloomers, slips, stockings: what nonsense! She found one of her mother's plain cotton shifts in a trunk and slipped it on without bothering with undergarments. She passed through the empty kitchen and stepped into the back-yard. There had apparently been a shower during the night, for when she took a few steps toward where her mother was sitting, the red mud oozed up between her toes, gooey and soothing.

Her mother was skinning a rabbit. She sat on a stump with a board across her lap, and on another plank nearby were two rabbits already skinned and washed.

Her mother looked young in the strong light, happy. Her glossy black hair was pulled tight about her head and braided into a single long rope down her back, with a streak of gray running through it. Her mother's face was wider, more aboriginal, than her own, the nose broad and flat. Here, Viktor! she thought. Here's your model.

You slept well?

Yes, thank you. I hope you don't mind if I wear your dress.

Her mother beamed. *It is yours now.*

Iola sat cross-legged on the ground with a gunnysack beneath her and observed with fascination as her mother made skillful slits with a knife on the rabbit's body then peeled away the fur and skin in one piece.

Mother, are you feeling well these days?

Yes, daughter.

And Father?

He got much older while you were at the war. It's a bad thing when the daughters go to war and the fathers stay behind.

Was he ashamed?

Worried, mostly.

But I'm home now.

Her mother nodded. *I wish all the young people would come back.*

They sat in a comfortable silence in the sun. It seemed to Iola that she was thawing, like the earth itself. After a moment, she went inside and returned with a hairbrush. Her hair had been pinned up in coils since she left New York on the train. From the shortish style of a wartime nurse, she had, in Paris, let her hair grow, so that uncoiled it fell in a fan to the middle of her back.

Her mother butchered the game into many more portions than the family could eat.

Why so much food?

Her mother grinned, and her eyes twinkled.

Your father has a surprise.

She was suddenly aware of his absence. The food, a "surprise": it all spelled visitors for dinner, in her honor. Her heart sank. She didn't feel like being in public, not today, not after such a fine morning.

Who is coming?

It took her mother a while to answer, then, obviously breaking a promise, she said, happily, *Your teacher. She and a man are coming to see you. Your father, he went to Anadarko to show them the way.*

Thank you for telling me.

She hurried through the kitchen and into the front room, where she pitched the hairbrush onto her rumpled bed covers. She dropped heavily to the cot for a moment, then jumped up, too agitated to sit.

Her father probably imagined that she would be happy to see Alice, but he was mistaken. Seeing her would require suiting up in emotional armor. Iola felt like a recuperating patient whose newly won strength shouldn't be put to a strenuous test.

A "man" was with Alice? Her curiosity increased the burden of dread: it might be Tom Quick, whom she also had no desire to see. If not Tom Quick, then some stranger (Alice's beau?) whom Alice and her father would expect her to impress with her skills at acting white.

They would naturally expect her to be properly attired—shoes, corset, the entire panoply. Here, on her first day back, being put on display as a trophy! She wouldn't do it. She would greet them as she was.

A half hour later, thinking of her father's embarrassment, she dug out her clothes, removed the shift, and had climbed into the bloomers and corset before thinking: What if the "man" was David? How would she want to appear to him?

So she changed again.

She offered to help her mother, but her mother insisted on treating her as a guest. She walked away from the house and into a thicket of wild flowering plum trees, where, hidden, she wept a moment with fists clenched.

She heard the jangle of harness from the road and the chug of an auto's engine but stayed hidden. After a moment, her father, Alice, and "the man" were coming out the back door, obviously searching for her.

The "man" was not Tom Quick; nor was he David. A stranger, he had the unmistakable stamp of the rural Protestant ecclesiastic—khaki trousers, a white shirt buttoned at the neck and a dark woolen frock coat, a hat with a rounded brim and a short, flat crown. Iola groaned. Fresh-faced, in his mid-twenties. Spectacles.

"Iola?" her father called.

Sighing, she stepped out of the thicket and walked toward them, hopping over puddles and raising the hem of her mother's shift like any white matron. She fixed her lips into a smile.

Alice was rushing forward heedless of the red mud, beaming with delight, arms outstretched. She had lost weight, Iola noted, and she realized at once that Alice was younger than she had once thought. Alice was a peer now, no more "adult" than she.

Alice clutched her in a bone-bending hug, which she halfheartedly returned.

"Oh, child!" she gushed. "How grown-up you look! I've missed you terribly."

"It's good to be here."

If Alice was upset by Iola's going "back to the blanket," she held her tongue. Iola hoped that her appearance would reveal her present state of mind and heart. Her father, however, was clearly uncomfortable about it, and the stranger appeared to be taken aback.

Alice introduced him as the Reverend Youngblood, now at Chickasha. He said he was newly arrived from North Carolina and had offered to drive Alice here to get a feel for the country and the people.

"And of course I've heard so much about you from your teacher! I do hope you will tell us of your work overseas!" His professional heartiness only thinly disguised his skepticism.

Her father led them into the front room, where he placed four unmatching chairs into a quadrant around an invisible table. When they sat, their knees almost touched, and they had to plant their feet under their chairs to keep from knocking each other in the shins. As the only person without shoes, Iola felt crude, and her embarrassment itself increased her resentment.

Rather than remain a quiet, tactful newcomer, the Reverend Youngblood repeated his desire to hear about Iola's "work."

The special, sanctimonious lilt to "work," equated it with some holy mission which Iola might have endured with the grace of a martyr. Did he think Iola had been a missionary in France? Did he confuse repairing bodies with saving souls? The Red Cross often perpetuated this confusion by depicting nurses as angels.

She offered a vague comment about her daily duties, making herself sound more like a serving girl than a medical functionary.

"I understand you suffered the loss of your husband there." The reverend had arranged his features into a lugubrious expression; it might have been something he had learned to do at seminary when in doubt, and Iola could tell he had been saving the condolence for insertion at the earliest opportunity.

She nodded, then shot a glance at her father. Apparently he had told Alice this information, and she had relayed it to this garrulous stranger!

"The Conway lad was a member of your tribe here?"

She suppressed a laugh. His presumption that the "lad" was a Kiowa her age not only amused her, it fueled a bitter mischief.

"No, he was a Philadelphia Conway." Her father looked at her. He was hanging on to her every word. She had never told him more than that she was married to a soldier named Conway and that he had died.

Iola smiled. "The Conways belong to an old tribe of bankers and railroad magnates."

The reverend continued to smile, his head bobbing. She wasn't certain he believed her. Her father did, but looked astonished, and her conscience pricked her for having told him so little.

"As you might guess, he was a black sheep," she went on. She could spin out quite a tale if she desired, and they would have to pretend to believe it. "It was said that the great-great grandfather had lusted after a few Mohawks in his day, but not a single Conway had ever done something so audacious as to *marry* an Indian."

Alice chuckled nervously. The reverend's brows rose slightly. Iola gave Alice a narrow look of reproach for having been the agent of Youngblood's presence, at which Alice looked away sheepishly.

"I see," the reverend said quietly. He had the look of a scolded puppy.

A pall of silence draped them. Her father looked as if he regretted having orchestrated this event, and Alice shuffled her feet. In a fashionable brown wool suit and with her lost weight and seemingly renewed youth, Alice looked as much a stranger as her companion. Still, catching Alice's lively eyes, Iola felt the old bond.

To fill the void, Alice asked, "Do you have any plans for the future?"

"No."

Another silence. The reverend twitched. "Sister Roberts and I," he said, "were wondering if you would consider staying here and helping us translate the Word of the Lord into the tongue of your people." He glanced at Alice, revealing his misgivings.

"The church will pay, of course," he added.

"It would be cheaper for the church if you learned Kiowa and did it yourself."

"Yes, that's certainly true!" the man said enthusiastically, with an innocent air. "It's one of my ambitions. But it might take time, and, well . . . perhaps you could tutor me while you work."

"I can't do it because I don't believe in it."

"You mean you think your people should learn the Bible in English?"

"No, I meant that I don't believe in the words of the Christian Bible."

Her father involuntarily grunted in surprise. She had forgotten him in this tug-of-war, and she remembered too late that she had not yet told him of her loss of faith during the war. He bolted up from his chair and left the room, murmuring an apology for his exit. Alice looked uncomfortable but not shocked.

"I see," said the reverend blandly. He might have been reacting to a mere technical difficulty, as if she had told him she couldn't make it on Mondays because her father needed the wagon.

"You have converted to another faith?" Alice asked quietly. She sounded faintly hopeful.

"Not yet. I'm looking."

"You make it sound like choosing pastry." Alice smiled wryly, and suddenly she seemed more familiar, but Iola also felt irritated at being patronized.

"Perhaps it is."

"How can you live without believing in something?"

Hearing a plaintive note, Iola softened her answer. "As easily or as hard as you can living a lie."

Alice nodded. "And the Lord Jesus Christ did not die for your sins?"

"That's not an idea that I can understand at all."

Alice grinned. "Let me explain it to you again."

"You know that I'm familiar with the catechism. It doesn't matter. The agony I saw in those hospitals could never be paid for by a man who knew he was immortal."

"But men make men suffer, not God."

"Why should I worship a scheme of things in which God will not intervene to prevent the suffering of the innocent?" Iola said. But then she added, "Oh, I know what your answer is, Alice!"

"Because the suffering of the innocent is proof of the freedom God gave man to choose between good and evil!" Alice piped in, grinning. For an instant, the reverend almost vanished and they were teacher and pupil again sharing the room in Wetoka.

"I suppose you've become a Darwinist," said Alice. "You consider the story of the Fall a fairy tale?"

"I don't think about it much any more. In France, it seemed very remote."

The reverend stirred. "But wouldn't such a story be extremely timely under those conditions? And what about all those letters we read throughout the war, boys writing home thanking God for having survived and testifying as to how the experience rekindled their faith?"

"Who would publish anything to the contrary?" Iola asked wearily.

This had apparently never occurred to him, and Iola could see his mind turning on the notion that a grand malign conspiracy might emerge from the murk of the war. Pondering her comment, he looked like an earnest seminary student. Alice smiled merrily, Iola cracked a grin. Sparring had been fun. Her father's wrath notwithstanding, Iola felt lighthearted all at once, the dread of this visit dissipated now that she had declared herself.

She led Alice along the beaten path to the outhouse and waited a distance away for her to return. Then they walked slowly side by side back toward the yard.

"You don't like my friend."

"No."

"I don't either, really."

"I thought maybe he was a beau."

Alice gave a short laugh. "No, he was only a professional obligation who had an automobile. And I can't say that I find your presumption particularly flattering!"

Iola, stung, wanted to say, Why not him—didn't you have a soft spot for the likes of Tom Quick?

After a moment, Alice said, "And I have the feeling you don't like me, either."

Iola stopped walking. They were standing under the chinaberry tree near the wagon, and she reached up to pull down a handful of the hard green berries, which she palmed and gripped in her fist. Alice peered at her with frank intensity.

"It's natural, you know," said Alice, "that pupils who once looked up to a teacher should come to feel, well, *overly influenced* is one way you could put it. They have to separate themselves, cut themselves away."

Iola was annoyed to have Alice belittle her turmoil by making it a mere example of a principle.

"That doesn't make me less angry. When I was in France there were times when I blamed you for my being there—you made such a good little citizen out of me."

"You went to France because David Copperfield married that woman."

Iola had an impulse to deny it, but any attempt to refute something so obvious seemed foolish. "Yes, that too," she said. A moment had arrived when she might ask about David, but Alice spoke before she could gather the right words.

"This may surprise you, but I don't believe a good many of the things I once taught, either. I'm not a stone, I change. I know what you were trying to say to me in there, and all I can tell you is that I've come to be sick of the wrathful Old Testament religion; I'm tired of the idea that religion is only Commandments."

Iola was genuinely surprised. "What now?"

Alice shrugged. "I don't know. But this is why I'm working for the state of Oklahoma and not a church."

The reverend and her father were walking toward them; soon they both felt the constraint of the men's presence, and Iola enjoyed being like a co-conspirator with Alice.

After they had eaten, the Reverend Youngblood declared his intention to visit the Wichita Mountains Preserve because he had never seen a live buffalo. Alice felt duty-bound to accompany him, but he also invited Iola's parents, who were delighted about the prospect of making a journey in an enclosed automobile, so Iola felt forced to go.

The ride took several hours, and in a few especially muddy spots, the men had to get out and push the car out of the bog while Iola steered. Conversation with anyone but the Reverend Youngblood was impossible: no sooner would she and her mother begin speaking about her cousins or about her grandfather than would the white preacher interrupt them. He demanded explanations of weather patterns and nomenclature of flora and fauna as if they should surely appreciate his willingness to learn, as if he had a holy duty to learn and thus they had no right to withhold information. Iola thought, this white man has come here all the way from North Carolina, brought his sickness with him. He had the white sickness that made people leave where they were born and go off to convince those in the new place that their religion and their customs were evil and that their punishment is to give up their land and resources.

They reached the Preserve shortly before sundown. They parked near the gates, where her grandfather had spoken, butterflies on his hat, almost thirteen years ago. Youngblood, Iola's parents, and Alice all walked to the fence and stood watching a trio of bison grazing in the distance. She stood just behind them. She didn't want to look at them.

"Very interesting, the variety of God's creatures!" the reverend said heartily. From where they stood the bison were about the size of her thumb, but the reverend still waxed enthusiastic over them. She stepped up to stand beside Alice, then, as if by tacit agreement, they strolled away.

"I'm going to strangle that man," said Alice.

Iola laughed, no longer angry—the white preacher was simply a fool. She drew a breath.

"Alice, do you know where David is and what has happened to him?"

"I know something. I wouldn't have come here empty-handed, knowing how you felt, although so far as I knew you and he might have been corresponding."

Iola laughed ruefully. "Well, hardly!"

Alice shrugged. "Do you know about the incident at the hotel?"

"What incident?"

"Someone tarred and feathered a friend of his, a German woman who was staying there, but people are saying that he was the real target."

"To be tarred and feathered?" Iola was alarmed.

Alice shrugged. "Worse. A lot of murders have been happening all over the oil fields. People talk about a sort of crime syndicate, but nobody says anything for certain."

"Is he out of danger now?"

"Yes, I think so. David had his friend put in a hospital in Tulsa, then he and his wife left rather quickly for Los Angeles."

"What is he doing there?"

"I can only tell you what Tom has told me. He—I mean Tom—travels to Los Angeles quite a bit because he has oil interests there. I understand that David lives in a large house in Santa Monica and that his wife aspires to be a motion-picture actress." Alice sighed, obviously sorry to bear this news.

"Excuse me, please," Iola murmured and walked away from Alice. Alice respected her need for privacy and turned back toward the group at the fence.

Because of the recent rains, the pasture grass was high and luxuriant, and a certain swelling of moisture and warmth hung like smoke in the waning sunlight. Iola retraced her steps along the creek where the buffalo had run, then she stepped into the field where the herd had come thundering down on her. She remembered running toward David and the herd, carrying the stone, meaning to hurl it at him, and then at some point as the heads of the buffalo grew too large suddenly she was afraid, she turned, tried to run, heart pounding, looking back, seeing them, him, the horse coming on her, then his hand stabbing under her armpit and nearly wrenching her arm out of its socket. . . .

She sat down slowly in the empty pasture, cross-legged, bent forward until the grass was higher than her head and dropped her face into her hands. She could hear the hooves.

PART

THREE

1923 — 1929

17

We were down in the arroyo holding our horses steady by their bridles, staying quiet. Little Thunder, he had crept up to the edge of the ravine and was keeping an eye out to the west, across a wide flat, where the wagon train was supposed to pass through a gap—they had a name for it, but I don't recall it—and come down along where we were hiding. Yellow Calf was up on the ridge above the gap, and when he saw the wagons coming, he would signal to Little Thunder, then we would all get on our mounts and come up out of the arroyo and attack them.

It was about noon, and it was hot where we were standing down in the draw. We had not eaten for a pretty good while, and my stomach was growling. We were wearing our best finery, though. We were proud. I had a big ax with hawk feathers on it that I had sharpened up good—it would take a big bite out of those white men, I said. Big Moon, Lone Bear, Two Feathers, and Eagle Wing were there beside me, and we were all getting nervous and happy at the same time, grinning and twitching like we had bugs crawling on us.

Little Thunder, he went sssst! and we mounted our horses but kept down low and didn't move. We waited, my heart was going like a drum in my chest, then he hollered and we whooped like they told us to even though it wasn't right and charged up out of the ravine.

The wagon train was still a pretty good way off, and they looped the first wagon around to meet the last one's tail so they were in a big circle. We went on, riding hard and yelling, waving our lances and axes and rifles, and when we reached the wagons, they were firing at us with their guns from behind the wheels. A couple of us got hit in the first volley and went rolling off the horses, but the rest of us, we went around and around, hollering loud as we could. This went on for a little while, them shooting, us shooting back, some flying off our horses, some of

*them jumping up and flying backward when we put our lances through
their chests, then finally we got to rush right into the center of the circle.*

*We fought hand-to-hand here. One soldier in a blue coat knocked me
off the horse with the butt of his rifle and we went to wrestling there in
the dust. I rolled on top of him and almost chopped his head open with
my ax, and he spun away and cussed me real good. Then I got up and
went to the first wagon nearby, where there was a white woman in a
bonnet—I was pretty excited you can guess!—and a little girl beside
her, and I jumped up on the wagon spokes and grabbed that girl around
her waist and took a few swings at the white woman who started screaming and jumped up and fell over the seat into the wagon in a faint, so
just to make a big show I hacked at the seat with my ax a few times,
then I took that little girl and ran back to my horse.*

*There was fighting all over. There were dead soldiers and dead In-
dians, just dead and wounded people all over the ground, some of them
crawling and making terrible faces, and any blue coats and Indians still
standing were trying to hack and stab and shoot each other. It got our
blood up, I mean it. But I wasn't supposed to stay around. I got on my
horse and had that child with me and rode off. Everybody else came
after me, and we rode back down into that arroyo. We got down and
started laughing and clapping each other on the back. Yellow Calf said,
That was almost as good as fighting Custer! I was still feeling my heart
make my blood go like that drum in my body.*

*Right when we were laughing the most, Mark Ortega came running
down into the arroyo, and he looked upset. He was one of the Carlisle
people, had on shoes, he was always playing the one who could read.*

*You guys better get serious, he said. Old Wart on Nose is hopping
mad at you.*

Us? we said. How come?

You went too far, he said.

*He didn't have a chance to say anything more because it wasn't a
second later Old Wart on Nose came up himself in the truck that the
man who had the picture box drove. He got out and just about fell down
the side of that arroyo to get to us as fast as he could.*

*He started screaming at us, jumping up and down, yelling. I told him
to calm down and talk soft and slow and we'd try to listen to him. He
came over to me.*

You! he said. What's your name?

Jack Little Tree, I said. I had told him that many times, but he couldn't tell us apart.

I told you to slug that soldier, I never said a single thing about taking a swing at him with that ax—what in Sweet Jesus' name are you trying to do?

Kill him, I said. But I winked to show I meant a joke.

He said, Then you go up to the wagon and you swing that goddamn ax at my leading lady! Do you have ANY GODDAMN IDEA who that woman is?

Pioneer white woman, I said.

That's her CHARACTER, goddamnit! he yells at me. She's a very important actress and her name is Mary Pickford! If anything happens to her, I will have my throat cut! And what do you mean by taking that ax to our props, too?

Well, he didn't wait for an answer from me. He had things like that to say to everybody there. Sure I knew it was Mary Pickford. She'd played Indian women a few times, too, and we had all seen Ramona. But up there on that wagon seat she was just a pioneer white woman and that fellow in blue was a white soldier. I was born too late to fight Custer like Yellow Calf had, but I am a Sioux, and I have my pride.

What happened was, Old Wart on Nose wanted us to do it all over again, so he left and we waited down in that hot draw with our stomachs growling for the signal to come again. Before it came, though, Old Wart on Nose sent a couple of his prop men down there with us to wrap cloth around my ax blade and to blunt some of the lance tips. We tried it again and did it the way he wanted. It wasn't as much fun as before when my blade had made the soldier and the pioneer white woman afraid of me, but—Ha!—it gave me satisfaction that Old Wart on Nose had had to worry about us running wild.

The hotel lay in the shadow of the elevated tram that took tourists up into the hills. The women in the lobby were dressed for the warm Los Angeles weather, and Iola felt leaden and dowdy in her dark wool suit. The desk clerk asked, "Is there only this one bag, miss?" and turned to take a slip of paper—a telephone message—from a pigeonhole on the wall behind him.

From Lenny. *Thinking of you.*

As she and the bellhop stepped away from the desk, she was aware of the clerk's scrutiny on her back, as if he were still wondering whether to allow her to register. Indian-looking woman. One bag. A message from a lover?

The third-floor room was stuffy, so she tugged at the cranks on the casement window until both halves swung out. Cool but dusty air crept in and she stood a moment looking at the view of the hills to the northwest. She was sweating under the woolens. The weather had been dry and cold in Santa Fe, with hard blue skies and the sun glistening on snow in the Sangre de Christos. She undressed to her slip and stockings and sat on the bed fanning herself, then lifted the telephone receiver and gave the clerk the number of the Los Angeles chapter of the Greater Federation of Women's Clubs. Once connected, she made an appointment to see Mrs. William Poynter the following afternoon.

After a few moments, she lifted the directory, and, with her heart beginning to pound, ran her finger down the columns of C's and stopped at his name. Her hands were trembling.

What should she say?

Say you are here on business.

She sighed, committed the number to memory, shut the book, and placed it in the stand beside the bed. Well, she *was* here on business, and there was no reason why David Copperfield could not be included in it. She would not mention the note she had given Tom Quick the day she left Wetoka for Europe, and perhaps he would have the good grace to presume that she regretted having written it and had outgrown it or changed her mind.

The telephone at his house rang four times before a male voice said, "Hello."

"David?"

"No, Mr. Copperfield is out of town but he's expected back this evening. This is his assistant, Wilbur Smythe. Would you like to speak to Mrs. Copperfield?"

"No, thank you."

"Could I help you or give him a message?"

Had it not been for the man's courteous insistence, she might have merely hung up, but his professionalism caused her to slip momentarily into her own for protection.

"Yes, maybe. I'm with the Western Association for Indian Defense in Santa Fe, and I wanted to discuss a matter of mutual concern with him. I'll only be in town for a day or so. David and I are old friends. If it's possible," she began, then hesitated, drawing in a breath, "I'd like an appointment to see him tomorrow morning."

"I could pencil you in for eleven, but I'll have to confirm it first with him when he returns. You are—"

"Mrs. Conway," Iola blurted out. She was on the verge of correcting herself when Smythe said, "Very good, and your telephone?"

She gave him the hotel's number.

Cursing herself, she called the front desk to say she would be receiving calls for a Mrs. Conway.

She had not gone by that name since leaving Anadarko two years ago. She realized now why she had given it: David would have no idea who "Mrs. Conway" was. If he agreed to see a "Mrs. Conway" sight unseen, Iola would appear—that would be one surprise—and appearing as a married woman or widow would be still another. After the humiliation of that pathetic letter to him, she was glad that "Mrs. Conway" suggested that she had found someone other than David to love. But it was a dreary, even pitiful, facade, and her deviousness made her feel ashamed. Had she been thinking clearly or swiftly, she would not have done it.

The twilight air was cool; through the screenless windows she watched the last ribbons of violet light descend slowly over the unseen ocean to the west. She lay in her slip under the top sheet, listening to autos on the street below, feeling tired and hungry, but more the former than the latter, so she couldn't force herself to go down to the dining room for supper. Her excitement about being in a new city and her anxiety about the possibility of seeing David had flogged her nerves raw.

Another new place. Was it the influence of the missionaries or some Kiowa wanderlust in her blood that made her sew this new experience to her memory like a badge of progress? Alice, way back then, put little pins on her blouse for reading well. First place. Best little Indian girl anybody ever saw. Most promising. Most likely to become a white person.

What had happened to David since she last saw him in Wetoka? She wasn't surprised that he had a telephone—even her parents had a radio now, the primary delight of which to her mother was turning the knob to make the white man's voice shut up. The "secretary" had not surprised her, either, because it suggested that he was still surrounded by whites who could work him like a mine.

Would she care to speak to Mrs. Copperfield?

No, thank you.

When the moon had risen and flooded the hotel room with a cold blue light, Iola rose from tossing in bed, retrieved a glass of water from the bathroom, and sat by the window. It would be hard to get any rest tonight.

In the morning, as she was oversleeping, Lenny woke her with a call from Santa Fe. He just wanted to tell her how lovely she had looked in the plaza with those huge, flocculent snowflakes falling into her hair and melting on her cheeks. She thought about how the snow had gotten caught in his goatee, looking a little like some breakfast grits had stuck there; when he had tilted his head, the flakes had landed splat on the small round lenses of his glasses. She was both amused by and ashamed of the disparity between the snow's having made her beautiful and him only comical. But only Lenny would use a word such as "flocculent" while paying a compliment.

He had called to remind her that she was the most beautiful woman he had ever seen, he said. She laughed and said that didn't sound like something a Trotskyite should say to a woman. After they hung up, she felt more confident about seeing David, even though it seemed wrong to use one man's adoration to prop herself up for another man's scrutiny.

She inspected herself in the mirror, trying to assess what David would be seeing for the first time in six years. Her face had narrowed, sharpened, time cutting away at baby fat and carving its lines into harder but also more dramatic configurations. Her eyes seemed larger, her forehead and cheekbones more prominent, and now the lines of her full mouth seemed more exaggerated.

She was satisfied with her face, but annoyed that the clothing she had brought from cold Santa Fe—pieces from her summer wardrobe hauled out of a trunk—smelled of mothballs. She put on a simple dress of blue cotton with an ankle-length hem, but since she hadn't worn it in months, it made her feel off-center and disoriented, very little like herself.

In the dining room women were wearing up-to-date bowl-shaped hats, knee-high flapper's dresses with scoop necks, low waistlines, and short sleeves. They exuded a playful but dangerous insouciance. Her own dress with its matching jacket made her look like a stenographer from Cleveland. She wore an overly large hat with sprouting peacock feathers—a burdensome thing—and felt ill at ease for being Kiowa and so inappropriately dressed. She didn't ordinarily give much thought to her apparel; it didn't deserve, she believed, to be the subject of anxiety or concern, and being unable to ignore it irritated her.

Her stomach was too jumpy to tolerate much breakfast, but she tried to finish an order of hotcakes, thinking she should fortify herself. Then, carrying the breakfast like a stone in her stomach, she boarded the trolley downtown. It rocked and creaked like a leaking ship; the smell of ozone mixing with the hot air of the coastal basin made her queasy. She tried to concentrate on what she might say to David about her work. She wouldn't tell him that she had stayed around Anadarko after the war to please her father, out of guilt and the creeping sense that she had failed him.

She might tell him how she and Vera had done a health survey on reservations for the Red Cross, but she could hardly stand to think about what had happened, let alone relate it. (She might say it was a sickness survey, to begin with.) She felt confused and would like to talk about it with David but had no confidence that he might be helpful or serve as an appropriate sounding board. Working in New Mexico among the Pueblo peoples she had begun to believe that when you brought "primitives" a so-called civilized culture, you risked transforming if not corrupting them. For the past forty years the worst white men tried to exterminate red people, while the best-intentioned tried to save them by disguising them as whites. Lately she had been goaded by the suspicion that teaching Indians to be white was, in the long run, destructive. Under Alice's influence, she had been encouraged to erase the Kiowa in herself. Now she wondered if she hadn't been cheated.

Walking from the trolley stop, she arrived at David's address at precisely eleven. Heart racing, she was let into the front door by a Mexican servant, who explained that Mr. Copperfield was not back yet from his morning walk. She was shown into the study, where she circled about, too nervous to alight on either of the two leather chairs or the velvet sofa. A huge oriental carpet covered the varnished floor. Mahogany tables with ornate legs were set beside the chairs, with a matching coffee table before the sofa. A clutch of white peonies in a Zuni vase cast round shadows across the faces of the magazines—*Saturday Evening Post*, *Photoplay*, and *Vanity Fair*—on the table. She automatically attributed the flowers and magazines to David's wife.

A piano stood centered in the room like an insect of some gargantuan order, its one glossy black wing cocked toward the ceiling. Her eye swept past it to a glass-fronted cabinet which held several rifles in horizontal ranks. On one wall was a mounted elk's head with antlers shaped like palm leaves. Another cabinet held a display of arrow and spear heads. Opposite the fireplace wall, bookshelves reached from floor to ceiling, filled with volumes that seemed widely eclectic—Bacon's histories, Gibbon, an elementary Latin text bearing a library's white patch. Curious, she took down a translation of Goethe, opened it, and found marginalia scrawled throughout in blue ink and an unfamiliar hand, the comments in German and apparently scribbled with some passion, to judge by the exclamation marks.

Once again, she was absorbing David through the props and fixtures of his life, the way she had that day at his cabin. How much of what was here was due to the influence of the lady of the house? And would it still be the blond singer? She stood stock-still to listen for sounds issuing from other rooms. If the wife were home, she was rude to leave Iola unattended, though Iola was thankful for it.

A large library table, obviously used as a desk, occupied the center of the room. She moved closer, curious to inspect the disheveled papers spread over the oak surface. A ledgerlike book lay open, its pages filled with a bold but childlike cursive, and she bent forward to glimpse a few lines—*they cooked up a jimson weed tea they used in ceremonys, and they had a temple that is described as a great circle surounded by feathers from birds they sacraficed.* She wanted to pry further, but guilt held her back. She circled the table slowly, trying to read the type and script from a distance, as if keeping in motion and keeping her hands to herself might be sufficient restriction to pay for the privilege of prying.

When she turned, she saw a large man through the windows—a *Kiowa!* she thought—strolling up the driveway. Unmistakably, it was David. He had let his hair grow long and wore it in two braids, with a red band about his forehead. His face looked deeply tan against the white shirt open halfway down his sternum. Those wide, full shoulders —she had forgotten. His bulk was still taut, dense, though his waist seemed slightly thicker, girded by a leather belt with a silver buckle. His khaki trousers were rolled to his shins. He had a smooth, rolling step, a relaxed authority, easily planting the end of a fishing pole into the ground with each stride.

She caught her breath: he looked so . . . complete! And with his hair long, like the old days! Seeing him from this distance struck an old spark she had imagined, had hoped, had been extinguished by the war and the ensuing years.

She turned from the window and sat on the sofa. It was silly to get carried away by a brief glimpse, and, besides, she had no intentions of doing anything but pay a visit. She had a pretext—no, a *reason* and a good one—for being here. He was a man of means and she was a person who raised funds for a cause that he might contribute to, and the fact that they had known one another was merely a fortuitous circumstance that could work in her favor.

Her stomach lurched; she listened for noises which might allow her to trace his invisible path through the unknown interior spaces; finally, at the sounds of footfalls outside the door to the room, she rose.

He had removed the headband, rolled down his cuffs and traded the sneakers for dress shoes, buttoned his shirt and slipped on a blue suit coat.

"Mrs. Conway?" he asked from across the room. When she grinned and stepped forward, he laughed uproariously and her heart bounded. *Set 'Alma!* he blurted in Kiowa. He came forward, not meeting her eye, and she looked away from his face—this sudden immersion into Kiowa habit sent a pang through her blood.

Standing before her, he wavered, holding out his arms in a helpless way as if he might have been inspired to hug her but suddenly thought better of it. Finding nothing else to do with those outstretched arms, he clapped her lightly on the shoulders with his palms.

"What a surprise! I've been down to the beach. I would have come back sooner had I known it was you." The English broke the spell, and she was able to look at him directly; she cocked her head to look up into his dark brown eyes, and felt a sudden heat on her cheeks.

"I shouldn't have been so secretive," she confessed. "It was an oversight." She wished to straighten out the matter of her married name—to say that she was a widow—but there didn't appear to be an opening for it: he was guiding her across the room.

"Well, no matter. Please sit down!"

She sank clumsily into the sofa, calves quivering, while he heaved himself quite casually into a chair facing her. His pleasure in seeing her was a joy; it calmed her some.

"Yolanda!" he hollered. Turning to Iola, he said, "Excuse me a moment," then leaped from the chair, stuck his head into the hallway. *"Dos cafes, por favor!"* He came back, smiling, striding quickly and easily, his braids swinging.

She caught herself smiling. His brows cocked in query.

"Your hair," she said.

He chuckled. "Well, at first it was for the pictures. As a matter of fact, I only got back last night from being on location for a month in the desert. I have been a Sioux, a Paiute, a Comanche, every kind of Indian you can think of. It's all the same, though," he said. "The cowboys or the cavalry always win."

"I don't get to see pictures much," she said apologetically.

"Oh, it's not a particular accomplishment to ride a horse for these people and fall off of it when you are shot. For me it's what white people call a hobby. It's brought me many friends, though, because there are a lot of us doing this. We even have some Apaches from Czechoslovakia. All it takes is a big nose and black hair and some war paint." He laughed again—she could not recall David Copperfield ever having laughed in the old days, and this rich baritone rumble he had either acquired or had learned to let loose was very becoming.

"But now, here is something else," he went on, more earnestly. "When I'm out there riding, doing that, it makes me think of the stories people used to tell about the old days. I suppose it's the next closest thing to having lived then."

Her mind turned on this idea, quickly inserting objections to it that she didn't want to raise—wasn't this a mockery? She had said she "didn't get to the pictures much" as if they had not been available to her, but in truth she had only meant to be tactful. She had stayed away from Westerns ever since she had seen, years ago, a picture about an Indian who had gone to Carlisle and had become a football hero. He fell in love with the white heroine, but when the girl's father rejected him as a suitor, he went berserk, donned a war bonnet, got drunk, tried to kill the father, and was dragged off to prison. Ostensibly this picture had sympathy for the hero, but the sodden sentimentality of it was built on the idea that civilization was only a thin veneer and a savage will always be a savage. Over a decade ago, she remembered, a group of Cheyennes, Shoshonis, Arapahoes, and Chippewa had gone to Washington to complain to Congress about their portrayal in moving pictures.

"Yes, I suppose," she said lamely. Some light flickered in his eyes, as if he were remembering the old Iola—the haughty girl given to judgment.

"What I was on my way to say, about my hair," he continued, "was that wearing it this way, well, it has allowed me some measure of pride in my difference."

"Ah!"

"You approve?" He grinned.

"Oh yes," she said, laughing. "I'm working right now in Taos and Santa Fe with the Western Association for Indian Defense. We're trying to stop the government from forcing the Pueblo tribes to become such good Americans that they forget how to be who they have been for longer than any white men have lived on this continent," she said eagerly. She was afraid she had rushed too abruptly into her business here, but his talk of pride ushered it in naturally. "And there are legal matters too, such as fighting in the courts to get parcels of land stolen by the federal government back in the hands of the people to whom they really belong."

"Have you been there long?"

"No, not really. After I came back from Europe I went home for a while. Then a friend who was with the Red Cross as a public health nurse came to visit. She was on loan to the Bureau of Indian Affairs to do a survey of health conditions, and she hired me to help her. We spent the better part of last year traveling all over the West to reservations. We found pretty much what I thought we would—tuberculosis, syphilis, high rate of infant mortality, not many doctors and most of them lame or bitter, and not many hospitals and most of them filthy and ill-equipped. Lots and lots of trachoma—"

"Sore eyes?"

She nodded. "Sore eyes. The Indian Service had some circuit-riding 'specialists' who went around doing trachoma procedures, but a couple of these men were unfeeling butchers. One took his patients' eyelid between his thumb and index finger and pulled it away from the eye then ran a toothbrush behind the lid to scrape out the granules and he didn't even bother to disinfect the toothbrush from one to the other. It made me sick. Sometimes he crippled the tissue so badly the lid would never come fully open again." Talking about the recent memories upset her, so she went on quickly, "We made up the report and sent it in, and the next thing we knew someone told us secretly that the report was going to be buried in Washington."

She shrugged. The Mexican maid appeared with a tray bearing two cups of coffee, along with a porcelain pitcher of cream and a bowl of sugar. David nodded and murmured thanks as she quietly set the tray down and padded from the room. His apparent ease with the servant bothered Iola; he had taken too easily, she thought, to being a man who is waited upon.

She reached for the cup of coffee and took a sip without putting sugar or cream in it; she did not like it black, but the idea of fully utilizing all the condiments the maid had brought unsettled her.

"Vera and I wound up our survey in Santa Fe, and I met people there who had just started working on some projects—some artists, lawyers and reformers, and some Indians, too. They're raising money to hire medical help for the Pueblos, and were trying to lobby against the Bursum bill. They're also trying to go up against all the local reservation agents who are sending reports back East that say the Indian dances are 'immoral' and 'bestial,' and young girls are deflowered during them—"

David laughed. Iola permitted herself a wan smile, but wouldn't take the absurdity so lightly.

"Well, I'm sure you know what they could say. So a lot of church groups have been pressuring the Commissioner of Indian Affairs to stop all native dancing and to find measures to 'protect' the 'rights' of Christian and 'progressive' Indians to be safe from temptation," she said contemptuously. "We're trying to counteract a lot of very foolish and destructive nonsense."

David gave her a sly grin. "Oh boy. Next thing, you'll be doing the Feather Dance."

He almost got a rise from her, but she held back. She set her coffee cup on its saucer; she had drunk more than she intended, but she would drink no more.

"The Bursum bill, I believe I read about it," he said seriously, understanding she meant to chastise him by ignoring his jibe. "Interior Secretary Fall and Senator Bursum are looking to give some reservation land to whites who've settled on it?"

"More or less. It deeds reservation land to non-Indian claimants, and it involves some water rights, too. The whole thing has become more complicated because oil was found on the Navajo land. Anyway, all this lobbying effort takes money, for lawyers, for expenses. That's why I'm here in Los Angeles. To raise funds. The California chapters of a national women's group may agree to work with us." She hesitated, thinking it was far too soon for a sales pitch, so she looked away and fell silent.

He also grew strangely quiet; he might have been trying to determine if he was on her list of potential benefactors, and she felt uneasy about appearing to be only exploiting their mutual past.

"My grandfather died four years ago," she said after a moment, trying to obscure any mercenary purpose and to make her visit a social call. "It was when I was in Paris after the war. I came back too late for his funeral, but it was good to be home for a while."

David nodded. He smiled faintly. "I wonder if the old man ever forgave me for stealing that horse."

Iola laughed; now she felt at ease, locking this old link between them. "I think he was as happy seeing those buffalo running as he was angry with you for taking the horse."

"It didn't please you any."

She blushed furiously. "I was young."

Iola told him about the tribe scattered across three counties—who had died, who had married, about those like Morris who had not come back from the war. He asked about her experiences during the fighting; she gave a report such as she might have delivered to a public audience, and omitting the story of her loss of faith left her dissatisfied. She wanted to explain how she had come to repudiate Alice's influence, and was caught between the indignity of admitting to having been a fool and the indignity of being eager to rebuke herself.

During a pause, he said, "And you've gotten married since last I saw you."

She flushed. "I'm a widow," she said. "The war."

"I'm sorry."

"No, no—I mean he was . . . yes, he was killed in the war, this boy. But I meant more that, you see, the war was not why I'm a widow but why I was married, also."

This sounded terrible to her ears—she was dishonoring Conway by trying to minimize his importance simply to . . . to make it appear as if she'd never loved anyone else?

"You were married long?"

She shook her head. "Only a few days. It was an impulsive thing to do."

"Well," he said, "I can see how, in the war, the confusion people were feeling, it must have been a good reason. At the time."

She waited; he seemed to be leaning forward inside, some weight there about to topple toward her.

"Better that than some other ways," he uttered at last.

Her heart took flight. She had been struck by his aura of well-being, of health and self-assurance—and this painful utterance was the only sign of unhappiness. He was verging on a pronouncement about himself, and though she wanted to help him say it, she likewise heard an ancient Kiowa voice that gravely respected privacy: *Do not touch another's mind with your own.* That, and his own reserve, kept her from asking, David, do you love her? Are you happy? She suspected he was not, and it tormented her to realize she had snatched greedily at any evidence of his misery.

She didn't know whether to close this box or rummage through it.

"Do you have children now?" she asked finally.

He looked surprised, even shocked, and she regretted asking a question whose answer was obviously painful. After a moment, though, he smiled, then chuckled.

He rose and held out his hand.

"Come," he said. "I have none and I've got many. Let me show you."

Perplexed, she let him take her hand in his warm strong grip as he pulled her up from the sofa. His touch set off a surge of vibrations running through her arm and down her spine, making her limp, boneless. Had he not touched her, she could have easily risen on her own; being helped, she suddenly needed his strength.

19

"About a year and a half ago, I was driving along, and I looked up into the hills right over *there*—" David pulled to the curb and pointed toward the hills above the boulevard. Iola saw an arid hillside covered with scrubby growth, an occasional house perched in a nook carved from the earth, sometimes a portion of it jutting precariously out over the slope.

He grinned. "Hundreds of red people were camping! Headdresses, breastplates, buffalo-skin lodges, open fires, cooking pots, deerskin dresses. It nearly took the top of my head off! I stopped the car and I got out and walked up the hill, thinking I was having a vision." He smiled. "You grow used to seeing things out here that aren't what they seem. I mean I thought it was only another set for a picture, but even from a distance these people were real to me, and I couldn't see cameras anywhere. When I got up there, I talked to a Sioux, who told me that a white man named Colonel McCoy had brought them all from the reservation, and they had been camping while waiting to be used in a picture —*The Covered Wagon*. Camping out that way—well, it was a good excuse to have things the way they were in the old days."

He sighed. "They're all at Inceville now, playing in Ince's pictures. That's how I got my first part. It was on that picture. It's still playing at Grauman's and the Sioux do a big show onstage each night before it runs."

He kept looking at the hillside and chuckling, as if he were seeing more there than she did. Once again, she was struck by how loquacious he seemed; compared to the taciturn youth she had known both at Anadarko and Wetoka, he was a veritable chatterbox this morning. And she, who usually had words for everything, had fallen oddly silent.

"There's a club not too far from here down on Cahuenga where a lot of us meet just to play cards and trade stories." He winked. "Lemonade in the front, a little 'firewater' in the back; many's the night I've used my auto here like an ambulance; it reminds me of how we used to have to carry those heavy bags of flour and sugar from the wagon into the mess hall!" He laughed. "You know, before that came along, I was just a lonely Kiowa miles away from anything that reminded me of home. I've got friends now. Jack Little Tree, Jimmy Young Deer and his wife, Red Wing. Jack's directing shows, and Red Wing got her start in *Squaw Man*. I'd say she's been in thirty pictures easy since then, and Jimmy puts together an Indian float for the Tournament of Roses Parade every year." He chuckled. "People ask what kind of Indians we are, we say 'De Mille Indians.' "

He slowly pulled away from the curb, keeping his eyes on the slopes.

His story about the "tribe" he now belonged to and his confession of loneliness conjured a picture in her mind of a man who lived apart from his spouse.

"Didn't your wife come out here to be in pictures, too? I believe she was a singer back in Oklahoma." She struggled for a casual note to hide the intensity of her curiosity.

"Well, yes," he said flatly. She thought he was going to drop the subject, he sounded so abrupt, but then, after a moment, he added, "She hasn't been as lucky. She appeared in two pictures, small parts, but the man who directed her was murdered. People say some lover did it, but nothing has ever been proved."

Iola vaguely recalled a scandal, but she did not keep up with motion-picture gossip. Was his wife jealous of his success? She felt so small, to be spying for a crack that might reveal an ugly truth about his marriage. Alice had always hinted that the woman was only after David's money. Did David know this? If he did, why would he stay with her? For love? She had half expected to find him beaten and servile, like a kept beast, still in thrall to his blond goddess. And yet he seemed to be in perfect control of his life. Whatever had happened to him these past few years had given him strength and authority.

He steered with his left hand; his right lay flat on his thigh, the long brown fingers splayed. His hands looked strong. His nails were manicured, and this additional suggestion of wealth and indulgence disturbed her. Stronger, though, than her objection was the quickening in her pulse as she took in the size of those hands, their warm clay color. Lenny's white hands had torn and dirty nails, their knuckles ink- and tobacco-stained; his were the hands of both scholar and proletariat. Cool and small. David's large hands, warm, on her breasts.

She flushed and looked away.

"David, I want to apologize for something."

He remained silent, puzzled.

She was thinking, I want to apologize for having once thought you were unattractive, but said, "That day you ran away with the buffalo, I didn't know how much you needed to go or why."

He nodded, and gave her a glance whose intent she could not fathom.

"It's been a good thing."

Maybe, she thought. Was he referring to having become rich or to having become the husband of a white gold digger? Or to his smooth assimilation? Toward her own she had countless mixed feelings now. It had brought her a good deal of agony and a nameless dread. It made her rootlesss, unable to place herself comfortably either among her own people or among whites.

He chuckled. "I forgive you for cussing at me."

She frowned. "I suppose I'm also apologizing for how in Wetoka I acted like I should take charge of your life."

"The old man's granddaughter always thought she knew best for everyone, eh?"

She heard a faint undertone of triumph and thought, perhaps he's become a trifle too proud.

"It's obvious you've done well for yourself." She didn't fully believe this yet—not all of the evidence was in—but saying it might draw him out.

He told her with pride that he had learned to invest in real estate. The boom had just begun when he'd come here, carpenters were putting up bungalows all over the hills, and he realized that white men were going to build on every inch of vacant ground along the coast. "It's all going pretty fast. Some people say that sooner or later there'll be houses all the way from downtown to the ocean." David chuckled. "That's the one thing that can be trusted, you know, this spreading out"—he made a sweeping gesture—"so I thought it would be wise to buy the carpenters and the lumber, too."

When she didn't respond, he added, "Every Kiowa should be handed a fortune on a silver platter. It's a very quick education in the ways of the world."

This undercurrent of bitterness—where did it come from? Was he referring to his wife? She felt furious at this woman for having hurt him, and tender, protective toward him, which seemed wholly inappropriate and irrational considering how long they had been apart. He was more attractive now than ever before, but he was a stranger, and it was foolish to let thoughts such as *he's not happy with his wife* into her head. She was here on business, nothing more. Perhaps also for old time's sake, tribal feeling.

"Where is Miss Roberts?" he asked suddenly. "Do you hear from her?"

"We've exchanged letters over the past year or so. She's in Oklahoma City working for the state department of education. Things there are in an uproar now with Governor Walton's impeachment. The last time I heard from her she said it was likely that if he went down she would probably go with him—she's stuck her neck out and campaigned pretty hard to get people to support him. She believes that the Klan was behind the impeachment drive."

"I read about that." He wheeled the heavy auto into an intersection and gave an arm signal out the window. Just ahead were the buildings of downtown, and she thought automatically that David could return her to the hotel and she wouldn't have to ride that trolley again. "She's a good woman," he went on. "She always meant well."

"So much for good intentions," Iola said sardonically.

David looked surprised.

"I guess I don't believe so much in Kiowas becoming like white people any more," she added. "It's only brought them grief."

"That's not true of me."

Of course not! thought Iola. Somebody handed you a fortune on a silver platter, by your own words.

"Is it of you?"

"Yes and no," she said, hedging. "I suppose I would rather be an educated Kiowa moving about in a world that never really accepts me than to watch my children go hungry or die from disease. But I also can't accept that those are the only alternatives."

She sat up and assumed her characteristic posture for arguing, as she had done so many hours in Paris or Santa Fe, talking into the night over kitchen or café tables about immigration quotas, preserving cultures, and the efficacy of the so-called melting pot. She thought of her mother's serenity and apparent inability or *refusal* to be Americanized—was that the state to aspire to? She wanted to remain as much a Kiowa as possible in these times, and she repelled everyone's attempts to drag her into a more assimilated condition.

"I had a period there in France where I was very angry with Alice. You know how we were taught that the whites had all the right answers —the right medicine, the right law, the right religion, the right color. And I was just like any good colonial child, I tried to learn my catechism so I would be accepted and saved from being Kiowa. But in France all that came unraveled, David. Alice seemed stupid to me then—how could anybody have believed in the *justness* of white civilization? I couldn't deny the power, but I could deny the goodness! What those people did to each other in France, David, the scale of it. Those huge armies, and all the ingenuity of their machinery put to use for killing one another! They *use* their beliefs as excuses for their action. They don't act out of a need to keep to their convictions. Our tribe had a grand way of looking at the world, and it's disappearing quickly. The missionaries are chipping away at it."

"I prefer my house to anybody's buffalo-skin lodge," he said calmly. He seemed bewildered by her outburst. "I'd rather play at being an Indian on a movie set than to eat dung on the prairie, and I like this auto"—he chuckled and patted the dashboard with that large tan hand —"far better than any horse."

Certainly he liked being wealthy! He should take a trip home to see how some of the rest of the tribe lived in squalor and disillusionment: young men his age had come back from the war with terrible wounds and no rewards and now lived hand-to-mouth, without work or dignity. They had lost a language of their own.

"We were born too late to have the best of it," she said, feeling tough and icy inside. His inability to see the larger picture annoyed her. "They've robbed us of a chance to know the true beauty of the old way. You've been very fortunate in not having to suffer the worst conse- quences," she said pointedly. "As you said, you've been eating from a silver platter." It was a relief to be able to be angry with him.

He was grinning. When she looked at him, he said, "No one but you could apologize to a person one minute then criticize him the next."

She laughed, reproaching herself for not holding her tongue; she sank back against the seat, determined to assume a more impersonal, ambas- sadorial pose. She felt better thinking she had bested a weak and foolish part of herself that had flared up from the past to make her heart palpi- tate needlessly. She tried to ignore the echoes of his rejoinder because they only reminded her of how well he knew her character.

They weaved through downtown streets, where the traffic was heavy and people were milling on the walks. When she saw the tram tower, she thought she recognized her hotel, then, in a moment, they went by it. Presently, he was pulling to the curb at a three-story Victorian house that fronted on a park. Her obvious curiosity made him smile. "You'll see," he said. He gently cupped her elbow in his palm as they made their way up the walk bordered by blossoming flowers whose name was unknown to her: flowers in November, it seemed strange.

On a wide front porch were wooden ladder-back chairs set at random angles and two wicker rocking chairs with needlepoint cushions standing side by side against the wall; before them was a card table covered by oilcoth and strewn with half-filled glasses of a reddish liquid, alphabet blocks, and a wooden toy truck. Draped over the porch railing were a pair of child's knickers, stiff, having dried there in the sun.

Over the front door was a sign: "Heaven's Haven." Inside the foyer, Iola was hit with a cacophony of children's voices issuing from all over the house. Snatches of a hymn from upstairs, the discordant banging of a piano, a shrill voice yelling, "But that's mine!" and a thunder of footsteps. Crystal droplets in the chandelier shimmered and tinkled from the vibrations. David laughed.

"Hullo!" he called, cupping his hands around his mouth.

A woman appeared down the hall and came forward. "Oh, there you are!" She was tall, with flaming red hair pulled into a dated Gibson-girl bun. She had high cheekbones, deep green eyes, and a lace of golden freckles laid across the pale skin of her nose. She was stunningly beautiful. Her warm smile bespoke a deep, genuine pleasure in seeing David, and Iola felt an annoying twinge of jealousy.

"This is Mrs. Smythe," David said to Iola. "And this is a friend from my tribe, Iola Conway."

Iola politely murmured, "How do you do."

"It's nice to meet you. And it's Bobette." She grabbed David's arm. "Come along, Mr. Copperfield!" Her voice had a lilting, jocular quality that Iola envied—or, rather, it suggested a state of mind barely short of ecstasy that Iola herself would have liked to assume with David. The woman looked back at Iola. "The young ones get so impatient. And he's late!"

"Sorry," said David. "I'm slow this morning."

"Choose your punishment." Bobette pulled a yellow paper from the pocket of her large apron. "You can either eat lunch with us or take this bill from the roofers."

"You Irish eat too many potatoes," David joked as he took the paper.

They entered a classroom, where desks ran in two files, a portable blackboard bore monosyllabic words in a childish hand, and a map of the world hung on one wall surrounded by paper silhouettes of animals. Several children were gathered about a desk looking at a book when David was spotted; a girl in a smock yelped, broke away, and ran to him, grabbing his finger and trying to dig her hand into his coat pocket.

"No, you wait, Mae—you know that's not right!" He grinned, as the rest of the children surrounded him, yelling and pleading for something —it was bedlam.

"Children!" Bobette clapped her hands and they fell away, giggling. The boys were dressed in knickers and had bowl-shaped haircuts; the girls, their hair tied in pigtails, were in smocks, except for one in a white frock with pink flowers and matching bloomers.

It was this child whom David went to, giving her a mock ceremonial bow.

"And besides," he said. "It's Rachel's birthday so she gets first pick!"

The child, a homely brunette with a face as gaunt as any Iola had seen in France, grinned, then covered her mouth to hide the gaps between her teeth.

"Put her there, *amigo*." David held his large paw out before the child. "Seven big years, what a victory!"

Giggling and grinning sheepishly, the child grabbed his forefinger and shook it.

"Are we ready for a story?" Bobette asked. They all cheered and scrambled to the front of the room, where they sat cross-legged on the floor in a semicircle. David turned to Iola and stage-whispered, "When they're this young, they're a good audience. Two more years and it's all stuff for little children to them."

Iola eased into a child's seat, feeling absurdly large and strangely moved—it took her back, the desks, with their carved names and ink stains. She remembered being in front of Alice's classroom the day she told the class the buffalo were coming back.

"So what's it to be? Another Trickster story? Or something else?" asked David. "An old one or a new one?"

"You better decide!" called out Bobette, who sat on the teacher's desk, her legs dangling.

"Let's let Rachel decide," said David.

The birthday girl blushed and said shyly, "Rolling Heads."

"Rolling Heads!" thundered David. "What a bloodthirsty little paleface you are!" He turned to the others. "Are you all certain you can take it?"

They nodded; one boy yelled, "Sure!"

"Okay, here it is." David stood and stretched his arms upward, breathing deeply, eyes closed, giving the children the impression that he was preparing himself for a great conflict. They grew very quiet.

"Once a long time ago there was a village of people who lived far out on the prairie from here," he said. "Their chief had a daughter—well, we will call her Gertrude for now, eh? And the chief wanted Gertrude and the son of another chief to get married. That's the way people did it back then, you see—their parents said how they would be married.

"So Gertrude and this boy got married. Soon afterward, the boy went out looking for scalps with a war party. They came to a place where another tribe was camped, and they stopped to visit. While the boy was talking to the chief there, he saw *that* chief's daughter, and he fell in love with her. He wanted to marry her, too. He told the chief he was not married back in his own tribe, so pretty soon he and this chief's daughter got married, also. He asked his friends not to tell Gertrude that he had gone and gotten married again to someone else he liked better in another tribe.

" 'But what shall we tell her?' they asked him. And he said, 'Tell her I was killed and some people took my scalp.'

"So when the boy's friends returned home, they told Gertrude that her husband had been killed and scalped. Oh, children, how she cried!" David threw up his hands. "She would go out and sit by the river to cry, and the river would say, 'Please, do not cry, you are making me overflow my banks,' because her tears, you see, would run down her cheeks and down around her like a puddle and then run off into the river, like rainwater. She took a knife and cut deep gashes in her arms because that was the way those people mourned when someone they loved was dead—" David made a quick series of slashes with his finger cross his forearm, and Iola saw the little birthday girl wince. "She wailed so loud that the people could not hear the thunder, and she would not eat for months. She grieved for a long, long year, and the people got so tired of hearing her mourn, they made her go into the woods to do it.

"Well, one day, she was crying in the woods when a woodpecker heard her. When he asked her what was wrong, she told him, and he said, 'Those men were lying; your husband is alive in another village and he is married to another chief's daughter.' Gertrude told the woodpecker that she didn't believe him, so he said, 'I will take you to him.' She went back home and got some moccasins to walk in and some food and asked her little sister-in-law to go with her. Her name, of course, was Rachel." He looked at the child and winked, and some of the children giggled.

"Gertrude and Rachel and the woodpecker set out for the other village. They walked for ten days, and she grew very tired and discouraged, but finally, they came to a hill, and the woodpecker said, 'Look down into the valley; there is the village where your husband lives with his new wife.' And then he flew off.

"Gertrude and her little sister-in-law Rachel started to walk into the village. All the dogs started barking at them, and soon she was at the chief's lodge asking to talk to him. She discovered her husband inside with his new wife—" David stopped and looked very earnestly at the children. "Can you imagine how embarrassed everyone was? Well, her husband, he started confessing to everyone that Gertrude was his wife but he said that he had been forced to marry her. This made her cry. The chief became angry with his son-in-law and he said to Gertrude, 'Don't worry. He never told us he had a wife in another village; if he had told us I would not have allowed him to marry my daughter. So here's what I will do—I will call you my oldest daughter, and you can live here as long as you like.'

"Gertrude and Rachel stayed there for about a year, but Gertrude was still very, very angry." David paused a moment, shifting his weight, crinkling his broad brown brow with frowns. Iola had never heard the story told with such embellishment; she wondered if it wasn't more fascinating to her and Bobette Smythe than to the children. The other woman sat with her chin resting on her fists, like a huge child clad in adult clothes.

"For one thing, the man who was her husband still shunned her," David went on. "She wanted to get even, but she didn't know how. Finally, something came to her in a dream. The next day, she told Rachel to follow her to the river. When they got there, Gertrude started slowly wading into the river, and—now here's the strange part, children!—as she stepped into the water, very slowly"—here he leaned forward again, eyes wide, a look of horror on his face—"why, the water was just like a knife cutting her off as she went into it! And when she had sunk down to her neck, and the river had cut off her body, she said to her sister-in-law, 'Wrap my head up in a blanket and put it between my husband and his other wife when they are sleeping.'

"Rachel wrapped up the head in a blanket and did that, and during the night, the head swallowed both the husband and the wife right up!

Arrrggghhhh!" David roared suddenly and made a mock lunge for his audience.

There was a muted yelp from among the children, then nervous laughter and squealing.

"Then the head said, 'Sister-in-law, wrap me up and take me home.' Little Rachel wrapped the head in a blanket, and they started going home. The head kept saying not to be afraid of animals, because she, the head, could kill anything.

"Well—" He leaned forward and whispered hoarsely, "You and I know what the little girl was *really* afraid of, don't we! What would you be the most afraid of? Would you be afraid of some wild animals in the woods or this chopped-off head that talked to you and had already swallowed two people up?"

"The head!" everybody shouted.

"That's right! But Rachel couldn't let on she was afraid; she had to talk to the head and feed it and comb its hair just like they were the best of friends. But inside—oh, inside she was quivering and trembling, she was so afraid the head would get mad at her and swallow her up! So that night, when she thought the head was asleep, she took it and threw it into a hollow tree and started to run away.

"She ran all night long; in the morning she reached a valley where there was a river. The sun was now shining, and she was very, very tired. She longed to go to sleep and to eat something—" David's eyes drooped, he let his head nod, then suddenly he jerked it upright. "But when she looked behind her—" He stopped and looked horror-struck.

"The head was coming after her!" screamed a child.

"That's right; it was rolling down the mountain, swiftly making up the distance, and it was growling something fierce! Arrrawwwgh!! Well, the girl took off running again, she was panting hard, and sweat was running into her eyes so she couldn't see very well. She kept tripping over sticks and stones, and her heart was going thump! thump! thump! in her chest. She would dig into her bag as she ran and take out some grease and throw it on the ground, and the head would stop there and eat the greasy ground, but then it would start up again after the little girl.

"Oh, poor little Rachel ran for what seemed days and days and days! Finally, as the head was catching up to her and she knew that any moment she would be running out of breath, she stumbled into a clearing where two old women were roasting acorns over a fire.

"Oh, please please help me!' she pleaded with the old women. 'There's a head rolling down the hill after me, and it's coming to eat me up!'

"And of course the old women were very slow and deaf, and so they both said, 'Eh? What's that?' "—David imitated the old women, hunched over, cupping their ears with their hands—"And poor Rachel looked up the hill where the head was getting bigger and bigger. She pointed to it and shouted, 'Oh, please! Here comes a head that wants to swallow me up!'

"Finally the old women understood her. 'Quickly,' one said, 'get under my skirts.' Rachel did it, and when the head came rolling into the clearing, it growled and snarled and said, 'Where's that girl? I want to swallow her up!'

"The two old women said they had not seen the girl. And before the head could roll off, the two old women grabbed it up by its hair. They tied that head by its hair to a tree, then they put a great big black pot over their fire and tossed the head into the boiling water!"

He paused, then let out a sigh of mock relief. "And of course then little Rachel got safely home." He winked at Bobette. "Do you know what she learned?"

The children shook their heads in unison. "To be fair," said Rachel.

"Well, yes," said David. "And when you cheat or betray someone you might make them so mad they'll turn into a rolling head that wants to get even so bad it will eat up everything around it and you, too."

Bobette Smythe smacked her palms to applaud; the children followed suit, then leapt up to dig into David's coat pockets, where he kept pieces of wrapped hard candy. Within minutes the children had plucked them out and were walking around the room with bulges in their cheeks.

"Come see our turkey!" The birthday girl tugged on his finger.

"Are you finished with it already?" David asked her.

She nodded and pulled him toward the door.

"We're making Thanksgiving decorations," Bobette explained to Iola, then turned to the children. "It's almost time for lunch. I want you to wash your hands and go to the table. Mae, you tell Cooky to set two extra places." She turned to Iola, startling her. "You and Mr. Copperfield will stay, won't you?"

"It's kind of you, but it's up to him. He's my tour guide."

"Oh, he always eats with the children. Will you excuse me for just a minute?"

Bobette herded the children through the door, and in her absence, Iola idly strolled the length of the classroom. The room seemed empty without the children and without David's rich baritone—how expressive it had become. To be fair? Well, she could draw another point from the story, about marriage and jealousy. Hell hath no fury like a woman scorned, as whites said.

Iola had never seen David at play. He had found his true audience in the children. But then even with adults he seemed different, now, his presence warmer, more vibrant, confident.

Bobette came back as Iola was slowly turning the globe and tracing her finger across the Atlantic toward Europe. There was an awkward silence, then Bobette said, "I believe Mr. Copperfield said you were Kiowa, too?"

"Yes, we grew up and went to school together. How did you two meet?"

"Through my husband, Wilbur. He's Mr. Copperfield's assistant."

"Oh, I spoke to him on the phone, I believe." She could not have said why she felt such relief at having these connections outlined for her.

"Mr. Copperfield is both our bosses, I guess you'd say. We can't imagine working for anybody else." Bobette straightened papers and put books back on their shelf. "I used to work at the library, but when I graduated from the Normal he asked me to help him here."

"Help him?"

"Well, it was a kind of partnership, really. After my child was born, I was told I couldn't have any more, and I guess you know that Mr. Copperfield and his wife can't have any children?"

"No, I wasn't aware of that."

Bobette colored slightly. "I suppose I should have let him tell you that. But, anyway, that's why we started this. We've been going for about a year. We have a full house, now—twenty. They're all children that the county doesn't know what to do with. I think Mr. Copperfield would like to adopt one personally, but coming around almost every day is the next best thing. Even when he's out somewhere making pictures he manages to check on things."

Iola wondered why David couldn't adopt a child and hoped that Bobette would satisfy her curiosity without her having to ask. She felt guilty pumping her for information—this was none of her business. When it was apparent Bobette would not continue, Iola couldn't resist encouraging her.

"And Mrs. Copperfield would favor adoption?"

"Oh well, I don't know. She's very busy."

Bobette's tone was diplomatic. Iola decided not to pry further. Gesturing toward the classroom, she said, "Well, he certainly seems to enjoy being here. I know several people who'd be surprised to see him playing like a teacher." She smiled. "He wasn't much of a scholar."

"Oh? That's surprising. He studies all the time. He was at the library often when I worked there." Bobette smiled. "He told Wilbur he never much cared for studying until he realized it was how you kept people from cheating you."

Bobette led Iola to the dining room, where she sat next to David and ate the simple fare of boiled beets, potatoes, and meat loaf. She was too nervous to do more than pick at her food; instead, she watched David play patriarch to his young, put-together clan and eat with gusto.

Settling herself in the car for the ride back to the hotel, Iola thought: this is the last time I'll see him for a while, maybe forever. She wanted to tell him how good it made her feel to see him here, being appreciated, and taking pleasure giving.

"Would you like to go to the beach?" David asked as they pulled away from the house. The day had grown progressively warmer and made her languorous. In three days she would be back in the winter of Santa Fe, and his invitation tempted her.

"I can't," she said, genuinely sorry. "I have an appointment at three. If I go back to Santa Fe empty-handed, I'd just be too ashamed of myself. The woman I'm supposed to see this afternoon controls the strings to a pretty hefty purse."

He gave her an impish grin. "Suppose you got a contribution from me—then could you go to the beach? I'd like to take you where I walk everyday, and there's a café nearby where we could sit outside, have coffee and feel the sun on our faces."

She laughed. "Oh, David—that's called extortion! Now I can't say no without feeling I'm letting everybody down! That's not fair!"

"So we'll go?"

"No, no, I can't. I'm sorry. This woman is expecting me."

"Well, I won't make you a criminal," he said lightly.

But, clearly, he was disappointed. She knew she could easily cancel her appointment, make another, extend her trip a day or so—no one would question the added expense if she came back with David's contribution. Spending the afternoon with him sounded enormously appealing, and that was why she had to say no. There was Lenny holding her in the plaza in the snow, adoring her, fearful something might happen when she came here—had his intuition felt a shift in her attention while she thought more and more about contacting David when she came? To spend any more time with David would be dangerous, would disrupt the flow of her life, confuse her.

"Thank you anyway," she said finally. "It sounds very nice. Maybe when I come again."

"Will you?" he asked quickly.

"Oh, I don't know. We don't plan for me to, I didn't mean that. I just thought maybe in the future I'd be here again." Some instinct made her think *your work!* and she added, "I could always ask you for a contribution, anyway. It's still a good cause, whether we go to the beach or not."

He laughed in appreciation of her effort.

"Well, you go back and tell them you've got a big fish nibbling at the bait but you need another trip to hook him, and then we can spend a whole day at the beach."

She nodded. She didn't like this game all of a sudden. She didn't like leaning on their old connection to hit him up, and she didn't like his using his money as a means to get them together. But if the contribution were large, everyone in Santa Fe would say her scruples were too finely tuned and were becoming obstacles.

They merged into heavy traffic downtown and the going was slow. He asked her where she was staying, she told him, then they lapsed into silence for a while. It seemed there was something more she should say, that this would be her last opportunity. She was tempted to bring up the note. But she didn't know what to say about it—that it was false? That she hoped he hadn't felt he owed her anything in return?

"You're fortunate to have such a devoted pair of employees in those Smythes."

"Yes. Now *there's* a pair of married people who are happy," he said. "They're still the lovebirds. You never saw a man or woman who fit together better than those two."

He sounded wistful. She cursed her innocent question because it had led to his poignant answer. Today she had managed to learn just about everything about him except what she really wanted to know. Are he and the blond singer happy? No? Why not? And why are they still together?

He wheeled the auto to a stop at the hotel entrance before she could gather her wits. The doorman was trotting forward to usher her out of the car. She turned to David quickly, aware that it was within her power to have him move off again so that they could spend the afternoon together, but she said, hastily, so that she could exit before he might see how upset she was, "David, it's been so good to see you. I'm very proud of you!"

She squeezed his hand firmly, stepped down to the curb, and strode toward the entrance of the hotel so swiftly that the doorman couldn't catch her to open the door.

David drove away glowing from their reunion. He had enjoyed Iola's company and was surprised to see the intervening years had brought them a capacity for friendship and mutual respect. The change, he thought, was due to her mellowing—the haughty girl had grown into a much more humble woman; she had almost thanked him for saving her life.

He felt proud for having won her respect, and, because she was even more beautiful than he had remembered, her regard bestowed a special blessing. Several times he had slipped into an odd confusion while looking at her. He wanted to look at her face more than he was able to. To stare his fill was to risk making it obvious that his glances were not merely functional or curious; rather, they were more like strokes of a hand on the back of a pet whose glossy coat is irresistible to touch. This need to study her face reminded him of his old tenderness toward her as a child—that is, it recalled his old burden of unreciprocated feeling. His past resentment stood like a rock under this current, bending the flow. Still another cross-current ran against the first: Oh now you think I'm worthy, do you? The bitterness of his triumph was sweetened by his happiness at finally earning the approval of a beautiful woman he had admired.

What about this "Conway"? Iola's marriage had apparently not been a wise one. As he wondered about it, his mind turned back to his own. He was a moon orbiting around two planets; the farther he drove from the hotel, the more his lightness, his happiness, became so much air too thin to breathe. Their meeting had been too brief, their separation too long, he told himself, for her to affect him more than superficially. Block by block he was approaching the influence of a darker astral body, and the ebullient mood induced by Iola's visit dissipated like the aura of a lovely dream.

Thinking of Iola led him to consider his own marriage. He hadn't known what to expect from Laura as a wife. He hadn't known that each man and woman together are different from every other man and woman. His father had taken a wife by kidnapping a stranger, and had thereby cheated himself and his victim of the possibility of selecting a partner judiciously. Slowly, David had been realizing wives were not generic; a man might choose a woman who loves him, or a woman whom he loves, or a woman he is supposed to love but does not. The bride might choose a man who loves her but whom she does not love. In truth, he had taken a wife the way a man buys a very good horse. Other men would envy him; owning it added to his dignity and worth. Even when the horse refused to be ridden.

That night three years ago in the Wetoka hotel, her spirits had soared when he'd agreed to come here. Riding the train West, she'd been compliant, even willing in their lovemaking. They were driven in an open auto through Hollywood, where small frame houses and farms were intersected by a trolley line that ran past barns housing the studios of the moviemakers. Along Vine Street, pepper trees draped their tangerine clusters of corns, and they parked in the shade under one to eat oranges, Laura laughing and looking about, and, to his astonishment, hugging him. *Oh, I'm going to be happy here!* she kept saying.

It hadn't lasted. He'd tried to understand why her moods came and went. He was bewildered and hurt when she ignored him for long stretches only to turn on a whim and treat him, for a moment, as important. This waxing and waning of her attention was capricious, and he couldn't find anything in his own behavior that might be a catalyst to one mood or the other. In the past year longer lulls were interrupting her spells of attention.

Now he feared that her happiness had only been gratitude for the ride, that possibility had been her love potion. Whatever pleasure she had taken in his touch had vanished, just as she had all but vanished from his life.

Arriving home the night before after a month away, he had found that Laura was not there. Nor had she been home on several occasions when he'd managed to return from the movie location to check on the orphanage or see Wilbur. Or to see her. But he knew his trips were motivated less by business or longing for Laura than by his jealousy and fear. He had come back unannounced hoping to discover how she was using her freedom.

She had stayed out all night, and he had gone to the beach this morning bruised, angry, and suspicious. Laura always had alibis, excuses. He had once been on the verge of hiring a detective, but his pride wouldn't allow him to disbelieve her stories. Nor would it allow him to appear a cuckold to some detective. He preferred to think that his threats to leave her and do harm to a nameless lover or lovers were enough to keep her faithful.

He was tired of struggling with her. Sometimes it seemed foolish to continue their marriage. His companions at the War Paint Club were friends with their wives—they had children and homes in which they, the men, were the center, and their wives heeded their counsel and brought them the children to bounce on their knees. Other men's marriages seemed more sound, more like partnerships, and even if the men went out to drink and play poker or go to the fights, their wives stayed home and were faithful. How should he deal with Laura's refusal to be a dutiful wife? Their marriage had a tantalizing quality of never achieved dominance or pleasure; they played a bitter, if somehow exciting, game of tug-of-war. If she should suddenly surrender and become all a wife should be, would he be happy with her?

He couldn't answer—he couldn't imagine how he could best her. But he couldn't give up trying, either. He was ashamed to have a woman he could not break. Every time she threw him off, he would get back up, more determined not to be thrown. He wanted her to be proud to be his wife, he wanted a woman's loving compliance.

When he got home, her red roadster was parked in the garage. As he entered the house, he looked up at her bedroom window to see if she was watching for him. He could imagine her standing behind the curtains nervously concocting some witch's brew of an alibi for her absence last night.

After a quick look in his study, he stood in the front hallway and bellowed.

"Laura!"

In the stillness that followed, he heard only the faint tinkle of the glass wind chimes Laura had hung from the trees in the front yard. It infuriated her to be yelled at this way—"I don't answer to hog calls!" she'd say—just as it made his own blood boil for her to ignore him. A perverse impulse goaded him to make them both angry.

He checked himself from shouting again and went up the stairs two at a time. When he didn't find her in her bedroom, he went to her sitting room.

He paused to listen at the closed door. Sometimes in the afternoons her gramophone would be playing; there'd be the tinkle of glasses, murmur of conversation, laughter; sometimes he would barge in without knocking (it was his house!) to find three or four strangers lounging on the sofas and chaise longues, clouds of incense billowing around them. They would look up, startled, as he entered, and more than once he'd found Laura dancing in the arms of some young actor. Later, when they argued, she'd claim she had been "just learning the steps." These people would be more or less frozen in place for as long as he chose to interrupt them, giving him the maddening sensation of being a hunter scanning the landscape for small game that knew to move only when he was not looking.

Hearing nothing, he opened the door.

Laura, alone, sat on a green velvet wing chair by the window. She bolted up when he entered and raced toward him, arms out, the lapels of her robe fluttering like dark wings.

"Oh, David, I'm so glad to see you!" She hugged him and her moist mouth slid across his neck, while her body wriggled against his torso. He passed his palm over her smooth hips.

"Well, I'm glad you're glad," he said evenly. Her warm greeting surprised him and made him suspicious. He let go of her and she stepped away.

"Oh, I know you're upset with me for not being home last night. But you know I didn't think you were going to be here," she said in a cheerful mock-pout. "I've been having an *awful* time while you were gone, and I've been waiting on pins and needles for you to get back. Come—"

She took his hand and walked him to the window. Reluctantly, he followed. As they stepped into the light, he was dumbstruck by her appearance; in the month since he'd been on location, she'd grown pale and thin; her cheekbones stood out more, the flesh below them lank. They sat so close their knees were almost touching, and he noted how shadows underscored her eyes and how her hair was disheveled. She looked as if she had spent the night sleeping on the beach. Or in a gutter. She was not wearing any makeup, and her lips were the color of liver. In a month she'd aged ten years, and he was suddenly concerned.

"You don't look well. Are you sick?" He knew despite himself he sounded accusatory—as if she'd gotten sick only to avoid punishment or her conjugal duties—and he tried to amend it by taking her hand.

"No, but I've been taking care of someone who is, and it has just about worn me out. You remember Sylvia?"

He nodded. Sylvia had been on the production crew of *Sacred and Sinful Love*, and he'd met her in Laura's salon.

"The big girl?"

"Yes, with all the hair. David—" Laura leaned forward with a worried look. "She has TB, poor thing. I've been staying with her a lot because she doesn't have any family, and since the scandal a lot of people won't have anything to do with anybody who worked on Ronald's pictures because they're scared."

"I'm sorry to hear that. How long have you been helping her?"

"Since right after you left."

How tidy, he thought. "I wish you had told me or gotten word to me."

"I knew you were busy."

"But you made me worry, you know that." He got up from the wing chair and stood looking out the window. On the lawn one of their gardeners was leaning on a rake, talking to Laura's maid, and he wondered idly what went on between the household staff that he didn't know about.

"I know. I'm sorry," Laura said quietly.

Her contrition was too unusual. It signaled the arrival of a new Laura modeled on his wishes, but rather than feeling pleased, he was disconcerted, and wanted, inexplicably, to provoke her.

"She couldn't hire a nurse?"

"No. She hasn't worked in a year, like me."

He heard overtones of self-pity and solidarity with the unemployed

Sylvia. Them against the world, he thought. How could this Sylvia inspire such loyalty in Laura where he could not?

He sat back down, and as soon as he was settled, Laura rose and slid into his lap. She put her arm around his neck so that his nose was in her throat. Her warm hips pressed into his groin; he inhaled her perfume and grew painfully hard. She began humming and moving her hips gently in time with her song, stopping now and then to kiss his brow.

"I missed you," he said, and instantly regretted it, remembering his rage at her nightlong absence. His weakness for this woman was a curse!

She hugged his head closer, reached down and peeled the lapel to her robe back, then undid a button of her white satin pajama top so that her small white breasts with their pert nipples filled his vision. She took his hand by the wrist and laid his palm on her breast. He almost swooned with pleasure to feel her flesh against his hand. He bent down and lapped at her nipple. He wanted her so intensely it was like having sleep overcome him despite a desire to stay alert.

"Does it feel good?" she asked.

He was mute with longing. His mouth went around her small hard nipple; she parted her legs slightly so that his hand could stroke her inner thigh.

"It's nice to be wanted," she murmured. "You've been away a long time. Would you like for me to do something wicked?"

He was dimly aware she was making a request, but his mind had simply stopped working. She startled him by sliding off his lap and onto the floor beside the chair, shaking him awake, but before he could react, she was on her knees and had bent her head over his lap. She unbuckled his belt and looked up into his face, smiling.

After a moment, she had undone his fly and her fingers were reaching inside.

"You know, we should be nicer to each other. We should help each other more."

He closed his eyes. Her soft cool fingers closed lightly around him.

"Oh, David, won't you help me?"

He opened his eyes and was astonished to see his erection alongside her pale cheek.

"How?" he murmured.

"Sylvia needs a nurse," she whispered.

He looked away. He was heartsick at her transparent ploy but was also too aroused to resist.

"Yes. All right."

He shut his eyes again and felt, for only a moment, something slick and wet and warm enclose his flesh, her fingers moved, and he erupted within seconds.

"Goodness!" She laughed, pleased with herself.

He heard her slippers slapping quietly as she went into the bathroom. He opened his eyes. He had made a mess in his lap.

He was standing at the window in his briefs when she came back. She hugged him from behind.

"I'm glad you'll help."

"How much?"

She was quiet for a moment. "Five hundred."

He unpeeled her arms from around his chest.

"I'm not a wise man when it comes to you, but I am not an idiot, either. That's as much as I pay Wilbur in six months' time. Now maybe you can tell me where you really were last night and why you need this money."

"What I told you was the truth! And why should I have to beg for every scrap I get? Why shouldn't I have my own money? Am I your wife or not?"

"I don't want to be your banker. I want to be your husband, and I want you at my side like a proper wife!"

She knotted her arms over her breast and rolled her eyes in disgust. "Well, you don't think I'd do *that* for my banker, do you!" She gestured at the chair. "Oh God, you are so thickheaded! You're the one who's always talking about why can't we get along better, but you always treat me like a criminal. You don't trust me, and you humiliate me by making me crawl for just a few dollars that I need to help a friend!"

She burst into sobs, hiding her face in her hands, and David stood behind her, helpless. He wanted to comfort her, wanted to believe her, but couldn't ignore his suspicions. She wept as if worn-out, heartbroken. He was unaccustomed to her crying in his presence—seeing her sob on-screen in *Sacred and Sinful Love* had shocked him, and the way she now tucked her chin into her breastbone and covered her face recalled that one brief scene.

"All right." He couldn't count the times she'd wheedled money from

him beyond her allowance, which itself far exceeded that his companions allowed their spouses, but in the past year she had demanded more
money, more often, and he had resisted more strenuously. But this
crying was extraordinary.

She stopped weeping and clasped his hands in hers.

"Thank you, David. She'll pay it back, I swear."

He shrugged. "I'm not doing it for her. I want to be your friend and
I want you to be mine."

Sighing, Laura stepped to the window again. She pulled a handkerchief from the green robe and blew her nose vigorously.

"I wonder if it's possible."

"Why not?"

"I don't know. A man and wife, you know, it seems like only in the
movies . . ."

"Well, Wilbur and Bobette—" he began, but she cut him off with a
nasty laugh.

"Yes, well, they are the perfect couple, aren't they?"

"They are friends."

"Then they probably trust one another," said Laura.

"Yes, and she probably doesn't give him any reason not to trust
her."

"Let's not fight, David. I don't have the energy for it," she said
quietly. "I'm going to take a bath."

David changed into fresh underwear and trousers, then, downstairs,
he told the cook that he and Mrs. Copperfield would be dining at home.
In his study, he looked through the mail that had accumulated in his
absence. Wilbur, who had free access to the study, had been coming
every day to tend to business. David sat down to the desk for an hour
and tried to catch up on what Wilbur had done, but he couldn't concentrate.

Iola had appeared out of nowhere and Laura was in an unusual state
of agitation. He was glad to be back and glad to have Laura here under
his roof. When they were home together, he felt calm. Tonight perhaps
she would play the piano and sing for him or they might sit here and
read together. He might tell her about the picture he'd been working on
—his biggest since last year's *The Covered Wagon*—and many hilarious
and interesting things had occurred that might give them an evening's
entertainment over a cigar and a brandy.

But Laura didn't relish his stories about working in pictures. No matter. He'd listen to her tell about what she had been doing for the past month.

Just before dinner, thinking he'd make peace with Laura, he fixed her a gin and tonic, with a lime slice clipped onto the rim of the glass the way she liked it. When he knocked on her bedroom door, she said, "Wait a minute." There was a rustling. "Come in."

She was seated at her dressing bench applying lipstick in quick little strokes. He was wearing a smile that suited the gift in his hand until he noticed that she'd put on a hat that matched her peach-colored dress, and a beaded purse lay in her lap. He set the drink on the dressing table's marble ledge.

"Thanks!"

Fretting, he sank onto the edge of her bed.

"David, before you say anything, let me explain. I have to go tell her the good news, don't you see?"

"She doesn't have a telephone?"

He watched her face in the mirror as if it were on a movie screen.

"Yes, sure, but it's not the same. Besides, I need to check on her."

"In a party dress?"

She shrugged. "We have good news to celebrate, thanks to you."

He snorted.

"David, you're not trusting me again. I thought we were going to be friends."

"Let me be friends with your friends. I'll go with you to tell her this good news."

She shifted her gaze back to her own face and contorted her mouth to inspect her teeth.

"I wish you could," she said finally.

"You wish I could?"

Furious, he bolted up from the bed and strode to the dresser, where he planted his fists on the marble tops on either side and hovered over her. She spread her nails before her face as if to inspect them calmly, but he caught a flicker of uncertainty in her eyes. He longed to dump the drink on her head.

"David, she's afraid of being contagious."

"You are so foolish when you tell lies this big!" He backhanded the glass of gin, and it struck the wall. To his gratification, she flinched.

"Your 'friend' can cough up her lungs for all I care. She's not getting any help from me."

He was striding out of the room, but Laura wailed, "Please, David, wait!" Her voice was so panic-stricken that even in the thick of their fight he was startled by it.

He stopped, and she rushed to embrace him.

"Please, David, please!" Her eyes were tearing again. "Don't fail me now."

"Tell me the truth, then."

He pushed her away, glowering.

"All right," she said quietly. "Yes, I did lie. But I was afraid you wouldn't help her if I told you the truth."

"Maybe I wouldn't. Maybe I won't. But I want the truth, anyway. Hearing a white person tell me the truth will be a new experience. I don't know yet what it will inspire."

"David, don't bother being sarcastic, I'm not up to it. I told you I would tell the truth."

He waited, and after a moment, she said, "The truth is that Sylvia doesn't have TB." She lifted her head and gave him a steady gaze full of either challenge or sincerity, he couldn't tell which. "But she is sick. She's a morphine addict, and she needs to go to a hospital. I knew if I told you that you'd be worried about my hanging around her crowd and you'd be less willing to help her. I told you you couldn't go with me because she wouldn't want strangers to see her in this condition."

"But her friends can."

"That's why they're friends. But she's got no choice, really. Like me."

"What do you mean, 'Like me?' "

"I mean if I had any other source to go to, I wouldn't be asking you for this because it only makes you angry and it humiliates me. I don't want to crawl for money. Do you think Bobette has to beg for anything from Wilbur? Wilbur *showers* her with proof of his love, David. I know you've seen that."

He sat down beside her on the bed. Her feet were small and white and neat in peach-colored sequined slippers.

"So you want the money to help your friend Sylvia get into a hospital to cure her morphone addiction," he said, as if trying the story out for himself. "I can't take her my money in person because she would be . . . ashamed? I am to give her the money to cure herself but she's not to be embarrassed by knowing that it was a gift?"

Laura sighed. "Suspicious, not ashamed."

"Suspicious?"

"Well, that's why I'm wearing this dress, David. She doesn't know she's going to the hospital yet. We—her friends and I—have arranged to take her to dinner and get her good and drunk and then check her in before she really knows what's happening. She's talked a lot about going, but she's been scared and she's broke."

David leaned forward and rubbed his face in his hands. The story had a hundred holes but it hurt his pride too much to demand that she fill them.

Laura laid her cheek on his back.

"I promise I'll spend all tomorrow night with you."

"I want a receipt from the hospital," said David.

21

At twilight, with David's "gift" in her purse, Laura headed on Wilshire toward downtown without a definite destination. It was too early to arrive at Sylvia's, and, besides, she couldn't go empty-handed.

She could drive down to San Pedro, there was time, but she'd have to call to see if Tom Quick was at his warehouse or had already gone back to Oklahoma City. He'd have the smuggled Gordon's on hand—Sylvia's favorite—but he might not be particularly receptive: the last time they'd met she'd slapped his face. Since then, he and David had gone to the fights together when he was in town, but Laura steered clear of him. Now she regretted having slapped him. She should have handled him with style rather than act like a schoolmarm whose virtue had been offended. Then she might have been able to go to him for the money.

Maybe it was still possible. She could apologize for the slap, chat with him a little. Having had his pride wounded, maybe he would be appeased if she asked for a loan; putting herself in his debt could be a form of apology.

What had he expected? He'd tried to kiss her and shove his hand between her legs when they were drunk and were having a grand time tearing up the roads in Griffith Park one night when David was on location for *The Covered Wagon*. Tom had seen her in *Sacred and Sinful*

Love, had invited her out and had obviously confused her life with her film role, though she had been in only one scene, and that as a nameless streetwalker who warns the ingenue against a slattern's life. It had aroused Tom's interest, anyway. She had relished his wanting her then, when her career seemed to be launched and she was Ronald's lover. She had had the world by the tail, she was gloating, and the slap was merely a punctuation mark that said: *You cannot touch me! I have ascended!*

Then was then. Ronald Traylor must have been laughing up his sleeve. To think she had let him put her on her hands and knees, for which he had tossed her a bone, you might say, in payment. She had one minor part, then he was murdered. And she was so far down the list of his girlfriends that she hadn't even been called before the grand jury.

And David, look at David! Without worrying about it, wanting it or trying for it, he had now been given roles in a dozen westerns after *The Covered Wagon*, which had been just about the biggest picture of 1922 and was still going strong. Shot on location in Wyoming, hundreds of extras. When he'd been out there last year, she'd tormented herself by picturing the crew and cast working, making jokes, listening to their director's voice. In her reveries, her jaws would grind their food, her inner ear absorb their banter, and she'd experience vicariously the pleasure of knowing that what you were doing was important and that your face would be flashed upon screens all over the nation, big as billboards, creeping into people's dreams. An interview with Lois Wilson in last month's *Picture Play* made her sick with envy. Lois said that conditions had been rough "but no more so than on any other Western." She said she'd had frostbite, they'd run out of supplies "and had to live on apples and baked beans for a while, but I loved every minute of the picture." Then she went on about the cold and the unexpected snow, and you could tell that she was proud as some actual pioneer woman for having endured these hardships. She bragged about the Conestoga wagons they had used, how people from all over the Middle West had lent them as props, then swung into a sickening song and dance about the Indian actors and actresses, even mentioning David by name, and wound up the whole nauseating mess by claiming she was now making big contributions to Indian schools. Press-agent crap.

God, there was no justice to it! And David came back glowing with his own importance, having found a place in the world to call his own.

With his hair long, like a savage. Playing Indian always brought out the worst in him. He went about the house for weeks strutting like a moronic, overgrown cock.

Well, she had bested him today, but it was getting harder every time.

She drove through MacArthur Park and through downtown only partly aware; she had begun to worry about a telegram which she had stuffed into her glove box. NEED LOAN. BAD TIMES. CAN DISCUSS IN PERSON IF NECESSARY. BK. Sending this message by Western Union had been incredibly brazen. He was trying to scare her. David might have been home to get it, but her luck had held, for once. The man in the uniform seemed vaguely sinister, like an imposter, and her hands had shaken terribly as she signed for the telegram.

She'd managed to put Bill Kale out of her mind so successfully that she presumed he'd forgotten she existed. Or hoped he had.

Can discuss in person if necessary. That was a masterpiece of ambiguity, so like him. If she didn't send him a "loan," he might come and get it; if she wanted him to come, he would. It was either a threat or an offer. But in neither case was he expressing a desire to come.

This was your proverbial other shoe, she thought. In the time since she had run away from Wetoka with David she had worried what Bill would do about it. She had imagined that he might show up and she'd have to explain herself. The truth was, that night in Wetoka, he had promised to do something about her marriage, but instead David had come back and told her he had seen Shingle. It put her at risk. She had worshiped Bill's coldness and his strength, but when it turned out that he was ineffectual—or at least hadn't had sufficient interest to protect her—she'd panicked.

Ineffectual—that was the best way to look at it. The worst way had come seconds later when she feared that her pressing Bill to leave his family had made him decide to sacrifice her. He had turned on her by making it plain to David that she was involved or was perhaps even the instigator. Any witness to what happened to either David or to the German woman that night would know that Shingle had been hired by Laura to drive her and David to be married, and Bill had so much power in that county she'd never be able to prove that Shingle had really been hired by Bill both times.

Now she wondered if there had ever been a moment in his life when he genuinely missed or wanted her. She'd possessed nothing he wanted badly enough that she could fashion his desire into a handle to hold him by. That made him dangerous. She had lived for four years dreading how he might react to what he surely saw as a betrayal—taking their "gold mine," as he put it, away so she wouldn't have to share it. That he might show up here had always made her shudder. The telegram renewed her terror: he had not forgotten.

What would he do if she ignored him?

He was capable of anything, she thought. She certainly couldn't trust him to look after *her* best interests.

Besides, Bill had done nothing to deserve any reward. While she'd had to endure the constant humiliation—the looks from men when she and David were in public that said *You dirty whore you fuck an Indian you'd fuck a nigger or a snake*, the looks from women that said *You couldn't get a white man?* or *I wonder what it's like* or *A million wouldn't be enough*.

She managed to get the gin at a speakeasy in Vernon for a hefty ten dollars. It was far more than she wanted to pay, but the night was critical and she felt the gift was required. She hadn't meant to stay, but the porter and a couple of friends were sitting at a card table in a back room—it was too early for a crowd to gather up front—sipping something made from potatoes, and they invited her to drink with them. It amused her to sit with three Negro fellows and share their liquor—they treated her like a queen. One had a guitar, and they all sang, "Bye, Bye, Blackbird." They praised her voice. The liquor was awful but its white-hot core stunned her brain into tranquility. She could have drunk a quart of it, but she wouldn't have been able to stand, and she didn't relish passing out in that particular place among those particular people.

By the time Laura arrived at Sylvia's big house on the Grand Corso in Venice, the party which had begun there earlier had withered into hard little knots of embittered drunks who'd already made their way through a case of good Scotch brought in from Mexico. Their generous hostess had provided it on the chance that Von Stroheim, for whom she worked as a set designer, might show up and might want something better than the acid whiskey from somebody's washtub that several of these listless drunks were imprudently sipping from a fruit jar with a zinc lid.

It took a minute for Laura's eyes to adjust to the dimness in the room. Sylvia had done the downstairs in Chinatown decadence with red paper lanterns and busily patterned carpets. On the walls she'd painted bunks like those in opium dens. The overall effect was suggestive of sin but ultimately harmless, mere pretense or parody, though Sylvia was known to favor morphine over liquor. Laura stood inside the doorway adjusting her eyes to the dimness when five figures emerged like a developing photograph out of the ruddy gloom. An electrician she knew who worked at Famous-Players/Lasky was reclining on a sofa; lying beside him was a young woman with blond bobbed hair and a short skirt. Her cheek pressed against the electrician's chest, her eyes were closed, and her mouth hung open. Sitting cross-legged about a low table were a woman Laura recognized as a scriptwriter and two stunt men dressed in the fashion of Tom Mix.

Laura stepped forward and stood by the table. They all fell into a silence that Laura first interpreted to be the result of her intrusion, but as the electrician yawned she chalked it up to lassitude. Had Von Stroheim been around, they would have been upright, most likely. In a corner a phonograph needle traveled over and over the last groove of a record.

"Sylvia here?"

The scriptwriter smirked, then raised her thumb. Laura left them to their ennui and walked through a hallway leading to a staircase, under which stood a couple necking—the woman was sandwiched between the man and the wall—and near them a trio of guffawing drunks clung to the newel post, their faces shimmering with sweat.

She hadn't been here in a while. She had taken advantage of David's absence this past month to extend her circle of acquaintances and pleasures. She had been more drunk than sober, had snorted more joy powder than was good for her, and had been embarrassed more than once to wake up with a man she hadn't known until the evening before. As far as finding work as an actress, the month had been a bust. She had become increasingly agitated, feeling the urge to go faster, faster. To catch up. Catch up to what, she couldn't say.

She reached the top of the stairs, gasping and grabbing for the banister. The raw hootch she'd drunk with the colored fellows made her head spin and blurred her vision; it had the nasty tang of a rusty nail. She felt exhausted; being so angry and unhappy wore her out. The bare wooden floors and red light surrounding her recalled a two-dollar whorehouse, doubtless one of Sylvia's intended ironic effects, but too depressing to be laughed at.

She lifted the bottle from its shoe box, was tempted to break the seal, but thought a modicum of self-control would be important here tonight.

She came to a bedroom in which a large tent had been raised so that crossing the threshold you stepped into the domain of a Bedouin chieftain. There were overlapping carpets, huge pillows with gold tassels and low tables with burning candles. The back of the tent had been cut away and on the wall Sylvia had painted a desert scene, complete with oasis and camel.

In one corner a man in a peppermint-striped seersucker coat was sucking smoke from a water pipe. A girl in an Indian princess getup sat beside him with her arms wrapped about her shins and her chin on her knees, her cheeks glistening with what might have been tears. Laura smelled hashish.

Low voices, then sudden laughter from an open doorway where the wall of the tent gave way into a bathroom. An overhead fixture cast a long trapezoid of cold light slanting across the carpet into the tent. Sylvia, in a loose red silk blouse, black sash, and red Arab pantaloons, was seated on the bathtub, gesturing to someone Laura couldn't see. Her blond hair hung like a long limp broom so far down her back that if there had been water in the tub, the tips of it would have gotten wet.

Laura walked in just as a woman in pants and no makeup was leaving.

"Laura!" Sylvia crowed. She rose from the tub to her full six feet and clapped Laura's shoulders lightly. "I'm so glad you came!" Her gray-blue eyes were perfectly round and large as fifty-cent pieces, the whites crisscrossed with a network of fine red lines. She was a pretty woman with a nose slightly too small for her wide face and full, fleshy mouth. "I thought you'd abandoned me!"

Laura flushed. "I've had a hard time getting away from the house lately." She shrugged and rolled her eyes, inviting Sylvia to picture her as imprisoned by David, whom Sylvia had met and found intimidating. "But I missed you, and I just had to come tonight."

Sylvia eyed her, as if wanting to hear more about her motive for being here, but Laura merely held out the shoe box. "I brought a present." She lifted the lid and presented the bottle.

"Shoes!" joked Sylvia. "And just my size! Shall we?"

Laura nodded eagerly. Sylvia broke the seal with a quick twist of her wrist, passed the bottle, and, drinking from it, Laura felt a gratifying burn at the bottom of her stomach.

They chatted for a few moments and Laura wondered, a little panicky, how their small talk would give way to something more substantial. She sat on the closed lid of the commode, aware that her peach-colored dress with the short pleated skirt made her look like someone going to a garden party, or a fashionable lady making an obligatory visit to a bohemian neighbor. The low-cut yoke allowed her rope of pearls to drape over her breasts, and she kept her eyes drifting lazily about the room as she talked so that Sylvia could look wherever she wanted without embarrassment.

Sylvia had worked for Ronald Traylor and found Laura crying the day that Traylor had lost patience with her on the set of *Sacred and Sinful Love*. Sylvia had coaxed her back into good cheer by poking fun at Traylor's phony British accent. A clump of wildflowers, a cartoon cut from a magazine—little gifts—had followed and suggested a need in Sylvia that Laura knew she couldn't meet; she'd tried to keep Sylvia at arm's length and yet not allow her to lose interest.

Finally, Laura leaned forward, rubbed her face with her hands, and sighed. Read my mind, she thought, and was gratified when Sylvia said, "You seem unhappy, dear."

Laura laughed bitterly. "Men!"

"Oh dear! I can remember that," sighed Sylvia.

The woman's large hand went gently to the nape of Laura's neck, and her strong thumb massaged the taut cords of muscle there. The gesture was meant to be soothing, but it only made Laura tense.

"Do you want to tell me about it?" Sensing Laura's uneasiness, she withdrew her hand and used it to lift the bottle again.

"Well, I'm pregnant."

Sylvia gave a low whistle. Laura kept her head bowed; on the back of one of her hands, she thought she spotted a faint darkening patch of skin that suggested liver spots. She put her palms together as if to pray and wedged them between her thighs.

"What about your husband?"

"He doesn't want children."

Laura lifted her head; as she slowly brought her gaze in line with Sylvia's, she was dimly aware that she was giving a performance, but her tears were not precisely false. Even if she were not pregnant at this moment, she had been before and had had to take care of the problem alone, with no one's help, and she *was*, she felt, in deep trouble. She felt woozy and vulnerable and afraid, so the tears were sincere, no matter if they served to move Sylvia to pity.

"Especially someone else's."

Sylvia's face melted. "Oh, you poor thing! And the father—"

Laura emitted a short, sardonic laugh. "*The* father?" She dumped her face back into her hands and wept. Drunk as she was, it was easier than she might have thought. Sylvia murmured, leaned forward, threw her long arm about Laura's shoulders, then pressed her forehead against Laura's temple.

"Sweetie, what can I do?"

"Oh, I don't know!" Laura wailed. "What can anyone do?" She straightened up. Sylvia's arm fell off her shoulders, and Laura reached down to tear a swatch of toilet tissue and blew her nose.

"There are ways to take care of these things," murmured Sylvia. "You're not without friends. I know people—doctors—who owe me a good deed or two."

"I know how to deal with this, but I don't have any money! He's rich as Croesus, but never gives me any. I try to save what little I make, but I couldn't possibly get enough in time, and you know I haven't worked in such a long while."

"Don't worry about the money."

Laura turned to Sylvia, tears streaming down her cheeks. "Oh, I didn't mean you. I mean, I couldn't ask something like that from you. I just didn't know where to turn."

"It's okay. I want to help you, don't you see?"

Because the moment called for it, Laura reached out blindly, found Sylvia's hand, and squeezed it meaningfully. The warmth and strength of the other woman's hand sent a curious sensation down her spine, and she wished desperately for an instant that she was capable of being sincere, of feeling true friendship. A still sober part of her snickered privately at this performance, and she felt contempt for the other woman for being taken in.

"I'm afraid I need a lot," she said.

Sylvia withdrew slightly, as if realizing she hadn't gotten the whole story yet, that Laura had been feeding her information like bait.

"How much?" Now Sylvia sounded like a dispassionate banker, and Laura realized she needed to make another plea before revealing a figure.

Laura sighed, rose unsteadily, and drew the door closed. She sat back down on the commode, letting her knees touch Sylvia's. She bowed her head, and her vision filled with the red silk of Sylvia's blouse. Kneading the other woman's long fingers, Laura thought absently, *she doesn't wear rings.*

"There was a man, back in Oklahoma, that I was in love with. He wasn't good for me at all, but I lost my head and trusted him completely, and—" She raised her head until she could see Sylvia's blue eyes swimming in tears of sympathy.

"He jilted you."

Laura nodded. "More or less. He knew things about me that no one else knew, things I wouldn't have wanted anyone else to know." She halted, unsure of how to go on.

"You don't have to tell me," Sylvia murmured.

"No, I want to! I trust you." Laura squeezed Sylvia's fingers. "I married David just to forget him; I thought when we came out here that that was the end of it, that I'd never hear from him again, and it was good riddance! I wanted to start a new life!" She said fervently, and suddenly she believed it. "Yesterday, while I was sitting at home worrying and crying about being pregnant, this man came to the door—"

"He's out here?" Sylvia said indignantly.

"No, this was a telegram messenger. The telegram said he wanted a 'loan.' You see, he thinks that because David has money that I do, too!" She fell silent, waiting for Sylvia to ask the obvious question.

"And if you don't lend him any money?"

"He didn't say, of course, but I know what he'd do—he'd tell David about me." She could feel Sylvia's mind turning on the next question, feel her wanting to be the kind of friend who asks no questions, and Laura knew that if she told Sylvia a would-be dark secret, the deal would be sealed.

"He'll tell David that I was a . . . a . . . whore!" she wailed, dropped her head against Sylvia's hands and sobbed. Sylvia eased her hands from under Laura's face, letting Laura's cheeks rest on her thighs.

"Oh, you poor kid! It's all right, don't worry about it, pretty baby! I'll take care of you," Sylvia crooned, leaning her own head down until Laura could feel the faint huffs of breath against her hair. After so many hours of worry, it was pleasant to surrender and feel safe, and she put her arms about the woman's thighs to hug her. Sylvia had not even forced her to give a figure: this was blank-check generosity. It made her feel chastised and somehow cleansed, as if forgiven for her sins. Laura's heart lifted in this closeness and trust; it didn't seem to matter that she'd lied—she told herself that even had she revealed the whole truth, Sylvia would have helped her, and somehow that exonerated her for lying.

She felt Sylvia shift about and heard a clicking metallic sound.

"Here." Sylvia cupped Laura's chin in her palm and brought Laura's face close to her own. Her blue eyes were bright with compassion. "I'll take care of everything. I'm just so glad you came to me. You need something that will make it all go away right now."

Sylvia's hand appeared in Laura's vision holding a syringe. Laura sat up, suddenly alert.

"Your offer to help made it all go away, Syl," she said, to make explicit what she felt she'd gained by implication only. "That would just be superfluous. Besides, I need to tend to business."

"Suit yourself."

Laura stood by while Sylvia aimed the needle at her own arm. She didn't want to watch and would have left, but she was waiting for Sylvia to give her something specific in regard to "help." She felt impatient. The needle suggested doctors to her, reminded her of David's "receipt" —the doctor who performed her abortion a year ago could probably be persuaded for a "fee" to write something on his letterhead, but she'd need to get hold of him immediately.

She feared that once Sylvia inserted the needle, the offer would be forgotten. Just when Laura thought she'd have to say something humiliating about the money, Sylvia, head bowed, said, "In the top drawer of my desk, at the back, an envelope. Take all you need." She sounded oddly abject and beaten, as if her own cynicism about people had once again been proved right despite a hope to the contrary. Laura felt guilty. She winced as the needle slid into Sylvia's flesh and thought, *I'll never stoop that low.*

"I'll see you later," she whispered. She leaned over and kissed Sylvia's brow the way a spouse might say goodbye to a busy and distracted mate.

Downstairs, in Sylvia's office, she opened the top desk drawer, found the envelope, and counted a thousand dollars in large and small bills. She shook her head: it never ceased to amaze her how trusting some people were.

22

Iola lay across the bed reading Hearst's *Herald-Examiner*. She'd read every word about the ex-Kaiser's possible return to Germany from exile in Holland; she'd turned to the news about Coolidge's and Secretary Mellon's tax-cut plan, but she couldn't force herself to finish the article, and, instead, skimmed onward through the paper. She looked for but found no news about the Bursum bill. Niels Bohr of the University of Copenhagen was resuming his lecture course at Yale on the structure of the atom; here in Hollywood, picture producers commented on the temporary shutdown of a studio, one of whom said, "Freelance actors and actresses who used to get $3000 a week are now offering their services for one-third that amount."

Ordinarily, Iola didn't read about the motion-picture industry, but since it was like an indigenous crop, as a traveler in the region she felt obliged to learn. She was astonished that people had had their weekly salaries cut down to a figure that approximated her annual wages. As Lenny would say, that pretty well put them on the other side of the barricades.

She took a second pass through the paper to distract herself, then, giving in, she put it aside and rolled onto her back, hands behind her head. An unsettling day, with David tugging at her heart and Mrs. Poynter turning out to be a wealthy, patronizing widow whose presence on the boards of charitable organizations had given her the airs of a duchess. She would not commit the Greater California Women's Clubs to support funding for the Western Association for Indian Defense. Mrs. Poynter obviously wanted to be courted further, and with more ceremony, before she'd relinquish the hesitation that brought her such pleasure. Iola thought, *She wants some man to come talk to her about it, not an Indian girl.*

She hadn't wanted to return to Santa Fe empty handed. David had made an offer, but it had been vague, and she knew that between intentions and a check lay many a deep arroyo into which the transaction could fall. She could press him, but he might think she was using business as a pretext; the thought mortified her. Especially since it was partly true.

When the telephone rang, she thought, Lenny, and made no move to answer it. By the third ring, she decided he didn't deserve to be shunned, so she hastened to catch the call before he gave up.

"Hello." She tried to sound cheerful.

"Iola?"

Her heart leapt. "David? I was just thinking about you," she blurted out.

"Yes?"

"My appointment didn't go so well," she said, then took a deep breath. So long as he had called (and why *had* he called?) she might as well plunge ahead. "So I was wondering if you wouldn't tell me something definite about your willingess to give us something. The people back in Santa Fe could stand some good news."

"I will give you a check for a thousand dollars—would that help?"

"Immensely!" She was stunned.

"I'll bring it to you now. If you don't have other plans."

"No, no," she said. "Please do."

As Iola combed her hair out a little too carefully it dawned on her that she felt as if she were going on a date. Her heart had been thumping like a drum ever since she had recognized his voice. She was elated about the donation, but no mere check would make her hands damp. But why had he called? Had he been groping for a reason to see her again, too? She hadn't given him a chance to speak. She thought of him in his house, calling her. His wife was absent? In another room? Iola hadn't set eyes on the woman since before she had married David. They couldn't have children, Bobette said. And David so obviously wanted them.

She studied her face in the mirror and thought of David's. They both had strong, bold features. The white woman might go away or perhaps David would outgrow her. The children that David and Iola might have would look—

Nonsense!

When she entered the lobby, he was talking to the desk clerk.

"Ah well, here she is, anyway!" He smiled at her, then dipped his head toward the clerk. "He was confused about your name."

Her ears burned, but David sensed her discomfort and took her lightly by the elbow. "Come, let's have some coffee in the dining room." He wore khaki slacks, a white cotton shirt, and a tweed sport coat. He smelled of bay rum. He was smiling enigmatically, as if to savor a secret pleasure.

The dining room was not crowded. With a boyish smile, David led her to a table by the window and pulled back her chair for her. You'd think he went to Harvard, she mused, although, on second thought, his manners seemed self-conscious to her: he was showing them off.

He signaled a waitress to their table, ordered coffee for them both.

"I'm glad you called," Iola said. "I was about to have myself a mope."

He laughed. "I'm glad, too. Here, let's take care of this." He reached into his coat pocket and slipped out the check. She looked at it—yes, it was real, the signature was there—then realized she'd left her purse upstairs.

"I'll get an envelope." He smiled at her confusion, pleased, she could tell, to have flustered her by his gift. After he went into the lobby, the waitress came with a pot of coffee, two cups and saucers, a silver cream pitcher. The waitress bristled with hostility barely held in check. Iola concluded that she and David were too red-skinned to suit her.

David returned and passed Iola the check inside an envelope with the hotel's name embossed on it.

"So your appointment didn't go well."

"No. But this makes up for it, David. You're going to be hearing a lot of thank you's from a lot of people, and I'm going to be the first—thank you very, very much." She grinned at him. "Also I suppose you know this will mean you'll be hearing from us again in the future."

"Well, I hope so." He gave her a meaningful look that shook her. "I had a good time today with you."

She dropped her eyes to her cup and felt her face go hot. "I did, also."

"It wasn't like it used to be, back when I had the ferry and you worked for the doctor, or back when we were children. Today you showed me your respect. We weren't fighting or trying to best each other. Today you showed me you could be my friend."

It was odd, she thought, how he spoke as if she had never declared her love. Something in his words told her that, to the contrary, he'd felt abused by her, or at least unappreciated.

"I felt it, too. Please don't bear me any grudges because of how I behaved when we were children, David."

He chuckled. Then he sighed, laid his cheek in his palm and idly stirred his coffee. "Oh well, you did make me angry many times back then. You were too important to yourself."

He was grinning and only meant to tease her, but she felt stung. A rejoinder flashed to mind—*Yes, unlike you I did try to take my future seriously*—but she held her tongue. And not for the first time today, she thought. She was reminded of how David could make her furious in a way that no other man could.

"Well, many people told me I was important. They can share the blame."

"And many people told me I wasn't," he said earnestly. "They can share the blame for that, too."

Neither his self-pity nor his apparent need to prove them all wrong was becoming. "It doesn't matter now one way or the other, I think."

"You're right. But what they said about you, it was true, you know."

"What do you mean?" She was prepared for an insult, but his soft, melancholy tone undercut her suspicion.

"It was how you should have been treated. What's happened to me has been luck. Hearing about your work today, what you do, it made me a little ashamed of myself. It made me want to do more than just write a check now and then. My father was always generous. We Kiowas have always believed that a man is rich only in proportion to what he gives away, and you made me see that I've become too much like a white man with my money." He grinned. "I should hold a giveaway."

"Oh, David! Good! I'm happy you want to!"

He said wryly, "Yes, I knew you would be pleased with me."

"It's a good thing, whether I'm pleased about it or not!"

"That's truly why I called. I have a plan, you see."

"A plan?"

He picked up his cup and saucer and put them to the side, then wiped the tablecloth free of spilled sugar and crumbs with his splayed fingers. Finished, he placed his clasped hands in the spot he had prepared.

"Yes. This has taken me a while, but do you remember how you and Miss Roberts always wanted me to give money to start a hospital or a school in Anadarko?"

"Yes, is that what you—"

"In a way," he said. "I want to start a foundation that does nothing but give money to good causes. Our children's home would be one, but I could build what they call an endowment so that plenty of money would be there for many other things."

"David, that's wonderful!"

He paused a moment, then flashed her a boyish, mischievous grin. "There's more to the plan. You see, I know this is a good thing all right, I know it should be done, but it doesn't interest me much. I like playing Indians in pictures and going to the fights and the races. I like being with my friends at the War Paint Club, and I like to read history and listen to piano music. I stay busy with Wilbur playing this white people's money game, but, to be truthful, I wouldn't want to spend any time worrying about this foundation and its money." He gave her a very steady, level gaze. "I want you to come be the person who has charge of it. You can be the chief, give out the money however you see fit. If you want to give it all to the Western Association for Indian Defense then you can do it."

She'd been too stunned to think, and it was much too important a decision to be made on the spot. Later, after they'd said goodnight, she sat at the window looking off to the hills where the lights from houses glimmered against a dark backdrop like stars. She tried to think clearly about the offer. She'd told him, "David, it's a great thing to do. You don't need me, though. You can hire a very able administrator with the right sympathies, can't you?" And he'd said, "Maybe I won't get around to doing it at all if I don't have you and your good influence to push me into it."

Gentle blackmail. As if to say, *If you don't take my offer then all this good will not be done. It will be your fault.*

Around midnight, she rose from the window with a heavy sigh, slipped out of her robe, and got into bed. Of course she wanted to do it even as much as she wanted to see that it was done. Was his offer also a way of saying *I want you here with me?* Had he created this foundation just to draw her here?

She knew she might accept his offer partly to be here with him. But she couldn't allow herself to take it if that were her only reason.

Lenny loved her and proved it day after day; he wanted to marry her. With Lenny, she would have a devoted mate who adored her, an intelligent, warm, sensitive, and witty man who'd doubtless be as good a father as he'd be a husband. Her youth was passing, and she yearned to have a family and children. David was already married and was so unprepared to express his feeling for her that he had to invent a foundation to lure her rather than say, *Stay because I need you and want you.*

And this foundation was the best evidence she had for his regard. Why should she throw away what she had with Lenny to be near a man with whom she had no future?

As far as doing good was concerned, she could continue to work in Santa Fe without feeling she'd cheated anyone by turning down the offer. David's philanthropy shouldn't depend on her being held hostage.

Once she'd decided to return to Santa Fe, she felt immensely sad and wept. Before she fell asleep, she consoled herself with the thought that her life had been reasonably good before she came, and she could expect it to stay that way. If she wasn't pleased with her decision, she was reconciled to it.

She awoke once in the darkness and guessed the time to be somewhere around three and fell asleep once more. Then her mind came half-awake in her slumbering body as the tide of the night ebbed out. She couldn't place herself. A classroom. A boarding school, a line of children—she knew they were Sioux—coming in the door, and the line went down the hall, out to the porch of the building, into the field and over the hill as far as you could see; as the children stepped forward, she would look into their mouths and their eyes and their ears, listen to their chests when they breathed and mark down in a folder what was wrong; the children kept coming faster, each one sicker than the last, and the white people were hurrying them through the line as Iola desperately tried to keep up. Outside the window the ground was stone frozen, and she kept hearing the peculiar sound of flesh going *ca-chunk* against the ice. When she turned to look she saw a horse lying on its side, tangled up in a barbed-wire fence. It was beating its head against the ice, again and again, trying to knock itself senseless. Nobody could do anything about it until they'd finished with the children.

She woke up sick and horrified and held herself very still in the violet light. The nightmare had juxtaposed and distorted two actual incidents from when she and Vera had traveled to do the health survey. Gradually, as the hotel room asserted itself, she shook off her nightmare.

Exhausted, she drifted into dreamless sleep. She overslept and yanked herself awake in panic when she realized the room was flooded with light. Feeling disorganized and rattled, she tried to pack. The suitcase wouldn't close, and she couldn't remember how she'd originally folded her clothes and placed the shoes and hats. She repacked the valise several times, but no matter how she tried, the case wouldn't close unless one garment was left out.

Weary and frustrated from struggling with the suitcase, she sat in the desk chair. She closed her eyes to rest them. The warm sunlight streaming through the window bathed her face. Lassitude overtook her, she dozed sitting up until jolted awake as if by an electric shock when the telephone rang.

"Yes?"

"I know you've been thinking about it," said David. "Can you give me your answer? I haven't slept since I saw you."

"Oh, David," she sighed. She sounded sad, but she felt oddly punch-drunk, a little giddy. "I can't get my suitcase closed."

His rich baritone laugh boomed in her ear. "That settles it, then. You'll have to stay! I can't tell you how happy it makes me!"

Back in Santa Fe, she packed her belongings and said goodbye to everyone. She never identified David as anything but a donor, but Lenny must have known—the abruptness of her decision to move could only be explained by a previous tie. Everyone was happy for her, pleased that she'd be in a better position to do good things. Lenny tried to hide his wounds by waxing enthusiastic over Iola's opportunity, bravely pretending that the common good was far more important than the needs of his single heart.

In the early spring of 1924, she moved into a boardinghouse and saw David almost daily as they discussed plans for the Copperfield Foundation. They rented a suite of offices downtown where Iola, David, and Wilbur each had working space. It pleased her that David was so directly involved in the enterprise because she was eager to be with him as much as possible during the day. Wilbur pointed out to him that this arrangement was more efficient than their meeting at the sidewalk café, but after a few weeks, much to her disappointment, David said he missed his morning walks on the beach. The offices made him feel too much like a person whose life was devoted to commerce, which made her wonder what he did when he was not working and whether he and Mrs. Copperfield did it, whatever "it" was, together.

So Wilbur went back to meeting him at the café, and they would both arrive at the downtown office around noon. Now and then Wilbur would come alone and report that David was spending the day with his pals at the club on Cahuenga, had gone to the races with Tom, or was reading in the library. And she wondered, What about his wife?

Iola coveted her moments with him during working hours. For the rest of 1924 and early 1925, he almost always drove her home and had time to park the car, stroll up the walk and through the door with her, stop to chat with the crippled landlady, drink a cup of coffee, and, once or twice, even stay to have supper with her and the other boarders. While accepting or declining an offer, he never once said, "My wife is expecting me" or "Maybe I should let my wife know I'll be late." He thus appeared to be a bachelor, and Iola still couldn't understand what he and Laura meant to each other or how they spent their time together.

Once during this period, Wilbur and Bobette invited Iola to supper. After Pearl had gone to bed and Wilbur had left to buy pipe tobacco, Iola and Bobette sat in the Smythes' cozy living room over cups of tea; Iola, feeling both relaxed and accepted, asked, "Do you know David's wife very well?"

"No. I've only met her a time or two. She's very pretty. I saw her in that last picture where she was a prostitute."

Iola listened keenly for a trace of irony but heard none. Oh, she was so ready to discover something bad! But the atmosphere here in the Smythe home discouraged it. The aging, overstuffed chairs wore their well-laundered antimacassars with the air of down-at-the-heels but genteel dowagers, and on the wall above the sofa hung a needlepoint sampler done by Bobette's mother showing the letters of the alphabet in modestly accomplished stitching.

Iola couldn't resist probing further.

"Have you ever heard him talk about her?"

"No."

"Me either."

They fell silent a moment, Iola letting the fact of David's not talking grow weightier by the moment as it hung between them.

"But Wilbur says he buys her a lot of things and gives her a very generous allowance," Bobette added, defending David against Iola's unspoken charge.

"You don't think it means anything, then, that he doesn't ever mention her?"

"Gosh, I don't know. I thought that since he was an Indian"—Bobette blushed suddenly—"I mean, I presumed that was why he was quiet about her."

Iola laughed. "Well, despite what you see in the Hollywood pictures, Indian men are quite the talkers when they want to be. They can complain or brag about their wives the same as any other men."

"I thought you would know his wife. Didn't he meet her in Oklahoma?"

"They did get married there, but I didn't meet her. I knew her by sight. She and I weren't—" She broke off, thinking *I'm about to say too much.* "Very well known to each other," she finished lamely.

They fell silent, and Iola could sense Bobette's mind turning.

"Have you ever thought of getting married again?"

Iola hesitated. Bobette had neatly skipped a few steps: she hadn't asked if Iola was a widow (obviously she'd heard it), and the placement of her question suggested that she had an inkling of Iola's unrequited yearning for David.

"Yes, I have. Just before I came out here there was a man in Santa Fe, his name was Lenny. He wanted to marry me. But . . ." Iola shrugged.

"You weren't in love with him?"

"No. But I respected him. He really loved me, still does, I imagine, and I think I broke his heart. He's a good man, and he'll be a good husband and father for some woman."

"A lot of girls would settle for that."

"You didn't."

Bobette smiled. "No. I was very lucky. I *am* very lucky. Was your first marriage a good one?"

"No. It really wasn't much of any kind of marriage."

Bobette looked puzzled and curious, but Iola couldn't bring herself to tell the dreary story of her marriage to Conway. In lieu of reciting the painful details, she said, "Anyway, I've learned what I want. I'd rather not have any marriage than to marry for the wrong reasons or to have someone marry me for the wrong reasons."

"Good for you," Bobette said, smiling.

Iola wanted to steer the conversation back to Laura and David, who were, to her mind, people who were married for the wrong reasons, but she didn't want to sound like a gossip.

Soon after this conversation, Iola went to see *Sacred and Sinful Love.*

Laura was not on the screen for more than a minute or two. The young handsome hero has heard that the girl he loves was once a prostitute, and so he goes to investigate; he finds her friend—played by Laura—and quizzes her about his true love's past, and the friend, weeping (too much, Iola thought) pleads with the hero to forgive the woman he loves. The actress was pretty but gaunt, wasted, appropriately degraded from having walked the streets. So powerful was the image of the woman on the screen that for a few days Iola went about thinking of Laura as a prostitute who wanted to reform only to have to remind herself that Laura had only been playing a part.

On another occasion—a Sunday afternoon in May—David showed up at her boardinghouse unexpectedly and said, "You remember once I promised to take you to the beach?"

They drove out in his Packard and met Jack Little Tree and his wife, Dove Tail, at Malibu. She thought at first it was an accident, but it turned out David and Jack had already arranged it. Iola had accompanied David to a War Paint banquet (why wouldn't Laura go?), and, as much as she enjoyed meeting his Indian-actor friends—and felt a little less alien herself in Los Angeles because of them—she disliked being David's date. During the banquet people who didn't know David well presumed Iola to be his wife, causing her the excruciating embarrassment of having to correct the misapprehension while wishing it were true.

Her discomfort was less severe with Jack Little Tree and Dove Tail, but still, she felt manipulated—the other couple had apparently been expecting them, but David had not told her they were to form a foursome, and for a moment when they were greeting one another, she was surprised. While David and Jack strolled up the beach, working at their cigars, Iola and Dove Tail sat on a blanket and watched the Sunday afternoon promenade through their sunglasses. Dove Tail was pregnant and Iola eyed her rounded abdomen with envy.

"What're you hoping for?"

"A girl." Dove Tail laughed. "I'll tell you. If you ask when Jack's around, though, I'll have to say a boy."

"That's what Jack wants?"

"Sure, wouldn't David, too?"

Did she presume that Iola was David's mistress, that she would know the answer to such a question? Iola cringed, but tried to ignore her discomfort. Maybe Dove Tail only meant David was probably like most men.

"I don't know what he would want." She needed to end any speculation that she and David were lovers. "He doesn't tell me much about what's in his heart." She took a breath. "Maybe his wife would know."

"Doubt it."

"Why?"

Dove Tail shrugged and looked away. Iola guessed that she was reluctant to offend. After a long moment, though, Dove Tail said, as if divining every nuance of emotion that Iola had felt since first hearing of David's marriage to the white singer, "They marry them to keep on top. They don't let their secrets be known to the enemy."

"What do you mean?"

"Well, David, he got a lot of money all of a sudden and needed something to buy to prove to everybody he was a big man, better maybe than a lot of white men who weren't rich enough to buy her. Marrying an Indian woman wouldn't prove nothing except that he's just an Indian. That's the way I figure it."

It seemed so bald, so cynical; it hurt Iola to think that Dove Tail must feel so little respect for David. She was about to rush to his defense but held back, seeing that, in truth, what Dove Tail had said was not wrong.

"Why don't you think that he loves her?"

Again a shrug. "Is she here?" Dove Tail said finally.

At last, on a spring afternoon in 1926 when David held a party for the Heaven's Haven children at his home, Iola encountered the real Laura for the first time since Wetoka. Laura looked very little like the haggard streetwalker from the film. She wore a flapper's shift that left her sleek arms bare and showed the roll of her stockings just above the knees; Iola was struck with begrudging admiration for those well-proportioned limbs and their fair skin. Her throat, her collarbone, her neck—she exposed much of her flesh. She was flushed and smiling as she moved toward a trio of young men standing at the buffet table on the back lawn. She laughed too loudly while poking her head into their circle, demanding and receiving their undivided attention. Her eyes were bright lacquered marbles, and as she jabbered full steam at all three men at once she kept those thin white arms in motion, her hands flitting about to playfully tug one man's earlobe and give another a jocular punch on the arm. She was an outrageous flirt and, unlike the woman in the picture she'd portrayed, didn't appear desirous of reforming any aspect of her behavior.

As Iola, Wilbur, Bobette, and Pearl came across the lawn, Laura broke away from the trio to greet them. To Iola's surprise, Laura shook hands with the firm, decisive grip of a man.

"You're the one from David's tribe in Oklahoma?"

Iola dumbly nodded yes.

"And you've come out here to help him give away his money?" she continued, deadpan, then winked at Wilbur to show she was only joking. "Oh, I'm sure it's for a good cause." Laura laughed as Iola stood mute and helpless. Looking off beyond the buffet table, she saw David playing blindman's buff with the children. She gathered her wits sufficiently to form a sentence—"We certainly believe there are good causes to spend money on"—but when she turned back, Laura was walking away, head cocked over her shoulder, hand extended up as she waggled the backs of her fingers at them in a sort of digital "toodle-loo."

Iola felt stung, intimidated by the blonde's brashness and self-possession. She was, moreover, disconcerted by Laura's knowledge of her life. Had David talked to his wife about her? How much had he told? She thought ruefully that if he'd told Laura anything, it would mean he felt closer to Laura than to Iola. For the rest of the afternoon, Iola felt that Laura had put her under surveillance and was silently accusing her of trying to steal David away.

Eventually, two parties were in progress at the Copperfield's, one on the lawn, one upstairs in Laura's salon. Laura's guests from the film studio became drunk and loud as the day wore on. Their laughter and singing upstairs could be heard above the children's voices through the open French doors off the second-story balcony.

David was tense and distracted all afternoon. Iola knew he was angry. She suspected that the job she was performing—blowing noses, wiping ice cream from blouses, directing traffic to and from the food table, and managing games—had been intended for Laura. Knowing David's desire for children, Iola guessed that he had wanted Laura to play hostess and nanny so that she could get used to the idea and perhaps even warm to a particular child.

Gradually she sank into a blue mood that left her feeling profoundly alienated.

"You look tired," Wilbur said as she was absently cutting pieces of cake and putting them onto plates.

"Yes, I am. A little." She looked up, caught his glance: it was laden with more sympathy than one would deserve for merely being tired, and she understood that he meant to console her for having to suffer such close proximity to the Copperfields' marriage. Guessing that her secret desires had been the subject of the Smythes' pillow talk, she reddened.

"Actually, I was thinking of when I was doing the health survey, about how those children were so less lucky than these. I wondered if I really should be here doing this. . . ." She raised her metal scoop, though her "this" had not meant ladling ice cream, precisely.

"I'm glad you are, and so is Bobette," said Wilbur, understanding. "The Foundation will help a lot of people, you know that."

"Handling money," Iola said with a sour twist of her mouth, "even money for good causes . . . Maybe I think I should get back down in the trenches."

A commotion on the upstairs balcony interrupted them. Laura and two young men were standing at the rail singing "For He's a Jolly Good Fellow." With Laura's arms draped over their shoulders, each man had a drink hoisted and pointed toward David, who stood below, watching. One young man slipped an arm about Laura's waist, dragging her dress up her thigh as they swayed.

The song might have been a friendly tribute to David under other circumstances, but given the afternoon's tension, it hinted at mockery. The children were galvanized by the grownups singing so boisterously, and Bobette, nearby, said, "Come on, children, let's start cleaning up our mess!"

David stood stock-still, a cake-smeared knife in his hand. The muscles along his jaw tightened under his tawny skin. After a minute, he tossed the knife onto the buffet table and walked to the house.

The younger children had grown tired and cranky; Bobette had the older girls prepare the younger ones for leaving, while Iola volunteered to supervise the older boys in taking plates into the house. It wasn't until Iola was in the large, tile-floored kitchen that she suspected she had come inside for ulterior motives. When the boys went out for another load, Iola went to find David on the pretext of telling him that the children were almost ready to leave.

When she came down the hall behind the staircase, she heard David's and Laura's voices close by, so she halted, thinking it would be rude to intrude on them in their home.

"David!" Laura was mewling fitfully like a child. "Let go of my arm!"

"I don't want you to be like this!"

Iola moved forward, not knowing whether to declare her presence or to allow them their privacy. In the darkness of the corridor, she edged closer and saw them standing at the foot of the staircase, David holding Laura tightly at her wrist with his left arm until suddenly he released her.

"I don't like the way you behave around those men."

"I'm just having fun, David!"

"Don't drink any more."

"All right," Laura said. Unexpectedly, she gave him a childish, mock pout that opened into a silly grin. "Don't be so gruff, you old bear!" She giggled, then fell into him, wrapped her arms around his neck, pressed her slim form into his loins and began moving her hips and murmuring profanities in baby talk. Iola flushed and crept backward, glimpsing David's face: eyes shut, teeth clenched in pleasure and exasperation, as if he knew he was being manipulated but couldn't resist it.

She fled to the backyard, where the cool air seared her burning cheeks. She was nauseated. She tried to get the children rounded up and to avoid thinking of what she had seen. After a while, David and Laura emerged from the house, Laura at his arm, eyes glittery, waving to everyone, saying goodbye to the children, shaking Iola's hand, Bobette's hand, Wilbur's hand, scruffing the children on their heads, saying, "You children come back, now," while David beamed with the smug complacency of a country squire.

Later that evening, Iola could think of nothing but the astonishing things she'd witnessed at the Copperfields'. Gradually, an understanding came to her: Laura offered David various kinds of torment. She made him feel anger, lust, pride, defeat, humility, then gave him back his self-esteem by making him a conqueror. Iola thought, groping for the right word, she *seduces* him. It didn't mean merely that she inspired a carnal desire. It meant "bewitching," or "hypnotizing"; it meant keeping his mind and his feelings aroused and focused on her. He was like a liquid mixture in a bowl that needed constant stirring, and Laura was the stick. Laura's strength was David's weakness. She was in control, and that was why she stayed. No matter how angry he might be at her, no matter how she might humiliate him, she could always appease him and make him imagine his pretty white wife doted on him. She would be free to make her next move while he basked in his delusion of good fortune.

Thereafter, Iola feared Laura's power. Disenchanted and heartsick, she spent several weeks feeling she'd made the wrong decision to come to Los Angeles. She felt defeated, lonely; David had promised her nothing but a job, of course, but hadn't something more been implied?

Along with her confusion, Iola couldn't shake her disappointment at David's letting himself be manipulated by Laura, losing his dignity. She wondered if her own love for him wasn't misplaced or blind; she wondered if he could ever leave Laura.

From then on, she struggled to keep her feelings for David neatly circumscribed by their business relationship. When he had a thread hanging from his coat, she didn't brush it away as an excuse to run her hand across his shoulder; once when he complained of having a lash stuck in his eye, she gave him a compact mirror rather than use the occasion as a pretext for bending her face close to his; she didn't invite him to share lunch at her desk; she declined his offers to take her home after work.

She spent the month of March on the road in New York and Santa Fe, and on her return to the office, David burst in, beaming, and grabbed her to him.

"My but I've missed you!" he said.

Through April, there he was, pressing her to go with him to War Paint Club socials, to lunch, to the races, seeming hurt when she declined. It was very hard to say no to him, and the rejection on his face always caused her a pang of regret.

On the first of May he brought her daisies, placed them on her desk, and asked her to dinner.

"I have to work tonight. Thank you just the same."

"I'll work with you."

Later, when they were alone in the office, she gave him a stack of mail-outs to fold and to insert into envelopes, thinking he'd find the work tedious and leave.

They worked quietly side by side for a while, then he said, "I need your advice."

"My advice? That's usually Wilbur's department."

"The advice of a woman is what I mean."

"Just any woman will do?"

"No," he frowned, as if Iola's gigging him was something he knew he deserved but didn't like. "A friend, a woman friend."

"David," Iola said sincerely, "if there is anything at all I am to you, it's that, for certain."

"Yes. I can trust you."

He took her silence as a promise of loyalty, and said, "You see, I don't know what to do."

"What's the problem?"

He shrugged. His hands absently folded the sheets of paper in thirds. Iola waited, mute. She would not prompt him. Finally, he gave out a huge sigh.

"About a month ago, I hired a detective. I wanted him to find out how Laura was spending her time. She was never home, day or night, and she would lie to me—" He turned toward Iola, and his dark eyes were blazing with wounded anger. "The detective says she's been going to several places, some of them the homes of her friends, where she takes drugs. He gave me his report today."

Iola was surprised to learn that he'd received this news so recently—his mood had seemed wholly normal. He was very good at hiding his pain.

"I'm sorry to hear it."

"You see, I don't know what to do about it."

"Do you think she's in danger?"

"Danger?"

"Of doing harm to herself."

"Yes," he said. "There's that."

And what else? Iola wondered. As pleased as she was to have David confide in her, and as pleased as she was to learn something about his relationship to Laura, she was irked at being put in a position to suggest a course of action that might help them, even if it gave her a small measure of power over Laura's fate.

"What do you think I should do?"

"If I were your wife, I'd want you to do whatever was best for me whether I knew it or not at the time and whether I liked it or not at the time. I'd want you to know what I really needed and be firm in making me do whatever was really in my best interest."

He took Iola's hand. "Thank you," he said earnestly. "That's what I needed to hear."

She didn't see him for four days, then she learned from Wilbur that he'd placed Laura in a sanatorium. David began to haunt the offices morning and evening, clearly at loose ends. No one was allowed to visit Laura for a while, although she could call home. He acted as if he were lonely, as if his wife had, indeed, been a companion to him when she was well. Iola didn't invite him to talk to her about Laura, but he seemed so forlorn that she was unable to turn him down when he invited her to the pictures, to dinner, or for a walk, one evening, along the beach near the Santa Monica pier where he used to stroll each morning at dawn.

There was a half-moon, light enough to see the surf throwing out a silver rope of foam as it came onto the beach and their footsteps filling instantly with black water behind them. He talked for a while about the other people he usually met walking on the beach, then he pointed out the home of a well-known studio head.

"Every Sunday night he has a dance party on a wooden platform down here, with two orchestras, a fox-trot band and a rhumba band. Sometimes Laura used to come by herself and stand out here in the darkness so she could identify the stars who were dancing. There's always somebody like Billie Burke or Mary Pickford around."

The picture of Laura hovering beyond the reach of the festive lights evoked a rare flicker of sympathy in Iola.

"Well, she got to be in pictures."

"Not enough," said David. "She's always been jealous of me."

He was quiet a moment and they walked toward the lighted pier.

"I took your advice, you know."

"Yes?"

"I put Laura in the hospital."

"I heard."

"Well, you didn't hear how I did it, because nobody knows. I followed her myself one night to one of these houses of her friends. They were having a party. I went inside and picked her up from the bathroom floor and threw her over my shoulder and put her in my car—she woke up kicking and screaming, but she was too doped up to do much—and then I drove her to this hospital." This was obviously difficult for him to tell; Iola wanted to interject a dozen questions but held her tongue.

"She said she hated me for it."

"You did the right thing. Wilbur told me something about it. You probably saved her life. Maybe she'll come to see that."

"Maybe." He sounded doubtful. "Maybe it was a mistake."

"Why? Because of how she feels?"

"I meant my marriage was maybe a mistake."

Iola reeled inside but simply kept one foot moving ahead of the other toward the distant lights. Between them she could feel the tension grow taut as a cocked bowstring. She tried to read his face but couldn't. He was unhappy, that was all she saw. Fearing he would change the subject and the moment would be lost, she stopped walking and gestured toward the ground. He removed his jacket and spread it on the dry sand; they sat together, she on his lee side, feeling his warmth and smelling the aroma of his shirt.

"David, did you never wonder about my marriage?"

"To this Conway man?"

"What other marriage would I mean?" Was he acting dense merely to make all this difficult for her?

"Yes, I have wondered."

"What did you wonder?"

"What kind of man he was."

"Why that?"

"Because he was a white man. That surprised me, but only in a way. You were always closer to them than most of us. But you were also so proud."

"That's the pot calling the kettle black, David!"

He ignored her reproach. "I thought he must have been a very special man, probably educated, maybe a doctor."

"You didn't wonder if I loved him?"

He shrugged. "Why else would you marry him?"

She sighed. Couldn't he see that from his own case? Or was that his case? She refused to believe that David could love, or have ever loved, a woman who treated him so badly. She wrapped her arms about her shins and stared at his profile until he turned to meet her gaze.

"I want to tell you something important. It's about my marriage. Nobody knows this. It's not that it needs to be a secret, you understand, only that I haven't wanted to tell it." She drew a few long breaths, then said, "You have to know first of all that before I'd been in Europe very long I got heartsick from seeing so many people die—soldiers, women, children, old men. I learned pretty quickly that when it comes to suffering, everybody has a knack for it no matter what their color. And when it comes to making people suffer, these white armies had a talent for turning their populations into cannon fodder.

"It was a living nightmare, David. By the time Conway came along I was just thinking that death was everywhere all the time and that all of the people all over the globe were going to be killed and mutilated by this war—I was thinking that this war was the end to life here, period, the end of humankind, no thanks to white men.

"At first Sergeant Conway was just another casualty to me. We were working out of a circus tent set up in a potato field a few miles behind the lines, and he was brought in to us. He had been wounded; his insides were like a sieve, and he was . . . leaking blood inside while the doctor and I stood around his cot and joked with him so that he wouldn't know what was happening when it came. He knew, anyway. He took a fancy to me. He told me he came from an old Philadelphia family, but then he winked like it didn't matter now. He was redheaded, and he had a face that a lot of white girls would have envied, sort of boyish and fine-featured, and he had a very merry smile despite his pain."

She lapsed into silence a moment, the memories flooding back to her.

"He knew he was going to die, so he convinced the chaplain to ask me to marry him before he did. He was such a pleasant boy I was touched, and the request seemed safe enough because he was only another casualty who was bleeding to death. So I held his hand while the chaplain stood at the foot of his bed and recited from the Good Book. We could hear shells from German artillery go overhead and explode a mile or so to the other side of the potato field. There were rumors that the Germans were about to mount a counteroffensive, and I guessed that if he didn't die from his wounds, he'd never survive being moved if we had to retreat."

She glanced at David. He seemed attentive, but he was not looking at her. His gaze went out toward the horizon, and eventually her silence caused him to turn to her.

"David, this isn't easy to tell!"

"I'm grateful to hear it."

She nodded. "You see, the chaplain asked me to pray for him. I'd stopped believing in what the missionaries had taught us about being Christian, David—the Germans were Christians, the French, the English, the Americans—but I thought if it would help, I mean that I knew it couldn't hurt, so I did pray for Sergeant Conway."

She sighed and averted her face from David's gaze. "So long as he was dying, I felt free to pray that he would live. I hung around at the end of his cot for a day watching him slip under, and the grief that I anticipated feeling was very . . . well, the only word I can think of is *comfortable*, David. I didn't know that, though, until Chaplain Wilkins came up to me the evening after Conway and I were married, and he was grinning as if he'd witnessed a miracle. He said, 'Your groom's getting better! Your prayers are being answered!'

"I just hadn't been prepared for that to happen. For a few hours I was very confused; I kept thinking I should feel grateful and relieved, but it wouldn't come. That night was very hectic; we were getting new rumors that the Germans were about to advance, so we knew that we might have to retreat. French refugees came swarming back from the front. We could hear artillery banging away all around us throughout the night, so we were very tense because we didn't know exactly where the war was going on at any given hour.

"I just tried not to think and to stay busy. Later that night, when I went in to see him, he seemed to be asleep. But then while I was feeding a soldier next to him, he came awake and grabbed at my arm. He scared me. When I turned around, he was sitting half up, and his eyes were burning like he had a fever. He said, 'You saved my life, angel.' And Wilkins was standing there smiling and sort of blessing us. I gave Conway's hand a squeeze as if to say I was happy to see him so well, but then I went out of the tent as fast I could.

"I looked for some place where I could just be alone to think, and ended up sitting in the middle of an empty field. I could hear shells going overhead and there were flares in the distance." She paused a moment, the images washing over her, recalling suddenly how the French railway gun seven miles to the rear of their position kept flinging huge projectiles that did a whirlagig whistle overhead then landed miles away with a flash and an impact that she could feel in her haunches. The noise, the confusion of the lights, the way death was in the very air —the malevolence of it all was bewildering and made her despair.

"David, the marriage, it was supposed to have been like a last rite. He wasn't supposed to get better. His death had already been decided by the extent of his wounds. The marriage had only been a gesture of consolation." Iola blew out a breath. "The truth is that while I sat there in the middle of that field, I started to feel that he'd betrayed me, that he'd reneged on his part of the bargain. I couldn't get these bad thoughts out of my head—I was . . . I was wishing—" She faltered, unable to articulate her thought.

"I understand," David put in quickly.

"I tried to chastise myself by going back on duty at midnight. I just kept on working for hours and hours in the badly wounded wards, and when the head nurse finally ordered me to go off duty, I went down to the canteen that stayed open all night for the doughboys and poured coffee and washed cups until dawn.

"Somehow I managed to burn all my anger and guilt out that way. I started back for the hospital tent. I thought I'd go see Conway and try to show him that I was pleased he was getting well. I felt resigned." She could recall trudging in the hazy half-light along the muddy road, which even at that hour was crowded with troops, mule-drawn ammo carts, and ambulances. She had vowed to devote herself to his infirmity; everyone had to make a sacrifice in war, and hers would be the folly of a good deed.

"But as soon as I stepped inside, the chaplain stopped me and gave me a sorrowful look. I just felt numb, and he had a hard time believing I wasn't in shock and that I'd understood what he had to tell me. But the truth was I just didn't know whether to feel glad or sad."

"Yes, I can see why," murmured David.

She felt better for having revealed part of the story but anxious about telling the rest.

"When I came back to the States, I intended to see his mother in Philadelphia. I didn't want anything from her. I only wanted to tell her about how brave her boy had been and how painlessly he had died. I thought that she'd want to hear from someone who'd known him during his last moments. When I called her from New York, she'd already been told about our marriage by the chaplain. She seemed very happy to hear from me and was excited about my coming to visit."

"Did she know you were Kiowa?"

"I'm coming to that. I got on the train in New York, but I couldn't make myself get off in Philadelphia. I knew she'd be shocked to see me, and, besides, her son had really meant little to me. Later I wrote her a little about myself. I told her what I'd known of her son and made it clear that I'd make no claim on their family since our attachment was too slight. An attorney replied that the family respectfully requested that I revert to my maiden name and offered compensation for me to do it."

"Yes, well, they were *white*, weren't they!" David snorted with disgust. He smiled at her. "And you kept it to spite them—I remember when you first came here, I met you as Mrs. Conway."

"Maybe it was to spite them. But in a way it hurt my pride to keep it. I was slow to understand why I used it for so long after I came back."

She closed her eyes and went silent, her pride too great to offer him this gift without his showing he wanted to know. At last, he asked, "Why did you keep it, then?"

"Because I wanted to be known as a war widow."

"Why?"

"This is hard to say and hard to explain, David. When I told people I was a war widow, then they made certain assumptions about me, about the condition of my heart. They thought that I'd loved my husband and that when he died, I'd grieved and probably put my heart away in a trunk, so to speak. My potential as a mate, for them, had already been used and whatever remained had been sealed and put away, you see?"

"Yes, but why would you want people to think that?"

"Because," she began, then faltered and had to wait for her heart to stop pounding. "Because it was true in spirit if not in fact. I mean even before I met Conway I'd loved and lost and grieved and put away my heart in a trunk, and so long as I was 'Mrs. Conway,' nobody was going to ask difficult questions of me, including myself."

She was trembling and had to stop speaking. He turned to look at her, confused and troubled to see her on the verge of tears. She thought, He won't be so stupid as to ask who I mean, will he? She'd told him in many words that took a long and looping route about the truth: *I didn't love my husband. My marriage was a mistake I made because I was in love with you.*

He leaned toward her and kissed her very softly on the lips. When he eased back, she pushed forward slightly, and he kissed her again, with more passion. Her heart was hammering as she passed her hands over his cheeks. Her lips parted and she felt his breath in her lungs.

"Come," he whispered hoarsely when he broke off the kiss. He rose and slipped his arm about her waist and clutched her closely to his side as they walked up to the pier then across the street to where he'd parked the Packard in the shadows beneath a line of palms. He let her in on the passenger side. Was he going to take her somewhere? Was that kiss all they would have or was it a prelude?

When he got behind the wheel, he leaned toward her; she tilted her head to make it easy for him, and he kissed her long and deeply once more, then his lips moved down her neck.

"Oh, I've wanted to do this for so long," he whispered.

"Yes." She clutched him around the neck as his lips went to the hollow under her throat. Down the street people were strolling to and from the pier. His movements rustled against the leather seats, and she could hear her own quick breathing. Lights from the passing autos flickered against the roof of the car. When she felt the lapels of her blouse being tugged back so his mouth could reach lower, she almost panicked.

"David," she whispered, clutching his head to stop him, but after a moment she pressed his mouth between the tops of her breasts, aching to have him.

24

Saturday, June 26, 1926

"Somebody downstairs for you."

"Oh? Thank you," Iola called back to the voice outside her door. Her heart skipped, and she spun on her dressing bench to see her clock. David was fifteen minutes early. In the silent house, most of the other boarders were sleeping or were out. The landlady was at the parade with Alice. Listening, Iola thought she heard in the distance a clash of cymbals, thud of a bass drum. Below her second-story window the leaves of the lemon tree shimmered in the breeze.

She sat perfectly still, breathing deeply and evenly. When she lifted her comb to her hair, however, her hand was trembling. She wore her thick black hair bobbed now, and today it was truculent; she couldn't locate her habitual part with her comb—it was as if it had been erased or like a cut had healed while she slept—and the result in the mirror made her feel a stranger to herself. She hated to care about it, especially today. She could only gain Laura's resentment if she showed up at the hospital looking attractive. It would be small of her to enjoy such a petty victory. She hoped that if she couldn't control her pleasure at Laura's fall, she'd at least keep her gloating well hidden.

However she looked it would probably be better—more healthy, at any rate—than Laura. What had Laura been going through the past few weeks? What changes in her would they see today? For Iola, it seemed as if years had passed in that short time. The last week alone had held enough thrills and terror to make the preceding two and a half years serene by contrast.

A flatulent "boomp!" of a tuba came faintly through the window. It was too bad she couldn't talk to Alice about her difficulty. When Alice had arrived last fall, Iola had hoped that she and Alice could reach a new understanding, one between equals; however, Alice seemed far too busy breathlessly extolling the virtues of her own mentor to be curious about Iola's unhappiness or confusion. And they had soon quarreled. Alice supported the national campaign to ban Indian dancing and ceremonials because they encouraged "lewd and lascivious" behavior. Those had not been Alice's words; indeed, since she'd joined Sister Aimee Semple McPherson's flock she was even more tolerant of what her former superiors would have called the baser human appetites—but on the whole, she was still guided by the old malign moon of the missonary: Indians should be farmers not hunters, they should not drink or be idle, and, above all, they should become Christians, and that meant giving up their old pagan religion as exemplified by the ceremonial dances.

Iola had been too proud to talk to Alice about what had occurred between her and David, but now she wished she had, or could, still. Events were moving swiftly toward a crisis, and Iola needed another woman's advice and comfort, particularly that of a woman who had always believed that Iola and David belonged together.

It wasn't only the quarrels that kept Iola from pouring out her heart to Alice. She was afraid that Alice might be judgmental about what they had done. And Iola wouldn't be able to describe her feelings with precision to Alice because they were a tangled bundle of confusion. The first few days after she and David had made love, she had thought that everything would be different from then on. She had replayed the evening a thousand times, how they talked on the beach and she felt so close to him, then their kisses, how they embraced in the car after they had driven to a private overlook, his hands on her, their words, their breathing, the rustle of their clothing as they removed it, the chiaroscuro of shadows on the ceiling above his shoulders, the aroma of the leather seats and his masculine flesh. The memory was so vivid it overpowered the reality she seemed to slumber through for the next few days. When she pressed hard on her memory to give her accurate images, she had to admit their lovemaking had been furtive, hasty, and clumsy. But, oddly, recognizing that didn't make her disappointed—it inspired thoughts of a next time, when mistakes could be amended.

She refused to think about his wife then. For those several days, when he popped in and out of the office, she always gave him a meaningful smile. Twice she excused herself to retrieve something from the supply closet, hoping he'd follow her there and kiss her. When he didn't, she worried. Did he regret their making love? Did he fear that she was regretting it? She waited, but he made no mention of planning a next time. For two weeks, he said nothing and either was very busy or wanted to be perceived as being so. He wasn't cold to her but seemed unaware of her need to have this extraordinary event acknowledged.

But on Wednesday of this week, he had conferred with two visitors in his office for three hours. Wilbur told her they were lawyers who specialized in divorce, and she was stunned. Then she was able to rationalize David's behavior, believing he had been grimly buckling himself up to perform the difficult task of asking his wife for a divorce. His remoteness to Iola had been ceremonial, in a way—his grandfather or her own might have fasted for four days in a spirit quest on a mountain before pursuing a very significant goal.

Thursday, he said, "I'm going to be allowed to visit Laura at the sanatorium on Saturday morning. I'd like for you to go with me."

"Certainly," she offered warmly, trying to restrain her excitement and hope.

But yesterday, she'd lost her confidence. What was she supposed to do for him—offer moral support? Stand by him as his ally or new consort? Before leaving the office last evening, he'd said, "I'll come by about eleven in the morning? Would you bring the green ledger?" She replied yes, wondering if her role was only to play secretary.

She tried one last time to comb her hair in its usual way, then surrendered to its unruly insistence. She was as ready as she could be. Looking out the window over the top of the lemon tree, she tried to guess the temperature, then raised the sash and inhaled the balmy air laden with the aroma of citrus blossoms. After one last, despairing look in the mirror, she took the green ledger of Foundation accounts from her dresser and went down the stairs to meet David.

Waiting for Iola to descend, Tom Quick caught himself, once again, struggling to unearth any aspect of his personality that she might find appealing. Or even tolerable.

He'd worked on his costume, anyway. Respectable, but sporty: a bun-colored Palm Beach suit, spats, white shirt, necktie with natty red pencil stripes on navy, the whole shebang set off perfectly by the straw hat he was spinning nervously between his hands. But finding the correct expression to wear on his face worried him. Anything but hang-dog, lovey-dovey, moonstruck. Preferably earnestness to match the check he'd give, and maybe aw-shucks modesty and a blush to follow up her thanks. As usual, he worried his would-be reason for being here wouldn't seem sufficient, that the guise was thin as water spilled on a table and she'd be privately laughing at him.

Footsteps overhead made the chandelier shiver. The parlor in this ladies' boarding home was a baklava of suffocating fabrics. An oriental carpet was overlaid with throw rugs of clashing design and color; the coffee table was covered with lace and religious pamphlets; the ancient horsehair sofa and chairs wore large disintegrating antimacassars; the frosted lampshades were like inverted bowls dumping out the lurid flowers painted on their glass, rims dripping with tassels or beads. Hefty velvet valances hung over draped windows, not so much keeping out the light from this fine morning as tinting it the sea-green color of the drapes. The whole effect was feminine and stuffy and made Tom feel he'd stepped into a greenhouse full of Venus flytraps.

He'd waited in the parlors of brothels with this same restless awkwardness, but here he knew he wouldn't leave calm, spent, whistling as he strolled to his car. Here there was no promise of anything but humiliation and a scrappy bone of encouragement he'd gnaw for weeks until it was in splinters. Then he'd be forced to come again, just to look at her for a few minutes. Since Iola had moved to Los Angeles, he'd seen her six times, each on his initiative, each after an agony of hesitation, each time cursing himself for both his cowardice and for his perverse willingness to punish himself. She was a peculiar drug he needed in regular doses to cure an ache but taking it only made the pang pang more.

In the corner stood an upright floor-model radio with a top like a church cupola. Copperfield had bought into the company that made them, a local firm, just before the uproar over Sister McPherson's "disappearance" had tripled local radio sales. That Indian had the Midas touch, it was incredible. But then the poor devil had that wife to contend with, and there but for the grace of God . . .

He wanted to turn the radio on for distraction but was reasonably sure the dial had been set by the proprietress of this fortress for female virtue to KFSG: Kall Four Square Gospel. He had had plenty of Aimee Semple McPherson lately and would get even a bigger dose later today at the parade. Assuming the posture of a brainless, mealymouthed disciple with his ear glued to the speaker might square his reputation with the landlady, but it would have little effect on Iola. Her reservations about Alice's conversion to McPhersonism had given Tom a small peg to hang his boater from; they could cluck their tongues together over the blindness of a mutual friend. Iola didn't know, of course, the root of Tom's irritation with Alice's religious fervor. Worrying herself sick during Mrs. McPherson's disappearance, Alice was unable to feel the pleasure that normally overwhelmed her moral objections to having his hands roam over her flesh. Unlike Iola, Alice did not object to any essential part of Tom's nature. She hated the sin but loved the sinner. If they ever compared notes his goose was cooked. Iola had no idea that he and Alice had rubbed bellies a few times back in Oklahoma, and Alice didn't know he carried this torch for Iola, so he had a personal interest in the outcome of their present antagonism. It would be nice someday to become a straightforward person with no secrets that could shame you.

He heard her coming briskly down the stairs. He rose quickly and bumped his knee against the table. Good God, how this woman rattled him!

"Hullo!" he shouted up the stairwell as the dark blue blotch of her dress emerged. "I hope you weren't too busy, you know I hate to drop in on you like this, but I was in the neighborhood, and . . ." He trailed off, the lies sounding like handsaw music twanging in the air.

He realized he was standing in her way at the foot of the stairs and crabbed off sideways to let her step down. "I had a little something," he went on. "Had a little luck, thought I'd pass it on." He was on the verge of adding "to someone who is less fortunate," but a blessed restraint spared him at the last minute of humiliating himself by blowing his own horn. Being around those damned McPhersonites had him talking like a preacher!

"Hello, Thomas," Iola said with an amused lilt in her voice. Her tone was a new development that matched the slight, wry smile with which she greeted him. He was afraid it meant she thought him a fool. He had no idea why she had taken to using his full name; schoolmarms had always called him "Thomas."

He waited, hoping, and was glad when she offered her hand. She was carrying a large green ledger tucked under her left arm. He took her hand, feeling her cool, smooth flesh, and worried that he would hold it too long.

"Come sit down," she said, moving into the parlor.

He eased down on the sofa hoping that she'd choose to sit beside him. She set the book on a lamp table, then floated down into the chair where he had been sitting, lightly, her arms gliding down upon the dingy antimacassars. Her long skirt billowed for a moment before lapsing like spent breath upon her thighs. The spontaneous ease of her motions awed him: her limbs were fluid, supple, her movements glowing with grace.

He noted the entwined filaments of premature gray that shone in her dark, pulled-back hair like a sliver of moonlight. It was understandable that her face grew more sculptured, more beautiful every year, but altogether unfair—it made her at once more unapproachable and more desirable. As a business executive she was solid and earnest and quite capable; he knew from talking to Copperfield that she was deadly serious about her work and spent long hours at it, and this only increased his admiration for her. Being an executive had given her a cool, self-contained air that seemed to put her beyond his reach. The angles of her youthful figure had been smoothed over by a busty ripeness that always reminded him that she had been married and thus wasn't a goddess that no man could have. That magnified his exasperation. He'd have been happier were she a haggard spinster who'd lost her looks through the manly calling of business and as punishment for having rejected him.

As usual, he had to break the silence. He tried for righteous indignation, but it was an ill-fitting shirt: "Did you hear about that fellow in Arizona saying that Aimee didn't act like anybody who'd spent a day walking in the desert because her shoes weren't scuffed, she never asked for water, and her clothes weren't even sweaty?" He couldn't care less if Aimee Semple McPherson sheared every one of her sheep and made up a thousand lies to explain her disappearance when everybody knew she'd been shacking up. The papers said it was a "love nest" in Carmel. He was not one to condemn anyone else for acts of dubious morality, but he hoped to strike a harmonious response in Iola.

"I know," she sighed. "Poor Alice."

She meant poor misled Alice, the poor woman had lost her mind. Tom could fill her in on more details but it would involve describing how Alice wriggled in torment when he laid his hand on her thigh.

"It looks to me like me and you—" He grinned. "You and I are the only living humans in all of Los Angeles to accuse her of being a mortal woman."

Iola looked puzzled.

"Sister McPherson, I mean."

"Oh."

There was a pause wide enough to back a truck into. She would wait for him to fill it, and he swallowed back his resentment.

"So how's the boss man?"

She gave him a curious glance that measured him for something. "I'm a little worried about him. Maybe you—" she began, then faltered. He understood that he was being considered for trust, and his heart soared.

"What's up? Just tell me, I'd be glad to do anything I can." She rarely encouraged his and Copperfield's friendship. Aside from being surprised, he was curious—he and Copperfield had gone to the fights a month before at the Armory, and the Indian seemed in good spirits. Tom couldn't mention it, though, without incriminating himself: he had talked Copperfield into following his bet on this new Swedish kid instead of the favored McDougal. "What can I do?"

"I'm not sure, Tom. It's . . . Laura."

Tom nodded. That Copperfield was having trouble with his wife was no news. But he was surprised that Iola would get mixed up in it.

"I don't know if you've heard."

"Heard?"

"That David put her in a sanatorium. For addicts."

Addicts? Had that plea for money been for drugs? He hadn't seen Laura in three months. After she'd slapped him for feeling her up, he'd kept away. Then, three months ago, she was on his doorstep looking like spoiled fruit, her breath like engine fumes. She was more disheveled than any ridge-running white trash he had seen in a month of Sundays. She'd asked for money—a rather large amount that she'd explained away with vague, conflicting lies. She let him know he could have her body as repayment.

He'd turned her down. Why, he wasn't sure. Maybe it was to humiliate her and maybe it was to keep from humiliating her.

Possibly it had been a mistake—it certainly had made her furious. Not two days after Laura had gone off in a huff, Copperfield asked him for an audit of royalties on that old Oklahoma allotment, and Tom was sure that Copperfield was only a ventriloquist's dummy saying *fuck you*, from Laura. He'd produced a satisfactory accounting, though not a true one. He had shaved a few points here and there. If they started digging into what went on in Oklahoma, he thought, an audit of Laura's behavior might turn up some surprises, too. Nothing that could be proved, probably, only the fishy stench of her and Kale being seen together at least once too often. She'd best take care when she started yelling for the books to be opened.

Iola knew none of this, he was sure. His knowledge didn't make him feel superior, only dirty.

"I'd say she's in pretty good hands then," Tom said finally. A word or two condemning Laura might be received with sympathy and might serve as fibers in the cord he was struggling laboriously to weave between Iola and himself. But some odd chivalry—honor among thieves? —made him resist belittling Laura. Iola was frowning, lost in thought. He said, to prompt her, "But you're worried about *him?*"

"I think David's been considering divorce," she said sadly.

"Did he say so?"

"No, but he's met with divorce lawyers this week."

He nodded as if he understood. But he was altogether baffled. He would have thought that Iola would be overjoyed to hear that her precious blood brother had finally managed to shake the hold of his gold-digging wife. But he knew Iola well enough to realize she wouldn't influence Copperfield in a weak moment for her own advantage. Such selflessness made him want to howl with exasperation, since he was not the object of it.

"I guess it's his business," said Tom politely.

"Oh, I know we shouldn't meddle, Tom." Her "we" suggested a cozy mutual enterprise, and he appreciated it. "But I'm worried about him— he's not happy at all. And I'm afraid he might do something hasty that he'd later regret just because he's angry."

"How do you suppose I could help?"

"Talk to him, maybe. Let him know what you think. Let him work out what he truly wants so he won't act out of anger."

"I'm not sure what I think." He supposed Iola wanted to encourage Copperfield to get rid of Laura and couldn't do the dirty work herself. That was the way your high-minded person worked. Once Tom had allowed Copperfield to talk himself into getting a divorce in a nice, cool, rational manner, Iola could step in and claim him without feeling she'd gotten soiled in the fray.

"You want me to help him decide to do it?" he asked, testing.

She looked a little horrified. "Oh no!" she yelped. "Not if it's not what he really wants!"

"Oh," he said, confused.

"I know I'm not being very clear. He's just so blue now, you see, and I can't seem to help."

"Well, I'll do what I can." What he could tell Copperfield would put him one up on Laura, but he was reluctant to start the cycle anew.

"I'd really appreciate it. It's hard for me to . . . well, we talk about a lot of things but not about her."

Tom fidgeted. Copperfield's divorce was not in Tom's best interest. But he couldn't think of a single good reason why Copperfield ought to stay married to Laura, except that divorce might complicate his financial affairs. He wondered suddenly if Iola had any fear of Laura's lawyers getting their hands on the Copperfield Foundation funds.

Iola was looking at the miniature pendulum clock on the mantel. She glanced back to catch Tom staring at her.

"We're driving out to see her at the hospital," she said. "Maybe you'd like to come along? He's due any minute."

He laughed before he could catch himself. "Well, thanks just the same. I'm not so sure she'd want to see me." Or you, he thought. "Besides, it might be better for him not to know that we've been talking." He winked to tighten the string around them, and she smiled back.

With Copperfield about to arrive, he felt the need to get on with his own business.

"What I came for was—" Here he lifted a haunch, reached back, and pulled his wallet out. Like a workman, he still carried it in his pants pocket.

"Oh yes," she said. "I'm sorry I—"

"Okay," he said, waving her off. "It's no big deal. I just had a little windfall like I said and I thought the Foundation might use it maybe at the orphanage or something." He removed the folded check from the sweat-dampened leather and was disturbed to see it had gotten soiled during the many days it had taken him to work up his gumption for the visit. "Sorry about the condition of it."

She took the check and gingerly opened its wings as if reading a very small, delicately bound book. Waiting for her response, he lifted his hat as overture of departure.

"That's very nice of you, Tom." That the amount—$1,500—impressed her only made him uncomfortable, since the origin of the money was a good tip on a horse. Or else he could think of it as Copperfield's rebate on what Tom had managed to shave from the royalties.

Iola walked Tom out to his Ford and shook his hand. "Thank you again, Thomas, it was very generous of you."

He gave her a nervous grin as he started the engine and pulled away.

He took her momentary good cheer away with him. When he popped up unexpectedly this way a little like a bashful genie, he usually banished her habitual melancholy. He enhanced her self-esteem as a woman, and the way he fretted and chattered and self-consciously wrung his hands amused her. She blamed him for corrupting David, but she'd come to blame David as well. David might have been an innocent and gullible young Kiowa when Tom Quick met him, but now he had to be held accountable for what he did of his own free will.

Maybe she'd been a little thoughtless in enlisting Tom's aid to help David make a good decision about his marriage. But, expecting David when she had come downstairs, she'd been flustered and let her concerns surface, and she'd recruited Tom so she wouldn't feel so alone with her anxious thoughts.

Now she stood on the curb waiting for David and replaying their conversations of the past week. What did they add up to? Would he divorce Laura? Was this visit to the hospital meant to break their marriage? Why did he want her along—a witness? To stand the two women side by side and compare before making his pick?

She tried to calm down by tracing the patterns on the shredded bark of a eucalyptus tree in the parkway. Moments later, David arrived in his Packard; she waved to discourage him from getting out to open her door and slid into the passenger seat without ceremony.

He looked very handsome in his dove-colored suit, so she turned her attention to the large houses along Highland as the car eased away from the curb. Sometimes he didn't bother with the courtesies with which both Kiowas and whites were expected to behave, and since he'd failed to greet her when she got in, she punished him through her opening remark.

"Tom Quick came to see me this morning."

"I'm glad you are going to the hospital with me," he said. It was not a response—he was too preoccupied to have a conversation—but an expression of what was on his mind. "I want to pay Laura's bill with the Foundation money and give them a donation, too." He nodded toward the ledger in her lap. His wife's hospital bill! And a donation intended merely to ensure special attention! She had better things to do than to write checks like that. Besides, his signature was as good as hers.

"Is that all you wanted me for? To write a check?"

He looked uncomfortable, keeping his gaze dead ahead even though she stared at his profile. Oh, he didn't like for her to make him reveal his motives, did he!

"You could write the check yourself."

"Yes." An awkward silence fell, then, without turning, he reached over and squeezed her hand. "I need a friend to help me have a clear head."

She didn't answer.

"I don't know if you realized it or not, but I've been talking to lawyers this week about divorce."

He waited for Iola to express shock, elation, or sorrow; she said nothing, and only thought, *It's about time you told me that!*

"But it's hard to know the right thing," he went on. "When you're rich, getting a divorce is very complicated."

"Would the Foundation endowment be affected?"

"I think that money could be put in a trust beyond my control."

And Laura's reach, Iola thought.

"But the money is not so important, anyway. I've tried to help her become a good wife. I think I've been a generous husband. But she can't be handled and she has a contrary spirit that keeps her from letting herself love me. I want and need a wife who isn't my enemy, who will be a mate. I need a wife who will be a friend"—he gave Iola a piercing look—"the way you are."

Iola blushed. What was he saying?

"I don't know whether to give up on her or forgive her."

He fell silent. Iola realized that he'd reached the question he'd invited her along to answer—should he leave Laura? And he was, it seemed, really asking more: *Will you be there for me if I do?* He wanted reassurance that if he cast off a "bad" wife, he'd be guaranteed a "good" one in exchange. She couldn't say that the prospect of being the better trade pleased her. She wanted no responsibility for his divorce and didn't feel it fair of him to extort a commitment from her now. If he wanted to divorce Laura, then let him do it—then he could court her and find out.

But after what had occurred between them that night, how could he wonder? She bit her lip to stanch a threatening wave of tears.

"David," she said finally, "I think you should do what your heart says. I'm sorry I can't say more than that."

25

Saturday, June 26, 1926

The veranda overlooked a sweeping lawn that descended to an avenue bordered by eucalyptus trees; beyond, across the avenue, a row of house tops stretched under a rim of ocean that hung on the horizon like glittery bunting.

Now, just past noon, the air was clear, and Laura could see tiny horizontal dashes on the blue scrim of water. Boats. Sometimes the water in Lake Michigan was green as mint jelly. She would wear her blue sailor dress of German linen trimmed in white with rows of sou-tache braid on the collar and a little blue anchor embroidered on the dickey. Grum always made her put on thick white stockings to go with it, even though everyone on the boat except she and her grandfather would be dressed for swimming.

Papa's worsted bathing suit was also blue, with narrow white bands on the sleeves. He would race toward her, snarling "I'm going to get you!" and she'd run, her school shoes slipping on the varnished deck; she'd grab the mast and whirl around it, keep it between them, giggling so hard she could barely breathe. He'd pretend to trip and couldn't catch her, so she'd have to bait him, waggle her fingers in her ears and stick out her tongue. Soon his attention would flag and she'd let herself be caught. He'd lift her up, her legs would spread around his waist, and she'd throw her arms around his neck and hug him, his beard and handlebar mustache scratching and tickling. Feeling his warm body against hers, the light dancing on the polished deck, the gulls hovering with their wings jigging like a tightrope walker's arms—she could imagine it through Mum's eyes, Mum back in the mansion on the North Shore gritting her teeth and angry at nobody ever knew what.

Papa let her fit the ends of the fishing pole together to make one long rod. They'd sit with legs dangling over the edge of the boat; he'd yell, "Dinnertime, fish!" and she'd scoot close so his thigh warmed her leg and lay her cheek on his bare arm to feel the little wiry hairs against her face, close her eyes and hum. She hoped a fish would be hungry, because if he didn't get one soon, he'd want to play the scary game. Even though he was a grown man, Grum would yell at him to get down off the mast, but he would just keep shinnying up it until the bottoms of his feet looked small as eggs and it hurt her neck to watch him. Grum would yell, "You could fall and kill yourself, you know!" and she would pray, Oh, please, Papa don't fall! At the top, he'd sway, his weight making the anchored boat dip from side to side. He'd yell, "Goodbye, cruel world!" then jump. She'd watch him sail through the air in a crouch, holding his nose, plummeting like a big blue boulder so fast it looked like something invisible and bigger than him had a grip on his body. Then a crash in the mint-colored lake and the plume of white that was the water sticking out its tongue after swallowing him.

He'd stay under, hiding; it was inconceivable that he could breathe, because her breath came in tormented gasps as she raced to the rail to try to see the top of his yellow head under the water. "Papa!" she'd scream. He'd trick her, swim under the boat, cling to the anchor rope at the stern where she couldn't see, or wherever she wasn't, and she'd think that even though he didn't drown last time and had been teasing, this time he wasn't. When she burst into tears, he'd pop up, say "Peek-aboo!" and expect her to laugh.

Laura leaned back in the porch chair and put her fingers against her eyes to stop her tears. She sat very still until she could breathe slowly, without a hitch. He had only been practicing, she thought. By the time he got it right two years later, creditors had confiscated the yacht, Grum's fortune in tanned buffalo hides had wafted away on the winds of the commodities market. Papa judged the distance between the gallery railing and the floor of the Exchange sufficient: there was more space on the floor after the Panic of '93; you could take a dive and not hit anybody.

Hard to forgive him still. She and her mother had to move to Lombard where the little wop kids called her "bastid" because she had blond hair and wasn't Italian. They wore rags, stank of garlic, fish on Fridays. Nuns clamping the muscle at the top of her shoulder in their claws when she said the wrong thing or spoke at the wrong time. She could thank the Irish trolley conductor for the pleasures of parochial school. Her Mum had married him out of desperation—she could see that now but not then—and whatever feeling she had for Mum had withered. He told her he was a medical student. Laura's head hurt to remember how he'd leaned over her bed on the night following her first Communion, hissing "Princess," whiskey on his breath. He meant *You think you're too good for me, don't you!* And she had. When his palms passed over the front of her white nightgown, she spat in his face.

She blew her nose, smoothed the skirt of her gray cotton dress. David was late. She felt herself wilting like a cut flower and pulled her compact from her pocket to check her appearance. Like other patients expecting visitors, she had groomed herself too much, with the result that the more she did the worse she looked. Having lost the knack for doing her hair, she had tucked it into a bun. She had foregone makeup but for a bit of red lipstick, which she applied by clutching the wrist of the drawing hand with her other hand to stop the shaking. In the compact mirror, her face looked a little blotchy, but it was no longer skeletal. She'd put a few pounds back on. Being upset by childhood memories was a good sign, too; her doctor would endorse it, saying pain meant life.

Another good sign: the clarity of the vista before her eyes. Weeks before, sitting here, she'd only felt the cold metal of the lawn chair penetrate her shaking muscles and jangling bones. She hadn't even noticed the ocean in the distance. A scumble of haze clouded her perceptions, and every cell in her had been writhing, turning her concentration inward. It was a marvel how the flesh healed itself when you stopped abusing it. This morning, for the first time in months, she had the power to turn her limbs this way and that when she chose and not when and how her addiction told her to. But still, her hands trembled when she raised them from her lap to the sunlight to scrutinize them. Her nails were bitten to the quick and her skin showed freckles too large to be called by that name.

Down on the lawn a woman was knocking a croquet ball with a mallet ringed in red around its hammer. In her white cotton dress and large straw hat she looked as if she were at a Victorian garden party instead of at a sanatorium trying to lift her head from a cloud mist of gin. Her husband wore ice-cream pants and a blue blazer, and as they moved to their balls, he put his arm around her like a friend or a brother; they laughed, and the man leaned over and delicately laid a kiss on the woman's cheek like a schoolboy overwhelmed by his own tender regard. When you get sick they walk around you as if on eggshells, everybody said here. Wrong thing to do.

She'd never had a man treat her this "wrong" way. Something in the connection between the couple on the lawn had always eluded her— now he was holding her hands, his head bent down to her face, and they looked like honeymooners. Pals, lovers, like those idiotic Smythes.

It was hard to know if love was as real on the inside as it looked from the outside. It was hard to know whether "true love" existed or was all movie bunk. The terrifying thing was to think it was out there but you'd never be able to get it because of who you were and who you picked.

Since coming here, she'd slowly realized that while others seemed to have a love of mutual equality, Laura could surrender only to whoever conquered her—you saw a white flag waving from the other trenches or you waved one yourself. Once she had believed her machinations were a sign of strength, but now they only spun a thin web over a void. Looking at the downward spiral of her life, she'd recognized the truth: nothing had made her happy. *If only I could . . .* she used to think, then fill in the blank: could get richer, get a leading role, get drunker, higher, lower, stronger—*then* I'd be satisfied. It terrified her to think that nothing she'd ever do would fill that void.

The couple on the lawn ambled toward the porch, arm in arm, and Laura thought that the moment the camera of her eye quit filming them they'd break apart to become separate lonely people who'd only been imitating bliss. She looked away to rob them of an audience, but the woman spoke anyway.

"Hello."

Laura nodded as they passed through the doors. The woman's eyes flicked about like those of a spooked horse, a new nervousness there since the morning when she and Laura had talked of the husband's impending visit. He wanted her home with her children, but she claimed she was not ready yet. Visiting days sent tremors through the hospital you could feel the moment you came awake; everybody was on edge, expecting and dreading too much, embarrassed—not about being seen by outsiders as a patient, but about being an insider seen with someone from beyond the walls. When the doors locked, the patients were a world unto themselves, kin in their afflictions, but when the doors opened old troubles drifted in like an insidious gas.

Looking down to the border of the lawn, Laura saw David coming up the flagstone walk, Iola at his side. She wanted to run inside before they spied her and busy herself with something—playing the piano in the lounge, maybe—so they wouldn't know she'd been waiting.

As usual, Iola wore a dark blue suit, though she'd set it off with a white blouse and white shoes. Watching them advance, Laura felt ugly and old. To her surprise and envy, they made quite a handsome couple with their glossy black hair, erect carriages, and wide faces the soft, deep color of tanned leather. Maybe they *were* a couple. She wouldn't be surprised; she wasn't blind to how Iola looked at David, and while Laura had been dead to the world any number of bargains might have been struck.

From this distance she couldn't see David's braids but could tell by the way his hair curved smoothly back from his forehead that he still had them. He looked fit in the gray suit and she noted his grace, his dignity, and the authority with which he strode. Oh, how the world had been turned upside down! Who'd believe she'd first seen him clomping along on the streets of Wetoka in torn-up brogans, overall pockets bulging with items he'd come to town to purchase, hair in a bumpkin's bowl-shaped cut. And Bill saying with a bitter sigh, "There's the richest man in the county and he doesn't even know it. Another oil-rich savage who can't count to ten!"

He was wrong. David definitely knew how to count, with a vengeance. To this day, Bill still refused to believe she couldn't merely steal from him at will. Regular as Christmas there'd be the telegram or the letter and once a telephone call, demanding a "loan," and the voice nastier each time. His implicit threat of exposure wasn't half so worrisome as imagining how he could harm her if she made him too angry.

She believed her only hold on David was the desire she could arouse. That was frightening, too. She was well over forty now, and she couldn't stand to see her body in a mirror, all those bones sticking out, her breasts saggy, their upper slopes almost vertical. Only her ability to tease, to promise but not satisfy, was left.

How could she keep him now, this man who'd decided for inexplicable reasons to be responsible for her? She'd detested how he'd allowed her to use him, and now felt guilty. He'd proved by bringing her here that he loved her, hadn't he? None of her so-called friends had cared. The sad truth was that on this planet only this man cared enough to save her from killing herself. Without him, she'd not only be poor, she'd be alone.

The irony was that that hulking savage had become desirable to women. Were she a stranger who knew only that he was a philanthropist, movie actor, and wealthy entrepreneur, she would connive to meet him. Odd how the power of money could make a man handsome.

Well, you cannot have this handsome stranger because he's already mine!

Laura rose as they came up the steps and stood with her hands demurely folded, smiling in welcome. "I hope you're not afraid of witches," she joked to both, though neither seemed to understand she was making fun of how she looked.

"Laura, it's good to see you," Iola said, coming forward. Her brow was furrowed with solicitude, and the implied sympathy would have touched Laura had she thought Iola sincere. The ledger tucked under Iola's arm reminded Laura her stay depended upon sweeps of Iola's pen. Iola and the hospital's director would no doubt talk about her behind her back. "I hope you feel better soon," Iola added as she turned to pass into the foyer.

"Thank you," murmured Laura.

David looked grave and a little helpless. She stepped to him, nervously rose on her toes and pecked his cheek, smelling his bay rum and the afterscent of cigar, then led him by the hand to the railing.

"This is a wonderful place! Look out there—" She pointed to the vista of sky and sea, afraid for him to look at her or to look into his eyes. "Today it's so clear you can see sails. It reminds me of my childhood. I'd so love to have a boat again!"

She paused and searched the lawn for something else to talk about. "And we play croquet after lunch and supper sometimes." She nudged him playfully. "Sometimes at night people dance here on the porch, but the only partner I could find is an old man with a hump on his back who's shorter than me!" She laughed, sounding delirious to herself. She was desperate to have him see her as a restored woman, a young, joyous woman capable of giving him pleasure. The trembling in her arms flowed like a drug through her body, and she was afraid for a moment she'd faint. She grasped the railing with both hands. She wished he would say something.

"David, I want you to know that I really appreciate your bringing me here. I'm sorry if I said otherwise. I'm all the way off the dope, and I feel alive again."

"Good."

The word sank into her ear with a cold weight. Surprised, she glanced up; he was looking out toward the avenue, frowning.

"What's the matter?"

He turned his dark eyes to her. She could feel him churning inside, see his temples throb slightly.

"It didn't please me to have to put you here."

So, he was going to lecture her? Had he any idea of the agony she'd gone through these weeks, her body like a rubber pretzel some devil knotted and unknotted, her cells screaming until she thought her skull would burst?

"Do you want me to say I'm sorry for all the trouble I've been?"

"I want to know first of all how you got that way. Who did this to you?"

"It doesn't matter, David. It's all in the past, believe me." She tried to hook her arm through his and pull him close, but he straightened his elbow, the loop collapsed, and her arm fell to her side.

"I say it does matter."

"But why?"

"Because I want to know."

She had an instinctive fear against naming the people from whom she'd bought morphine and opium.

"Nobody did it to me. I did it to myself."

"Who supplied you with the drugs?"

"I got them from friends."

"I wouldn't call them that."

"Oh, David. Please don't be so . . ." *hard on me* she almost said, but she remembered to hide, as she'd always done, her weakness from him. " . . . So gloomy. Let's not talk about that right now."

"Come sit down," he commanded, leading her back to the chair. He eased a hip onto the railing, crossing his forearms over his thigh, casually it seemed, but his hands were flexing into fists. On the lawn, two nurses walked a young man between them. He took small, tentative steps, as if the close-cropped grass were somehow treacherous.

"We live very different lives," he said slowly. "For a long time I've sat by and watched you ignore what you knew I wanted a wife to be. I've tolerated your behavior because I always believed that you could some day love and treat me the way a wife should. I no longer think that's true."

"David, you're very important to me, believe it!"

"Yes, I believe you need my money, Laura."

"Do you really think so little of me? You think I would have stayed with you just for your money? Do you think so little of yourself?" And fearing that he might ask why she *had* stayed if not for the money, she told herself it was because she respected and admired him, appreciated his strength: didn't the whole world kow-tow to him now?

"David, I admit it was once partly true. You have to admit that when I came waltzing up to you in your garden you weren't exactly what my mother would have picked." She tried to smile, to conjure up nostalgia, but his face was a wall. "But you're not the same now, and neither am I."

"Do you love me?" A plaintive note sounded under his question.

"Yes!" That sounded too bald. "I respect you, admire you. I'm not a woman who can be"—she searched for a word and couldn't find precisely what she meant—"demonstrative," she finished at last. "I feel about you the way you feel about me."

He chuckled bitterly. "Well, I feel angry! Being with you chips away at my self-respect. Being with you is the only part of my life I would like to change. I want a woman who keeps my house and my children and who is my wife before she is anything else."

"You can't make prisoners of people!"

"I have a right to ask my wife to remain faithful," he said fiercely. "If she won't agree to these conditions then I will divorce her."

The word struck her like a slap, but he wouldn't have used third person, she thought, if he'd really meant it.

"Do you want to draw up a contract for us to sign?" she asked acidly, but she was afraid.

"No." He looked at her, and she saw that he was on the verge of tears. "We are not happy together; we can never be happy together. The papers have already been drawn up. You'll get all the money you'll need."

She was stunned. Her mind whirled.

"Who have you been with, David? Did *she* put you up to this? God, I can't believe you'd do this to me while I'm here! You don't mean it! How could you kick me when I'm so down!" She burst into tears that were astonishingly real.

"I said you'd have all the money you need."

She turned away, suddenly empty.

"There's not enough money, anywhere, David, to be all I need." Knowing she could walk away with a portion of his fortune and never have to see him again was not a bit consoling. That *he* could reject *her*, he, who'd still be barefoot and stinking like a goat had she not civilized him!

She fought to keep her voice under control. "David, this isn't fair, you know! You haven't even given me a warning, you aren't giving me a chance—"

"Of course I have. I've told you many times over the past few years exactly what I expect from my wife."

It was true. She simply hadn't taken him seriously.

"You just don't know how hard it is to be or do anything when you're an addict except find ways to get what your system is screaming for, David. I know I could be a better wife to you now." She tried to sound matter-of-fact. She still had too much pride to beg.

He shrugged as if indifferent, and that infuriated her.

"I won't make it easy for you!" She glared through her mist of tears. "I can get lawyers, too, and I can go to court and—"

"And tell about the men you've let lie on you to get money to pay for your drugs?" David cut in, his black eyes flashing.

She blushed. He'd had detectives following her, then. "If I have to. I don't care about my reputation."

He rose to leave, and she panicked. She rushed up, pressed herself against him and laid her cheek against his large warm chest. She held him tightly, this person who was the only human standing between her and total isolation, the only human in whom she was capable of inspiring desire, anger, perhaps even love. If she could only get him into bed for five minutes she might turn this all around again.

"Oh, David, please don't make me beg! Just give me another chance. You owe me that, David, because that night in Wetoka at the hotel, I made you come here because I didn't want you to be killed. I know it really hurts you that I slept with other men"—she tried to get him to meet her gaze—"but oh, David, the dope, you don't have any idea of what it will do to a person! And I couldn't get money from you, could I? I was too ashamed to ask for it!"

He tilted his chin downward until she could see his eyes. She knew now why he hadn't wanted to meet her gaze: she could see fear of succumbing to her pleas. He just needs a *reason*, she told herself, maybe not even a good one, to keep me.

"David, please, I'm not making excuses for myself, but I didn't have any idea of what this stuff could do to you, and the people who sold it to me, they didn't tell me I could get hooked, and then before I knew it I was doing 'favors' to get it. God knows you're embarrassed by what I've done, but it makes me feel like trash too. If there had been any way I could've been strong enough to resist it, I would have, David, if only to keep from hurting you. I'm stronger now, believe me, I'm ready to be a mother to your child. We'll adopt one of the orphanage kids! Please, just let me have another start with you!"

She shuddered and held him closer. He peeled away her clutching arms and appeared to be finished with her.

"Tell me who did this to you."

This fixation of his baffled her, but she understood it was the key.

"What will you do!"

He pushed away from her, turned toward the door.

"David, wait!" She had no idea why it meant so much to him, but she collapsed back into the cold metal lawn chair and told him of Sylvia and the "doctor" on the Gower Street lot, omitting details of her sexual escapades, making her voice small and tremulous. She wanted to sound naive, an innocent who'd accidentally stumbled into a coven of witches whose powers had overwhelmed her.

And as soon as she'd told her story, she knew that she'd been suckered: he was only bluffing. He wouldn't have gone to court and let the world see the horns on his head, let his friends and acquaintances know how strangers had abused his *property* behind his back. He had far too much bullish pride. He'd extorted the information for revenge, and divorcing her would take away his justification to have that revenge.

She also believed now that he already had the names—he'd wanted not information, but a confession.

"David, what are you going to do about them?"

He shrugged.

"Oh, David, I want you to take me home! Give me another chance, please?"

"I want my wife to stay at home unless I give her permission to go somewhere. No matter who she is or what she wants to do, my permission comes first. If she goes out to the market, I want to be able to know that's where she went, and I want her to return when I say, without fail. I want my wife to think of her home as the place where she is the happiest, where she can watch over our children and the regular acts of common life."

"Yes, I know that now, David," she said eagerly, knowing, really, that he was describing a prison. "I'd like to be the one who does it."

"We'll see."

She had won a stay. Relieved, she rose and went to embrace him, but before she could, she saw Iola standing off from them, waiting with the ledger. David walked to the stairs, Iola flowed into his side, and they descended in step to the flagstone walk. Laura needed badly to seal her tentative victory. Iola's presence inhibited her, but she swallowed her pride and called out to their backs.

"David, I love you!" Startled, they both looked back, and she reddened at having hoisted the flag of her nakedness for Iola to see. "You won't be sorry!" she added impulsively, and the stricken look on the Kiowa woman's face more than evened the score.

After they had disappeared through the trees, Laura stepped down from the porch and stood in the hot light on the lawn. Her stomach churned. She eased down onto the wooden steps, almost faint. Good God, what had she done! If she'd kept her mouth shut, she'd be a free woman now with a decent settlement, and she wouldn't have to answer to him. The minute she'd coaxed him back into a semblance of submission, she'd lost interest in the game. She had been caught up in sparring with him, but now, exhausted, she felt no spark of energy or life. At this moment, he could divorce her *and* kick her out naked without a penny and she wouldn't lift a finger to stop him.

She dropped her forehead to her knees and wrapped her arms about her shins. She rocked slowly and tried to get a good solid breath to still her shaking.

She felt something in her hair, opened her eyes and saw a rose tumbling down the steps to rest beside her shoe. She picked it up by its short stem, thought someone had tossed it at her and looked back at an empty veranda. When she turned back toward the street, she was astonished to see more roses falling like rain—another near her foot, still another in the croquet court, going *plip!*, making the tiniest, softest sound, then a third carved a slow vertical arc from the tops of the trees to alight on the lawn like a miniature parachutist.

She glanced up, squinting into the strong sunlight. The sky was perfectly clear. She held the flowers in her left hand and smelled them. They were real. Where in the world had they come from?

26

Saturday, June 26, 1926

What should a man do when another man takes his wife, or when a wife betrays him or their tribe? People tell stories. Once a brave and his wife were going across mountain country and a storm came up with strong winds and hail, so they found a cave and went into it. When the storm died off, they discovered a stranger in the cave from an enemy tribe. The brave and the enemy fell to fighting hand to hand, and when the brave had his enemy pinned on the ground, he told his wife, Get my spear and stick him! She got the spear, but when she started to spear the handsome enemy, he looked into her eyes with love and nodded for her to stick her husband instead. The wife was tempted, and so she tried to kill her own husband. But her spear thrust missed, and the brave was able to grab the weapon from her and kill the enemy himself.

He scalped the handsome enemy, and they walked back to camp. He told the chiefs and all the warriors what his wife had done. Her brother was so ashamed by her behavior that he got his bow and arrow and shot her through the heart.

Another time, they say, a man called Chief of the Red Tipi was holding a smoke in his lodge and he sent his wife out for more firewood. She did not come back. She ran off with a young man who had been waiting for her outside. The next morning the chief went about camp, calling out, My wife is missing, will anyone help me find her? He could have been quiet about it and just taken some of the young man's horses or even killed a few, but letting everyone know this way meant he would have to do something more serious. Since the snow was on the ground, it was easy to track down the wife and the young man. They were sitting around a fire, shivering. When the young man saw the chief coming, he ran off and left the wife to face her husband alone. The chief told his wife, This mule I am riding will drag you home, maybe drag you until you're dead. But when the chief was putting a rope around her waist, she sneaked an arrow from his quiver and hid it in her dress. She put her arms around him and told him she loved him, and when he kissed her, she pulled out the arrow and stuck him in the throat. Then she tied him onto the mule and took him home. When she got back, her husband's people found her and killed her.

Some men whip their women, but you should not cripple them. They say that in the old days many warriors would cut off their wives' noses if they caught them in bed with another warrior, but I know of only one case, myself. Once when the chief Big Bow was away on a war party, his sister caught one of his wives in bed with Gomgiete. When he came back and heard about it, he cut off her nose. Her brother got mad and had a big fight with Big Bow. They got a death grip on each other and neither one could move. Two medicine keepers had to come and force pipes into their mouths and make them smoke, then the fight was over.

But plenty of other times another of Big Bow's wives—this would be Onkima, she was a famous beauty—would run off, and he would not do much about it. She ran off once with Dohasan, who was onde like himself, and nothing happened. She ran off with Guitadla, also a famous and brave warrior. This time Big Bow's brothers took two horses from Guitadla, and Big Bow's sister Dombedai cut off Onkima's hair when Onkima came back. Many times a man's female kin will raid the offending warrior's female kin and chop up their clothing and food and lodges with butcher knives.

Many times a man will not punish a wife because wives are women, and that is that. A woman is foolish and will believe any story a man tells her to gain her love. She might not realize that a man might steal her away from another man just to get even for some wrong the man has done him or to raise himself in people's eyes.

If both men are great, both onde, they are expected to behave with civility and courtesy. A man who is onde will be sure in himself and can forgive another man. Here is a story about a famous chief named Gule. Once a brash young man stole his favorite wife and took her on a war party. When the war party returned, Gule welcomed his wife back and asked politely about her health. He told her to prepare for a feast. Then he invited the young man to his tipi and all his relatives and the warriors who had gone raiding. They all came, and they were all nervous, especially the young man. But Gule got up and said to the young man, I thank you for bringing my wife back safely and for taking such good care of her on your trip. I want you to take a horse from my herd and take my wife and make her happy. The young man was very surprised, of course, and he got up and said, This is why you are a great chief. You have offered me the hand of friendship and have given me your horse. I am not worthy to be your friend. I was wrong to take your wife, and I ask your forgiveness, and I pledge to be your friend the rest of my life. Please take back your wife. And so Gule took back his wife.

If another, lesser, man had acted the way Gule had, he would be thought a coward, but Gule was too great a warrior and a leader to make a big kick about a wrong that had been done to him. A very great man may simply overlook a friend's indiscretion if they are equal. But if a great chief steals a common man's wife, there's not much the husband can do if he does not have many kin on his side and cannot face the warrior down. To ignore the insult is to lose what little honor he might have, though. He might take a chief's horse and that's the end of it.

What a man does about these insults depends not so much on the wife but on the other man. If he is an equal, a friend or relative, and has abused the friend or relative's trust, it is one thing. If they are not related or equal, and have had past trouble between them, then that has to be considered.

The only thing certain is—if an enemy or someone from another tribe *takes your wife, your honor will be stained forever if you do not make him pay with his blood.*

David sat behind the wheel in the alley, itching for darkness to descend. While waiting, he watched people pass across the alley's mouth, women in red and gold silk, bell-shaped sleeves covering all but their knuckles, and men in black silk and pigtails. He felt a kinship with these Orientals, also a trace of envy: they'd banded together into tribes here, were self-sufficient, enclosed in their Chinatown. The scent of strange vegetables and meat steamed or cooked in ways foreign to him wafted into the alley. A few men in European suits and derbies walked by.

He wanted to smoke a cigar but didn't—the glowing tip might call attention to him. The report he'd gotten from the detective agency had been accurate so far. It had led him to the house on the Grand Corso in Venice and to the man on the Gower Street lot known as "the doctor." In her confession at the hospital this afternoon, Laura had confirmed his name but had neglected to say what he had known from the report—that his activities included "exchanging sexual favors for narcotics." Her "confession" corroborated both the detective's list of names and her habit of lying.

The man named in the report had shown up shortly after eight-thirty and entered the hotel across the street, where he kept rooms for business in the evening. He also owned a chunk of land in Topanga Canyon where he was building a mansion enclosed by a high wall—considerable assets for a man whose income was ostensibly derived from wages as an electrician.

But a wall a mile high would not prevent him from coming to justice. And not by the slippery and labyrinthian means of white courts. Gripping the wheel, David felt an old identity slip under his skin, a war song rising from his gut. He opened the Packard's glove box and drew out a beaded band which he slipped about his forehead. He was wearing Sioux moccasins and heavy denim jeans girded by a wide Navajo belt set with conchos the size and weight of silver dollars. He'd worn these clothes in a two-reeler he'd just finished shooting and had walked off the location with his costume. Dressed this way he might draw unwanted attention to himself, but the dark, vengeful mood it helped to support made it worth the risk.

The pictures the detective's report conjured in his head shamed and enraged him. White men had taken advantage of her, seduced her, humiliated and degraded her. You did not do that to the wife of a Kiowa!

As a red man, he was accustomed to minor insults from white clerks and waiters, to the contempt of white ladies on the streets. But some humiliations no man could tolerate and retain his self-respect.

He reached into the glove box and drew out a knife. The deer-horn handle was worn smooth from years of use, and the blade was the length of his stacked fists. He'd bought it from an Apache on an Inceville picture, and he was sure it had already been plunged into live red meat, some of it human.

He stepped out into the shadows of the alley, closing the door softly behind him. A line of autos sluggishly inched forward in front of the hotel, and people crowded the sidewalks, venturing out for supper and shopping. The strangely inflected click and whang of Chinese and the melancholy sounds of oriental instruments rose over the chug and pop of motors.

He strode through the lobby and to the elevator cage near the counter where the clerk sat reading *Photoplay;* he waited, tense, as the slow, groaning machinery descended from overhead and rattled to a stop before him. Taking the stairs would have been quicker and easier, but stealth would have made him more conspicuous.

He emerged from the elevator into a dim hallway. Of the four ceiling light globes, only two were illuminated. He padded quietly to the end of the hall, where he found room 321. He cocked his head against the door and heard the soft jangle of ragtime. The space below the door leaked light. He tapped gently three times. He imagined Laura standing here, almost faint, leaning against the doorframe, waiting for the man to pierce her flesh with his needle, then plunge his cock into her when she was limp and pliable.

David struggled not to slam his shoulder against the thin door and thrash through the splinters into the room.

"Who is it?"

"Laura sent me."

After a moment, the door cracked open, and one gray eye with a swatch of fine blond hair draped across it appeared. It was the "doctor," the man the report had identified as Robert Bates.

"I was just leaving."

"I need help."

"Not tonight."

A safety chain stretched across the gap between the door and its frame; David gave the door a smart slap with the heel of his hand, thrusting with his weight behind the blow—the chain popped and the door swung in and struck the other man's face. David slipped into the room, saw the man squatting on a hassock with both hands pressed to an eye, then closed the door gently behind him. The man was barefoot and wore a red silk kimono embroidered with snow-covered mountains and birds perched on the branches of cherry trees.

"I didn't like your answer."

"Obviously," Bates said wryly.

Bates removed his hands from the eye and looked into his palms as if expecting to find blood. His head was small for his bulk, and his face had acne scars bridged across his crooked nose like buckshot peppering a paper target. When he peered up at David, he wore an expression of sour disgust. His eyes flicked from David's to the black-lacquered Chinese table just beyond his reach upon which sat a pearl-handled derringer. He wasn't a gangster, as David had expected—he had no bodyguard. David picked up the derringer and slipped it under the waistband of his jeans, pulling back his deerskin vest to show the handle of his knife. The man kept patting the wound the door made when it struck his face.

David sat in a wing chair to which the man's hassock was a companion. He surveyed the room: no "bed" to which Laura might have been carried, but a Victorian chaise longue stood along one wall. Next to it a fern stand on which rested a black telephone. Two other chairs, posters from Parisian art shows, those French lamps Laura favored—the place was cramped but fashionable. Had he met this man in Laura's salon?

"Do you know who I am?"

"No, unless you're from Marcos."

"I'm not from 'Marcos,' but you can make another guess." David pulled the knife out of his wasitband—the point had begun to dig into his loins when he sat down. He held the blade up. "This was uncomfortable. It has a sharp point, you see."

Bates smiled as if he thought he could joke his way out of this. "Well, if you insist, I'd guess you're Laura Copperfield's husband."

"Do you know where she is?"

The man gave him a puzzled, half-relieved look, obviously thinking David was here merely to locate a fugitive wife.

"In the hospital? I mean, I thought—"

"No, that's right. You know why she's there?"

The man looked away. "Hey, it's a free country! People come to me, they want something to make them feel good—I don't go asking! I don't make anybody do anything! I'm really sorry to hear Laura lost control, but me, when she asked, it wasn't my place to say no." The man gave a helpless little smile and raised his palms in the air.

"Just a civic-minded fellow," said David. Bates was more baby-faced than David had pictured him, far less pernicious; his "evil" was only that vapid absence of attention or care that could characterize the way white men did harm to others.

Presuming he was to be interrogated, Bates relaxed, his gaze wandering about. David flipped the knife over and jabbed at the man's knee with the point. Bates yipped and rubbed the wound with the heel of his hand.

"Pay attention. You were thinking of escape. I want you to concentrate on my questions."

Bates nodded.

"Now, how did she pay you?"

"Cash." His lips jerked into a half smirk he tried to hide by literally wiping it off with his fingers. "I can't afford to do business any other way."

David leaned forward and brought the knife up slowly until the point of it rested on the soft flesh under the man's jaw.

"I don't like for you to smile. You understand?" The man couldn't nod without pushing the knife point into his jaw, so he blinked and swallowed. It would be so easy, David thought, to shove the knife up through his flesh and skewer his tongue with it.

"She always had money?"

The man's irises clung to the bottoms of his eye sockets as he tried to keep the knife in sight. "Yes," he said from between tightly clenched teeth.

"Always?" David pushed the knife up a little.

"I can't talk," the man hissed.

David moved the knife down to the man's jugular vein.

"Yes?"

"Not every time."

"And when she didn't?"

The man shrugged.

"What, you didn't care? You took an IOU?"

There was a long silence in which David grew impatient. The snow-covered mountain on the right breast of the man's kimono quivered.

"You'd better not lie."

"Okay. If she didn't have money, we'd work something out."

"Work something out?"

Bates's Adam's apple bobbed once, and he looked away. "I would watch."

David blinked, puzzled.

"Watch? Watch *what?*"

"Well . . . " Bates gave David a sheepish smile. "You know, just watch." When David pressed on the knife, he said quickly, "Watch her move, dance."

"That was as good as money to you?" David realized he sounded more bewildered than threatening.

"She would be . . . without some clothes."

There, in the room, the ghost of David's wife arose, nude, posing, and the man sitting in David's chair, moving his eager gaze over her breasts, her angular hips, the fine hair on her mound. David's stomach rose into his throat.

"That's all that happened?"

The man nodded too eagerly.

"You are a very easy fellow to please, then."

"The Chinese have a saying about the different gates to heaven, my friend. I meant no harm. I never touched her."

"I believe you." David leaned back and brought the knife away from Bates's neck. The other man visibly sank with relief and stretched out his legs to relieve a cramp. David looked into the man's fear-struck eyes and slowly bent forward again. He softly patted Bates's head, felt the greasy blond hair under his palm.

The man braced himself and shuddered from David's touch.

"Close your eyes."

The man hesitated, trembling, then his quivering eyelids shut. David gently inserted the point of the knife into Bates's left nostril, and the man jerked, stiffened.

"I want to believe you, but Laura has said many things about the time she spent here with you."

"What did she say?"

"You tell me."

The man didn't dare open his eyes with the knife still up his nostril.

"She would lie down sometimes and . . . pretend."

"You made her do this?"

The man squirmed. "Yes."

"What else did you make her do?"

David yearned to slam the knife up through the man's crooked white nose. He twisted it slightly, and Bates blurted out, "Another person, a man, just once, but it only happened once, I swear it!"

David could see Laura drugged on the couch, her body covered by a white man's while this other man sat watching. Suddenly he felt queasy.

"She didn't even know, you see, it was like she was asleep and no harm was done, and it was only once."

David sank back into the chair and, stunned into momentary helplessness, regarded Bates. He was afraid he'd vomit. He took several long, deep breaths and said, "I'll punish you only once, then."

Before the "doctor" could register his words, David bolted up from the chair, dragged him upright by the lapels of his kimono, and shoved him toward the bathroom, prodding him with the knife.

"Hey, what—"

"You fix yourself a big dose first."

"What? Why?" he sputtered.

"You know, so you'll be asleep and you won't hardly know what is happening to you. Just once."

"What're you planning to do?" Bates screeched. As he tried to spin around, David caught one arm and yanked his wrist up between his shoulder blades. He took the derringer from his waistband and shoved the muzzle against the man's ear.

"You fix it, you hear? I want to watch."

For several seconds, Bates's breath came in heaves.

"Do it!"

Finally, the man staggered into the bathroom, where he sank down on the lid of the toilet, opened a small upright enamel cabinet nearby and took out a vial and syringe. He tried several times to stab the syringe needle into the vial, hands trembling violently. Eventually, he drew the syringe full of pale liquid and waited for further instructions.

"Use it!"

The derringer pressed to his ear, Bates pulled back the sleeve of the kimono and pushed the needle into his arm. He pressed the syringe slowly until all the liquid had entered his protruding vein. They waited in silence, with a curiously cooperative patience, until the man's chin drooped down to his breastbone. David watched with fascination as the man's shoulders slumped, his torso sagged, and he tumbled slowly from the commode seat to collapse, as if poured, to the tile floor.

Standing over him, David arranged his arms to lie peacefully folded over his chest. The kimono lay open, exposing his round pale belly and his shrunken penis resting harmlessly on his testicles.

It was not worth cutting off; the man never used it. David bent down and pulled back one eyelid. He saw a pale gray iris jellied with a numbed glaze.

He liked to watch, did he?

Quickly, David drew the sharp blade of the knife softly across the gelatinous surface of the open eye. He opened the lid of the other eye and was about to slice through the second pale iris when he hesitated. How much punishment was for justice and how much to satiate his desire for revenge?

The instant a flicker of compassion had begun to shine through his anger, he shut it out deliberately, reached down and ran the blade across the untouched eye.

He left the bathroom, went to the telephone and called an ambulance. For a moment, he sat, very quietly, on the chaise longue, tortured by images of Laura naked in the room. He'd expected his revenge to purge his anger. He did feel washed out, hands trembling as if he'd just finished lifting something heavy, and the tendons in his limbs, taut as harp wires for hours, now sagged, slack. But his mind hadn't been eased by what he'd done. He felt as much a victim as the man lying on the bathroom floor, as if Laura had made fools of them both.

He'd spent his fury on this complete stranger, his heart was still heavy, and suddenly the punishment looked too severe for the crime. And he still couldn't be certain he'd reached the bottom of things. That was the way it was with Laura. She lied. By what she said and what she left unsaid. He recalled something she'd blurted out today—she'd brought him to Los Angeles so he wouldn't be killed? Who'd want to kill him?

No sooner had he begun to remember his last night in Wetoka than he heard the ambulance bell on the street in front of the hotel. Quickly, he went to the window opening onto the alley, slipped through and descended the fire escape.

27

Saturday, June 26, 1926

"Mmmm! I'm going to put strawberry jam on mine!"

Alice was poking into his electric refrigerator, shoving bottles aside on the lower shelf, while Tom tended the hotcakes in the huge copper skillet. The four yellow discs the size of headlamps had been poured perfectly so their beautifully crisping rims didn't touch. His fine craftsmanship in producing these picture-perfect cakes warmed him with satisfaction. Otherwise, it hadn't been a good day.

"How about you, Mr. Quick?"

"Maple syrup. It's in the pie safe."

Just before she straightened from her stoop, his eyes left the cakes to take a tantalizing snapshot of her rounded buttocks arched in the air, the cloth of her dress dipping into the crack between her cheeks, and his interest in the evening was restored.

She was humming a hymn as she set the plates onto the table with a clatter. The percolator on the back burner was chortling, sending pleasant wisps of coffee steam into the air. He wanted to take his straight right then, but he would play the perfect host and wait for Alice to doctor hers at the table: half coffee, half cream, two spoons of sugar—it was just another dessert for her. He really wanted a snort of hootch, but taking one in front of Alice would spoil his chances.

"Here you go, toots!" He carried the pan to the table with the handle wrapped in a handkerchief and spatulaed two cakes onto Alice's plate.

"Mmmm! Thomas, you'll make some woman a nice little wife someday—these look posolutely, absatively delicious!"

Ordinarily he took her chiding in good stride, but since she'd kept him in an itchy state of randiness all day, he was annoyed. He'd given her the two perfect cakes and now regretted it. He took the others, slightly overcooked, onto his own plate. He poured coffee, feeling resentful. It was bad enough he had to cook for her to get her in the mood —a lot of women got hungry after sex, but Alice you had to prime by stuffing her first—but he didn't need her making jokes about it.

He poured syrup in curlicue dribbles like tangled fishing line on his cakes and was about to dig in, forgetting, when Alice said, "Dear Lord . . . " in that voice.

He ducked his head and stared at his cakes, thinking Dear Lord, I forgot the butter.

"We thank thee for this food . . . " Tom waited, his stomach writhing. A long or short one? He'd had a snootful of religion today and having to endure grace at his own table seemed unfair. Good taters, good meat, Good Lord, let's eat!

"We thank thee for this glorious day and for restoring our Sister to us by your miracle! We thank thee for keeping her with us so that she may do her good work here on this Earth. . . ." Alice's eyes were closed and her hands flattened together, fingers pointed toward the ceiling over her plate.

Tom sighed inwardly. He was sick of Mrs. McPherson, disgusted by that tumultuous arrival at the train station today, the thousands of supporters coming in chartered buses, battalions of firemen and police, rooftops and balconies and second-story windows choked with well-wishers and sightseers: you'd have thought it was the pope! The Temple band played "Wonderful Savior!" and the Fire Department band struck up "Praise God from Whom All Blessings Flow." There were speeches and prayers, then she was carried in a high-backed wicker chair decorated with roses and carnations, followed by disciples carrying Bibles and strewing flowers in her path. People reached out to touch her clothing. From an airplane roses came cascading down like soft red hail.

He'd tagged along patiently with Alice, driving in the parade past the packed sidewalks of Sunset Boulevard and to Echo Park, where the Temple rose from a horizon of human heads. Alice had dragged him into the packed sanctuary to hear the Sister lead a chorus of ecstatic praise-giving and recount her kidnapping, her imprisonment in the desert shack, her perilous escape, and her arrival in a little Mexican town. It all stank like fish to Tom, but he wasn't about to argue his point amid six thousand fanatic devotees.

He'd imagined that Alice would reward him for his compliant stewardship by sharing her joy in bed. He should have known better. After they'd first done the dirty deed back in Oklahoma, it was six months before she'd let herself be alone with him again; as a political appointee to the State Board of Education, she'd been concerned about a possible scandal.

Now it was Sister Aimee and the Lord. Alice had been in a frenzy since he picked her up at noon; if he had a nickel for every time she'd said "the Lord" today, he wouldn't need his investments in the oil on Signal Hill. You'd think the Lord was deaf or feebleminded, the way they kept shouting the same message at Him.

Alice always loosened up when she visited him in San Pedro, perhaps because nobody here knew her, perhaps because away from the influence of her brethren she was more natural. She would even ride on the back of his new Indian two-popper. She always made him put her up in the suite he reserved at the Seaside Hotel when she came. Once he'd talked her into staying at the apartment; she'd been mortified the next morning to realize that the only staircase out led into the busy offices of Quick Oil downstairs, which she hadn't really noticed in the dark. She remained in his apartment—"like some soiled streetwalker" as she put it —until after lunch, when she could descend safely, pretending she'd gone up that morning and not the previous night.

But she didn't mind the place, for which he was grateful. The upper story of the building had been one large room, barny as a gymnasium with the distinctive but not unpleasant smell of hemp. He'd partitioned off rooms with studs and wallboards. Some day he'd get around to painting, hang a few pictures. In the meantime, the place was quite comfortable, with a woody, industrial atmosphere he liked. Two kitchen windows looked out on the harbor, and he liked to sit in the dark and watch the lighted masts inch into port. Some ships carried in their holds cases of good liquor he secretly cargoed in from Mexico.

". . . And our sins, past and present, dear Lord, help us to stay strong."

Tom took his napkin from his lap and set it on the table in disgust. Her grace had wandered a good country mile away from the subject of these poor cold cakes. The spiritual passion of the day was still fizzing like seltzer in her blood. Maybe she was arming herself against his inevitable approach; or maybe, just maybe, she was asking for forgiveness in advance? These lapses under his hands cost her agonies of remorse and guilt. Why couldn't she just accept her "sin" the way he accepted his own?

Well, the answer was that she was a better person, no doubt about it.

The posture of her arms pushed her ample breasts together, and a damp ring of sweat ran along her white collar. He didn't know why he was cursed with an itch for her, but on the few occasions when he'd managed to turn out the lights and strip her down under the sheets, her loose, spongy flesh had had a peculiar magnetic quality he'd never encountered before. She smelled of soap, and her sweat had a sweet pungency that aroused him. She wasn't attractive like the slender young bobbed-hair whores he could buy by the dozens, and he was always caught between calling himself a fool and struggling to find ways to wallow on her again. And, boy, was she a lot of trouble!

It was a good thing he didn't love her.

"Amen," she said.

"Thank the Lord!" Tom crowed.

"Tom!" She laughed, then fell at once upon those perfect but cold cakes, smearing them with a thick layer of strawberry jam.

"You sure you didn't leave anyone out? How about Coolidge, I didn't hear one word about old Silent Cal. And while you were at it, you could have asked for a good geology report on my wildcatter out in Bakersfield." He took two bites, then scooted his plate forward to clear a space for rolling a cigarette.

"Now, Tom, that would be a selfish prayer." She winked. "Fortunately, the Lord knows maybe even better than you do what you really need."

Strangely, it put her in a good humor to hear him grouse about her evangelical passion, a trait he could never quite fathom.

"What do you think about these reports of her not being thirsty after that long walk in the desert and of how her clothes weren't torn? I heard on the radio today that a guy in Tucson, some kind of government inspector, claims he saw her there a week ago."

"Anybody who does as much good as Sister Aimee does is bound to have enemies who will scrutinize every word of her story and find ways to create doubt, Tom. I hope you're not going to be one of them."

"I'm not saying she wasn't kidnapped; I was just asking."

Alice eyed him narrowly. "What do you think?"

"I think maybe she was kidnapped, maybe she wasn't. Maybe she needed to take a vacation. Who knows? Just like you and me, the woman steps into her bloomers one leg at a time."

He was tempted to suggest that Sister McPherson might even have a lover, but the mere mention of the evangelist's undergarments had been enough to set Alice off: she began to clear the table and wouldn't look him in the eye.

"I know she's mortal, Tom. All those weeks that I feared she was dead certainly proved that! And nobody's perfect." Her voice had a little tremolo that could, he knew, swell into a symphony of blubbering if he didn't back off. Alice stood at his sink, her head bowed, the dish towel pressed to her face.

"I spent years hearing a lot of stuffy preachers yell damnation at people, Tom, getting up behind their pulpits and making like Jeremiahs and hating everybody and everything."

He walked up behind her and slid his arm about her shoulders, feeling the heat of her back against his arm. Her eyes were teary, but she'd brought herself under control.

"I didn't mean anything, I'm sorry."

"And you know, when I first heard Sister Aimee preach in Oklahoma City, it was like lightning! She was somebody who knew that the Bible was full of *love*, Tom. It was all that heart that spoke to me. I'd always thought there was something wrong with *me* until that day. I've never been as happy as I've been to watch her work and help her—nobody does more good for people: she feeds them, clothes them, loves them, she makes them *feel* the love of God! And a lot of these dried-up old men resent her power. They think that religion is all about rules!"

"I know, sugar," he murmured. "I'm sorry—"

"I'm not upset with you, Tom." She smiled weakly and hugged him, pressing her breasts against his torso. Her aroma shot into his nostrils, reviving him. "It's been a very emotional day," she said. "I can't even think about her without wanting to bawl."

She wiped her tears with the dish towel and finally laughed. Tom washed their dishes, and Alice dried them, using the same towel, which gave him the sense that when he next used the plates they'd have an invisible sheen of her sorrow clinging to their surface. After he'd stacked them, he led her into his "parlor" on the pretext that it was cooler there. The room was a bare-floored square with wallboard that still showed nailheads lined like stitching on the butted edges. There was an old horsehair couch, a floor lamp, and a crate for an end table.

He sat beside her in the dark, cuddling her under his arm. After a respectable interval, he gently kissed her damp, warm cheeks. She inched closer, fitting her large form into his side, slipping her arm around his neck and pulling his head down so their lips met fully. But when his palm pressed the top slope of her breast, she sat up.

"Tom, I just can't. It's a sacrilege. I shouldn't have come here tonight; I should be at the Temple on my knees."

"Maybe so," Tom sighed. Alice typically said something in this vein at this stage of their petting, but tonight her resistance would likely be insurmountable. "I know I'm not good for you."

She smiled and hugged him. "Of course you are! You think I don't like it when you make love to me?" She gave him a merry kiss on his mouth then backed away. "It's not hypocritical for you to do this, I know, because you don't believe it's wrong."

Thus she nicely diced the laws to his advantage. He'd never known how she managed this, and now it was clear she thought of him as a missionary thinks of a heathen—living in ignorance of the rules.

"The only way I can justify it," Alice said slowly, looking away from him, "is that you're the only man I've ever had. I'd always thought I'd never have one, never be able to get one. And you're not just any man. You're kind and strong." Tears glistened on her cheeks in the half light from the street that came through the window. "So I may fret and moan and carry on about my sin because I do worry about it more than you could imagine, but I know I can be forgiven because my weakness isn't really lust, it's love."

He'd heard that word so many times today in a religious context that it took him a moment to realize she wasn't speaking of missionary or heavenly love. The old gal was stuck on him. And it took guts to say it first that way.

"Me?" He was as pleased as he was incredulous.

"Well, you needn't let it scare you any," Alice said with a nervous laugh. "My life is plenty full already. I'm not inviting you to the altar, Tom. Think of it as a gift with no strings. You're my one vice, I guess. Everybody ought to have at least one, don't you think? It's good for humility. My real shame is that when we're together it's so good I never mind too much paying for it."

"Alice, honey, come here." He drew her back down into his side and hugged her. "I don't know of any woman—and I have to tell you, I've had a few—who I'd chase through a mob of holy rollers just to cook a couple of pancakes for. There's something about you I can't get shut of."

"I'm glad to hear it."

She craned her head back, and he gratefully fit his open lips on her warm, soft mouth, feeling the tip of her tongue on his. She sank into the couch, limp in his arms, only her mouth moving passionately, her breath caressing his cheek. He grew painfully stiff in his trousers and had to shift. When his fingers reached her breasts again, she stiffened. "No, Tom!"

"Oh, Alice, sugar! Just above the waist, please!" he whispered back. When she didn't answer, he unbuttoned her dress, folded her stiff corset away from her breasts and feathered an erect nipple with the pads of his fingers. Alice groaned, squirming. Well, maybe there was half a chance now. He licked the hollow of her throat, slowly trailed his tongue down the soft slope of her breast, and lapped gently at her nipple.

"Oh, Tom!"

It was not a protest. He laid his right hand on her thigh and stroked his way down into the hollow between her legs. Her thighs waggled apart.

"Oh, Alice, sugar, I want you," he moaned, the words rushing out beyond his control. "So sweet, your lovely breasts, I could kiss you for days and days and days," he babbled, pressing his nose into her deep, soft cleavage, imagining her warm thighs around his waist. She wrapped her arms around his head and smashed his nose against her breasts. "Oh, my sweet Tom," she crooned. "Make me a sinner!"

Just as he was scrambling to get his trousers off, a huge *pop!* thundered through the loft.

"What in the world!" Alice sat up, startled.

Tom, mouth agape, craned his head toward the hallway.

"I don't know—"

"It sounded like a gunshot!"

Then thrice in succession the explosions came again.

"What *is* it?"

When his wits returned, Tom knew the evening was ruined.

"Aw, it's nothing," he muttered. He got to his feet. Another explosion thokked against the walls from the adjacent room.

"Nothing!"

"Just some stuff. Chemicals somebody stored here."

"And that smell!"

The pungent odor of hops wafted into the room.

"Don't worry about it. It's nothing."

"Well, aren't you at least going to look?"

"In the morning."

"But all those *explosions*, Tom! They're bound to have wrecked something, and maybe there's a fire . . . ."

"Okay," he said crossly. "I'll check it out."

He groped down the dim hallway until he found the right door, opened it and was almost KO'd by the boiling-hot mists of hops and yeast. He flicked on the light to find that five of the twenty-four-bottle case of home brew he'd put there to age had exploded, coating the walls around them with damp foam. Goddamnit! He should've kept it in a cooler place.

When he heard Alice behind him, he slammed the door shut. But she'd already seen something.

"Just chemicals, no problem."

"Oh, Tom!" She gave a huge sigh. "I wasn't born yesterday. You've been making liquor."

"Well, not liquor. Just beer."

"Oh, Tom! And all the times you've sat in the Temple with me and heard Aimee preach about drinking! How could you!"

"I get thirsty," he said sourly. "I'm just a crud, oil-patch trash, Alice."

"Oh, you're not going to get out of this that way. You always think you can get around me and twist my arm by putting on that long face and playing the fool or trying to act sorry, but I am so, so disappointed in you!"

"Well, goddamnit, woman! I'm getting just a little tired of people being disappointed in me! I'm a little tired of always having to apologize for being just an ordinary human being. I'm not high-minded, goddamnit! I'm not a saint! I do all kinds of things you don't know about!"

He hadn't meant to go so far, and shut up quickly. He could hear her mind working on "kinds of things," and it suddenly came to him that he was weary of hiding. Maybe he should tell her. Maybe then she wouldn't feel so all-fired good about him, and he'd have her troublesome love off his back. Let him confess his sins and they'd see whether she'd continue to love him or go running off to Sister McPherson. All that phony compassion for sinners!

"I'm a bootlegger, Alice. I bring in liquor by the tons from Mexico, then sell it to drunks who beat their wives. Since I charge a high price, they use their last pennies for it and their poor children go without supper. But I don't do it for the money, you know I don't need money, I do it because I like the feeling of being an outlaw."

"Oh, Tom, you can't mean it!"

"And I gamble at the racetrack and at the fights, and I've been known to cheat people at business deals if they don't keep a close eye on me."

"You sound like you're bragging!" Alice said hotly.

"Not about that. But here's what I'm proud of. I could walk out of here right now with a ten-dollar bill and inside of an hour I'd find me a whore happy to spend the night with me here making the beast with two backs. And contrary to what your good buddies at the Temple might tell you, she'd be right cheerful to do it, also. I know, because I've done it a time or two."

Alice sank slowly down the wall until she was sitting cross-legged on the floor.

"You're forgetting that I know a thing or two about prostitutes, Tom. They might act cheerful with a customer, but you've never had to tend one who's been beaten or humiliated by a man or consoled one who's thinking of killing herself because she's got no reason to live," she said quietly.

How coolly she accepted his insults! Was she trying to goad him? "I don't care about that. I just pay my ten dollars, Alice, take what it buys me. Like I said, I'm just oil-patch trash, and that's all I ever will be."

"And I said you can't expect to sidestep your responsibility by jumping on yourself before anybody else can. That's getting to be childish, Tom."

This pose of calm serenity—oh, the eternal superiority she displayed!

"And I don't know why you're telling me all this," she went on. "Maybe you're a little afraid of what I said earlier tonight about loving you, and maybe you're just trying to prove to me I don't, but—"

"Don't get fancy."

"But I know you're not nearly as tough as you act, Tom."

"You don't know a goddamn thing about me, that's what I've been trying to say!"

"Don't curse at me."

"Goddamnit, woman, this is my goddamn house, I'll cuss all I want to in it, and if you don't like it, right there's the goddamn door!"

"I'm afraid you have me at a disadvantage, Tom, I'm miles from home."

"You call that zoo a *home*?!" he screeched.

"Tom, what's really wrong?" she said in the voice of a patient school-marm coaxing a belligerent boy into letting down his guard. It drove Tom into a frenzy.

"Goddamnit, you tell me! You know everything about me, right?"

"I know you're unhappy."

"Well, give that lady a blue ribbon!"

"But why are you unhappy?"

"You tell me, you know it all."

He couldn't say why he felt like fighting, but he resented Alice's robbing him of a clean, purgative exhilaration by not putting up her own dukes. Her equanimity made him want to scream.

"Maybe," Alice said softly, slowly, "it's because you need to let the love of Christ into your heart."

Tom burst into laughter.

"Tom, don't sneer. He won't abandon you; He loves you."

"Yes," said Tom, aiming an arrow at her heart, "but Iola doesn't."

As they drove back in the inky blackness of a moonless 3:00 A.M. to Los Angeles, Alice sat mute as a stone. Tom knew he couldn't unsay that hurtful truth, and trying to qualify it or sand off its edges would only make it worse. Better to pretend it hadn't been said, and maybe it'd fade from her memory.

But confessing love for Iola—it felt good to have said something *true* for once. He'd been half hoping Alice would take it as a friend and help him win Iola. He'd hoped she'd put aside her personal interest in him and do the Christian thing, make a sacrifice. A martyr to the lions.

When they reached the Temple, it was almost dawn. In the gray light, disciples were gathered on the lawn in a prayer vigil. Alice looked ghastly; old and exhausted. He'd done this to her, this cruelty, and he suddenly felt deeply sorry that he had abused the trust and kindness of the one person in the world who was his true ally.

He shut the engine off after pulling to the curb, thinking they would talk—talking would be a form of punishment for what he'd done, at least—but the instant the engine went dead, Alice bumped her door open with her shoulder and stepped wearily out like an old cripple.

"Alice—" Tom said, feeling helpless. She turned and looked back into the car.

"Tom, I guess I always knew your heart was set on her. The signs were there all the time, I don't know why I didn't realize it." He could see she was fighting not to cry. "It's a good thing to tell the truth. But you shouldn't have said it the night I told you I loved you. I said I had a full life, and I meant it; I can live without the love of a man, and I can live without loving one, but loving you has made me feel . . ." She couldn't go on; she whirled and walked swiftly up the walk toward the Temple, fists clenched at her side.

28

Los Angeles 1926–1929

The day Laura left the sanatorium, David arranged a homecoming celebration. The "guests" were merely the household staff and three families with squawling brats—friends from the War Paint Club, among whom she felt like a captured pioneer woman. The staff, Indians, children, and the Smythes and their child all sat at the dining-room table to eat tamales and beans, food for poor Mexicans. He surrounded her with his friends and employees (she noticed Iola was missing) to make a show of force, not so much to let her know how much she was regarded, she thought, but, rather, how much he was.

When all the guests had gone, she waited in his study while he smoked a cigar and sipped brandy. She wanted to crawl up the stairs to her room and sleep for a year, but she sat, not drinking, hands folded in her lap like a dutiful wife.

"I'm going to give you a radio station."

He chuckled at her perplexed expression. "Well, not to have, or own. To use. It's a little station up in the hills that used to broadcast fire alarms and news to people living up in the canyons. I bought it a while back."

"What am I supposed to do with a radio station?"

"You've always liked to sing. You want to be a singer still, don't you? You can go there and sing over the air, if you like."

He seemed immensely pleased with himself, which only made her wary. She was reluctant to assent to anything he might be smug about.

"I'm not sure I'm strong enough for that yet."

"You will be."

He grinned as if he had a secret. This mysterious manner, this attempt to charm her, was frightening: she'd already seen, in *Variety*, the item about the studio electrician who'd had his eyes slashed by an unknown assailant. She was no longer sure of what he might do to anyone who crossed him; it was odd to think that David might be more dangerous than Bill.

"I *want* you to get well," he added, more plaintively. His need of her cooperation reassured her. "Just as I want you to continue to be my wife, and forget whatever has happened between us. We'll start out fresh again, and you'll never have to worry about being threatened by so-called friends."

She didn't have the energy to start anything; she was simply hanging on to her hard-won health, trying to catch her breath, trying to learn to sit upright without vomiting, to stand without feeling dizzy. All his talk about a future only wore her out, gave her a feeling of dread. She just wanted to get through the afternoon so she could sleep.

"Don't expect too much of me, David, please."

"I understand. But there will be rules, you know."

"Rules?"

He went to sit behind his desk, like a goddamn banker about to tell her an overdue note wouldn't be extended. How he'd learned a white man's arts so artlessly!

"Yes. Such as when you go to the radio station, that's where you will be and you'll not go there first without getting my permission. You won't go to the movie studios, and you won't see any of your old crowd. When you leave this house, you'll take someone with you, and yo:;'ll come back when I tell you to come back. You won't drink and you won't take drugs. You'll be in your bed by midnight, and you must be up when I say, taking charge of the house and telling the servants what to do. You will be in charge of things when we have guests."

A rage at his arrogance flared up but lacked fuel. She could only think, *Do whatever he says, whatever he wants, until the time comes to give it back to him in spades.*

"Is there anything else?"

"Only this—you've come back here because you asked me to have you here."

"What does *that* mean?"

"It's only something to remember when you're tempted to ignore my rules or to defy me."

She was certain it meant he wanted her to be wholly pliable when he came to slobber and poke at her. But even the distastefulness of that couldn't outweigh the apathy that hung on her bones. These rules added up to a total surrender of her will, her independence, her freedom. She thought she could easily have watched him die in agony before her eyes without protesting, but she wouldn't be able to raise a finger to vote for it.

"What do you hope to get from this?"

He smiled. "Peace of mind."

She snickered and looked away.

"I see you're not happy to hear this, but I know you well enough to say that though you think you'll hate living this way, in time you'll come to appreciate it."

She would have denied this to his face were it not that she couldn't answer the simple question, *Why are you willing to put up with this?*

She slept dreamlessly for three days, rising from her bed only to use the toilet. In doing this, she knowingly violated his rules, but her bed was a warm dark cave that enclosed and protected her. Yolanda appeared now and then to feed her posole or chicken broth; David would be standing at the foot of her bed sometimes when she came up for air, as it were. He seemed more concerned than irritated at this violation, and she would groan, "Oh, I'm so very tired, David!" like someone dragged from the surf after almost drowning. He seemed content to have her bedridden—the peace of mind he wanted she was able to give him this way.

Once he asked, "Do you want me to call a doctor?"

"No," she murmured. This chasm of sleep had become, inadvertently, a means of resistance. No one came to visit—was it because she had no real friends, or was David keeping them from her?—and no one inquired about her health but David. In her waking moments, she felt deeply bitter that her life had reached a point where no one but a man for whom she had contempt cared if she lived or died.

On the fourth day when she awoke, Yolanda was standing at the window, one cheek glistening. Unaware of being observed, she aroused Laura's curiosity. She'd been in the household for a few years, ducking Laura's wrath or impatience. It was strange to see her crying. What was her last name? Did she have family? A husband? Laura had slept herself silly, to boredom, and suddenly this other person's life seemed a strange and marvelous thing.

"What's the matter?"

Yolanda jumped. "I'm sorry, señora. I didn't know you were awake." A flush rosying her cheek, she hurried to the nightstand and with eyes averted picked up glasses. "Do you want anything?"

Now fully awake, Laura was suddenly ravenous. She almost shunted the girl's distress aside to place an order, but her curiosity was too great. She scooted up, wrapped her arms about her shins, and patted the bed beside her. "Sit down."

Reluctantly, the girl sat as if the mattress were glass. Laura could smell her own perfume on the girl and was touched—such a small, harmless theft implied a compliment.

"Tell me why you were crying," Laura said gently, although she felt she had the authority, if not the right, to require an answer. Yolanda wept for several minutes. Laura found the girl's weeping strangely arousing. She slipped her arms about the girl's waist and held her. Haltingly, Yolanda said she was pregnant and the father had gone back to Mexico. She'd left her husband, an older man, for this boy who'd run off, had even abandoned her two children to an aunt. She'd sinned so terribly she was afraid to go to confession. "Oh, don't you worry," Laura gushed. "I'll help you!"

Laura held her and rocked her for a while. What a strange and delightful way to begin a day! She had a flood of various emotions—interest in solving a problem, curiosity, a faintly maternal concern that arose from the implied trust and power granted her. She could help this child—well, she was a woman, surely, but blubbering in Laura's arms she seemed very young. The girl's physical warmth, her scented flesh, aroused in Laura a drowsy, lazy sensuousness, a vague yearning for flesh to meet flesh. Not that the girl could be a lover or even a friend—she was a Mexican servant—but she might become like a pet brought in hungry and wet from the rain to be dried, stroked, and fed, a pet grateful for acts of kindness which cost Laura little to perform. Since Laura had been put under house arrest, it would be wise, she thought, to seek entertainment here.

Eventually, being held by her mistress made the girl uneasy. She pulled a tissue from her uniform pocket and blew her nose timidly, then rose, leaving a cold hollow between Laura's arms.

"I'm sorry, señora, it's nothing. It will pass."

"I said I would help, Yolanda, and I will." Laura swung her feet to the floor and sat. "But first I need some breakfast—I'm famished!"

After Yolanda had gone, Laura yawned, stretched, and, inexplicably, smiled. A sentence floated into her mind: *Life begins anew when desire awakens.* Desire? Desire meaning not lust, precisely, but a yearning for an attachment to the rest of the world.

When Yolanda returned with her breakfast, she told the girl to go back to her husband and to beg his forgiveness. "Tell him the child is his own, and that that's why the boy went back to Mexico. Tell him that I'll pay the doctor's bills and that I'll give his child a gift on every birthday until he's grown if he'll take you back. If he doesn't believe it, tell him to come see me. If he won't do it, tell him I'll call the law."

For several weeks after her resurrection, she greeted David pleasantly because she'd learned that this baffled him. He expected resistance to his rules. She knew from Yolanda that he asked all the servants for an account of her activities while he was gone. The advantages to having an ally on the staff quickly became obvious. When the time came, she knew that Yolanda would be a chaperone she could leave somewhere while she went wherever she wished.

She stayed at home. Having to ask David if she could go out would be too galling; there was pleasure in not giving him the satisfaction of saying yea nor nay. But her unexpected compliance only aroused his suspicion, and he was wary of her breezy, amiable demeanor. She did exactly as he'd asked: she supervised the running of the house, changed rooms around, requested new furniture, began a landscaping project in the rear garden. Her mind was not wholly occupied by these activities, but there came to be a kind of safety in doing them.

Gradually, she felt the power of her own authority return. She took delight in being able to command the staff without being imperious, like one accustomed to having servants—unlike David, who still hadn't learned the knack and who, Yolanda said, grinning, could not stand to be in the same room with her without telling her to get him something whether he needed it or not.

During this time, he would come to collect his debt and subject her to the test of his control. Yet he appeared abashed, guilty that her reward for these weeks of good behavior would be to endure his heaving over her. She endured it easily, found it perfectly tolerable so long as his mood implied it created an obligation toward her. Beyond that, she was surprised to find herself wishing he hadn't finished so quickly. The proximity of another human body was a pleasant novelty after being celibate so long.

It started one Sunday, following her exemplary behavior at one of his parties for the orphans where she'd played the dutiful hostess and mistress of the house. She'd helped Smythe's Pollyanna wife ladle punch and dole out cookies and candy. She'd known what David wanted and had done it to build up credit. Watching David up close with the children, she saw a side of him that she'd forgotten could be exploited.

When he came to her bedroom that night, she sensed it had less to do with lust then with his old, nagging desire to have a child. It seemed a shame to her then that she'd had two abortions: as a father, David would be doting and helpless, and being his child's mother might have given her a fulcrum to lever his weight.

"Do you want to go anywhere?" he asked after he'd risen from her bed and dressed.

Ah, now he wanted to exercise his authority!

She shrugged.

"Well, I want you to go to the radio station; I want to turn on my radio and hear you singing."

She smiled to herself. She had had no idea that her passivity would turn out to be a tool. Now he *wanted* her to go out.

"I'll play the piano here and sing if you like."

"I want to be able to hear you in my auto."

"So you can be sure of where I am?"

"No, I'm proud of your singing—I want other people to hear it, too."

"Well, that's nice, David. Maybe I will."

And maybe I won't, she thought. Oddly enough, by complying with his rules she'd acquired a certain power over him.

"You can go other places, too," he added, as if puzzled.

"I thought you wanted me to stay right here like a good little wife and keep my pretty little head occupied with domestic matters."

"Well, yes, I do."

She laughed at his consternation. "But you never imagined I'd do it so readily and now that I am, you don't know how you feel, do you? Why do you want me to go other places? Do you want to test me and spy on me?"

"No, I don't want you to feel like a prisoner."

"David, I'll feel like a prisoner so long as you think I have to have your permission to move about."

"Well, I said you could go places, didn't I?"

She didn't bother to ask where, because she didn't want to hear his list, no matter how long it might be. And besides, where would she go? Who would she want to see? She had no friends. The idea of trudging around to the studios made her nauseated—having to beg for favors, struggle desperately to disguise or to utilize her age. After ten years of hard work, of debasing herself looking for parts as an extra—no, that dream seemed altogether gone now.

What party could she sneak off to where she wouldn't be tempted to become a lush or an addict again? At least now she'd begun to be able to look at herself in the mirror. She was looking healthy and could dress in the best clothes available to any woman on the planet.

Dress for whom, though?

Months slipped by without her awareness. She felt as if she had fallen into a trance. She redecorated rooms they hardly used, feeling like a museum curator. Redecorated, the house was becoming alien to her; room by room, the places where she could identify her self and any aspect of her old life grew fewer. She had a fantasy that as each room underwent upheaval, then restoration, she'd close each door and lock it, and, eventually, she'd be standing on the rear stoop, after locking the rear door, with nowhere to go, without even the *desire* to be anywhere.

She read *Photoplay*, but less of it from issue to issue. She tried to learn to crochet but lacked the patience and the discipline to finish any piece. She tried to learn to cook, but everything tasted like everything else. She'd sit at the piano and play snatches of songs, bored with each before she'd reach its ending.

When David gave up on her going to the radio station, she knew it was time to do it. The small staff of engineers and announcers made a fuss over her—she was, after all, Mrs. Copperfield—and she played a grand piano and sang vaudeville tunes for an hour each day.

To her surprise, she received mail. And David, who had one of the first automobile radios in Los Angeles, told her how he'd turn it on when they were shooting up in the canyons and her voice would serve as a pleasant background for the crew eating or taking a break. These gratifications were small but real. It began to matter that she went there every day; she looked forward to it. It was her time alone, her time to have an audience.

Sometimes she'd go up to the redecorated salon where she'd once entertained and gaze out of the windows. She sat in the new chairs so seldom that being in them was like trying them out at a store. It was hard to tell if they were truly comfortable, and she had the feeling she'd be asked to move any moment. There, though, she was free to contemplate her circumstance.

Rich girl. When everything is given, ennui becomes a natural part of life, she thought. As a child, she'd never had to imagine how to obtain a desired object. Those long hours of fantasizing about possession, the slow steps toward attainment were lessons of patience, dedication, and discipline, lessons she hadn't learned. When the money was gone and *he* had deserted her, she'd kept waiting for someone to hand her goal to her, to hand *herself* to her. She'd spent her life bouncing between men whose weakness was contemptible but useful and men whose strength was appealing but untrustworthy. It had been strong men such as Bill Kale who had stirred the deepest longings and sunk the deepest hooks in her. She met Bill Kale when she was hardly out of her teens, earning money for secretarial school as a singing and dancing waitress. He was older, dashing, and apparently wealthy; his faintly criminal air and cruel wit appeased some deep-rooted anger in her. He believed he was superior to "mongrels" and "scum." She'd believed it, too.

She remembered her pride at having attracted his attention. She'd tried to act tough and worldly to please him, but he could tell she was a virgin. They got drunk on good champagne in his hotel room. Later, when they'd gone out looking for breakfast, he'd slipped the stub of his burning cigar into the breast pocket of a sleeping bum. They staggered around the corner and laughed themselves breathless.

When, years later, she'd come looking for him in Wetoka, she was stronger, wiser, less intimidated than intimidating. He owed her, she thought. For her virginity and for running. He had a nice life there, with the wife, the lovely children, the family's bank. But it hadn't turned out right. He'd failed her, turned on her when she pushed him.

David, she thought, you were supposed to be like that bum sleeping off a drunk with our cigar burning in his pocket.

The terrible thing was that David had become the new Kale, this version abased, a counterfeit. She wasn't drawn to David, she only feared his power, and his power didn't reside in his person the way Bill's had—it was in his money, his employees, assistants, spies, companies, houses, land. She'd misjudged everything: Bill Kale, David's luck (all good), and her own (all bad), and, above all, David's strength, his character, the wily way he could not merely survive but thrive in a white man's world.

Living under David's rules had brought equanimity to her life, she had to admit. Her life was without discomfort, but empty—like sleepwalking. She was waiting, once again, for someone to hand her a reason for existing. David took her compliance to mean that she was content, that his grand scheme for her recovery had worked.

He was therefore alarmed when, in the summer of 1927, she asked if she could begin seeing her doctor at the hospital again. She didn't tell him the extent of her regression, that she'd been so afflicted with a nameless dread and profound melancholy that Yolanda had to take her by the arm and drag her from bed every morning. David sought to soothe and occupy her with a toy—and she admitted it was a marvelous one: he bought a forty-eight-foot sloop, and together they sailed it to Santa Catalina and up and down the coast for days at a time. It brought back memories both pleasant and painful to her of Lake Michigan and her father. She seemed to be feeling good again, and her doctor suggested she do volunteer work at the hospital.

Laura's efforts to be an angel of mercy were sincere in her own fashion. She was able to amuse herself in a significant way by becoming involved in the lives of the patients. Because she'd been a patient herself, she imagined she shared a bond with them that allowed her an uncommon understanding of their plight. She called florists and wheedled free bouquets for everyone; she wrote letters for those too addled or medicated to concentrate; she held hands and listened to stories of woe; she helped serve meals; she distributed magazines, and for Christmas of 1927, she produced a pageant assisted by Alice Roberts and members of the Angelus Temple choir, in which she played a wise man in a sumptuous blue velvet robe she'd had tailor-made for the occasion. When she sang "O Little Town of Bethlehem" as a solo, she removed the wise man's cumbersome hat to let her blond hair fall to the shoulders of the blue velvet robe, and the applause seemed unending.

One Sunday morning in January of 1928, she went to the hospital's recreation room to place a vase of gladiolas on top of the piano in preparation for the afternoon's visitors.

The room was empty except for a young man she'd never seen before who, nevertheless, looked strangely familiar. He'd wheeled the piano stool over to the aquarium and was sitting, transfixed and unshaven, with his nose pressed to the glass. She was on the opposite side of the tank and saw his face through the water. He appeared to be mugging.

"What's wrong?"

He moved his head very carefully back from the glass and turned to her with a dull-witted, gradual awareness; he might have been a tiny diver ascending slowly from the bottom of the tank and into the air.

"Are you a nurse?"

"No, I was a patient. Now I'm just a volunteer." She gestured toward the flowers.

He turned back to the aquarium. "It *looks* peaceful in there."

He watched the fish. They hovered, their tissuelike fins undulating in the water like hair, then, like blinking, they suddenly shot forward without apparent purpose. Laura noted the young man's pale blue eyes, long hanks of yellow hair dangling across his forehead; he looked like a young British pilot, both innocent and slightly damaged. His eyes, gray with a faint wash of blue, were riveted on the depths of the tank with a ferocious intensity that contradicted his boyish features.

Then she placed his face: he'd been a child motion-picture star back in the teens.

"Are you Darrell Sanders?"

He reached up and put his hand on the tank. "But if somebody gave it a hell of a shake," he said, looking up at Laura, "or maybe accidentally bumped into it, then life wouldn't be so ducky ha ha ha in there, would it?"

His arm went rigid as if he were about to shove the tank over, and Laura wondered if she shouldn't call an orderly. After a moment, he let his hand drop.

"No, I'm not. He was bewitched by a wicked queen." Suddenly he gave her a winning grin and winked. "You're very pretty, aren't you!"

She laughed. "My name is Laura."

"I think I'll call you 'Lolly.' "

"All right. But why?"

He sighed, slapped each side of his face with his hands, and made his eyes look mournful.

"I wish I could tell you."

"Is it such a big secret?"

"To me it is. If I knew what was going on in my own mind, would I be here?"

They both laughed.

"Well, if you're not Darrell Sanders, then who are you?"

"The committee hasn't issued its report yet."

"What committee?"

"The ones called 'they,' as in 'they made a man out of him.' "

Laura smiled. "Until they do, what should I call you?"

"How about 'Darrell Sanders'? You seem to know him already, so that could be a convenient short cut for us."

She nodded, still grinning. He turned back to the tank. "It's like a crystal ball," he said somberly. "And I see some terrible things in my future, Lolly."

He fell silent. "Such as?" she asked softly.

"Scrambled eggs and chipped beef on toast," he said, deadpan. "And I'm not kidding."

She couldn't tell if he'd lured her into playing an unwitting straight man or whether she'd unearthed some peculiar phobia. He stared at her evenly, revealing no hint of how he'd meant to be taken, and she decided this was a test.

Equally poker-faced, she said, "If you think that's the worst you have to face, then you haven't seen the oatmeal. Instead of putting raisins in it, they put in little dried-up cockroaches, and they grind up their wings to make a kind of dust that looks like cinnamon, only of course they won't admit any of this. Sometimes you get something between your teeth that feels crunchy like a nut but it's not."

He paled and gave her a look of guarded suspicion, as if he doubted her sanity.

She cracked a grin. "Gotcha!"

He smirked. "No you didn't, Laura. You just forgot that I was a professional actor in my childhood."

She didn't learn what Darrell officially "had," as, over the next few months, they became fast friends. She speculated that his difficulty related to his mother, who apparently ruled his life as if he were still in knickers and still had a motion-picture career. He received a letter a day from her and a personal visit once a week, and he told Laura long-winded "fables" about a "wicked queen." Laura began to wonder if poor Darrell had simply aped madness as a means to escape his mother. He was twenty-nine and no longer had any steady income other than the money his mother had invested from his working years. "I'm glad she did," he admitted to Laura finally, dropping the guise of discussing her in fable form, "but I can't be grateful, because it was my money to begin with. She always reminds me that I'm supposed to feel grateful, and sometimes even tells me which words to use to express my gratitude— like she was my *director!*" he wailed. Oh, Laura knew! Laura sympathized. She told Darrell fables about a tyrannical king!

"I tell you what scares me," Darrell said once when they were playing gin rummy in his room. "I'll be honest with you. I have daydreams about her getting killed or being drowned or something and I'm afraid that it will really happen because I wished for it. Then I'm afraid that she'll never die and I'll never get to have a life without her, and then I get afraid that when she *does* die I'll be alone. I'm afraid of fire and heights, too, by the way. And I'm afraid if I tell you all this you won't like me anymore, you'll think I'm a pansy."

Such candor amazed her. She was astonished at his trust in her. She said, "I think you're very brave to tell me those things."

"Shouldn't I trust you?" he asked, alarmed. "I mean, I thought we were friends."

"Oh, we are! I mean, I suppose I've never had a friend who'd tell me something like that."

"Good! I like to think that I can give you something."

"You do."

"Let me give you the chance to tell me something important about yourself so you'll feel somebody else knows you."

For a moment, she panicked.

"You want to hear a secret, is that it?"

"Yep." He fanned his cards out before his eyes, then turned them to face her. He lacked one card to gin. "Now that you know what's in my hand, you can help me go out or try to stop me. When we know what's in each other's hands, we can play against the cards and quit playing against each other."

A secret.

"I used to be a morphine addict, and that's why I was a patient here."

"Oh, for pity's sake, Lolly! All the doctors and the staff know that!"

"You didn't."

"You said you were here for a medical problem—that's the only one I know of—"

"Well, you didn't know it was for morphine."

"So what? God, I dredge something up from the dirty old sludge at the bottom of my heart, and that's the best you can do? Don't you understand this is an opportunity for you, and not something for me?"

He laid his cards face up on the table, removed hers from her hand and held her fingers between his palms. "Tell me something that only I will know so I can feel close to you." He gave her a long, sorrowful gaze and her heart melted. To have a friend!

She looked down at her hands in his palms, took a breath. "I don't love my husband."

They were silent for a long moment. Finally, Darrell let out a long soft whistle. "Oh, Lolly," he whispered. "That's a good one. A treasure. I guess I have to know next why you stay with him."

"Why do you stay with your mother?"

"Oh, I never said I didn't love my mother—I only said I hated her."

"I stay because I have nowhere else to go right now."

"Oh, I bet you do."

She flared inwardly and regretted having been so honest. "Well," she said defensively, "it would be hard."

"You like his money."

She looked at Darrell. He wasn't goading her, only coaxing her to be honest.

She sighed. "Yes. Now you know two secrets. And that's all you'll get tonight!" She scooped up her cards.

"Okay," Darrell said, picking up his own hand. "I think we're going to be really good friends, now." He grinned and pulled a card from his sleeve that he'd apparently already drawn. "Here's my gin card."

Soon they were wallowing in their mutual candor. One night, they slipped up to the roof with a bottle of wine she'd smuggled in. They sat side by side on a stack of roofing tile while he told her about having tortured the cats in his neighborhood when he was a child, and how he was once so jealous of an infant brought onto the set for a scene that he stabbed it with a hat pin when no one was looking.

"Haven't you ever done anything wrong as an adult?"

"Have I ever been one?" he joked. "All right," he said. "I write filthy anonymous letters to old women."

"What do you say in them?"

He blushed. "I don't want you to know that."

"Why not?"

"Because I'm ashamed, that's why."

"All the more reason to tell me."

"Someday. Not yet."

"But I told you about my abortions, and my husband doesn't know about that. Tell me what you say in the letters; I'll bet you can't tell me something about yourself that's worse than what I could tell you!"

"Are you daring me?"

"Yes."

"Okay." He stretched out his legs and took a long swallow from the wine bottle. The night was moonless, and the lights from the city washed the sky a shallow gray. "Well, I tell them how much I admire their clothing, their faces, then I write about their bodies, and I go into detail about their parts, you know." He sighed. "I make them think I'm a secret admirer or something. And just when I think they're feeling real complimented and rosy, I say something . . . ugly."

She jostled him with her shoulder. "Yes?"

"Okay. I say I'd like to put my organ in their mouths." He sighed hugely.

"That's it?"

He nodded.

"And that's the word you use?"

"Yes."

"Well, you *are* a naughty boy!"

"You shouldn't make fun of me, Lolly."

"Aw, I'm sorry." She patted his forearm to appease him.

"Your turn now," he said hurriedly.

She laughed. "Don't be so eager to hear the dirt!"

"But it's like we're uneven."

"Okay. You remember I told you about the fellow who I got my morphine from, the electrician?"

"Yes."

"He made me dance for him."

"How?"

"I started out with my clothes on, and he had his gramophone play a dance song by Paul Whiteman, I think, and—"

"What did you have on?"

"Different things."

"Oh, it happened more than once?"

"Yes."

"What about your underwear?"

"Usually tap pants, camisole top."

"Uh. Tell me what happened."

"Well, then I took off my clothes while he watched and . . . did himself."

She could feel her face burning in the darkness, although this was probably the least shameful scene she could have described from that period of her life.

"Huh!" he said. "You took off the underwear, too?"

"Yes."

"Could he see everything?"

"Yeah, Darrell," she said dryly, "he could see everything."

They were silent a moment, then Darrell said, "That makes me hot thinking about it." He turned to face her and grinned. "May I see your breasts?" he asked evenly.

Were it not for the little hitch in his voice, he might have been asking to browse through her stamp collection. Momentarily shocked, she looked away to gather her wits. They'd been blown willy-nilly into a sexual moment that was altogether unexpected. For the seven months she'd known him, they'd been playmates, brother and sister, buddies. Laura had been an only child, and her bond with Darrell was unique to her experience and very pleasant. It was precisely because he'd been indifferent to her as a woman that she had allowed herself to trust him so completely.

She wasn't certain how to respond. His request seemed harmless enough, couched in the spirit of childlike curiosity.

"Well, they're not very big," she said slowly. "But if it would please you . . . "

"I bet I don't like them big. I like them just your size."

He got on his knees between her legs and unbuttoned her blouse. She undid her brassiere. Cool air swept over her torso, then his soft warm hands stroked her breasts. For a long time he inspected her breasts with his hands and fingers, being exceedingly gentle, then laid his cheek against them and she felt his tongue licking delicately at her nipple. His caresses conveyed no urgency, and the idea that he would go no further —not without her prompting—aroused her.

"What do you think?"

"They're beautiful," he whispered. "If they were mine, I'd show them to everybody."

She hugged his head and rocked him a moment. "Darrell, have you ever had a woman?"

"Yes."

"You can tell me the truth."

"I am." He chuckled. "You think I'd tell you about those letters and then lie about never doing it with a woman?"

"Maybe. A lot of men would."

"Well, I'm not lying. When my mother had this boyfriend who didn't like me, she tried to marry me off to a daughter of a friend of hers, and we did it a couple of times. But I just didn't think it was—"

"It doesn't matter, anyway. I just want you to know that you can have me if you like."

His hand grew still on her breast. "Thank you. I truly appreciate that, Lolly. Maybe I will. Sometime. I don't have to do it right now. I like just being close to you and touching your breasts." He leaned back from her then brought his face close to hers. He gave her a goofy grin. "Besides, here's my most shameful confession as a man: I've already just done it in my pants."

By the fall of 1928, the rooftop had become their secret hideaway. They became lovers but felt they had to be discreet and kept apart during the day. David seemed to suspect nothing. He knew where she was every day and evening, and the chief psychiatrist was always ready to praise her generous efforts on behalf of the patients to him. She made a practice of coming home to David early enough and often enough to keep him contented.

This affair with Darrell was good for her, she thought. It brought out a maternal need in her to protect him, teach him, nurse him. She almost always took the lead when they made love, guiding him through their pleasures with imagination and humor. They giggled during these lessons, their mood lighthearted and joyful. She teased him about how quickly he came and he teased her about being a randy old slut. The more adept a lover he became, the more confident he grew; there was a period of several weeks where he acted like a spoiled brat, strutting about like a rooster with a yard full of hens, until she called him down on it.

She thought she was making a man out of him, and though she was proud of that, she was not certain the ultimate result would please her. If he became just another man among all the other men she knew, his appeal to her would be lost.

One evening in early October they quarreled on the roof. It was two days before her period, and she felt bloated, sluggish, bothered by a constant headache. She wanted Darrell to comfort her, but he kept trying to get her to lie still on her back, like him, and watch the Perseid meteor shower. She felt rejected, cross-grained, bored.

"Darrell, do you think I'm worthless?"

"Of course not, Lolly."

He must be humoring me, she thought. "What am I good for, then?"

He pointed into the sky. "There goes one. Look."

"I don't want to look. I want to know what am I good for." He sighed. He half-turned onto his hip and gave her a bemused look. "You were good for what ailed me."

"What ails you?" she asked, then realized with a jolt that he'd used the past tense.

"I needed a real woman to show me the ropes." He laughed. "Or, rather, the knots."

"And now what?"

"There goes another," he said. "Come on, Lolly, once a year!"

"I don't care if they're like Halley's Comet, Darrell, you're more important to me!"

"Okay, take it easy."

They lay side by side in a bruised silence.

"I asked now what," she said truculently.

He sighed. "Now I'm going to leave the hospital."

Her heart stopped for an instant. "When?"

"Next week."

"Oh, God, Darrell! Why didn't you tell me?"

"I am telling you."

She rolled over and jabbed him sharply in the ribs. "Look at me!" With weary good humor, Darrell turned to face her, propping his head up on his hand and elbow.

"What about us?" Laura asked.

"I'd say we can go on just like now."

"We can? But what about your mother?"

"I'm not going to live with her any more."

"Boy, Darrell! This is really big news here."

He squirmed with glee. "I know, I know. Dr. Samuells and I have agreed to confront her about my being on my own now."

She felt proud for him, yet an uneasiness made her shiver. "What do you think she'll do?"

"She'll say you go right ahead and see if you can get along, but I know you can't because you're not getting a penny from me, and maybe I'll be there when you fall flat on your face and maybe I won't—you'll just have to take the chance."

He fell onto his back again, fingers laced across his chest. Laura wasn't part of the struggle between Mother, Doctor, and Darrell. Laura's time with Darrell at the hospital had been precious to her but was, perhaps, impossible to transport to a new locale, a new circumstance. She envisioned him moving about freely in the world, a different person from the one she'd known and taught, one who might make choices she couldn't predict. Or influence. Without realizing it, she'd come to rely on his being restricted.

"What will you do for money?"

"I've got some ideas."

"Example?"

"I've been talking to that missionary you know, Sister Alice, about directing a movie. Aimee McPherson wants to produce some biblical stories for film," he said matter-of-factly.

"Darrell, that's wonderful!" she gushed, though she was wounded to be hearing the news so late. Alice hadn't mentioned it to her. She tried to squelch her jealousy. "Maybe there's something I could do to help."

"Maybe so," he said flatly.

His lack of enthusiasm for her help was painfully obvious. She and the hospital were to be put behind him; to him she'd been just another form of therapy.

"Oh, Lolly—" he began, but she sat up suddenly, scrambled on top of him, straddled his hips and pinned his arms down with her knees. She leaned over his face, furious—yet this was all so much like horseplay that it was hard to keep from laughing. But she wasn't joking.

"I ought to spit in your face!"

"Lolly!" he laughed. "What's the matter with you!"

"You're not telling me what you really mean to tell me!"

"And what's that?"

"That when you leave here you want to be free to practice what I taught you with a bunch of silly little girls."

"That's not true. And even if it were, how about you and your husband? Don't you do it with him?"

"So it's true! And you've been trying to justify it by thinking about me and David, haven't you?"

He flared and, with a heave of his hips, tossed her onto the blanket. She landed hard, pressed her face into her hands and tried not to sob.

"You don't love me!"

"Yes, I do."

"You don't really love me!"

"Yes, I do, damnit!"

She ran the sleeve of her sweater across her eyes and looked up at him.

"All right, then. Would you do anything for me?"

"What do you have in mind?"

"You can't ask that, Darrell!"

"Okay, yes, I really really love you and I'll do anything for you," he said, exasperated.

Unsteadily, she stood up and walked to the edge of the roof. She looked over the knee-high parapet topped with red Spanish tile.

"If you love me, you'll jump off of here."

"Don't be silly."

"I'm serious! If you don't really love me, I'm leaving here now and I won't ever come back!"

He shook his head, blew out a breath, and walked to where she stood beside the parapet; they looked out over the rooftops and down to where he might land—the shuffleboard court. Without ceremony, he startled her, stepping up onto the parapet and facing her. He put his heels together and his palms flat along his thighs, as if about to execute a fancy dive.

"I'm going to let myself lean backward, and the only thing that will keep me from falling will be if you grab me before it's too late. Okay?"

She nodded, fascinated. He closed his eyes. She didn't know what mad impulse had led her to challenge him like this. She was sure he'd never let himself fall. She would call his bluff, not make a move to save him, she thought, and his humiliation would be her trophy for the day.

He leaned back slightly, but only from his shoulders, pushing his pelvis forward.

"You won't do it."

He smiled beatifically, opened his sky-blue eyes, and gave her an intense look of longing, pain, and ecstasy. He began leaning backward, rigid as wood, and she recalled suddenly that he was not merely her lover—he was a patient in this hospital and thus not exactly sound of mind. He would tumble over backward unless she grabbed him.

Which she did. She yelped, bounded forward, and dragged him down off the parapet by his knees, while his arms were windmilling for balance.

"Oh, oh, you silly darling!" she moaned. "You would've done it! You do love me!"

She kissed his face madly, stroked his fine blond hair, tore open his shirt and licked his chest, his flanks, and his belly with her lips and tongue. He returned her kiss passionately, taking her breath away. But no sooner had she rolled over on her back and pulled him on top of her than he sat up suddenly and said, "Now you do it."

"What!"

"Do you love me?"

"Madly!" She kissed him. How grand she felt now!

"Then you jump off the roof."

His eyes were twinkling but his mouth was a dead-set line. "If this is going to be a one-sided thing, I'm giving up on it right now."

"Okay."

She stood on the parapet, back to the yard below, facing Darrell. Her palms broke into a sweat and her knees quivered slightly. A slight capricious breeze tugged on her body as she stood balancing. She hadn't noticed it before. Darrell stood in front of her a little more than an arm's-length away.

She closed her eyes and tilted back her head, feeling the breeze gently push on her, and she flicked her eyes open to see if he had moved forward. He hadn't.

"No use trying to fake it. I won't lift a finger to save you until after you've already leaned past the point where you can save yourself. This won't be any trouble for you if you really really love me and trust me." He sounded faintly bitter, and she realized he was angry at her for having tested him. "Of course"—he bent forward and gave her a wink that made a mockery of a wink—"you *are* depending on a goddamn loony who's locked up in a loony bin to save your life, you do realize that, don't you?"

She tittered. "Don't tease me, Darrell!"

"Maybe you were right." He gave a short laugh, like a cough, that was either the laugh of a maniac or the laugh of someone imitating a maniac just to confuse her. "Maybe I do plan to set myself free when I leave here. I'll have lots of silly little girls. Maybe this is my first act of liberation!"

"If you don't love me, then I *want* to die!" She would have liked to mean it. She closed her eyes, took a deep breath, felt a strange exhilaration as though she might be ascending and not falling, and a millisecond later felt his strong arms enclosing her hips and his face burrowing into her belly as he pulled her off the parapet. A moment later, they were locked in each other's arms, rolling on the roof, babbling and weeping with enormous gusto.

One evening in September of 1929, she came out of the hospital in the evening to find Bill Kale leaning against her car. He hadn't seen her, so she whirled to walk in the opposite direction. At the croquet courts, she sat on a bench in the shadow of a tree. From there, she could see her car, and Kale beside it, smoking, rolling his head back in that distinctive way to pop his neck, stretch the muscles. What did he want? How did he know she was here? Sunday was the only day she came to the hospital, now that Darrell was out. Otherwise, she was home, where she and Darrell used her salon as a filmmaking office, or at Darrell's tiny apartment.

What did Bill know about her life?

She shuddered to think Kale was here to make trouble and ask for money. Her life had been almost perfect this past year with Darrell. She loved him and together they'd make a movie. Maybe she would even star in it. She wasn't going to let Bill Kale upset her life. He'd intimidated her before, but not now, she thought.

As if to prove her own courage to herself, she rose from the bench and strode purposefully back to her car. She hadn't seen Kale in over ten years; he'd put on weight, his hairline was receding, his tie was loose around his neck, and he had a day's growth of beard.

She stood before him with her hands in her coat pockets. He flipped his cigarette butt away and grinned crookedly.

"Hello," he said. "Come give me a kiss."

She almost bolted, but he took her in his arms, wedged his knee between her legs and cupped her hips with his hands. He tried to kiss her, but she shoved him away.

"Do you *mind?*" she hissed. "What right do you think you have to treat me like that?"

He seemed amused by her anger, and that brought back an old, unpleasant sensation in her.

"I take it you're not happy to see me."

She stood away from him and folded her arms across her breasts. Heavier, grayer, obviously exhausted by travel or drinking, he was neither as frightening nor as dazzling as he used to be. She smiled to disarm him.

"You didn't give me a chance to be."

"You're not going to tell me it would've helped if I'd called ahead, now are you?"

"No. I meant I don't see you for more than ten years and you treat me like a whore. How could you expect me to be happy?"

He held his palms up like an apprehended burglar. "So you're a lady now. It figures; you're too old to be a whore."

Outraged, she said, "I don't know what you're doing here or what you want, but I tell you this—I don't want you in my life, and I don't even want you *near* it!" She began to shake her finger at his face. "You're poison, and I'm not about to get mixed up with *you* again, you hear me?"

He gave her a nasty grin. "Get your goddamn finger out of my face before I break it off."

Having spent her anger, she felt a little afraid. "I'm sorry," she said crossly. "But you can't expect me to be happy to see you after all I've heard from you these past years is 'send me money.' "

"Get in the car," he said. "Let's talk."

She decided that the sooner they got through whatever he had to say, the better. He slid behind the wheel, so she walked around the front of the car—he tooted the horn and laughed when she jumped—and got into the passenger seat. She was glad they couldn't be seen from the hospital, but she didn't like being alone with him.

"Burrrudddnnnt!" He made the sound of a car engine and gripped the wheel. "Nice car. Packard."

"Actually, it's David's."

"Everything belongs to him, right?"

"That's right."

Kale lit a cigarette, using the lighter from the car and making a show of admiring it as he did.

"So aren't you going to ask me something like, 'What brings you to our fair city of Los Angeles, Mr. Kale.' " He did a bad imitation of a simpering female voice.

"You want money."

"Yes."

"I've told you twice before that I do *not* have access to David's money, Bill. I wasn't lying! You just don't know how ignorant and simple that man is *not!* He gives me an allowance. He has accountants! Why won't you believe that?"

"You don't seem to be hurting."

"I pay the price! You hear me, I PAY THE PRICE!" She sat bolt upright and clenched her fists against her thighs, feeling the rage surge so swiftly she feared she'd go berserk and begin pounding him with her fists. "If you'd done what you were supposed to do, then I wouldn't be here, if you'd done what you led me to think you'd do, then we'd both have that money. But no, you bungled it. Or maybe you wanted it all and thought you'd just let me take the blame!" She was trembling.

Kale dropped his look of disdain and contempt. "Things didn't work out right. It wasn't anybody's fault." He shrugged. "And you don't need to go around playing the innocent lamb, do you? You knew what was up, and you didn't have the guts for it, and that's the truth. You can tell yourself all you want that I made you do things, but as far as I'm concerned you married that goddamn Indian with your eyes open. And you ran out on me."

She lay her head back against the seat and squeezed her eyes shut. "I don't have any money of my own," she insisted. "That's the truth."

"He has a life insurance policy, right?"

"I don't know; he doesn't keep me informed."

"I must say, you haven't been very resourceful. You might recall that we took one out for him. Besides, the laws protect widows, even in the event there's no will."

"He's got lawyers." She meant to suggest that anything they might do would be subject to scrutiny.

Kale laughed dryly. "Look, Laura. I need money. You understand? I'm not interested in what your problems are—it's obvious you're not working at helping me out." He sighed, stretched, then, to her surprise, opened the door and stepped out of the car.

"You can either share your good fortune with me or I can tell your husband about your boyfriend," he said.

"That won't matter," she said, shaken. "I'm going to tell him, anyway."

"Don't make me laugh."

"I mean it. You've got nothing you can use on me to make me give you anything. So you can just crawl back home to your pasty-faced wife and those fat little toads you call your children."

She glared at him, her jaw set. Standing up to him this way gave her an odd thrill, but she knew she was on a roller-coaster ride. Every muscle in her body was tensed for flight if he should open the door and come at her.

He cackled and slapped the sill as if she'd made a good joke.

"Okay, so long, kiddo. It's been nice seeing you. Think of me when I'm gone, you know, *use your imagination!*" He made a movie madman's face, rolling his eyes. "Keep me in your dreams. You'll be hearing from me one way or another."

He strolled away with an overblown saunter, whistling merrily. She sat stonily for a moment, then suddenly felt afraid. Yes, she'd planned to tell David about Darrell, but in her own time, on her own terms, for better reasons. And Bill could tell Darrell about himself, too. He could easily upset all the plans that she and Darrell had been making for so many months to get their picture launched and to secure their future together, so many delicate arrangements, including a plan to ask David to finance the project.

She leaned to the window. "Bill!"

He stopped as if on an expected cue, came back to the car, grinning. "You called?"

She couldn't look at him. "Sorry. You got under my skin, I guess."

He waited for her to go on, and when she didn't, he said, "So what now?"

"So what now?" Puzzled, she turned to look at him.

"That was your line. You ask, 'So what now?' "

She swallowed. Her heart was pounding. "So what now?" she asked, her voice thin, trembling. Whatever he says, she thought, I don't have to do it. I'm only stalling him, buying time.

He laughed merrily. "What now? Just as before, Laura. Don't worry."

PART

FOUR

September 1929

29

Saynday was coming along one day when he met Ant on the path. This was back in the time when Ant was just one big round ball and what to do about death had not been decided. After Saynday and Ant greeted one another, they sat down in the shade of a prickly pear to rest and to talk.

Nephew, said Saynday, I have been thinking of changing the world. Things have stayed the same for a long time, and now many people are old. They must die, but I think they should come back to life after four days.

No, said Ant. Do not let them come back to life. Old people have lived their lives and they need to make room for new people who come along to enjoy life.

But you know, Nephew, said old Saynday, sometimes young men and women die before they are old, maybe in a fight or maybe in an accident. We should have a way of bringing them back after four days so they can finish their lives.

Well, no, Uncle, said Ant, let them stay dead because it was their own fault. Let staying dead be a punishment for them.

I thank you for telling me your thoughts, said Saynday. Now that I know what you want, this is the way it will be. From now on, when people die, they will stay dead. They shall not return to this world. Now if you will excuse me, I will go see some more of my world.

Saynday went off and Ant went home to her lodge. Some time later, her way-behind little one got sick and was about to die. Ant was full of sorrow, and she sought out Saynday.

Oh, uncle, she said. Let things be the way you said. When people die they can return to this world after four days.

No, said Saynday. You have already said that when people die they should stay dead. Those were your wishes, and it shall be that way.

Ant went home, and the very next day her son died. She mourned for her boy and wailed in sorrow, but he did not come back to life. She felt so bad that she sang this song:

I wish I could break my back in two!
I wish I could break my back in two!

Right then, her back looked as if it was going to break. She still felt so bad that she sang more:

I wish my neck would break in two!
I wish my neck would break in two!

Right then, Ant's neck looked as if it was going to break. That is why, today, only a little piece holds Ant's neck and head and her body together.

And that is why people die at any age and do not come back.

30

Saturday, September 28, 1929

Fog wafted in swirls across the channel. It was still early morning, and the onshore breeze fanned a wet hand across David's cheek as he curled the wheel of Spider Old Woman on a starboard tack toward Santa Catalina Island. He kept an eye on Laura, who was posted in the bow pulpit, one hand gripping the jibsprit for support. She peered ahead as a lookout. With her white trousers glowing against the mist and her gray sweater melting into that same background, she was all long legs, a flash of white hands, a nape of neck, and blond hair whipping in the wind. She loved the salt spray in her hair and on her face, and, no matter how cold it was, wouldn't wear a hat.

She waved at him, ruddy cheeks framing a wide grin. How healthy she looked this morning!

"Three-mile buoy off the port bow!" she yelled, giving him a mock salute.

"I've been thinking it over," said Wilbur. Seated across from David in the wheel pit, he wore a woolen watch cap and a denim jacket. David thought the cap looked peculiar over Wilbur's narrow face; he wasn't accustomed to seeing Wilbur in casual attire.

"I think this is a case where, with your money in this, you can keep a hand on how things go. And if it's going to have sound, you're already ahead there. We can sell or lease our own system to the company."

David looked at Iola, who sat clutching a green woolen blanket around her shoulders and head so that only her face and fingers were visible. She reminded him of her mother that way. She caught his gaze.

"Well, it's none of my business," she said. He was surprised, having expected her to express concern that Foundation money might be mingled in the project's budget.

Laura was looking back at him, pointing off the port bow to the rusty three-mile buoy bobbing in the water, its bell clanging. Three sea lions sleeping on the bell housing awoke, groaning, as the sloop swished by, and a cow slid off the ledge into the gray water.

"Don't be scared, silly!" yelled Laura. "We're just passing by!"

David chuckled, his heart swelling like a sponge dropped into warm water. For the past several months, she'd been full of good spirits and a willingness to obey. It was hard not to mistrust her; still, her ebullience today seemed so genuine. It was her birthday, her thirty-eighth she said, though he believed that number to be a fiction.

"How about this Sanders fellow?" David asked quietly of Wilbur. Sanders stood inside the doorway to the cabin below talking to Alice, who was warming her palms around a mug of tea while listening to him relate what was—to judge by her smile—an amusing anecdote. Sanders had boyish good looks and a quick-witted charm, and David had spent many evenings over the past few months chuckling at his tales of mishaps and feuds on picture sets when he was a child star. But David found him too flighty to fully trust as a director.

"You know as much as I do," said Wilbur. "He grew up on movie sets. He's got a lot riding on this, that ought to be reassuring. It's a comeback, a sort of resurrection, for him."

"That happens to butterflies, too."

"He seems serious about this to me. He's passionate about this project. And he seems to feel he owes a lot to Laura for helping him out at the hospital."

It was hazy to David how this project had come about. An agreement

between Sister McPherson, Alice Roberts, Sanders, and Laura had resulted in the FourSquare Gospel's putting up money for a script by
Laura and Sanders about the life of Ruth. Sister McPherson wanted a
picture for her disciples that would illustrate good Christian conduct.
She'd even come to believe that using an actress who was a reformed
morphine addict would be an asset.

Laura had pitched into the project with a zest David had never seen
in her before. She kept the door to her new office open, and invited, no,
coaxed David to come in and listen to her and Sanders read their work
aloud. He was jealous of the time she spent with Sanders, but relieved
to see her stay at home. He loved when she'd dash downstairs, screaming his name, burst into his study and say, "Listen to this!," and proudly
read him dialogue she'd written.

She performed on her radio program sporadically now, and he missed
hearing her voice.

"Oh, I'll go back to it later," she'd say. "I promise. But right now
. . . well, this is so exciting for me!" She'd fling herself into his lap,
peck him on the cheek, then run back upstairs to her writing table, and
he'd be left with a tautening in his groin and a state of mind incapable
of reading about the Spanish conquest of California. When her partner
would finally leave, David would go up to her office and stand behind
her as she wrote, then he would touch her shoulders, slide his hands
down over her small breasts. She would put down her pen, rise, and
embrace him, then lead him to her bedroom where he'd receive his due
as her husband. He wouldn't have said she'd learned to enjoy being his
wife, but came to him with less resistance; she was more humble and
obedient now, though there was, lately, an inexplicable sorrow in it.
Once he dozed off beside her and came quietly awake to find her staring
at the ceiling, a tear building in the corner of her eye. He shut his eyes
and pretended to sleep.

If Laura's most passionate hobby was writing scripts in their home,
then so be it. Until yesterday, he hadn't thought it would lead to much:
he'd had enough experience with the motion-picture business to know
that whatever she wrote might not ever leave their house, and had even,
in some small way, counted on her essential failure to go beyond dab-
bling. She and her partner, the boyish fellow who had, she said, an
unnatural obsession about his mother, were like playmates. It was hard
to take their writing seriously. But if Sister McPherson wanted to pay
them to do it, fine.

Yesterday morning they'd read him the final scene of Ruth on her deathbed. Then they'd asked him to put up money for the production —Sister McPherson could not (would not?) put up funds to proceed without outside financing.

He hadn't said no. He hadn't said yes, either. The request brought back bad memories of Laura moving among the picture people, sinking into addiction and promiscuity. Despite that, he found himself edging slowly toward accepting the project. Alice Roberts would be a liaison between the production and the Angelus Temple, and that was reassuring. Above all, his money would buy him the right to keep an eye on things: far better his money and control, he thought, than someone else's.

They had apparently put the touch on Tom Quick, too. He was below in the sloop's stateroom auditioning some youngster with large breasts he'd discovered on the Santa Monica Pier. If Quick had told Laura and Sanders he could put up money, he was bluffing, David knew. The glut of oil on Signal Hill and elsewhere had driven the price far down, and Quick hadn't had the foresight to broaden his interests.

Watching Laura now, David felt charitable. She'd become the wife he'd wanted, so it seemed fair to grant this request. Neither Wilbur nor Iola had given him a reason to say no. It might be a fine touch to make his announcement over dinner tonight as a birthday gift.

Smiling, Laura hunched her shoulders in query—she had sensed the need to come about by looking at the sails. David checked the compass —the course for Catalina was 185 degrees—then waved to let her know he was coming about to a port tack. Patches of the thinning fog sailed past the boat in tattered wisps; beyond, he saw blue sky or, in the far distance, the hazy outline of Catalina with the two humps that had misled Cabrillo's pilots into presuming the presence of two separate upheavals of the continental plate. The boat lurched as it turned, and from under her blanket Iola's arms flew out to grab at her seat—she looked a little green. David smiled: she was no sailor; she was a woman born for the plains.

Laura fell to trimming the jib and tightening the canvas by running the wrench through the spiked ratchet along the gunwhales. She moved across the deck with the ease of a gymnast. Laura's love for sailing the boat—not merely being a passenger—was something she and David had in common; she could sail it as well as he, perhaps better. The boat seemed to calm her, to calm them both.

The Smythes' child came up on deck. "Here gulls! Here gulls!" she screamed. Her copper-colored hair flashed as she scampered through a sunbeam and to the rail, where she pitched a slice of bread overboard.

"Come here!" Laura called to her from the bow, laughing. Pearl clutched a hunk of bread in her right fist and held out her left arm for balance. She looked uncertainly across the expanse of varnished deck between her and Laura then began to inch along.

"Be careful!" yelled Wilbur, though the railing came to the girl's chest. Laura came over, took the girl's hand, and led her to the bow. There, they flung bits of bread into the air for the gulls to catch. David watched Laura bend down, listening to the child, smile as she helped her tear the bread. He felt heartened. Watching Laura's progress toward health these past few months had been like holding a soap bubble on the end of his finger. Now, though, he believed she'd make it. They could adopt a child, tighten the knot that bound them loosely together.

Most of his adult life, he considered, he'd been blessed with what most white men could want or ask for: money, an interesting life, freedom from need, even some small degree of fame as an actor in Westerns. He was proud of his heritage, but prouder still of having torn himself away from ignorance, poverty, and disease that so many of his Kiowa kin suffered. He was respected and feared by scores of white men, as much, he liked to think, as some of the old Kiowa chieftains who'd fought on the plains; he'd achieved the equivalent of a warrior's glory in a new world where the lance, rifle, and horse no longer counted. He had found confidence in himself, in his ability to create whatever his imagination might conjure; in this he knew he was a far cry from the passive youth who had so dumbly poled that ferry. There had been but one sorrow in his life: his wife's lack of love and respect for him and his failure to bring sons into the world. Now he could imagine two lines— one his life and one Laura's—easing forward through time, not quite parallel so that they would soon meet.

"Look!" Laura was calling to them. David emerged from his reverie to see her pointing ahead. The fog had burned off, and in the far distance where the sea melted into the shore stood the glimmering crescent of the new Avalon casino.

The undulant curve of Mount Orizaba rose from the water far off the bow, and Laura estimated they were forty minutes out of Avalon. She hadn't seen Darrell since they'd boarded at San Pedro, and she missed him. Soon they'd anchor in the harbor and go location hunting with Alice, Tom, and Tom's date; later, the entire party would celebrate her birthday at the casino. She feared she and Darrell wouldn't have a chance for a tête-à-tête. She was determined to carry out her resolve, but she needed to get Darrell's agreement first.

Beside her, Pearl stamped her feet.

"I'm cold," she whined.

"Okay, sugar, let's go below," Laura said, relieved.

The sun broke out just as Laura stepped through the portal to the cabin and yellow light suddenly billowed around the forms of Bobette, Alice, and Darrell standing about the ship's tiny sink, Alice with a mug of steaming tea. Laura thought they looked like figures in a wax museum, her entrance the cue needed to make them come to life.

"Hello." She gave Darrell a friendly pat on the bulky shoulder of his fisherman's sweater, but smiled at Alice.

"We've reached an understanding, Alice and I," Darrell said, winking conspicuously at Alice. "We've decided that she's going to marry me!"

He'd obviously been flirting with her, the way he charmed, almost by compulsion, every middle-aged or elderly woman he met by kissing her hands and telling her how beautiful she looked. It annoyed Laura, but here it only seemed a good strategy for diffusing suspicion.

"Let me be the first to congratulate you, Darrell!" Laura grinned. "But, Alice, I'm afraid you didn't get much in the trade."

"I told him I'd wait until he grew up or until after the Second Coming, whichever came first," cracked Alice.

Laura moved to the rear of the galley, giving Darrell a furtive but significant look as she turned. She heard Bobette let out an undignified grunt as she tugged off one of Pearl's damp shoes; being a mother made a washerwoman of even the most sophisticated flapper, thought Laura. At times, though, when she and Darrell were making love, a voice in her whispered *Let things meet and grow.* She sometimes caught herself wondering if having Darrell's child might force her to tell David, as she knew she must. Her happiness and love for Darrell made her want to do things right, to be honest. She could picture their future, hers and Darrell's, maybe poor, living in a cottage along the coast, writing, making movies, passing their toddler between their desks and taking long walks on the beach. Being with Darrell made her feel younger, but she was, in fact, almost too old to bear children, which worried her.

Having to hide galled her. It seemed unjust; their love became less holy, less noble the longer it remained a secret. The love she felt was like some god under whose judgment they stood.

She stopped at the main stateroom, found the door locked. A wry smile crept to her lips—Tom and his chippie were in there. How lost he seemed now! It was hard to believe she'd once thought she needed him.

She stopped at the door to the second stateroom, waited for Darrell to look at her, then flashed him a smile of invitation before she ducked into the room. Inside, she stood expectantly for a moment; the curtains had not been opened, and the room, hardly bigger than a large closet, was cool and dark.

After a moment, she heard him in the hallway. "I'll get the charts and maps and we'll have a look," he was saying to Alice, and Laura winced at the easy way he lied.

He came through the door grinning like a naughty boy, and she felt an invisible force push her to him. Their mouths met, tongues dancing; she could taste his tea; she pressed every inch of herself against him. "Put your hands on me," she groaned, as one palm was already cupping her hip, and the other climbed under her sweater, slid under the waistband of her trousers, then into her V, feverishly. She slid up onto his knee, ground herself against it, and heard him moan, "Oh, God! Five minutes and we could do it!"

She tugged playfully at his earlobe like a gentle schoolmarm.

"I'll take five days," she said, laughing. "Weeks, months, years!"

He bent down and they bumped heads. He quickly raised her sweater over her breasts and cocked his head to lick her nipples through her silk brassiere; she looked down to see the material grow translucent from his saliva and show the stiffening buds.

"Let's take your pants down!" he whispered, grinning.

They fell onto the bunk; he slid between her legs and pushed his cock up against her trousers.

"You take yours off!" she teased. "You're such a silly, impetuous boy!"

He smacked comically at her neck, and she laughed. She began to move against him slowly, provocatively, lifting then relaxing her hips.

"Wouldn't be hard."

"Yes, it is," she joked. "I should have worn a dress. And no underwear."

"You smell good, like salt air." He began to kiss her breasts again, but then drew her sweater down.

"I better find those charts," he sighed.

His chin hurt, pressing against her breastbone. He apparently thought they had been daring one another to see who would be bold enough to risk discovery, and, inexplicably, his giving up made her blood boil.

"I don't care who knows any more."

He let out a huff of exasperation, then got up and went to look inside the bureau.

"There aren't any charts here. You're just evading me."

"I want people to know, too."

"I wonder."

"I just think there's a time and place for everything."

"I think you're ashamed of me." She could feel her chin tremble—she was angry and aroused at once, about to laugh or cry, or both.

"Darling," he gushed. He sat beside her and took her hand, kissing her palm. "Don't be silly! You know I think you're so very swell! And I love you!"

She pulled her fingers from his grasp, pressed her hands palm to palm, and wedged them between her thighs. "I know," she sighed. "I feel all out of control, that's all." She looked off across the room to restore her calm—meeting his eyes was dangerous: she could fall into them and drown. "I just don't know how much longer I can stand this, you know, sneaking around, not being able to see or touch you except in secret."

"I thought you liked that part."

"I did."

"What happened?"

She shrugged. What, indeed, had happened?

"Maybe you have somebody else," she said after a moment, surprising herself by this accusation. She heard in her own voice the tone of the injured striking out blindly.

"Oh, you know that's not true!" He began kissing the side of her neck, her earlobe, and her cheek to cajole her, but she pushed him away.

"How can you stand it, then?" She felt tears welling. "I mean, you must go home at night and lie in bed and think about what's happening to me at home, with David! Don't you? How can you stand to think that I have to make love to him? Don't you even want to spare me that?"

Darrell shrugged sheepishly. "I guess I don't think about it because I don't want to."

"I wish I could avoid it that easily!"

Darrell continued to stare at the floor, a reprimanded child. She'd fallen in love with him because he wasn't a tyrant like David or a manipulator like Bill Kale. Now he seemed disturbingly helpless just when she needed him to guide her.

"I'm sorry."

"I don't want you to be *sorry!* I want you to help." When he had no response, she knew she'd have to do it alone.

"I want to tell him today. You said the right time and place. This seems right to me. I don't like the idea of asking him to finance our picture and hiding our love from him—it isn't fair. Despite everything, I do have some respect for him. I do owe him something, you know."

Darrell groaned in disgust, stepped to the dresser, slammed it with his fist, threw up his hands, and screwed his mouth into a pout—an adult's version of an infant's tantrum, she thought.

"I can't believe it! I just cannot believe what I'm hearing. Since when did you become Saint Joan? I love you, you know, but you have to remember I know a lot about you that even David doesn't know, so don't try playing Ruth on me! Don't play the martyr!"

Yes, she thought, some of that was true: it might seem out of character for her to be considerate of David's feelings, but loving Darrell made her forget who she had been or who she was supposed to be. Loving you has made me a better person. Or made me want to be one, she wanted to say.

"What do you care if I tell him now?"

Darrell was silent, squirming inwardly. She knew he wouldn't be candid; he'd only say whatever was expedient.

"Never mind!"

"No, I want to tell you," he rushed in. "I guess I'm just happy with things as they are. We're not just lovers and friends, Laura, we're also partners in a pretty darned important enterprise. If we do things right and keep our wits about us, we can build a good future for ourselves with this thing. I love you dearly," he said, scooting closer, again putting his arm around her neck and breathing hotly on her cheek. "I just think we should wait, that's all, not until he makes up his mind about the money, I mean it's not really relevant, just wait until we've got this picture off the ground and can devote all our time to ourselves. If you told him now, you'd have to move out—have you thought about that? I mean, sure, you could come live with me, but you know my place, with those two tiny rooms. We couldn't use the house for an office, and we'd have to move right when we're getting the busiest. And I'll be real honest with you—if I don't get this picture off the ground, I'm nowhere."

She was silent a moment. She knew that he didn't want his mother to call him a failure.

"Okay." She still felt wounded but allowed herself to be calmed by his insistence on practicality. "Maybe you're right."

Darrell leaned over, parted the window curtain.

"Almost there." He bent toward her. "Feel better?"

She sat, eyes down, hands wedged between her thighs. She nodded, then sighed to stop herself from sulking. "Yes."

"Well!" He slapped his thighs, satisfied, like someone proud of having coaxed a suicide off a bridge rail. "I guess I better go find those charts. You know where they are?"

Props! Disgusted, she raised her head and glared at him.

"No, you'll have to ask David."

He nodded, his eyes darting away, then went out the door. She could hear his tuneless whistle—his transparent impression of nonchalance—fade down the passageway.

31

Saturday, September 28, 1929

They came ashore by launch at Avalon and were met by porters in plumed hats, knee boots, and wide-sleeved blouses. Along the beach front strolling troubadours and cigarette vendors dressed like flamenco dancers were plying their trade for the weekend crowds flocking to the new casino. David hired two taxis for the trip to the St. Catherine Hotel at Descanso Bay. Sanders chose to stay alone at the Atwater, exhibiting, David thought, a mildly admirable desire to avoid obligation. It was nice to see somebody pay his own bills, but since Sanders had asked David to finance his project, that made it a trifling gesture. David sent Iola, Quick and his girlfriend, and the Smythes in one cab, while he, Alice, and Laura took the second and shared their extra space with their luggage.

Laura was quiet, subdued ashore, as they went along Crescent Avenue, while Alice chattered about each sight they encountered. The sun had burned away the fog; it was a marvelous California morning, the air balmy and slightly cool, and the light was stuffed into the surroundings so that the purple and orange bougainvillea tumbling down walls looked electrified. Alice lowered the window, stuck her arm out, and dangled her fingers, playing with the wind like a child in a warm bath.

At the St. Catherine, David made the arrangements for the day's activities. Laura and her party would scout locations at Two Harbors, while he, Iola, and the Smythes would take an inland tour and picnic near Middle Creek Ranch. Dictating his desires, doling out crisp big bills from his wallet to the desk clerk, he felt the pleasure of his own importance heighten his enjoyment of a very fine day. He savored the staff's civility, and stopped at the notions counter to buy a cigar as if to underscore it.

Feeling expansive as he headed for his and Laura's room, he wished the plans had been made differently, or, rather, that Laura would have chosen to go with him on the picnic. But he knew how happily engaged she was in this project, and he didn't want to spoil her pleasure by insisting that she come with him. She hadn't invited him along, either —she probably felt that his advice would only cheat her of the pleasure of making her own decisions.

He startled Laura when he came through the door without knocking. She was removing her sweater when she saw him, and turned modestly away.

"You scared me!" She looked over her shoulder and gave him a nervous smile.

"Sorry."

David stood by the bed in a block of sunlight. The porter had thrown open the wooden shutters, and a hummingbird was suspended momentarily in the frame, as though looking in. David's cigar lay flat planes of blue smoke a foot apart in the dazzling light. In the shadow by the closet, Laura was slipping on a red blouse, the backs of her shoulders showing pale smooth flesh moving like water over stones. He stubbed out his cigar and crossed into the shadow by the closet, where he pressed his mouth onto Laura's neck. His large hands gently palmed her breasts, and the smell of her perfume made him swallow.

"You don't have to leave for an hour," he whispered.

She kept still in his arms, neither wholly pliant nor quite frozen, as if waiting—which usually meant she was agreeable. He took her passivity to be the proper demeanor for a white lady, a wife. It never failed to arouse his pleasure in the notion of control, of bending her limbs and stroking her flesh however the mood might strike him. He slid his hand over her belly, then between her thighs.

"David." She twisted away.

"You could stay—" he began, but she moved to the window, her fingers working the buttons of her blouse.

"I want to talk to you about something."

At first he thought she was angry, but then, stepping to her side, he saw her chin quivering. "What is it?"

"Sit down, please."

He complied, anxious and curious, and watched dumbly while she eased down sidesaddle onto the desk chair.

She shook her head. "This is hard. I want you to think about something."

He wondered if "something" had to do with the request for his support of their project, but her expression was so tormented he knew she meant something more serious.

"I want you to know how grateful I am for everything you've done for me, especially taking me back and letting me get well. No woman could've ever asked for a better husband, David. Surely I didn't deserve it, considering what . . . " She broke off. He was pleased by this unexpected gratitude and praise, but he understood it was only a prelude to bad news.

"David, there comes a time in your life when you want things you've always been afraid to ask for, to even ask yourself to try to get, when you feel there's not much time left and you want to live how you want to live."

"Yes?" His spirits were plummeting.

"David," she said softly. "I need to be free."

"Free?" Did she mean his rules? "I understand that, Laura. I think you've earned it, and I don't see now why you should have to account for yourself—"

"You don't understand what I mean," she said, as if to herself. She was looking toward the window, her right cheek flushed in the light. "I mean truly free, David. To make my own decisions about my life. I need to be dependent on myself, not you. I don't want to feel like your child any more."

Her words carried no anger, only sadness. He'd never known her to make a request without being flirtatious, or, upon refusal, belligerent.

"You don't have to."

"Yes, I do!" she burst out. "Oh, this has nothing to do with you, really! It would be the same with any man, any marriage, don't you see? I'm not talking about how you could let me do more things, I'm talking about having to ask in the first place!" She flashed him an irritated look that, in turn, angered him.

"You've never shown in the past that you are able to take care of yourself very well."

"Oh sure, you would throw that up to me!"

They fell silent, nursing their anger. David was, beyond that, perplexed—what did she want, really?

"David," she said quietly, "I need to live apart from you for a while." She leaned forward with a pleading expression that seemed theatrical to him. "I must find myself."

He tried to understand. Did this mean she was "sick" again? Would she sink back into the gutter from which he'd rescued her?

"It's not a good idea for you to do that," he said quietly, trying to coax her gently away from the notion. "I know it's been hard living under my rules, but I only made you do it for your own good, you know. Very soon, believe me, you'll be much more on your own."

"David, you're not the one who can tell me when that time is coming!" She looked away. "Oh, I'm not getting this across very well!" She gave a groaning sigh. "David, I am *going* to live alone for a while. I just want you to get used to the idea."

"No! I won't allow—"

"You have no choice, David. I'm not your slave."

"No, but you are my wife!"

Laura cocked her head, her green eyes glinting. "Only by my choice, David. There's no law—"

"Of course there is!" He was on the verge of shouting. Good Lord! What a perverse creature she was! No sooner is she healthy than she immediately stirs up trouble! "I will not have you setting up your living quarters elsewhere than where I—"

"Then you will not *have* me!" She bolted up from her chair. "Oh, I knew you'd make this hard!" Her head bobbed toward him, pecking the air. "Divorce me, then!"

Her vehemence startled him. Her despair was so profoundly different from her ebullience of the morning that he refused to believe her state represented her real feelings: some wild, weird thing was careening through her blood.

"Well, of course I won't do that," he said calmly.

"Then I'll divorce you!" She was breathing hard, her shoulders heaving.

He chuckled nervously. "On what grounds?"

"On the grounds that I'm not good enough for you!"

He smiled: who could understand a woman? Rising, he came toward her to slip his arms around her—there was no fight between them but rather a storm within her over something he still didn't understand. He wanted to comfort her.

"Of course you're good enough for me."

The instant he touched her shoulders, she jerked away.

"Just remember what I said, David. Things are going to change. I just wanted to give you warning. I felt I owed it to you." She yanked a blue cardigan sweater off a hanger and threw it over her arm.

"Just how do you think you could get along without me?"

At the door, she said, looking at him coldly, "You can keep your money."

After she left, he stood at the window. Out to sea crisp white triangles of sails melted to blobs behind a skein of tears. He wanted to sob like a child, but he refused to allow himself. He'd lost her—no, he'd never had her, it had only been an illusion, a spell she had cast so she could bide her time. He'd been a fool again.

32

Saturday, September 28, 1929

On the leeward side of the island, Iola, David, and the three Smythes set out their picnic baskets in a meadow. The sunshine was brilliant, the heat moderated by a breeze from the ocean just below the cliffs nearby, and they ate cold roast chicken and potato salad. Iola was anxious to have David to herself—she'd been gauging his spirits all day, looking for the right moment to speak to him.

After lunch, they all climbed down the bluffs in search of caves along the charcoal-colored pumice. Stooping, they entered a few where, damp and cool but protected from the sea breeze, they saw starfish and sea urchins clinging to the rock, awash in the undulating surf. Playing docent, David told Pearl how the Pimugnans ate things from the sea. But marine creatures held little interest for Iola, and she saw in the murky shifting darkness of the ocean only something unknown and unreasonable.

Impatient to be alone with David and claustrophobic in the caves, she announced she was going back to the meadow to take some sun, hoping he might join her. She hiked back to where their picnic basket was perched on a boulder surrounded by heads of giant yellow coreopsis. She bundled a blanket as a pillow and lay on the ground in the warm light, eyes closed, wondering what words might be best to tell him.

She'd spent the last night churning in bed, reviewing the past few years, goading herself into action. The enthusiastic assistant she'd hired back in January had proved to be capable of running the Foundation now without her.

It had taken a long time to reach this point, to feel able finally to leave. She prayed she'd have the courage to stay on the path.

When David took Laura back after her hospitalization, Iola believed he did it out of pity; she believed he wouldn't leave his wife so long as she was "crippled," and, indeed, Iola wouldn't have wanted Laura's abandonment on her conscience.

So Iola had waited through the winter of 1926 and the spring and summer of 1927 for Laura to recuperate. Iola had remained watchful and patient, but the opportunity for her and David to be intimate again never came—neither tried to arrange it. She kept herself from thinking about David too much by working hard and traveling on business. The Foundation had grown to support a half dozen rights groups, three orphanages, and a medical clinic. If she stayed in the office she'd get buried under correspondence—she'd become, she saw ruefully, a kind of Mrs. Poynter.

Laura recuperated, but David seemed more enthralled than before. Iola began to give up hope. She tried to pretend she could live beside him as a friend and partner as well as she might have lived alongside him as a wife, and she tried to reconcile herself to being a spinster.

In March of 1928, her father died of tuberculosis. She went to Anadarko for the funeral in the church at Hog Creek. She sat in the congregation, dressed up like a white woman, beside her mother, who wept and ululated and obviously longed to gouge her own flesh but perhaps was discouraged from it by the sermons she'd never really appeared to be listening to all those years, and Iola, struggling to not embarrass herself or the whites in attendance, sat poker-faced through the service, clenching her jaw. At the cemetery, she held herself stiff and erect. Only when they'd come back to the frame house at the end of the dusty lane did she feel herself cracking open. There, left to themselves, Iola joined her mother, her mother's sisters, and her mother's sisters' children as they grieved like trapped wolves. She tried to comfort her mother, but her mother didn't need her comfort—her own sisters were clinging to her like mourning shawls, and Iola endured the guilt of having become a stranger through her absence. The keening voices pried away at that part of her self she'd kept locked inside for so long; when she opened her mouth centuries of her kin sang through it in mourning, liberating her, bonding her to family, to tribe.

Days later, as she was leaving for Los Angeles, her mother gave her a piercing look that said not even three sisters were an adequate substitute for the care and love of one's own daughter, one's *only* surviving child.

Back in Los Angeles, she kept on grieving. Weeks dragged by without her being aware of David except to think that her father would have been pleased if she and David had married. In the few letters he'd written during the last years of his life, Iola's father had groused good-naturedly about not having a grandchild and twice made reference to "the lad who ran the buffalo." She hated herself for not having been more attentive to him—for not knowing he was very sick. For a while it seemed she owed it to her father to marry herself off. She regretted having left Lenny so rashly. She dated sporadically, even allowing Tom Quick to escort her to pictures or concerts, and his attention allowed her the luxury of believing she was capable of inspiring romantic interest in a man. But she knew now that if she were ever to have a husband and a family, she had to forget David. Not only had she been cheating herself these last years of the chance for happiness, she'd also been limiting her contribution to the betterment of the world, or at least to her own people.

She was silently rehearsing her speech to David when she heard footsteps in the matted undergrowth of the meadow. She opened her eyes. David was strolling up the incline toward the boulder, alone. Her heart gave a minute flutter as she sat up.

"Where are the others?" she asked.

"They went down to the beach."

She was afraid to ask why he hadn't joined them, for fear his answer wouldn't be the compliment she wished for.

"Look—" he said. He was grinning, pointing to a far ridge. For a moment, she saw nothing out of the ordinary, then there they were: three buffalo, small as dogs from this distance, grazing on the hillside.

She laughed. "How'd they get here?" Their presence seemed magical, propitious.

"I've seen them before. A long time ago somebody brought some over for a Western." He chuckled. "It was *The Vanishing American*. A few got loose. They've bred in the wild here."

"Oh, David, let's go see them up close."

He shrugged, then grinned. "All right. You're sure you won't run out in front of them if they stampede, will you?"

She laughed, her heart aching. It seemed right, this sudden descent into their common past, and she hoped it would ease them into talking about her future.

She walked beside him, the blanket bundled under her left arm, and, her heart pounding, passed her right arm through the crook of his elbow as they went slowly up the hillside. If she were going to say goodbye today, she wanted to be close to him.

"Did you hear what I was telling Pearl?"

"About the Pimugnans?"

"Yes."

"Some." They paused momentarily while he stepped up onto a ledge, then held out his hand to help her. She took it, feeling his strength as he drew her up beside him, almost into him. They stood close, his body blocking the wind, his scent coming to her so unexpectedly that it was all she could do to keep from flinging her arms about him and saying, I have to leave!

He gave her a peculiar glance as if he'd divined that something was working beneath the surface of her expression, but he turned away as they started up the incline. She was afraid she'd frightened him, so she didn't take his arm. The buffalo seemed closer now, but were still a few hundred yards up the hill and to the right, on the far side of an arroyo they'd have to skirt.

"Well, I've been reading about them. Two Spanish priests wrote diaries on expeditions here. One of them was with Cabrillo. You know how it is reading these—it's hard to see what really was because of what they believed of themselves. One of them said the Indians here were cheerful and smiling. The Pimugnans cooked up a jimson-weed tea they used in ceremonies, and they had a temple—well, it was only a flat meadow down at Two Harbors that one priest said was a great circle surrounded by feathers from birds they'd sacrificed. They worshiped the eagle and the raven. One expedition came up on this place and found the Pimugnans gathered around a couple of large ravens in the center of the circle. One of the Spanish soldiers shot them with an harquebus and the priest said that the Indians 'began to lament and show great emotion.' The priests tried to convince the Pimugnans that the devil talked to them through these birds." David snorted. "It's a tiresome story, you know. The evidence the priest had was that he'd seen the ravens strolling up to the women on the beach who were cleaning fish, and the women allowed the ravens to take the fish out of their hands with their bills."

He gave a bitter little laugh. "That's your superior civilization. You *know* what happened to the Pimugnans!"

"Yes?"

"What else? Along with the priests there came trappers, miners, soldiers, fur traders—the traders brought the Aleuts from up north, and they pretty well massacred the people here. Then the good padres rounded up whoever was left and took them to the mainland into the missions." He was quiet a moment. "In other words," he continued slowly, "the usual story."

He paused and she stopped beside him. His anger puzzled her; it was out of character for him to bc full of wrath at a generic enemy. Usually, she was the one to make these broad political condemnations of history and he was the one to pass it off as remote and impersonal—he'd never seemed to have much interest in grievances that were not specifically his own, while she tended to take on the burdens of all red men and women everywhere.

"White people!" he spat suddenly.

She wondered if he'd been insulted back at the hotel by an employee or a guest.

They continued making their way toward the grazing buffalo, but by the time they'd reached the high mouth of the arroyo, the buffalo had moved farther south along the ridge.

To their left was an ironwood tree with overhanging branches.

"Let's rest, David." He nodded, and she spread the blanket under the tree. She let him sit first, then she lay alongside him on her hip, close, looking up at his profile.

"David, do you remember the day you stampeded the buffalo?"

"Of course."

He didn't sound pleased by her phrasing, but she gathered her courage and plunged ahead.

"I hated you then." She smiled at him, but he was looking out to sea. The breeze had ruffled his thick black hair over his ears, and the shadows of the ironwood leaves played on his forehead.

"You've told me before."

"You saved my life, too."

"Oh, those buffalo wouldn't have run you down. They were too happy." He turned toward her and smiled, showing his strong, even teeth. "But you've never said that, my friend!"

"I know."

"Well, are you grateful?" he asked dryly.

"I . . . wish I knew!" she laughed suddenly, surprising herself. It was so unlike her to reveal her feelings to him! "Oh, I don't mean I don't thank you for the effort," she added hastily. What did she mean, then? Maybe that she had not used her time wisely since.

"It was bad enough to steal the old man's horse. I thought I better keep his granddaughter from getting run down."

She lay quiet a moment then bent forward to shed her shoes. She propped her feet on a thick root that lay like a gnarled leg under the blanket, and the hem of her cotton skirt blew up over her knees. A breath of wind stole up her thighs, tickling her. She shivered and scooted closer to him, lying in the quiet hollow of his large form; he smelled of cigars, sweet sweat, dusty flesh. She could not recall when they'd last been this close, and she recognized a stirring inside which she'd successfully quelled over these past years. It seemed unfair to be assailed by this aching for him. His right hand was laid across the hip of his khaki trousers, the long thick fingers splayed, casually, his nails clean and trimmed—the hands of a very vigorous gentleman. A former poleman on a ferry. They had softened since, but his knuckles still showed interesting nicks and scars, a map of his journeys to this time and place. She could imagine his hand on her thigh, her breast. It had been so long since that night at the beach, in the car. . . .

She shuddered with yearning, irritated with herself, with him. But grateful, too. She'd never felt so alive, so keenly attuned to the sensuousness of the world, as she did at this moment—the salt spray, the dappled sunlight raining through the branches overhead, the warmth of lying in the windbreak of his body, and her own blood oozing, slowed by the luncheon wine, through her veins. She exhaled slowly and found her courage.

"I wish I'd spent my time better since then."

He look puzzled, as if fearing bad news. In the distance, where the buffalo had been, the meadow was empty.

"What do you mean?" he asked softly.

She raised up to lean on her elbows. Her legs were bare, her skirt just above her knees, and, inexplicably, she suddenly remembered that David and the Poulants had once pushed her into the creek.

"I should be doing more."

"More what?"

"More than be an administrator for your Foundation. What I do for you any white could do for a monthly wage."

"Are you discouraged about something?"

"No. I just feel disappointed in myself."

"Disappointed?"

"Yes. I'm not being useful enough. I miss nursing. I want to become a doctor before it's too late. I'm not young, but I'm not too old yet, either. I want to go back to Oklahoma and work with people who need my help, David. I want to work in politics to change things."

It took him so long to reply that, at first, she thought he'd lost interest in it, and her heart sank. She lay back, looking up into the branches of the ironwood tree, struggling not to cry. She couldn't hear him move, or breathe.

But then he said, "It's true. You always had a calling, as the missionaries say. You were always proud."

Annoyed, she sat up and tugged the hem of her skirt across her shins. She didn't want to hear him talk about her this way; she wanted to hear how her leaving made him feel.

"I'm sorry, David. It's just that I'm tired of working with numbers and paper."

"Do you want to go to medical school?"

"I think so."

He brought his face close to hers. To her astonishment, his large brown eyes, with their delicate, almost feminine lashes, were glazed with tears.

"Well, you can go to school out here. I'll pay for it."

"Oh, David! I couldn't have you do that!"

"Why not? Aren't we friends?"

She looked away. How could she explain that doing different work was only part of it—that she needed to leave him? Couldn't he see it?

"Yes," she said, her back to him. "We're friends. But I can't take your money."

"Borrow it, then."

"I have to go away for a while," she said with a huge, shuddering sigh.

"A vacation?"

"More than that, David."

She looked off toward the sea, blinking back tears. After a long silence, he said, "Is there some fellow?"

Was there some fellow! The unawareness implied by his unconscious irony made her too melancholy to speak for a long time.

At last, she said, "David, do you remember when I left Wetoka that spring for the war?"

"Yes."

"I left a letter for you with Tom. Did you get it?"

"A letter?"

So Tom had not delivered it! All this time she'd thought that David had known how she felt. Even without that letter, she'd shown him in a hundred ways since she'd come to work with him. And that night on the beach, in his car, when she told him about her marriage—surely, he must have known.

"Can't you guess now what that letter I gave Tom said?"

His face darkened slightly, but he said nothing.

"Didn't you ever wonder why I went away in the first place?"

She rose to her knees and knelt close to him as he lay back, his brow furrowed, his eyes on her face.

"Yes, I wondered," he said.

"Don't you remember what I said that night we were together on the beach, about how I went away to Europe because I had loved someone and lost him? And did you really think that I came here to work for you because I wanted to run a Foundation?"

He shrugged helplessly. "I didn't know."

She bit her lower lip and held her breath, struggling to keep from sobbing.

"David, don't you know what I'm trying to say?" Her voice was weepy, broken. "Can't you say anything *back!*?"

"Yes!" He sat up and put his arms about her. "I don't want you to leave."

"Oh, David!" she sobbed and collapsed into his side. She felt his mouth on her cheek and his arms slipping over her breasts as he held her tightly.

"Don't go away," he whispered in her ear, his warm breath thrilling her. "I need you. You are my only friend."

Dumbly, she pressed the back of his hand against her cheek, holding his long thick index finger in her fist like a child, and compulsively kissed it, jamming it crosswise in her mouth and biting gently on his knuckle. Then it was as if a whirling dervish of a wind caught them and lifted them together, entwining their limbs; she rolled over, clung hard to him, felt his large warm hands groping over her cool thighs, their mouths locked together.

Their lovemaking had a timelessness and dreamlike intensity. They kissed, nervously, awkwardly, then she held him vised in her arms so that they could not see each other, pressing her cheek to his as he lay on her. The branches shifted with a sibilant stir in the breeze, and the light danced with the leaves, then the boughs were a heaving blanket covering them, hiding them, as she lay moving to meet him. Hours passed, it seemed, as the desire which had long settled like sediment to the bottom of her being was stirred by his passion. Her face tingled; she felt faint. The undulating light blurred; images arose to her mind, random, unbeckoned—a seashell, a horse being curried—as he stroked her, cupped her bare flesh, his chest vibrating against hers as he moaned; she moaned with him, a canyon wren flit through the branches, then a strange, unexpected storm swept over her, frightening and delicious, and she blubbered like a baby in his ear to feel his long hot spasms.

Later, they lay in each other's arms. Their skin cooled and their breath evened; as she came back to herself, it seemed possible again that they could be together. But no—she wouldn't let herself be swayed.

"I treasure your friendship and your companionship," he said. "I was afraid you would be offended by my making love to you again. But I meant what I said, about being my friend. I don't want to lose you, too."

"Lose me, too?"

"Yes."

"Who else are you losing?"

He was quiet for a long moment. "I haven't lost anyone else yet."

He sounded vaguely combative. The rosiness of her mood faded; she understood he was lying to her by omission. She wanted to know more, she had a right to now, she thought. But as soon as she felt her own jealousy, she chastised herself—she was leaving, she had no stake in the outcome of David's and Laura's conflicts. She said nothing more, and he surprised her by saying, after a moment, "I think Laura may be sick again."

"Sick?"

"Confused."

"Confused about what?"

"About herself. About me."

"What makes you think so?"

As she stroked his head, she could feel his temples throbbing.

"Something she said." Irritated, Iola began to think she'd have to prompt him word by word, when he added, "She said she wanted to be less dependent."

"What did she mean?"

"I'm not sure. She only told me this today when we were at the hotel. I think she meant she wants to be . . . free."

"David, forgive me for asking, but is there another man?"

David sat up suddenly, moving out of her arms. He looked startled. "I wouldn't think so. She's been very happy." His face was drained, stricken. She could see she'd planted a terrible suspicion in his mind, and she couldn't truthfully have said she regretted it. She didn't need to add that Laura's happiness could as easily be the proof of her unfaithfulness as of her fidelity.

David stared out to sea. Iola lay back and closed her eyes. He and Laura had quarreled at the hotel. Thinking he was about to lose his wife, he had clung to Iola. It was too clear. Their making love had meant little but a soothing diversion for him. It was Laura's leaving, not hers, that had brought those tears to his eyes. She was glad she hadn't blurted out *I love you, David!* during their lovemaking.

She was sick to death of the Copperfields.

"David, why don't you and Laura get away from each other? I don't know if you love each other, but it's obvious you don't like each other. You treat her like a prisoner and you squabble all the time. She lies and cheats on you behind your back. Laura's made a fool of you, and she doesn't respect you. You want me to be a friend, I'll be a friend—do yourself a favor and make yourself happy. If she wants to be free, let her go."

David looked shocked.

"Have you always felt this way?"

"Yes."

"Why didn't you say something before?"

"I did."

"When?"

"When I wrote that letter. And later that night on the beach, and especially in your car."

"I meant about me and Laura."

"I don't want to talk about Laura. I want to talk about us. Did you realize that I wanted you?"

He looked away. "Yes," he murmured.

"I thought you felt the same. Otherwise, I wouldn't have ever made love to you."

"Your story made me feel sorry for you. You deserved a better life. It made me feel sad to think you hadn't had a good marriage."

"Did you realize how much it meant to me that we'd made love?"

He looked uncomfortable. "I guess I knew you wouldn't have done that casually. I knew you felt something special for me, yes. But after that night, you never showed anything again. I was afraid I'd done something wrong, that you didn't approve of me for pushing it on you. I was sure you regretted it. The day we drove to the hospital, I thought—"

"Oh, I wasn't free to say anything, can't you see that?"

"Free?"

"You were asking too much of me for the little that you were giving. It was too dangerous for me. And my advice would have been colored by my feelings and would have been self-serving."

"But now you feel free to tell me to divorce my wife, that it will make me happy?"

"Yes, because . . ."

"Because?"

"Because I'm free. I'm going to do what I've decided no matter what you do about her."

He blanched, looked down at her in surprise. "You mean, what we did today doesn't change your plans?"

"Why should it?" she said hotly. "Did it change yours the first time?"

She saw that she had stung him. She put her hand on top of his and asked, gently, "Does what we just did change your feelings for me?"

"Yes." He leaned toward her, but she turned away so he wouldn't see her tears.

"I remember once at school," David said, "I watched you play alone in the barn. I was hiding in the loft. You came into the stall below where the horses were kept—they were probably out to pasture—and you stepped off dimensions there in the hay like a stage. Then you did a show, like a pantomime, but I couldn't tell what you were thinking about. You just went about from place to place, talking to yourself and playing different parts. Then you went and climbed the rails of the stall door like a ladder and sat on the top. I remember you were humming and swinging the door back and forth, kicking your legs. A hole in the roof let in a light beam big as a tree trunk. You swung very wide and stopped right in the beam and sat there a minute with your face up toward me in the light and dust. You looked so beautiful daydreaming in that light. I felt very tender toward you, then. I looked up to you. You were teacher's pet. Your family put you out of my reach, though."

He rose on one elbow to look at her. "I adored you. I used to stare at you so long in class I'd get dizzy. Looking at your face would take my breath. Your ears were so . . . fine and delicate!" He smiled painfully. "And the day the buffalo came back. You remember how I was punished for the joke we played on you with the pie?"

She nodded.

"When I was at the flagpole and had wet my pants and you gave me that blanket to cover up with, I . . . it confused me. I mean, I was embarrassed that you knew, but touched that you would help me. I always wanted to be your beau, Iola, and I turned those buffalo loose because I wanted you to think I was brave. When you were angry about it, I had to run away."

"Oh, David, I'm sorry!"

He shrugged.

"When I saw you again at Wetoka with Alice, I still wanted you, but I was bitter."

"Did you *love* me, then?"

David blinked, swallowed. "Yes."

"Then why did you marry Laura?" Her voice shook. "Why not me? I would have, David, then. I would have, oh, I would have!" He had wasted these years that they could have been together. "Oh, how could you not have asked me!" She began weeping, covered her face with her hands, and pressed hard to make herself stop.

"I was convinced you would say no," he returned firmly. "You only showed how you disapproved of me when Tom Quick found my oil. I married Laura because that's the wife I thought a rich Indian should have, she seemed willing, and it was her idea, in fact. I was ignorant enough to think she had some regard for me, and it pleased me to think of how it would make you jealous."

"It made me *sick*, David! Are you satisfied to hear that? It made me die inside. Yes, I did disapprove of you and her, but I swear it wasn't only because I was jealous. I thought she would use you, and I didn't want to see you hurt."

They lay separate and still for a while, each considering like panting swimmers the distance they had just crossed.

And now? thought Iola. She felt hopeful, yet something in this exchange reminded her of the many times she had approached donors who said they would pledge funds only to later renege when it came time to sign a check. Laura was still his wife.

"David, all this still doesn't change my plans," she murmured finally. "It only makes it harder to go."

He drew in a deep breath as if to start a long reply, but they heard the Smythes hailing them from beyond the grove that screened them from view. Before she could say "Kiss me one last time," Pearl burst into the clearing and came skipping toward them.

33

Saturday, September 28, 1929

"Your friend certainly knows how to have a good time," Alice said without irony. She kept her face averted from Tom and watched Esther in the arms of a stranger out on the huge dance floor of the casino's ballroom.

Tom hardly knew how to answer. He puffed on his stogie, blew a large smoke ring, then sent a smaller one through it.

"She's had lots of practice," he joked, but Alice failed to respond. After several drinks, Esther had become devastatingly uninhibited and pixilated, and ever since Copperfield had led her onto the floor, she had stayed there, dancing with men she met on the wing, so to speak. Some were movie stars or directors or press agents or just hangers-on, but to a man they could sniff out an easy make and had surrounded her like a pack of dogs.

It was just as well someone was enjoying this party. It was as doleful a celebration as he'd ever attended, and he was glad they were at the ragged end of it. Copperfield had gone out onto the balcony a while back; later, Smythe had given Sanders a message to meet Copperfield out there. Laura looked as if she were wetting her bloomers when it happened—he'd give five dollars to know what *that* was about—then she had left the table. Iola had not even shown up for the party, and the Smythes had left to put their kid to bed.

No one was left at the table to make him feel uncomfortable about Esther except Alice. But if Alice had anything catty to say, she was keeping it to herself. He felt almost at ease for the first time all day, partly as a result of Alice's presence and partly at relief in not having to entertain Esther, who had no tolerance for boredom.

"Do you want to dance?"

Alice chuckled and looked at him. She had on a black sequined evening gown that diminished her bulk and sculpted it into curves. He could not recall ever having seen her in such an outfit; though she was only in her forties, she resembled a society matron who might have been a beauty in her youth. Her hair was up high on her head, fanned out like a Spanish lady's, and she wore lipstick, which disturbed him in a way he couldn't quite pin down.

"I thought I heard you tell that young lady you didn't know how to dance."

"She's not a lady. And maybe I just wanted to sit a few out here with you."

A moment of comfortable silence fell between them; then, over the blat of trombones, came Esther's squeal of delight. Like a little piggy being slaughtered, thought Tom, and loving every minute of it.

Alice couldn't resist a coy smile that mocked him. "I suppose your choice is flattering to me. Anyway, I don't know how to dance and you know it."

"What I had in mind was we go out there, put our arms around each other and just hug belly to belly and sway with the music." It did not sound like dancing or even upright intercourse—rather, he'd made it sound like clinging to one another in sorrow, he realized. "It's not so hard," he added, struggling for gaiety.

"You have no idea how hard it would be." Alice glanced at him, then quickly looked away. Now he had upset her! "Excuse me," she murmured. She took her small handbag in her gloved fist and tucked it under her arm as she rose from the table. Walking away, she opened the purse, plucked out a handkerchief, and dabbed at her eyes. He sighed. He had hurt her again.

One good thing about Esther was that it wouldn't be possible to hurt her feelings. Her only interest in him was how he might help her career, and that meant he was safe with her. With Esther, Tom felt a certain equality and serenity, especially after he had spent the trip to the island wallowing on her youthful, willowy form. She was supple, willing. And stupid. Her "supple" matched his restlessness, her "willing" fit his lust. Her stupid matched his stupid. Esther was a transparent gold-digger passing herself off as a talented starlet-in-the-making; Tom was posing as a rich oilman who was producing a movie. She was a slut; he was born to be scum. *Scum Forever.* A family motto. He knew what they thought of Esther and of him for bringing her. In the cab to the hotel, as Esther chattered brightly, the Smythe kid eyed Esther with a curiosity so naked and awestruck it had to mean that Bobette and Iola had been talking about Esther and what the kid had overheard had been a real education.

Her charm had worn thin as the day wore on. On the motor launch to Two Harbors, she started hitting Tom's flask three slugs for his every one. "You're too quiet, Tommies," she cackled at him as they stood at the rail alongside Alice, Laura, and Sanders. Usually, this "Tommies" business made her seem cute as a bug (the way she said it suggested there were several of him and they were all teeny, like toy soldiers), but today, it only made him wince. She told them his traveling-salesmen jokes, sang them his bawdy drinking songs, she laughed too loud, and hung all over him for support. By evening he'd become short-tempered with her, but was a little ashamed at his impatience and unwillingness to perform trivial and harmless acts of chivalry. She inspired lust but not like.

He believed a true gentleman would treat any female, be she a wench or a princess, with respect and courtesy. Tom knew, however, he was no true gentleman. That was the eternally abiding sorry truth of his life. A gentleman wouldn't have treated Alice so shabbily; a gentleman would have sense enough to recognize the true value of a woman with such a bountiful capacity for love in its most wondrous forms of sexual pleasure and friendship, a woman who would be the most devoted and grateful wife a man could possibly have.

Since the night in San Pedro when he had foolishly blurted out to her that he was in love with Iola, Alice had been a friend, as always, but he'd never been allowed to put his hands under her skirts again, which had only made her more desirable.

He was sorry Iola hadn't shown up for the dinner party. With her present, he could have lined up the three women and indulged in fantasy. If he had to spend the rest of his days on a desert island with only one, would it be the brainy virgin who inspired a holy awe, the fleshy earth-woman who inspired feelings of tenderness and friendship, or the delectable little cunt who made his cock hard as a rock? So long as he was just daydreaming, he could include Laura too, who wouldn't be a bad choice if he didn't mind spending the rest of his life slipping his shirt on over the knife handle sticking out of his back.

The desert island game, he saw, was really his secret vision of marriage—you had to choose one and stick with her. Maybe it was time to marry. Maybe Wilbur Smythe was a dull stick because he was so profoundly happy it had put his brain to sleep. He pictured the Smythes together on Christmas morning in a cozy little cottage, drinking tea, Pearl in pajamas, snow on the windowsills. While Tom awoke, alone and hung over, in his converted warehouse. On the other hand, there was marriage such as Copperfield knew: a boxing match where his hands were tied behind his back and his wife came out with brass knuckles.

Everything would depend on his choice.

To his pleasure and surprise, Alice was returning to the table. To make up for having hurt her feelings, he leapt to his feet, banging his knees, dropped his cigar as his hands shot out to keep glasses on the table from tumbling, snatched up the cigar before it could burn the tablecloth, and managed to pull back a chair for her before she arrived, chuckling at him.

"Apology accepted," she said.

She knew every motion of his mind, which gave him the comfort of being known and the discomfort of not being able to hide.

In her absence, he'd drunk the rest of the flask in two large swallows, and a rosy flush tingled on his face. He felt generous. He stroked Alice's arm as if she were a cherished pet.

"You know, you and me are pals."

She drew her arm away. "What did you think of the murals downstairs?"

"Murals?"

"On the walls, Tom. In the theater."

"Well, I don't recall . . ."

"Or the panoramic balcony or this grand ballroom here?"

"I like them fine." He knew this mood in Alice. "Don't change the subject."

"Was there a subject?"

"You and me," he said grumpily. "And you know it."

"Well, Tom, *my* subject is how nice this place is and how grand it feels to be here. I feel all worldly and sort of sinful all dressed up this way—"

"You look wonderful, Alice—" he inserted, hours late.

"And I'm having a grand time hobnobbing with the glamorous Hollywood folks, and watching the beautiful women dancing with those handsome men, and listening to this wonderful orchestra." She turned away. "I don't want it spoiled."

"I wasn't counting on spoiling it."

"Well, I can always tell when you're feeling blue, and I know that the next thing after you're feeling blue is that you want me to comfort you. You want me to think you need me just so I'll give you a little comfort; if I do that, you'll feel better, and off you'll go again until next time."

Tom was stunned. It irritated him that she presumptuously anticipated he would ask her for anything—he was just feeling friendly, wasn't he?

"If I ever have a man," she said evenly, "he will give as good as he takes."

All this had come out so unprovoked—or provoked by so little—that Tom suspected she'd sorted it out in the powder room while drying her tears.

"I wouldn't wish for any less for you, Alice. You're the best woman I've ever known."

He felt all choked up, mushy, a little woozy from the hootch. Tears stung his eyes. He decided to let himself get carried away by the moment; it seemed a more worthwhile thing to do than sit sucking on Copperfield's cigar while his date dry-humped strangers on the dance floor. Besides, it was true: Alice was true-blue. She had a heart big as a gymnasium, and she was somebody you could gracefully grow old with.

"I really wish you wouldn't say that, Tom." Alice gave him the stern, forthright gaze he called her "missionary" look. "It's not kind of you at all."

He needed to make a gesture to certify his sincerity. He sighed deeply, looking at the chasm at his feet then to the far side where Alice sat. Sometimes you had to take a breath, squinch your eyes shut, and leap; otherwise, you'd spend your life with your toes hanging over the precipice. What he needed, he realized, was a friend he could fuck, a mate smart enough to understand him and tough enough to chastise him when it was called for.

He leaned over, pulled her to him, and kissed her loudly and sloppily on the check.

"Tom! You—" She tried to back away, but he held on and whispered in her ear.

"I want you to marry me!"

A tremendous sense of liberation flooded his heart as he spoke, but an instant later, he regretted his words—they were irretrievable.

"Oh, Tom!" she wailed, glaring at him. "How can you do this to me?"

For God's sake! he thought with exasperation. Here I propose to this woman who outweighs anybody on the floor, and she carries on like I'd backhanded her!

"Because I want you to be my wife," Tom insisted, but with less passion than he'd felt while proposing.

They were silent a long moment. Alice kept pressing out the folds of her black dress on her thighs. Finally, she raised her head and faced him.

"Tom, I appreciate the offer. But I have to say no."

He'd been half hoping she'd reject him, but the instant she did—God in Heaven! Wouldn't anything stay put or turn out right?

"But why?"

"Because of what I said before. You're feeling low. Ask me again when you're happy. I'd dearly love to be your wife, but I won't be anybody's consolation prize."

"Consolation prize?" he almost screeched. He was still being punished for having admitted he desired Iola. "Look, Iola would never marry me in a thousand years, and I would never ask her." He thought this would be an argument in his favor, but the moment the words were out, he saw that they condemned him; they told Alice where his heart truly lay.

"I'm very tired," Alice said quietly. "Would you see me back to the hotel?"

He almost said, "I can't leave because of Esther," when he realized his loyalty lay with Alice. He leaned over and hugged her awkwardly, her chair arm between them, then kissed her cheek again.

"Sure. And I will ask again. I promise!"

"Don't make any promises you can't keep."

They left the casino and took a cab to the St. Catherine, where he walked her to her room. Outside the door, she turned and said, smiling, "Tom, what would you have done if I'd have said yes?"

"Ordered champagne for everybody, gone to the bandstand to announce our engagement on the microphone, and we would've waltzed the night away. Then tomorrow we'd have gone to get Sister McPherson to marry us." He tried to load his reply with enough heart-rending details to make her profoundly sorry for rejecting him. He grinned at her.

"Oh. And now what will you do since I said no?"

"Shoot myself."

She opened the door. "Well, since this is your last night on earth, I want you to spend it saying goodbye to me."

They went inside and began grappling, sighing, and tearing at each other's clothing. He was so moved by their bodies pressed together under the covers and her hot breath in his ear whispering, "I love you, Thomas," that it seemed only natural—seeing as how he had proposed to her—that he reply in kind, "I love you, Alice!" and was struck dumb by the fact that he even seemed to mean it. That made his proposal right as rain. And the rejection all the more terrible.

34

Saturday, September 28, 1929

David sat on the hotel's pier mulling over the day's events. The late-afternoon shade slid across the beach and hung over the water at his feet. Making love to Iola, learning that she loved him, hearing that she was determined to leave—all this made him feel a tumultuous confusion of gratification and alarm. He regretted his past blindness and stupidity; he felt he'd been given an unexpected, wonderful gift only to lose it through negligence the moment it had come into his possession.

What had happened between him and Iola soothed his hurt from being rejected by Laura, but it didn't resolve his quarrel with her. Nor did it move him to give Laura what she wanted. How could Laura refuse to value him when Iola did? In his most rational moment, he might have thought Good riddance! to Laura and done as Iola suggested, but his dark mood provoked him to thwart or punish Laura even if it wasn't in his best interest. It was Laura's fault that he was losing Iola; if Laura hadn't manipulated him into taking her back after the sanatorium, he and Iola would've come together, he thought. Now it was too late.

Well then, it was too late for Laura to be "free," too. There may be no joy in keeping a woman who stays against her will, but there is also no joy in being left by a woman who wants to be "free." If being free would make her happy, he couldn't allow it. They—as man and wife—would be whatever it was in his power to make them be: if they couldn't both be happy, then they'd both be miserable.

She couldn't divorce him without his permission, could she? If he threatened to leave her without a penny, how could she live?

Was there another man? Who? Sanders, maybe? He was only a puppy.

Exhausted with tormenting himself, David left the pier and went back to their room. He found Laura in her blue velvet dressing robe, fresh from a bath.

"Oh, hello. Did you have a good picnic?" she said with courtesy but little warmth. She was determined to be civil, he could see, to be *superior*, and her condescension irked him.

"Yes. Did you find good locations?"

"Yes."

They spoke as if nothing were wrong, though the weight of their unspoken conflict made this small talk lugubrious. He waited for her to elaborate; if she were seeking an opportunity to pump up his enthusiasm in the project, this might be one, but she chose not to take it. She stood at the armoire, shoving garments along the rod in the wardrobe, obviously anxious about what to wear. Her robe parted, giving him a glimpse of her white belly, and a wave of yearning tinged with nausea swept him back to those afternoons in the Wetoka hotel when he would come, a supplicant, hungry for her flesh.

She held up a satin dress the color of ivory, studied its low waistline and solid, unadorned front that would rise to her neck and deemphasize her small breasts. During the past few years, she had stopped wearing low-cut dresses. She carried it into the bathroom, leaving the door open, and while she was absent, he worked himself up to the subject. He felt worn down by the last few hours of morose rumination and decided to be conciliatory. He had no real plan other than trying to win a concession, a moratorium perhaps, that would allow him to sort out his feelings later, when he and Laura were calm. He had that oddly thick-witted sensation of being at the mercy of his emotions yet not knowing exactly what they were or how they would make him act, and meanwhile events had suddenly exploded about him without warning and were begging a response before he was ready to give one.

"I've been thinking about what you said, what you say you want. I want you to know that I'm willing to let you have some independence, even though it hurts me to think that you want to live apart from me. But I will not give you a divorce right now, because I don't think you really know your own mind."

He kept looking out the window, tracing the loops gulls made over the beach in the distance. At his back, he heard a rustle as she sat at the dressing table.

"Oh, David!" she sighed. "Don't be stupid about this. I don't want to be unkind, but I wasn't asking for your permission—you can't *grant* me anything, don't you see? I'm going to do what I'm going to do. This is not negotiable!" She didn't sound angry, only exhausted and firm, and her unwillingness to compromise enraged him.

"I'll never give you what you want because you have never given me what I want!"

"What I want has nothing to do with you! Can't you get that through your head?"

He stormed out of the room, slamming the door so hard the miniature chandeliers in the hallway shivered and tinkled. Was there no end to the misery this woman could cause him?

Later, at the casino, he had to put on a public face, which reduced his seething rage to a low, slow burn. Iola did not appear for dinner, and his regret swelled until he felt bloated with melancholy and pity for himself. He played host at the head of the table, while Laura sat at the other end beside Sanders and shot David saucy looks of defiance. He watched them, looking for evidence that would corroborate the suspicion that Iola had planted.

His plate had just been removed by the waiter, who was asking if he wished dessert—he was saying no, nodding, adding "Coffee only"— when he looked to the other end of the table to find Laura and Sanders gazing at one another. He couldn't have said they were looking longingly or even lustfully into each other's eyes, only that there was such ease between them they could communicate without having to speak.

Laura concluded this intimate exchange by allowing a tiny flicker of a smile, meant solely for Sanders, to cross her lips. She looked up at David, flushed slightly; she confronted him with metallic eyes, serenely indifferent. She was gloating over his discovery of her true situation, he thought.

He wanted to howl, to leap from the table and pummel them both, but he buried his rage, sat still as a stone, barely listening to Quick's girl nattering in his ear. Sanders and Laura went to the dance floor, and before he knew it Esther had dragged him there, too.

Dancing with her didn't take his mind from Laura; it aroused his sorrow. After three fox-trots across the huge cornmeal-dusted floor, David wearied of Esther's insinuating her slender form against him, clasping her small hot hands behind his nape as she tried to stir him up. He kept searching the crowd for Laura and Sanders, allowing himself the grim pleasure of imagining them in bed together, seeing himself stalk them, watching the white-limbed spider-beast kiss itself (creating this scene in his mind's eye was like irresistibly pressing on a tender bruise), Sanders raising her dress—such were her uses of "freedom"—then the upraised pistol in the frame of David's vision with his own hand holding it and the pistol kicking like a rabbit in his fist as the bullets tore into their bodies. He wouldn't bother to ask, "Why did you do this to me?" Or he'd ask her to explain just to hear her weasel and crawl to avoid her fate.

Why did you do this to me?

He was trembling so much that Esther gave him strange looks. He stopped dancing, strode quickly to the men's lounge, where he vomited his dinner. When he came out of the stall, a Negro porter with a whisk broom in his hand and a towel over his arm asked, "You awright, suh?"

"Wet towel."

The porter ran the tap, flicking his fingers in the stream of water until it was hot, immersed a face towel in it, wrung it out, and handed it over steaming. David sat down, pressed the towel to his face, and felt the whisk broom swish briskly across his shoulders. The absurdity of it was strangely heartening. When he chuckled to himself he realized he wouldn't be able to kill either of them. But he did have to decide on the most useful, intelligent way to deal with them.

Leaving the lounge, he felt better. He stepped out onto the balcony overlooking the harbor. Lights from yachts and sloops glimmered over the dark waters; the air was crisp and fresh, and he stood at the white stone parapet, breathing deeply.

He was there only a moment when Wilbur appeared to say goodnight. "Pearl's nodding off and getting cross, and Bobette feels bushed." He thanked David for including them in the celebration, and David realized then he hadn't made his planned toast to Laura and the project at dinner.

"Is there anything you'd like me to do before we turn in?"

"Send that Sanders fellow to me, will you?"

Having given the order for Sanders to appear, David had to consider what to say. He examined his anger, turning it this way and that, looking for words. Shadows, old voices, said that Sanders had taken his exclusive property, that Laura had betrayed him, hidden from him— that these two had plotted against him. Worse yet, he had a sudden intimation that while she'd always been reluctant to make love to him, she must have been more than willing with Sanders—why else would he be her lover? And what could she get from him but that—he had no money. Sanders had stolen what David had never really had the pleasure to possess or enjoy, the surrender of Laura's sexuality.

They would be punished; it was only a question of how. But he felt more disheartened and sorrowful than enraged, and that displeased him: he was being unmanned at the very moment he needed most to be a man. Rage was not productive—a raging man blundered where a cooler one performed more artfully—but it was comforting. It was a transformed state of mind as absolute as sleep or lust. You did not have rage, it had you. You were only along for the ride.

David noticed Sanders suddenly hovering nearby, waiting to be acknowledged. Sanders took out a pipe, packed and lighted it. His tuxedo fit his compact torso perfectly; it was a more appropriate article of evening wear than David's white dinner jacket, and that, in addition to Sanders's boyish Ivy League looks, made David feel unpolished beside him. Once the pipe was lighted, Sanders set it in his mouth, then stood rocking slightly in his black patent leather pumps, his hands clasped behind him, as if merely taking the air rather than answering a summons to appear.

"Mr. Copperfield," Sanders murmured, as if greeting an acquaintance stumbled upon by chance. The pose of nonchalance and innocence infuriated David. He ignored Sanders and looked out to sea. Sanders remained silent; the two stood in quiet expectancy until David slapped at the rail, making his wedding band click on the stone, and Sanders jerked as if he'd heard a pistol hammer cocked. Such a pale enemy he had to confront! David had never thought him dangerous. Now he saw that no pleasure could be had from ripping his heart out in the grand style of a time past. All that was left was to act like a white man.

"Have you seen my wife?"

"She's . . . still inside, I would guess."

"You don't know?"

David—a good head taller—peered down at Sanders. The pipe clenched between his teeth looked like an absurd prop against his bland, boyish features.

"Well . . . " Sanders faltered, seeming to say: I don't know what I should say if you mean what I think you mean. "Yes. She's inside."

"She tells me she wants to leave me." David struggled to speak coolly, but saying these words made him writhe with shame.

To his astonishment, Sanders stepped forward with a look of condolence and patted David gingerly on the shoulder, the way a child might pet a zoo animal.

"I'm sorry to hear that, old fellow."

"You don't know anything about it?"

"Nothing at all." He grasped the bowl of his pipe in his fist and cocked the stem skyward along his cheek, while his other hand slid into his trouser pocket. The pose of a gentleman modeling evening wear. "Sorry." He smiled as if waiting for his picture to be taken.

"I'm trying to be *civilized* about this, 'old fellow,' " David said. "Do you know what my father would have done about a wife like this and to the man who took her?"

"No, I'm afraid not."

David smiled broadly. "Well, he would've cut off her nose and he would've had the other man's heart for breakfast."

Sanders looked as if he might make a cute or ironic comment but thought better of it.

"That would be unfortunate. For everybody." Sanders tried to chuckle, but something caught in his throat.

"I'm going to be a white man about this. I'm going to fund your movie."

Sanders blinked, confused.

"From this moment on, you'll be the director and producer, only you won't use my wife in it. You'll go somewhere else to shoot it, and if you ever set eyes on her again I'll treat you the way my father would have."

"But I—"

"Look, 'old fellow.' Maybe you don't have anything to do with this. If so, there's no need to worry, am I right? You had a partner, now get yourself a new one. Unless she means more to you."

Looking down, Sanders nodded. David couldn't tell if this meant he agreed to these terms or he was simply afraid.

"It takes no courage to steal a woman, 'old fellow,' only to keep her."

Call him a coward and he only stands looking at his shoes—Laura was more a man than he!

"I understand," Sanders said unhappily.

"Good. Now you get off this island before I change my mind."

If Sanders had stood a second longer without leaving, David would've driven the pipe through his ear and yanked out his tongue, but the man sensed his gathering rage and left abruptly, obediently avoiding the ballroom.

For the next two hours David wandered along Crescent Avenue, feeling unconsoled by his victory. Getting rid of Sanders would only make Laura hate him. He could break her spirit, but they would never be together as husband and wife.

He returned to the St. Catherine, where the lobby was full of revelers just returned from the casino who merrily hailed one another and shouted invitations to post-dance drinks.

David went straight to his and Laura's room. It was dark. He turned on the bedside lamp, illuminating and amplifying the emptiness, then flicked it off after noting that Laura hadn't been back since they had left for the casino. He removed his jacket and lay back on the bed. He was no longer angry, only washed out. Had Iola gone back to the mainland? Making love to her this afternoon was a misty dream now, leaving a residue of fondness and longing.

After a time, clipped steps in the hallway made him sit up, the tattoo of Laura's heels as unmistakable as her voice. He heard a key scraping in the lock.

"It's open," he said, just as she entered the room.

"What have you done with Darrell!"

He reached over and turned on the lamp. The light made her skin yellow. Her makeup had run, her eyes were red and her hair disheveled. She held a piece of paper balled in the fist clenched at her side.

"I gave him the choice of being your lover or having his movie. If you can't find him, then you know which he took."

Before he could react, she flung herself at him, kicking, swinging her arms wildly, her sharp elbow pounding into his gut; she was crying furiously, hissing between her teeth, clawing at his face. He managed to grab her wrists as they toppled over on the bed, her knees jabbing at his groin. He rolled her under him where she continued to struggle and writhe. When she sucked in a breath and drew in her cheeks, he jammed one hand over her mouth so she couldn't spit on him, and her teeth bit firmly into the heel of it. He endured the pain and stiffened his body, worming between her thighs, her dress shoved up to her loins.

She kept slapping at the side of his head with her fist, and he pressed himself into her crotch in a rage, pushing against the bunched folds of material. He gritted his teeth to keep from crying out with pain from her teeth clamping his hand; they were at a standoff, breathing like winded horses.

At last, her jaw went slack and her body fell limp under him. He removed his hand from her mouth and lay still. After a moment, he slid off her and stood shakily. She laid her arms over her eyes and forehead and sobbed quietly.

"He was weak," David said quietly. "When you pick a man find one who'll fight to keep you. If he was half as tough as you he'd be with you now."

"You'll pay for this, David. I hate you!"

"You should hate him. I did what any man would do to protect his home."

"You couldn't just let me go, could you? You couldn't bear to see me happy! You don't have any idea what love is, because if you did, you would want me to be happy. You can't love anybody because you're just a filthy savage!"

"Don't call me that!"

"Kill me if you don't like it. It wouldn't matter."

She sounded so despondent that he had an impulse to comfort her, but being the cause of her despair he couldn't. He went into the bathroom and inspected his face in the mirror. Two long red slashes arced across his right cheek, dripping blood onto the front of his rumpled white shirt. His left earlobe was bleeding. He turned on the tap, lowered his head to the basin, and splashed water over his cheek.

He heard movement in the other room, the door open and shut and her heels clattering in the hallway outside. He almost bolted to chase her until he thought, Why? Wearily, he picked up the paper wadded on the floor near the bed. He opened it and pressed it out. On a piece of stationery from the Atwater Hotel was written: "I hope some day you'll forgive me. But remember I asked you not to tell him."

Entirely in character. Sanders had laid the blame on her. Laura deserved better; David wouldn't have minded so much losing her to a man he could respect. He held the paper over the toilet bowl, thought of flushing it, then carefully folded it into quarters instead and slid it into his shirt pocket—not because it was a document that might serve as evidence against them but because it testified to the other man's ignobility. A pelt, a scalp, he thought. In a white man's world, you took them where you found them.

35

Sunday, September 29, 1929

A half-moon hung like a tipped cradle in the sky that night, and the light spilling from it momentarily caught the white material. Alice had been sitting at the window for an hour after Tom had gone, she told Laura later; she had been crying, drying her tears, and crying again, when the flicker of white out in the water caught her eye.

When she realized she was not seeing a swimmer, she bolted from her seat by the window and, still in her robe, hurried downstairs to the lobby, where a young man wearing a baseball cap sat at the desk reading the *Herald-Examiner*. It was well past midnight, and no guests were in the lobby.

"Come quickly!" she blurted out to the clerk. "I think there's someone drowning."

The lad grabbed a flashlight then sprinted out the door toward the beach. She followed, and, huffing and panting, they strode up and down the shoreline as he shined the flashlight over the breakers.

"Where'd you see them?" He sounded faintly skeptical and annoyed to have been put into a panic over nothing. Then, beyond the last cresting wave, a white thing—an arm?—bobbed up and down.

"There!" she exclaimed.

The young man saw it, too, and he kicked off his shoes, dropped the flashlight to the sand, and plunged into the white surf. Alice picked up the flashlight and trained the beam out to sea so he could use it as a beacon for his return, and once, while she held it, something heavy and dark sailed over her head and landed with a flop at her feet; startled, she spun and shone the light onto the sand beside her. A flying fish lay gasping for breath, its pale gill wings working uselessly. It had been drawn to the light. Alice fretted and paced, unable to see either the young man or the white thing, but then the young man and his burden materialized through the breakers, and he trudged through the churning surf with a limp form draped over his back.

The boy fell to his knees and let the woman tumble off his shoulder onto the sand, then he pounded her back. Alice stood, holding the light to the woman's head, shocked as the desk clerk shoved his hands hard against Laura's ribs and made her cough up seawater and bile. Once she was breathing, they made her sit up. Alice pushed the strands of wet hair out of her face.

"Do you see a rose?" Laura asked them, trembling.

"What, dear?"

Laura burst into wracking sobs and clutched herself tightly to Alice's bosom, shaking violently and bawling like a baby. When Laura was able to stand, Alice walked her up to her room, put her to bed, and instructed the clerk to bring a pot of hot tea. Laura was asleep when it came, so Alice drank it. Laura slept deeply for an hour or so, once groaning and murmuring "spiderface," then later slowly came to consciousness like an anesthetized patient and lay staring at the ceiling.

"How do you feel?"

"Did anything happen to anybody while I was asleep?"

"Not that I know of. Were you expecting something?"

"No." Laura turned to look at Alice. "Now what?"

"Now what?"

"Now what do you think you're going to do with me?" She gave Alice a glance that would have been malevolent had there been any energy behind it. "The last thing I wanted was to be dragged back into this shit-hole life. Thanks for nothing." She began to blubber.

"You're welcome," said Alice.

"So since you want it, you can have it."

"Have what?"

"My life. Now it's yours. I can't make any decisions about it."

"I'll tell you what," said Alice. "I'll borrow it for a while and see if I can't patch it up, and then I'll give it back to you. How's that?"

The idea that someone else would be responsible for her was faintly appealing to Laura.

"Whatever," she said. "It doesn't matter."

Alice slept in a chair next to the bed, and in the morning asked Laura, "Do you feel like eating anything?"

Laura shook her head, annoyed that she had to indicate a choice. Alice was reneging already, it seemed.

"How about some coffee?"

Laura refused to fall for a ploy to get her involved by citing a preference. She ignored the question.

"Do you want me to go fetch David?"

Alice watched as tears sprung instantly to Laura's eyes.

"Alice, you think I'm being silly, don't you? You think I'm being like a little girl who's holding her breath out of anger. You ask me about David as if you're going to tell Daddy on me if I don't behave." Her chin was quivering and she turned to face the wall.

"I'm sorry."

"Do you really want to help me?" Laura asked, recognizing, with exasperation, that by being forced to ask for help, she had been manipulated into assuming control over her life, or at least an interest in its continuation.

"Yes, of course I do, dear."

"Then keep David away. And don't tell him what I did."

"All right. But he needs to know where you are. I'm sure he must be worried."

"I doubt it."

Alice ignored her and rose to go.

"Wait!"

Noting the panic on Laura's face, Alice sat down again.

"Aren't you afraid of what I might do while you're gone?"

"No. Should I be?"

"Not really."

"Here." Alice leaned over to the nightstand, lifted her white Bible, riffled the pages, stopped, cocked it fully open, and slipped a white bookmark into the crack. "If you feel frightened by your thoughts, read a little of this." She smiled, lifted the bookmark, and waggled it. "Or this."

The moment the door was shut, Laura was jittery and almost bolted from the room in panic. An overwhelming anxiety surrounded her like bad weather. She leaned over and picked up the Bible, but her eyes wouldn't focus clearly on the small print and the only phrase she registered—"and ye shall be witnesses unto me both in Jerusalem, and in all Judaea, and in Samaria"—seemed like a foreign language.

Her stomach crawled upon itself and creaked like ship's rigging. When had she last eaten? She felt an emptiness that was as much exhaustion as hunger. She hadn't slept well in days. At dinner last night, they had—

Darrell had been beside her, leaning over to whisper like a best friend. He was the only man I have ever really loved, she told herself, mostly because he was as weak as I was. She needed Darrell the way you need someone to make you feel less alone when you're at your worst. They were alike; he was the only man she ever knew who wasn't either better than or beneath her. And David knew that. He knew nothing would hurt her so much as to have her love, the love that she'd waited all her life to feel, laid out before her eyes like a simple card trick.

She couldn't bear to think of either man. She got up from the bed and trudged into the bathroom, where she wet a washcloth and swabbed her face. In the mirror, her eyes were bloodshot, the pouches of skin under them discolored and wrinkled. She grabbed a fistful of hair and pulled it back from her face until the skin was so taut her eyes were the shape of almonds. She looked old, sexless, like one of those stern widows without a trace of vanity who stare haughtily back at the photographer.

She sat down in the chair Alice had occupied; she put her hands in her lap, but she quickly grew fidgety and breathless, so she picked up the Bible again. The bookmark was a large white card on which a poem had been engraved in ornate gold script:

> Lord, you washed away my sins
> With your precious blood.
> You saved my immortal soul
> By aching on the wood.
> Please let your Heavenly love
> Fill my heart with joy
> So I may greet you up above
> When the Gospel has Earth's time withstood.

The borders of the card were decorated by elaborately entwined rose vines whose many blossoms were each colored with a dab of pink. Those McPhersonites liked roses. The time when Sister Aimee had come back

so triumphant from her disappearance, airplanes had crisscrossed the
city dropping thcm by the bushel basket—or so Laura had read, and
had uttered a little *oh!* to have stumbled accidentally upon the quite
prosaic explanation of how she'd been tapped on the shoulder that Saturday she sat on the hospital steps after David had gone.

A day of darkest despair, she thought, hearing the words in her head
as clearly as if she'd spoken them. She rubbed one dab of pink with her
thumb, as if to test its integrity; it held, but the paper seemed very
faintly darker where her flesh had been. Odd that the roses would show
up again—she'd thought of that rose falling on her last night while
wading into the surf—it seemed very coincidental. Too coincidental.
Maybe it wasn't an accident. She shuddered, and the nape of her neck
suddenly tingled. A Sign, maybe of something good for once? As if
Something were trying to speak through objects and had her in its
regard.

Suppose it were a Sign that showed her how to become like Alice.
How nice it would be to belong to a group who loved you and told you
how to behave and what to do. You wouldn't be free, but that was also
the point—she'd proven she wasn't capable of using her freedom to
create something of value of herself. Maybe having it was a luxury she
couldn't afford.

You'd always feel secure, it would be a little like living in a convent,
away from the world, taken care of. You'd have someone or something
that wouldn't betray you. She pictured herself in a flowing white robe,
in a hospital, caressing the brows of the sick, the grateful smiles. It was
harder to imagine standing on street corners accosting strangers with
loaded and cocked pamphlets. She saw a quiet sanctuary, a candelabra,
her face canted toward it, eyes closed, the light buttery on her cheeks.
The scene shifted and she was behind a desk, dressed smartly in a suit,
dispensing funds to establish missions on Indian reservations.

Maybe the rose could be her secret talisman. No one would know
how she'd been *tapped out*, just like a sorority ceremony, such a light
touch, and with a fragrance, too!

She could not change the past. Darrell was gone, David had seen to
that. She felt her rage rise like a bilious dry heave and fought it back.
She breathed slowly, feeling a need to become serene, to float above
these thoughts that suddenly seemed worldly and unworthy; she laid
her head back and probed the darkness behind her eyelids for a rose,

but the image clung tenaciously to the gray void and was slow to materialize. Finally, she plucked it, tried to hold it for contemplation, but the red petals grew large and pale, faded to white, then elongated into fleshy appendages, a fat spider's legs. When she had come to the lobby yesterday after arguing with David in their room, a man standing near the front door quickly ducked his head and shoved the brim of his hat down low over his face, but she thought she'd seen the scar. Then he was gone. She'd told herself it wasn't Shingle; now she thought it could have been.

No sooner had these thoughts flitted through her mind than she felt the nudge of an idea so ugly she immediately suppressed it; she told herself that even a Shingle, a known expert in hijacking and murder, could vacation wherever and whenever he chose, and there was nothing anyone could do about it. It was a free country. " 'Lord, you washed away my sins/With your precious blood,' " she recited; she realized, with a start, that the "poem" was actually a prayer.

Is that how to pray?

"God, grant me . . ." she began experimentally, then stopped, unsure of how to proceed. "Grant me . . ." The finger of thought stopped on a bruise, then dug at it cruelly, and all at once she was afraid of her own wishes. "Grant me happiness," she concluded quickly. Should she say Ah-men or A-men as in ace of spades?

"Ah-men," she uttered. The soft A sounded more respectful.

She listened intently. An auto chugging along the street below bleated like a sheep. In a room above hers, a water tap squeaked and the pipe thumped. A knock on a door, a murmur, then a cart rumbled along the corridor, dishes on it chattering like props in a waiter's imminent pratfall crash.

When David came down to the lobby, Wilbur and Bobette were waiting near the door between two wrought-iron stands holding potted palms. Beside them their family trunk was upright like a faceless troll, and as David stepped up to them, Wilbur slid his hands about Pearl's ribs to boost her atop the trunk.

"Have you seen Iola?" David asked Bobette. She was wearing a green sundress that set her hair on fire.

"No, but Tom told us he was staying and to go on without him."

"And that girl?"

Bobette shrugged, barely suppressing a smile. "He didn't say."

David walked to the desk, where the clerk passed him an envelope embossed with the Hotel St. Catherine's crest. Trembling, he tried to juggle the envelope, the hotel bill, his pen, and his checkbook. The envelope, he was sure, meant Iola wouldn't join them. Was it too late to ask her to sail back with him?

"The woman who gave you this?"

"I believe she checked out and took the early steamer."

David sighed and slipped the envelope into his coat pocket. As he turned to find a porter, Alice was gliding across the floor toward him, her brows knitted. He was startled to recognize the look she once used to scrutinize him when he was her pupil, a look that ranged from displeasure to disapproval to disgust. Today's version was stout, though blunted by the mournful downturn of her mouth.

"David."

"Good morning, teacher."

Puzzlement flickered over her features, but she was too preoccupied with her mission to interpret what he meant. "Laura's not feeling well."

He searched her eyes to distinguish between "not feeling well" as a white woman's social excuse and "not feeling well" as an understatement of a serious medical condition.

She read the question off his face. "She's going to be all right." She stepped closer and laid her fingertips on his arm. "I meant that there's nothing seriously wrong. She's upset by all this business between you. If it's all right, I'd like to take her to the Temple and let her rest for a few days."

Did Alice want to keep Laura away from him because she feared that he might harm her? He had no idea what or how much Alice knew about him and Laura or Sanders.

"She's free to do as she pleases."

He meant to be sarcastic and heard an unbecoming twinge of bitterness in his voice. Alice explained that they would take the afternoon ferry, thanked him for a wonderful weekend party, and turned to go back upstairs. The words he had spoken echoed slowly through his mind, and he discovered, quietly and unexpectedly, that being able to utter that simple truth had swept over him like a bracing air through a window thrown open in a stuffy room. Letting her go relieved him of the burden of controlling her.

When the porter brought down his luggage, Laura's two bags were on the cart, so he had to have the clerk ring up to Alice's room to settle the matter of his wife's belongings. The counter had become crowded as guests who had just finished breakfast gathered to leave on excursions. They stood, conspicuously quiet, while the clerk held his hand over the telephone mouthpiece and, consulting David unnecessarily, asked, too loudly, "Mrs. Copperfield would like to have her bags sent to Miss Roberts's room?" David murmured "yes," then the clerk slapped the bell and literally shouted over heads of the loitering guests, "Front—take Mrs. Copperfield's bags back upstairs." Still another porter had to be rousted to get David's and the Smythes' bags to the curb, and during all this David felt the impatience of those waiting around him grow until it took on that inevitably racist cast: they were no longer being held up by another person, it was by *a rich Indian*. Everybody waiting knew he and his wife were separating, it seemed; the confusion about the trunks covered him with disgrace.

In the taxi, Pearl chattered the distance to the yacht club, obviously unaware of undercurrents that kept Wilbur and Bobette subdued. To David, they formed a melancholy quartet, though he suspected that if he also weren't here the Smythes might have a merry time sailing back alone. They were a family. Fighting back queasiness, he looked out the window to spot the boat lying offshore in the harbor with its anchor rope tethered to a buoy. It was too bad the Smythes didn't know how to sail it; in his present mood he was going to be terrible company. He was anxious to secure the privacy to read and ruminate on Iola's letter.

He put it out of his mind while they had their valises trundled to the pier behind the yacht club, from where they were ferried in a launch through gray chop to the boat. He hadn't checked the weather at the club and had been too caught up in the swirling aftermath of the night to take much note of it—this was unsailorly, he thought with wincing self-reproach—until he stepped down into the pitching launch. The flag atop his mast confirmed what the steady breeze on his face suggested— the wind was from the east, carrying desert haze even this far offshore. Most likely they wouldn't get a squall, though it would be nippy in the cockpit and the sun would show only thinly through a high veneer of cloud. Beyond the harbor were rolling swells capped with wind-formed ripples; it was probably safe to sail, he thought, but the ride would be hard on anyone who got seasick.

They climbed up the aft ladder from the launch and tugged the cases on board; then he and Wilbur carried them down the narrow gangway below to stow them.

"Where to?" asked Wilbur.

"There," David said, nodding with his head—his hands were gripping the trunk's leather handle—"our room." The pronoun seemed to bounce between the thin, varnished partitions. "We can store it all there," he added, meaning, to himself, to Wilbur, that the room would never be occupied again.

Wilbur wasn't much of a sailor, and David had to give him more instructions than any one person could absorb and perform competently without assistance. David sent him forward to release the mooring catch from the anchor rope and to winch the cable on the reel. Meanwhile, David set to unsheathing the mainsail, clipping on the jib and preparing to run it up. He caught himself missing Laura: these were her chores, and she did them eagerly—without her aboard to help him, getting under way was a clumsy affair.

He went to the cockpit after they were loose from the mooring and the sails lay rumpled about the deck like sheets of a giant unmade bed. The latches to the cover on the motor housing were loose—this struck him as strange, but he didn't dwell on it—and he had to firm the wing nuts on the cover before starting the engine.

David donned a slicker to block the wind, though the rustling it made when he moved always annoyed him. The wind blew stiffly into his face when he put the engine into forward gear and slowly curled the wheel to bring the bow about toward the mouth of the harbor. What was the proper compass setting? He couldn't recall it now. He'd have to hail Wilbur back topside to raise the sails once they were clear of the harbor so they could tack; then he would get Wilbur to mind the wheel so he could go below to check the charts.

He accelerated the diesel engine a notch. It would take a while to reach sailing waters, so he settled himself into an attitude of patience and breathed deeply. Without Laura, there was not nearly so much pleasure in working with this boat. She'd been a good sailor.

This is what you did when someone died. You said they were this, they were that. Good sailor, good singer, good actress on the stage or off, and he could honestly say she'd never put on a show that didn't keep him on the edge of his seat.

He wasn't so angry with her this morning. Alice had sounded as if

Laura had had an accident, then denied it. He wondered about it, though he couldn't tell if his wondering was inspired by compassion or curiosity. He was still too angry to let himself care, and he'd been given permission not to be anxious about her.

He felt indifferent. Or was pretending to feel it in hopes of inducing it, he couldn't say which.

She is free do as she pleases. . . .

The sentence became a litany, an invocation to master his troublesome attachments to the world. Thinking *She is free to do as she pleases* was like hearing the hypnotist murmuring *Your lids are starting to close*, each successive pronouncement carrying less weight as the voice fades into memory, time, dream.

It didn't hurt so much to say it now. She had done as she pleased, anyway, so nothing could be gained by insisting on having his way. It hadn't prevented Sanders from coming along and getting under her skin. David hadn't won much by running him off except the embittered pleasure of spoiling her happiness, and now that the triumph had paled, what he had done seemed uncomfortably selfish. He'd do it the same way again, only this time wish Sanders could stand up and say he truly wanted Laura, wish it for Laura's sake. Iola had said, "Make yourself happy." As if she were certain he could be happy without Laura.

Bobette's red head passed across the frame of the galley ladder as she moved from the sink to the table, carrying a teapot. How does it happen that one couple can be happy, in "love," and another couple never arrive at it no matter how hard they try, and with the best intentions?

He brought his knee against the wheel to hold it and reached under the slicker and into his pocket for the envelope. He hoped the letter was long—he wanted to think about Iola for a while, everything she might say could be something to gnaw on—but the envelope contained only a brief note. Its very terseness seemed a reproach.

"You said it changed your feelings. You don't know how that tempts me, David! But I have to go, for me, and if they've changed enough, then maybe you'll come to believe that I'm worth following and finding. But if it turns out I'm not and I don't ever see you again, still I say—aho! All that happened between us I will treasure as my most precious memory."

He ached. Never see her again? It seemed unthinkable, yet all too possible. From the time they were children he'd admired her beauty: to look at her face and her womanly form was to experience an oddly paradoxical combination of restfulness and excitement. A spirit residing in her drew his gaze to her eyes, her lips, and when his gaze touched her, that spirit eased out like warm light to stroke him, as if to sleep. After all these years she still had the Kiowa maiden's modesty and sense of decorum that often made her avert her own eyes when he looked directly at her, a formality and diffidence he found enchanting.

She knew his past, his roots, they had a bond that no one else could share, and many times when she was away from the city he had been lonely for her. It would be fitting—convenient, even—for them to be a couple. Besides, she wanted him, and her devotion would soothe his wounded pride. He and Iola, as a couple, could go back to Anadarko as respected, influential people in their tribe. It would appease that ancient need in him to be her equal, to be raised to the status of an onde family.

Was this what she had wanted him to say? To explain how and in what ways she was important to him? Would that change her mind? Out of shyness and confusion, he'd been slow to respond when they'd made love on the hillside, slow to explain how he felt, slow to *know* what he felt.

Iola's willfulness about leaving had aroused his pique, however, and he'd balked as if to an ultimatum. Now he saw that unless he bent, he and Iola would be dead to one another, too. The litany he murmured about Laura—She is free to do as she pleases—applied to himself, he knew, and Anna's admonition came back to haunt him: "You must find a new man, make him from the clay that God has abandoned, David."

Separated from Laura he was free to choose Iola; he dimly recognized that he should be jubilant, but he kept stalking around his new possibilities, poking at them gingerly with a long stick. He and Iola together as lovers, or husband and wife. As in a wedding photo. It was difficult to imagine clearly. Where was the part of him inside that hooked to the part of her inside?

He blinked as a sunbeam burst down through a tatter in the veil of cloud and hovered over the swells like a great yellow dirigible made of light. Bobette was ascending from below wearing a heavy gray cardigan over her green dress, one hand hidden under the too-long cuff, the other carefully gyroscoping a mug of coffee as she climbed step by step the ladder, fearful of spilling the contents.

Iola could still get a rise out of him by implying a judgment, he thought. After all these years, he still felt she was formidable in her opposition to his essential nature. It was hard to show her his true self because she wouldn't approve of it. She only had to say she was "proud" of him and the undercurrents of the compliment would wash his feet out from under him: she meant he had managed to come up to her standards, temporarily. She saw him as "a credit to his race." Since she was one, too, she thought, she imagined that they belonged together. Credit to His Race, and Wife.

But in the end it came to this: Did he love Iola? Was love necessary?

He folded the note and slipped it into the envelope as Bobette reached the top of the ladder and jammed her hand against the hatchframe to steady herself. Confused, he was feeling a little bit of everything when he was not feeling a lot of something in particular. Bobette came forward holding out the mug and smiling at him, and he was thinking that he would let time work to tell him what he felt. To see if, when Iola went, he would miss her or just be lonely with Laura gone. And, no, it wouldn't be necessary for him to love Iola to ask her to be his wife. But it would be desirable, and he wouldn't upset Iola with false pretenses, he thought, reaching forward to take the mug—

A fist of air clapped the mug, his face, took him high, a stinging an awful stinging, then falling, falling back into the air, he crashed through the water; surrounded, fighting, churning arms and legs, the left arm odd, frantically he climbed the invisible ladder of his panic under all that water, feet and hands pawing where there were rungs only in the mind, but at last, gasping, he broke back over the surface. Explosion. Things raining on the water. Something wrong with one eye. Someone screaming. The sky was a plane of pale white viewed through a red scrim and below it an angry boiling curl of black smoke rushing from a billow of flames that nested like a winged gargoyle in the stern half of his boat. Screaming. He gasped. The slicker was the skin of a boulder about his form, like another desperate swimmer riding his back, so he gulped in air and, weighted, began a sinking as sure as a fall but slow as a dream, shrugged off his rider as it choked him, then dug his way back to air.

A gurgle, a choked-back scream, near on his left. He whirled about, treading water, looking, his left arm moving more lightly, quickly than its mate. There, the red hair, her face a raw, raw red, blood on her head, thrashing and flailing at the water. She could hardly swim, the cuff of the sweater leaden with water slapping like a fish. Only her face with her head jammed back showing a jittery ring of water framing it like the cowl on a nun and her voice going *humt! humt!* as she gasped between swallows. He tried to shout, "Hold on!" but only croaked and struggled to push toward her as he hung upright in the water keeled by his shoes and sodden clothing, working to reach her like trudging in a nightmare while being chased. He was wrestling furiously, gasping, heaving in the loose but smothering grip of the water, then he was seeing his left hand was gone, blood screaming out of the stub and washing away into the gray sea, making, about him in the water, an aura of dark rose blossom.

PART

FIVE

November 1929

36

Jack Little Tree and Dove Tail saw her off at the station, and she dozed fitfully as the barren San Gabriels slid by the window. Later, when the train stopped in Barstow, she stood for a while to stretch her legs, then when the train lurched, steel hooves aclatter, to begin its long bleak haul across the desert toward Needles, she grew hungry. Dove Tail had fed her a full breakfast, and she'd eaten a doughnut while waiting for the train, but she craved something substantial.

She checked her purse and calculated she could afford one hot meal today. She reached into her suitcase and removed a large manila envelope, picked up the gray shawl her mother had given her months before, and walked on sea legs to the dining car.

At a table by a window, wrapped in the shawl, she eased the ledger-sized book from the envelope. The waiter came to give her a menu and announce that the chef had prepared a Thanksgiving special—turkey, dressing, yams, cranberry—and Iola nodded, only half listening.

She sat looking at the cover of the book until the waiter returned with her coffee, to which she added cream and sugar. Although she was not the only person seated alone, the lunch crowd in the dining car was noisy and convivial; flasks were hoisted in toasts, and a haze of tobacco smoke hung in the air.

She sipped the coffee. Then, finally, she lifted the fabric-bound cover and was instantly swamped by grief upon seeing David's clumsy handwriting, his awkward, troubled accommodation to English; she remembered how the intelligent content in his notes to staff had to struggle to poke its head through a thicket of language. A wave of sadness crept over her. Grief is like an illness, she thought. You grow well enough to get out of bed and walk about, then all of a sudden you feel faint and have to sit down.

She closed the cover and remained very still until her sorrow passed.

She had made up her mind to read the journal but still felt trepidation and no little guilt about it. She'd first discovered the journal in the desk he used at the Foundation office a few days ago as she was packing up the Foundation records. The Foundation had ceased to operate. No one had been paid in several weeks, as the assets had been frozen in probate. Since David's death, Laura had refused to keep the Foundation alive or to manage the businesses whose hired workers depended on whatever stability they could summon since the stock market had crashed. David's will had given half of his estate to Laura, a quarter to the Foundation, and a quarter to his family and the tribal treasury, but her lawyers had contested it. Then, out of the blue, a banker in Wetoka had filed a claim that he was the estate's executor and had still another will which bequeathed the entire estate to himself and Laura, and it had become clear that the fight for control of David's money would go on in court after court, year after year, until at last the inevitable would occur—Laura and the lawyers would get most, if not all, of it. The Foundation couldn't survive in such circumstances.

She didn't know whether Laura's neglect of the Foundation was malicious or unintentional. She had more or less disappeared into the recesses of the Angelus Temple at Echo Park like a novitiate. Iola had last seen Laura at David's funeral; Laura had not attended Bobette's. After the service, during which Laura had sung a hymn dressed in a flowing white robe, tears streaming down her cheeks, she had come gliding over to Iola, her robe billowing and trailing, her face looking like the mouth of a drawstring bag, and, bending forward, had dusted Iola's cheek with her own and murmured, "Thank you for coming," like a hostess. Then she had turned to Wilbur and cooed, "I pray for you and for your loss, my dear Brother." Later, Wilbur said, "The idea of that gold-digger dope addict whore praying for me makes me puke!"

Iola too had been furious at how Laura seemed to appropriate as David's widow all rights to grieve. Indeed, the funeral had been all her doing: not one iota of it reflected that David was Kiowa. The Four-Square people had been given complete control, and Iola had been unable to get word to David's sister, Standing Inside Lodge, in time. Iola had longed to grieve openly for David the way she had allowed herself to surrender when her father died, but no one in Los Angeles would understand, except for friends at the War Paint Club, and she'd finally sought consolation among them.

Thus she had kept the journal. Though she knew it was private and belonged to his widow, she decided to have it as her own. It was the one possession she managed to take from David's estate. Possibly Laura hadn't known it existed—or, even if she had, it would have been of no interest. For Iola, even without knowing its contents, it was a priceless record of his person.

She hadn't read it yet because she hadn't had sufficient leisure for reflection. And she'd been afraid. She didn't want to violate his privacy, and she worried it might contain something that would alarm or hurt her, in which case it would be unfair to read it because he couldn't explain himself more fully. He'd be forced to stand on his words without having chosen to do so.

But someone should know him, keep on knowing him, hold him in memory, she told herself. She would read it as a duty or favor to him. But when she lifted the cover from the front page once more, she realized she was looking to find herself in this book.

She skimmed through descriptions of his reading and came to a series of meditations on historical subjects—there was a long ramble about Satank, Satanta, and Big Tree. David wondered who had been right: Satank, who died struggling with his guards on the wagon ride to prison; Satanta, who endured imprisonment until he learned he wouldn't be released, and so pitched himself out of a window of the prison down in Texas; or Big Tree, who had gone strolling into the future to become a Baptist minister. But Big Tree was younger than the others, Iola noted, longing to take up this old subject between them again. She had told David once that her grandfather said the past was like river cane in some people—you keep chopping it down but it grows back unless you dig out the roots.

Her waiter arrived with her Thanksgiving special. As soon as she set the book aside to eat, a young white woman appeared beside the table with a toddler perched on her hip. The child was a brunette girl with big red bows in her hair and a dotted Swiss dress worn over frilly petticoats. The child regarded Iola with enormous curiosity from her saddle.

"May we sit here?"

"Yes, of course."

"Thank you." The woman lifted the child and stood her upright in the chair opposite Iola.

"You need a booster," said Iola. She caught the eye of the waiter, who brought the nesting chair and helped the child into it. The woman draped her gray wool coat over the back of her chair, exposing its oyster-colored silk lining. She removed her black wool hat and veil with several deft gestures, leaving her careful coiffure untouched. Once settled, she removed a fork from the child's fist, then dug into her purse to retrieve a pack of cigarettes. She offered one by showing the face of the pack—Fatimas—but Iola shook her head.

"How old is she?"

"Twenty-two months. Too old to carry, that's for sure."

"Is she your first?"

"Yes, my God!" the woman gasped. Iola would've liked to ask about her pregnancy and delivery, but the woman's outburst suggested that should Iola inquire, she might hear more than she wanted to.

The child, grinning, observed Iola with large brown eyes. She certainly doesn't look angelic, thought Iola: she looked as if she had four times more personality than her small body could comfortably contain, and Iola wished the tot had joined her without her mother.

"She's very cute." Iola smiled and winked at the child, who turned suddenly shy.

"She usually talks a blue streak, but cat's got her tongue right now. Strangers, you know." The woman's eyes skimmed lightly across Iola's shawl-draped shoulders then across her face and were neutral except for the faint hint that this neutrality had been hastily summoned. "We got delayed in Los Angeles or we wouldn't be traveling today. My husband is in Kansas at her granny's"—a nod here toward the child—"and I suspect they're all sitting down to a goose about now."

Iola wondered if a thumbnail sketch of herself was obligatory, but the woman looked at Iola's plate and said, "You're having turkey and dressing and cranberry? That's appropriate."

"It's the special."

The woman blew a long thin stream of smoke hard from between her lips then nipped at a tobacco bit on her tongue with a thumb and middle finger. Her nails were long and shaped but unpainted.

"Maybe I'll just have a club sandwich," she said, sounding a little as if such an order would punish everyone, including herself.

But when the waiter came she ordered the special, then turned her attention to dipping a napkin in her water glass and dabbing at the child's hands and cheeks. Iola watched quietly, not knowing whether to comment on what they were doing or to finish her meal in silence to discourage further contact.

When the woman's plate came, she hoisted her fork and knife with a ceremonial air, smiled wryly, and said, "I guess this is it, my Thanksgiving," and the declaration seemed to stand as a kind of grace said in lieu of the one currently being offered in Kansas.

The woman fed herself and the child from one plate, murmuring, "Okay, here comes the yams, the yummy yams from mummy!" never looking at Iola but, nonetheless, giving Iola the feeling that this was all for her benefit. When, finished, the woman had been given a second cup of coffee and lighted a cigarette, she looked up to Iola, smiled, and said brightly, "There, now I'm human again!" as if to acknowledge that she had been off-putting. "It's hard to travel with kids."

"I'm sure it is."

The woman leaned forward and rolled her eyes, "And it's *that* time again. That was the best thing about being pregnant."

Iola passed a hand across her abdomen. "Yes. That and feeling you can eat all you want."

The child was struggling to stand in the chair and was obviously growing sleepy and cross, so the woman stood, lifted the child, and planted her back on a hip. She took the child's arm in her own hand and, using the toddler like a marionette, waved goodbye.

They left an odd glow hanging in the air over their side of the table. Iola had an impulse to reach over to the woman's plate and take her uneaten roll. Resisting it, she went back to the journal. She began to skim the pages, glancing at the lines, not really aware of what she was in such a hurry to find until her gaze at last hooked on the barb of her own name.

"Dear Iola—"

Her heart jolted, she looked at the date—last year—but was too impatient to consider the implications of it and instead hurried on to the body of the letter.

"I've been thinking about that essay you wrote about Columbus, and how you won the trip to New York. You wrote about a crazy white man and for a prize you got to go to that zoo where they had saved a few buffalo after trying so hard to make them extinct. What got me thinking about this was that I was reading and thinking about him. I'd like to go back in time and go up against you in that contest now. Or I could help you write another essay. I'll tell you what to say, you do the saying. I can tell you Crazy Columbus didn't go out looking for the New World with an empty head. He had a skull full of notions as queer as any the white men ever said we had. He thought sick humans could be cured by prayer or having leaches put on their bodies or having their veins cut open or that their spirits could be healed through rites where high priests spoke mumbo-jumbo and waved tin cans on strings filled with smoking stuff over the bodies of the bewitched. He believed that God was really three people and that God had planted a Holy Seed in a Holy Virgin who gave birth to the God's Son, and the son had the spirit power to walk on water and to multiply loaves and fishes and bend the so-called laws of Nature. He believed that on the other side of the ocean there were tribes of black Amazon women who lived without men and yearned for them. He believed over there were cities made of gold. In a book I have it says Crazy Columbus believed that some place on this great big round globe was a real Earthly Paradise. He thought the Christian Garden of Eden was a real place somewhere. He said that the earth was shaped like a pear or like the breast of a woman who was lying down and the Garden could be found on the nipple, which would be the place on Earth closest to Heaven. He thought it was someplace in South America."

There followed a blank space, in which Iola was free to project the image of David grinning, laughing out loud, and slapping his thigh as he considered the lunacy of Columbus's notions.

Before reading it, she thought he hadn't sent this letter because it contained too strong an expression of his feelings for her. One reading of the contents dashed that hope, however. She couldn't say if she were relieved.

She quickly ran through the rest of the journal in search of her own name but found nothing. He hadn't confided much of anything truly personal here, and her only consolation was that Laura had not inspired any mention whatsoever.

Disappointment slowly crushed her. Fighting it, she looked back to the letter and tried to warm to the implicit posture he took toward her—"my chum," it seemed to say, "here, I know you'll appreciate this . . . " She eagerly absorbed the nice suggestion of friendship, of warm regard, in how he was thinking of their writing a new essay together or competing in a friendly way, and the very fact of his writing it at all while she was out of town meant that he had been lonely for her, had missed her, had been thinking of her. She could also count the nostalgic tone that apparently came from good memories of their childhood together.

Could such scraps build a case that he loved her? That afternoon on Catalina, he seemed to be like a great, top-heavy tree leaning, leaning, leaning toward her. Yet never fell. Would he have? It was terrible to realize that there was nothing outside her own skin to objectively corroborate what she chose to believe. She wanted more than ever now to feel that David had loved her. She could weave the evidence into an elaborately contrived tapestry that said so, yet the method by which this truth was derived gave her pain. If he had truly loved her, wouldn't he have said? Wouldn't she know? Wasn't love a thing of the heart, so strong it would sweep away her doubt, so strong it would have driven him to her long ago?

She sighed, looked out the window into the desert. On the horizon hung razor-edge serrations along the spines of purple ridges; in the flats lay a plane of steel gray like a lake shimmering in rapturous evaporation. Thinking he loved her was a comfort. But the truth was she didn't believe he had, at least not in the way she had loved him or in the way she would want a man to love her. Maybe he would have. Maybe not. She had the rest of her life to make up her mind about it.

The day came when the soldiers put chains on the warriors' wrists and ankles to send them to that fort by the ocean. I was only a very small girl then, and my mother was about as big as you with my brother. When they brought out the men to put them into the wagons, some women gave a war cry to build up the men's courage, and others were wailing and scratching themselves on their arms. Some women held tight to the prisoners and cried, I will die before I leave my man! or they begged the soldiers to let them go, too. I knew Maman'te's daughter, Red Dress, well, and she and I cried and ran beside the wagon that carried her father and your grandfather.

Was I afraid my father would die? Oh yes. You see, people died right away. Kicking Bird died, they said Maman'te smoked and made owl talk for it to happen, but then he himself died only a day later. A

Cheyenne tried to run away, and the soldiers shot him. Sun Chief and Steven Gote's father died of sickness because the prison walls sweat all day and night and made them cough.

Red Dress's mother taught us the first grieving song, do you remember it? No? Ah. You will have to come back to my school. I will teach it to you again so when you are sad you can sing it.

A story goes with the song. When the Half Boys were living with Spider Old Woman she taught them how to make lances and throw them to kill animals for their food. She said only kill certain ones and do not harm the others. One day the boys came home and found a snake in their lodge, and they killed it, even though it was only eating from a bowl. When Spider Old Woman came home, she cried because the boys had killed the snake. She said it was Old Man Snake, he had lived through the great flood. You boys have killed your own grandfather, Stony Road, she told them. From then on, men and snakes were never friends. Spider Old Woman felt so full of sorrow that she sat down upon the earth and sang this song:

> I am sitting by the willow,
> My tears are falling for you,
> Stony Road, your beautiful spotted body.
> Stony Road, your beautiful spotted body.

But too much talk of one kind can be harmful, so I should tell you about when the men came home. There was a dance and a big eat. Everybody was happy. The young men who came back found girls to marry and started having babies, and those babies helped people forget bad things that happened before.

Girls who are going to be mothers have to know certain things. Or they did when I was having babies. I don't know about you modern girls. You all want to have a white medicine man come look and help. Uh! We just took care not to jiggle the spirits. There was once a girl who was going to have a baby. She was always going to a certain big sandy hill to find wild turtles, because she loved to eat their eggs. She would open up the turtles and eat many eggs, even ones that were not shelled over. She kept doing that when it was two months before her baby was to come. Well, a long time more went by, and still she didn't get very big. She got very bad pains, as if she were being cut inside.

She had two san'tabe with her to attend the birth, and they got scared, so they called in a medicine man. Out of her came turtle feet and legs, then a human face. They choked that thing and buried it deep, and the girl died.

That is not a cheerful story, but a girl who is not greedy for turtle eggs need not worry. Here are some more things my mother taught me when I was going to have your brother. If a girl stares at any one animal too long, then her child might be marked. If she eats turtles or fish or raccoons, the baby will have six toes or six fingers. Also do not eat cat, rabbit, bird, possum, squirrel, dog, or alligator, or the baby might not come formed right.

You are smiling that way again. Well, just to be safe, I will not roast any alligators for you. . . .

Do you remember how to sing to a baby? They say when Sun Boy and his mother fell to earth and she was killed, he wandered about for a while until he found Spider Old Woman's lodge while she was away. He took food from her and hid. She knew a child had taken it because she saw the small footprints. She set out a ball and a bow and arrows the next day, and when she came back the bow and arrows were missing, so she knew the little thief was a boy. To catch him, she turned herself into a cockleburr, and when Sun Boy came by the door, she grabbed him. He struggled with her, but she calmed him down and put him to sleep by singing this song:

> Wa-ho Wa-ho-oooo . . .
> Go to sleep and do not cry,
> Your mother is dead,
> And still you try to feed upon her breasts.

This is the very first lullaby, and it's for grandmothers to sing to their grandchildren. To tell the truth, I did not think I would ever get to sing it. I am happy now.